D0434959

0 1 1 1 1 1 0 0 0 1 0 0 0 0 1 1 0 1 0 1 0 1 0 0 1 0 0 1 1 0 1 1 0 0 1 0 0
0 0 0 1 0 1 0 1 1 0 1 1 0 0 0 0 0 0 1 0 0 1 1 1 0 0 0 0 0 1 0 1 1 0 1 0 0
1 0 0 0 0 0 1 1 1 1 1 0 1 0 0 1 1 1 1 1 0 1 1 0 0 1 1 0 1 0 0 0 1 0 1 0 0
0 1 0 1 1 0 0 1 1 1 1 1 1 1 0 0 1 1 1 0 1 0 1 1 0 0 0 0 0 0 1 0 0 1 1 1
0 1 0 0 0 1 1 0 1 1 0 1 1 1 0 0 1 1 1 1 0 0 0 0 0 0 1 0 1 1 0 1 0 0 1
1 1 1 0 1 0 0 0 0 0 1 1 1 1 0 0 1 0 0 1 0 0 1 0 1 1 1 0 0 1 1 1 0 1 0 0 1
0 1 0 1 0 1 0 0 0 1 1 0 1 1 0 0 0 0 1 1 0 1 0 0 1 1 0 0 0 1 0 1 1 1 1 0 0
0 1 0 1 1 0 0 1 1 0 1 0 0 0 0 0 1 0 1 1 1 0 1 1 0 0 0 0 0 0 1 0 1 1 0 0
1 1 1 0 0 0 1 1 0 0 0 0 0 1 1 1 1 0 1 1 0 1 1 0 1 0 0 0 0 0 1 0 0 1 1 1 0
1 1 1 1 1 0 0 1 0 1 0 1 1 1 0 1 1 1 0 1 0 1 0 1 1 1 1 0 1 0 1 1 0 1 1 0
1 0 1 0 0 1 1 1 1 1 1 0 1 1 0 0 0 0 1 1 1 0 1 1 0 1 1 1 0 1 1 1 1 0 0 0
0 0 0 1 1 0 1 1 0 0 1 1 0 1 0 0 1 0 0 0 1 0 1 0 1 0 0 1 0 0 0 0 1 0 0 1 0
1 1 1 0 0 0 1 0 0 1 0 1 1 0 0 1 0 0 1 1 0 1 0 1 0 1 1 1 0 0 0 0 1 0 1 1 0
0 1 0 0 0 0 0 0 0 1 1 1 1 0 1 1 0 0 1 1 0 1 1 0 0 0 0 0 0 1 0 0 0 0 1 0 0
0 0 0 1 1 0 1 0 0 1 1 1 1 0 0 1 1 1 0 1 1 0 0 1 1 0 0 1 1 1 0 0 1 0 0 0 0
0 1 0 0 0 0 1 1 1 1 0 1 1 0 1 0 0 0 1 0 0 1 1 1 0 0 0 0 1 0 1 1 1 1 0 0
1 0 0 1 0 1 1 1 1 0 0 0 0 0 1 0 1 1 0 1 0 0 0 0 0 0 0 1 0 0 0 1 1 1 0 0
0 1 1 0 1 1 1 0 0 0 1 1 1 0 0 1 1 1 0 0 0 0 1 1 0 0 1 0 0 1 0 1 0 1 1 1 1
1 1 0 1 0 0 0 1 0 1 1 1 0 0 1 0 1 1 1 1 0 0 1 0 1 1 0 1 1 0 1 1 1 1 1 0 0
0 0 1 0 0 1 0 1 0 1 1 1 1 0 0 0 1 0 1 0 1 0 1 0 1 0 0 0 0 1 0 0 0 0 1 1 0 1

INSIGNIA

```
1 1 1 1 1 0 0 0 1 0 0 0 0 1 1 0 1 0 1 0 1 0 0 1 0 0 1 1 0 1 1 0 0 1 0 0
0 0 1 0 1 0 1 1 0 1 1 0 0 0 0 0 0 1 0 0 1 1 1 0 0 0 0 0 1 0 1 1 0 1 0 0
1 0 0 0 0 0 1 1 1 1 0 1 0 0 1 1 1 1 1 0 1 1 0 0 1 1 0 1 0 0 0 1 0 1 0 0
0 1 0 1 1 0 0 1 1 1 1 1 1 1 0 0 1 1 1 0 1 0 1 1 0 0 0 0 0 0 1 0 0 1 1 1
0 1 0 0 0 1 1 0 1 1 0 1 0 1 1 1 0 0 1 1 1 1 0 0 0 0 0 0 0 1 0 1 0 0 0 1
1 1 1 0 1 0 0 0 0 1 1 1 1 0 0 1 0 0 1 0 1 1 1 0 0 1 1 1 0 1 1 0 0 1 0 0
0 1 0 1 0 1 0 0 0 1 1 0 1 1 0 0 0 0 1 1 0 1 0 0 1 1 0 0 0 1 0 1 1 1 1 0 0
0 1 0 1 1 0 0 1 1 0 1 0 0 0 0 0 1 0 1 1 1 0 1 1 0 0 0 0 0 0 0 1 0 1 1 0 0
1 1 1 0 0 0 1 1 0 0 0 0 0 1 1 1 1 0 1 1 0 1 1 0 1 0 0 0 0 0 1 0 0 1 1 1 0
1 1 1 1 1 1 0 0 1 0 1 0 1 1 1 0 1 1 1 0 1 0 1 0 1 1 1 0 1 0 1 1 0 1 1 0
1 0 1 0 0 1 1 1 1 1 1 0 1 1 0 0 0 0 1 1 1 0 1 1 0 1 1 1 0 1 1 1 0 0 0
0 0 0 1 1 0 1 1 0 0 1 1 0 1 0 0 1 0 0 0 1 0 1 0 1 0 0 1 0 0 0 0 1 0 0 1 0
1 1 1 0 0 0 1 0 0 1 0 1 1 0 0 1 0 0 1 1 0 1 0 1 0 1 1 1 0 0 0 0 1 0 1 1 0
0 1 0 0 0 0 0 0 0 1 1 1 1 0 1 1 0 0 1 1 0 1 1 0 0 0 0 0 0 1 0 0 0 0 1 0 0
0 0 0 1 1 0 1 0 0 1 1 1 1 0 0 1 1 1 0 1 1 0 0 1 1 0 0 1 1 1 0 0 1 0 0 0 0
0 1 0 0 0 0 1 1 1 1 0 1 1 0 1 0 0 0 1 0 0 1 1 1 0 0 0 0 1 0 1 1 1 1 0 0
1 0 0 1 0 1 1 1 1 0 0 0 0 0 1 0 1 1 0 1 0 0 0 0 0 0 1 0 0 0 1 1 1 1 0 0
0 1 1 0 1 1 1 0 0 0 1 1 1 0 0 1 1 1 0 0 0 0 1 1 0 0 1 0 0 1 0 1 0 1 1 1 1
1 1 0 1 0 0 0 1 0 1 0 1 1 0 0 1 0 1 1 1 0 0 1 0 1 1 0 1 1 0 1 1 1 1 0 0
0 0 0 1 0 0 0 1 0 1 0 1 1 0 0 0 1 0 1 0 1 0 0 1 0 0 0 1 0 0 0 0 1 1 0 1
1 1 0 1 0 0 1 1 0 0 0 0 1 1 0 0 1 0 0 0 1 0 1 1 1 1 1 1 1 0 0
```

INSIGNIA

S. J. KINCAID

KATHERINE TEGEN BOOKS
An Imprint of HarperCollins Publishers

Katherine Tegen Books is an imprint of HarperCollins Publishers.

Insignia

Library of Congress Cataloging-in-Publication Data
Kincaid, S. J.
    Insignia / S. J. Kincaid.
       p.   cm.
    Summary: Tom, a fourteen-year-old genius at virtual reality games, is recruited
by the United States military to begin training at the Pentagonal Spire as a
Combatant in World War III, controlling the mechanized drones that do the actual
fighting off-planet.
    ISBN 978-0-06-209299-1
    [1. Science fiction.   2. Virtual reality—Fiction.   3. Video games—Fiction.
4. War—Fiction.]   I. Title.
PZ7.K61926Ins 2012   2011044634
[Fic]—dc23

Typography by Carla Weise
12 13 14 15 16   LP/RRDH   10 9 8 7 6 5 4 3 2 1
❖
First Edition

To my father and mother,
for encouraging my dreams and
giving me the strength to pursue them

THE COALITION OF MULT

THE INDO-AMERICAN ALLIANCE:

European-Australian Block • Oceanic Nations •
North American Alliance • Central America

MULTINATIONAL CORPORATIONS
(and sponsored Combantants):

Dominion Agra
SPONSORED COMBATANTS: Karl "Vanquisher" Marsters

Nobridis, Inc.
SPONSORED COMBATANTS: Elliot "Ares" Ramirez,
Cadence "Stinger" Grey, Britt "Ox" Schmeiser

Wyndham Harks
SPONSORED COMBATANTS: Heather "Enigma" Akron,
Yosef "Vector" Saide, Snowden "NewGuy" Gainey

Matchett-Reddy
SPONSORED COMBATANTS: Lea "Firestorm" Styron,
Mason "Specter" Meekins

Epicenter Manufacturing
SPONSORED COMBATANTS: Emefa "Polaris" Austerley,
Alec "Condor" Tarsus, Ralph "Matador" Bates

Obsidian Corp.
SPONSORED COMBATANTS: None

ATIONAL CORPORATIONS

THE RUSSO-CHINESE ALLIANCE:
*South American Federation • Nordic Block •
Affiliated African Nations*

MULTINATIONAL CORPORATIONS
(sponsored members unknown):

Harbinger

Lexicon Mobile

LM Lymer Fleet

Kronus Portable

Stronghold Energy

Preeminent Communications

1 1 1 1 1 0 0 0 1 0 0 0 0 1 1 0 1 0 1 1 0 0 1 1 0 1 1 0 1 1 0 0 1 0 0
0 0 1 0 1 0 1 1 0 1 1 0 0 0 0 0 1 0 0 1 1 1 0 0 0 0 0 1 0 1 1 0 1 0 0
0 0 0 0 0 1 1 1 1 0 1 0 0 1 1 1 1 0 1 1 0 0 1 1 0 1 0 0 0 1 0 1 0 0
1 0 1 1 0 0 1 1 1 1 1 1 0 0 1 1 1 0 1 0 1 1 0 0 0 0 0 0 1 0 0 1 1 1
1 0 0 0 1 1 0 1 1 0 1 1 1 0 0 1 1 1 0 0 0 0 0 0 0 1 0 1 1 0 1 0 0 1
1 1 0 1 0 0 0 0 0 1 1 1 1 0 0 1 0 0 1 0 1 1 1 0 0 1 1 1 0 1 1 0 0 1 0 1
1 0 1 0 1 0 0 0 1 1 0 1 1 0 0 0 0 1 1 0 1 0 0 1 1 0 0 0 1 0 1 1 1 1 0 0
1 0 1 1 0 0 1 1 0 1 0 0 0 0 0 1 0 1 1 1 0 1 1 0 0 0 0 0 0 1 0 1 1 0 0
1 1 0 0 0 1 1 0 0 0 0 0 1 1 1 1 0 1 1 0 1 1 0 1 0 0 0 0 1 0 0 1 1 1 0
1 1 1 1 1 0 0 1 0 1 0 1 1 1 0 1 1 1 0 1 0 1 0 1 1 1 0 1 0 1 0 1 1 0
0 1 0 0 1 1 1 1 1 1 1 0 1 1 0 0 0 1 0 1 0 1 0 1

0 0 1 0 1 0 1 1 0 1 1 0 0 0 0 0 0 1 0 0 1 1 1 0 0 0 0 0 1 0 1 1 0 1 0 0
0 0 0 0 0 1 1 1 1 0 1 0 0 1 1 1 1 0 1 1 0 0 1 1 0 1 0 0 0 1 0 1 0 0
1 0 1 1 0 0 1 1 1 1 1 1 0 0 1 1 1 0 1 0 1 1 0 0 0 0 0 0 1 0 0 1 1 1
1 0 0 0 1 1 0 1 1 0 1 1 1 0 0 1 1 1 0 0 0 0 0 0 0 1 0 1 1 0 1 0 0 1
1 1 0 1 0 0 0 0 1 1 1 1 0 0 1 0 0 1 0 1 1 1 0 0 1 1 1 0 1 1 0 0 1 0 1
1 0 1 0 1 0 0 0 1 1 0 1 0 0 0 1 1 0 1 0 0 1 1 0 0 0 1 0 1 1 1 1 0 0
1 0 1 1 0 0 1 1 0 1 0 0 0 0 1 0 1 1 1 0 1 1 0 0 0 0 0 0 1 0 1 1 0 0
1 1 0 0 0 1 1 0 0 0 0 0 1 1 1 1 0 1 1 0 1 1 0 1 0 0 0 0 0 1 0 0 1 1 1 0
1 1 1 1 1 0 0 1 0 1 0 1 1 1 0 1 1 1 0 1 0 1 0 1 1 1 1 0 1 0 1 1 0 1 1 0
0 1 0 0 1 1 1 1 1 1 1 0 1 1 0 0 0 0 1 1 0 1 1 0 1 1 0 1

INSIGNIA

CHAPTER ONE

NEW TOWN, NEW casino—same old plan. Arizona's Dusty Squanto Casino made it easy for Tom Raines, since he didn't even have to pay his way into their virtual reality parlor. He slipped into the room, settled onto a couch in the back corner, and looked over the crowd of gamers, taking them in one at a time. His gaze settled on the two men in the opposite corner, and locked onto target.

Them, Tom thought.

The men stood with VR visors on, wired gloves clenched in the air. Their racing simulation blazed across an overhead screen for anyone who wanted to bet on the outcome. No one would bet on *this* race, though. One man was a good driver— he navigated the virtual track with the skill of an experienced gamer—and the other was pitifully bad. His car's fender dragged across the wall of the arena, and the fake onlookers were screaming and dodging out of the way.

The winning racer gave a triumphant laugh as his car

plowed across the finish line. He turned to the other man, chest puffed with victory, and demanded payment.

Tom smiled from his solitary spot on the couch.

Enjoy it while you can, buddy.

He timed it just right, waiting until the winner started counting up his bills to rise to his feet and wander into his line of sight. Tom noisily rattled one of the VR sets out of its storage container, then made a show of putting on the gloves the wrong way, before painstakingly adjusting them so the cloth and mesh wiring clasped his arms up to his elbows. Out of the corner of his eye, he became aware of the winning racer watching him.

"You like playing games, kid?" the man said to him. "Wanna have a go next?"

Tom gave him the wide-eyed, innocent look that he knew made him appear a lot younger than he was. Even though he was fourteen, he was short and skinny and had such bad acne that people usually couldn't guess his real age.

"I'm just looking. My dad says I'm not allowed to gamble."

The man licked his lips. "Oh, don't you worry. Your dad doesn't even have to know. Put down a few bucks, and we'll have us a great race. Maybe you'll win. How much money do you have?"

"Only fifty bucks."

Tom knew better than to say more than that. More than that, and people wanted to see it before taking up the bet. He actually had about two dollars in his pocket.

"Fifty bucks?" the man said. "That's enough. This is just car racing. You can race a car, can't you?" He twisted an invisible wheel. "Nothing to it. And think: you beat me, and you'll *double* that fifty."

"Really?"

"Really, kid. Let's have a go." A condescending chuckle. "I'll pay up for sure if you win."

"But if I lose . . ." Tom let that hang there. "That's all my money. I just . . . I can't." He started walking away, waiting for the magic words.

"All right, kid," the guy called. "Double or nothing."

Ha! Tom thought.

"I win," the man said, "and I'll get fifty. You win, you get a hundred. You can't beat that. Take a chance."

Tom turned slowly, fighting the laughter rising in his throat. This guy must already taste his easy fifty bucks since he'd fallen for the act so readily. Most casinos had one or two gamers who practically lived in the VR parlors, fancying themselves gods among men who could beat any chump luckless enough to enter their territory. Tom loved the way they looked at him: as some scrawny, stupid little kid they could easily con. He loved even more seeing their smiles disappear when he wiped the floor with them.

Just to be safe, Tom kept up the act. He made a show of fumbling as he strapped on the VR visor. "Okay, you're on, I guess."

Triumph rang in the man's voice. "We're on."

They were off. Their cars roared to life and tore furiously down the track. Tom mentally ticked off the laps, taking it all very deliberately. He made a few token mistakes here and there. They were never enough to slow him down much, just enough to ensure he was lagging behind the other car. The man, puffed up with confidence and certain of winning, whirled his steering wheel with great, lashing sweeps of his wired gloves. As the finish line appeared and the man's car turned at the right angle, Tom finally let a grin blaze across his lips.

One flick of his glove did the trick. He rammed his car forward and clipped the guy's back fender, then floored his gas. The man bellowed in rage and disbelief when his car swerved off the road in a rain of sparks.

Tom's car sailed past the finish line while the other car crashed and exploded in the arena's side ditch.

"What—what—" the man sputtered.

Tom flipped up his visor. "Whoops. I think I *have* played that game before." He tugged off his gloves. "Wanna fork over my hundred bucks?"

He watched, fascinated, the way a vein began popping out and fluttering in the man's forehead. "You little—You can't—You're . . ."

"You're not gonna pay me, then?" Tom cast an idle glance toward the man's recent victim, now sitting on a nearby couch. The bad driver was suddenly interested in their exchange. Tom raised his voice to make sure the man could make out every word. "I guess no one's playing games for money in here. Is that it?"

The gamer followed Tom's gaze to his victim, catching the implication: if he wouldn't pay Tom, then the other guy shouldn't have paid *him*.

The man spluttered a bit like the engine of his wrecked car, then jerked a hundred bucks out of a wad from his pocket. He crammed the bills into Tom's hand, muttering something about a rematch.

Tom flipped through the bills, completely enjoying the man's outrage. "You want a rematch, I'm game. Double or nothing, again? I could really use another two hundred dollars."

The man turned a curious shade of scarlet, cut his losses, and fled the room. As for the newbie on the couch, he gave Tom a grateful thumbs-up. Tom returned it, then stashed the bills in his pocket. One hundred dollars. Usually he had to pull off the bet with a few more gamers to make enough for a night's stay—VR sims involved such low stakes, after all—but at a dive like the Dusty Squanto Casino, a hundred would be enough for a room.

Tom's mind already whirled with the promises of the night ahead. A bed. Television. Air-conditioning. A real shower. He could even come back here and play games *just for fun*.

The ghastly realization hit just as he reached the door: he was at a casino with a VR parlor.

He had absolutely no excuse for missing school this afternoon.

TOM STAYED IN the VR parlor and logged into the Rosewood Reformatory sim for the first time in two weeks. In four years at Rosewood, he'd never skipped such a long stretch of school before, and he'd already missed most of class today. Just the sight in his visor of Ms. Falmouth's avatar and her virtual chalkboard killed any lingering satisfaction over his victory.

She immediately focused her attention on him. "Tom Raines," she said. "Thank you for gracing us with your presence today."

"You're welcome," Tom said. He knew it would just annoy her, but it wasn't like she had a good opinion of him to be ruined.

To be fair, he missed class a lot. Mostly not on purpose. Mostly he missed school due to losing access to an internet connection. It was just another hazard of having a gambler for a father.

Tom's dad, Neil, usually saved enough money to pay for a roof over their heads and some food at the gift shop. But some days he got totally cleaned out at the poker tables. It happened more and more in recent years as the last of his luck deserted him. When Neil squandered their money, and Tom couldn't find any sucker to bet against him in the VR parlors, they had to skip on small luxuries like hotel rooms. They ended up in a park or at a bus station or lying on benches at the train station.

Now with Ms. Falmouth and his entire class watching him, Tom tried to think of an excuse he'd never used before to explain why he'd missed the last ten days. He'd missed school so many times, he'd repeated himself a couple times by accident. He'd already lied about going to the funerals of all his grandparents, and even a couple great-grandparents, and there were only so many times he could say he "fell down a well" or "got lost in the woods" or "got hit in the head and got amnesia" before even *he* thought he sounded like a colossal idiot.

Today, he tried, "There was this massive cyberattack on all the local VR parlors. Russo-Chinese hackers, you know? The Department of Homeland Security came in and had to interview everyone in a ten-mile radius. I couldn't even access the internet."

Ms. Falmouth just shook her head. "Don't waste your breath, Tom."

Tom dropped into a seat, irrationally disappointed. It had been a good lie this time, too.

The avatars throughout the classroom sniggered at him, the way they always did, at Tom the loser who never knew what assignments were due, who never turned in his homework, who couldn't even manage to show up at an online class most days. He tuned his classmates out and occupied himself with twirling a pencil, which was trickier in VR than most people realized. The sensors of most standard-issue wired gloves had a strange lag time, and Tom figured honing his dexterity with them could only help him in future games.

He heard a whisper from beside him. "*I* liked your excuse."

Tom threw a careless glance toward the girl next to him. She must've joined the class sometime in the last two weeks. Her avatar was a gorgeous brunette with striking yellow-brown eyes. "Thanks. Nice avatar."

"I'm Heather." She flashed him a smile. "And this isn't an avatar."

Sure it isn't, Tom thought. People didn't look like that in real life unless they were celebrities. But he nodded like he believed her. "I'm Tom. And believe it or not, this"—he gestured to himself like he was proud of how very handsome he was—"isn't an avatar, either."

Heather giggled, because his avatar looked just like him, with acne and scrawny limbs and all. It definitely wasn't an image anyone would use to impress people online.

Ms. Falmouth turned back to face them. "Tom, Heather, are you done interrupting me, or do you need more time for your conversation?"

"Sorry," Tom said. "We're all through."

Tom hadn't seen eye to eye with Ms. Falmouth since he'd shown up for the first day of school a few years ago as Lord Krull from the game Celtic Quest. She'd yelled at him in front of everyone for being insolent, like he had done it as part of some elaborate scheme to mock her class. He'd just liked Lord Krull from Celtic Quest, that was all.

From then on, Tom always came to class as himself. He never signed on to the internet without an avatar if he could help it. It felt like he'd left his real skin behind, showing up at Rosewood as the same ugly, pale-eyed, and blond-haired Thomas Raines who tailed behind his dad in the real world. Never mind that he didn't believe for a second that the new girl sitting next to him really looked like her beautiful brunette avatar, and Serge Leon, in the back corner, was way too blustering to be a hulking six-footer in real life. He was probably four foot something and fat.

But Ms. Falmouth didn't seem to care about them. Whenever Tom was around, her radar was trained on him.

"Our subject's the current war, Tom. Perhaps you can contribute to our discussion. What is an offshored conflict?"

His thoughts flickered to what he'd seen in the news and on the internet, the clips of the ships fighting in space, controlled remotely by the top-secret combatants identified only by their call signs. "An offshored conflict is a war fought somewhere other than Earth. It's in space or on another planet."

"And the sky is blue, and the sun rises in the east. I'll need much more than the blatantly obvious."

Tom stopped twirling the virtual pencil and tried to concentrate. "Modern wars aren't fought by people. I mean, they're kind of fought by people, because people on Earth control mechanized drones remotely, but the machines do the actual fighting. If our machines don't get demolished by Russo-Chinese machines, our country wins the battle."

"And who is involved in the current conflict, Tom?"

"The whole world. That's why it's called World War III." She seemed to be waiting for more, so Tom ticked off the major players on his virtual fingers: "India and America are allies, and the Euro-Australian block is aligned with us. Russia and China are allies, and they're supported by the African states and the South American Federation. The Coalition of Multinationals, the twelve most powerful corporations in the world, is split down the middle between our two sides. And . . . yeah. That's about it."

That was pretty much all he knew about the war. He wasn't sure what else she wanted. He couldn't list all the tiny little countries allied with the two sides if he tried, and he doubted anyone else in the room could, either. There was a reason Rosewood was a reform school—most of its students couldn't cut it in a real, building one.

"Would you like to explain one notable characteristic about this offshored conflict, as opposed to wars in ages past?"

"No?" he tried hopefully.

"I wasn't really asking. Now answer the question."

Tom started twirling his pencil again. This was how Ms. Falmouth operated. She questioned him until he ran through all his knowledge, messed up, and looked like an idiot. This time he'd give it to her. "Dunno. Sorry."

Ms. Falmouth sighed as though she expected nothing more, and moved on to her next victim. "Heather, you two look to be making fast friends. If you're talking during class on your first day here, maybe you can list a notable characteristic for Tom."

Heather gave Tom a quick, sidelong look, then answered, "By going to war on other planets, and avoiding fights on Earth, we resolve issues through violence, but we avoid most of the consequences of traditional warfare such as debilitating injuries, human deaths, disruption of infrastructure, and environmental contamination. That's four notable characteristics. Do you want me to list more than that, Ms. Falmouth?"

Ms. Falmouth was silent for several seconds, perhaps stunned at how readily Heather had answered the question. "That'll quite do, Heather. Very well articulated. Offshored conflicts are practical socially as well as ecologically." She strode to the board. "I'd like you all to think of some ways the nature of conflict has shifted the consequences we face. . . ."

Heather took the opportunity to whisper to Tom, "I didn't mean to get you in trouble."

Tom laughed softly and shook his head. "You didn't get me in trouble. This is just Ms. Falmouth letting me know how much she missed me."

His gloves vibrated, signaling that someone was making physical contact with his avatar. Tom glanced down, startled, and saw her hand resting on his arm. Her voice was a breathy whisper. "You sure?"

Tom stared at her as Ms. Falmouth's voice carried on: ". . . exported conflicts serve several purposes . . ."

"I'm sure," he told her, so keenly aware of her touch she might as well have been next to him touching him in real life, too.

Heather's hand trailed down his arm and then slipped away. She nestled it back on her desktop. Tom found himself wondering what she actually looked like. Her avatar didn't even look like a ninth grader. Was she older than him?

"With the weaponry we use nowadays," Ms. Falmouth said beside the board, "we could destroy the ionosphere, irradiate the planet, vaporize the oceans. By exporting our wars and engaging Russia and China on, say, *Saturn* instead of on Earth, we can hash out our disagreements over resource allocation without the devastating consequences of traditional warfare, as Heather explained just now. In ages past, people believed that World War III would end all civilization. A famous quote by Albert Einstein: *'I know not with what weapons World War III will be fought, but World War IV will be fought with sticks and stones.'* But we're in the middle of World War III, and we're far from ending civilization."

Ms. Falmouth twitched her finger and the chalkboard morphed into a screen. "Now, I'd like to focus upon the current Intrasolar Forces. I want you to turn your thoughts to the teenagers who are out there deciding the future of your country. We'll play a short video clip."

Tom sat up straighter, watching the screen resolve into an outdoor view of the Pentagon and the tall tower jutting from the middle—the Pentagonal Spire—and then to a newsroom where a familiar teenage boy sat with a reporter.

It was Elliot Ramirez.

Tom slumped back down in his seat. Behind him, Serge Leon actually cried out in dismay, "Not *Dorkmirez!*"

Elliot Ramirez was everywhere. Everyone knew him— the handsome, smiling, all-American seventeen-year-old who represented the future of Indo-American supremacy in the solar system. He was in commercials, on bulletin boards, his bright grin flashing and dark eyes twinkling on cereal boxes, on vitamin bottles, on T-shirts. Whenever a new Indo-American victory was announced on the news, Elliot was trotted out to give an interview and to talk about how America was *sure* to win now! And of course, Elliot was front and center in Nobridis, Inc.'s public service announcements because they sponsored him. He was one of the young trainees who controlled American machines in outer space, one of the Americans dedicated to taking down the Russo-Chinese alliance and claiming the solar system for the Indo-American allies.

"How did you get the call sign Ares?" the reporter asked Elliot. "That's the Greek god of war, I understand. It says a lot about your battlefield prowess."

Elliot's chuckle flashed his white teeth. "I didn't choose 'Ares' for myself, but I guess my fellow soldiers thought it should be my call sign. They pleaded with me to take it. I couldn't refuse the appeals of my brothers-in-arms."

Tom laughed. He couldn't help it. Several female avatars whirled around to shush him.

The image on the screen flickered briefly to a battle in

space, where a vessel digitally labeled "Ares" was flying toward a dispersed mass of ships. At the bottom of the screen, the caption read "The Battle of Titan." The reporter's voice carried on over the image: ". . . great deal of attention these last few years, Mr. Ramirez. How do you feel about the public's fascination with you?"

"To tell you the truth, I don't see myself as a great hero the way so many people do. It's the machines that do all the fighting in space. I just control them. You could say"—and here the image flipped back to Elliot just as he threw a wink at the camera—"I'm just a kid who likes to play with robots."

Tom kept remembering the only interview of Elliot Ramirez he'd ever sat through before this one. His father was in the hotel room with him, and he'd insisted on watching the entire thing several times because he was convinced that the famed Elliot Ramirez wasn't a real person. He refused to change the channel until Tom was convinced of it, too.

"That's not a boy. That's a computer simulation," Neil had declared.

"People have seen him in person, Dad."

"No human being acts like that! Look how he blinks every fifteen seconds on the dot. Time it. And then look at his eyebrows. He raises them to the exact same height every single time. That smile, too. Always the same width. That's a computer-generated simulation of a human. I guarantee it."

"Who's the reporter talking to, then?"

"She's in on it, too. Who owns the mainstream media? Corporations. That's who."

"Right. So I guess cereal companies are putting a fake kid on their boxes, and Elliot's big sponsor, Nobridis Inc., is also parading around a guy they've never met? Oh, and don't forget all those people on the internet who say they've gotten his autograph. . . . They're *all* in on it, too, right?"

Neil's spit began flying. "Tom, I am telling you, this Elliot kid is not a real person. This is how the corporate oligarchy works. They want a pretty face to make their agenda look good for the masses. A real human being is unpredictable. Create a computer-generated human to be the representation of your organization? Then you control everything about that representation. He's no different from a logo, an action figure, a piece of insignia."

"And you're the only one in the world who's picked up on this."

"What, you think the American sheeple are going to question the corporatocracy? They're too busy doing their patriotic duty, gutting their own country to fund a war over which Coalition CEO gets the biggest yacht this year. Wake up, Tom! I don't want any son of mine buying into the establishment propaganda."

"I don't. I don't," Tom had protested.

He wanted his dad to be right. He really did. Even now, he studied Elliot and tried to see something fake and computer simulated about him, but he just saw a cheesy kid madly in love with himself who laughed at his own jokes way too much.

"What message would you like to leave viewers with tonight, Mr. Ramirez?"

"I want them to know, we kids at the Pentagonal Spire aren't making the big sacrifice. Saving the country's pretty fun! It's you, the American taxpayers, who keep the fight for our nation going strong. And thanks to Nobridis, Inc., the Indo-American alliance is more—"

"Saving. The. Country." Ms. Falmouth flipped off the video segment as Elliot launched into promoting Nobridis. "The next time you think you have too much homework, I want you to consider the burden on this young man's shoulders. Elliot Ramirez is out there forging a future for our nation, securing the solar system's resources for us, and you don't hear him complaining, do you?"

The bell filled the sim. Ms. Falmouth didn't even get a chance to dismiss them. Students began fizzling away.

Tom was normally among the first to sign off. He wasn't this time because just as he raised his hand to yank off the VR visor, Heather spoke up. "Are you signing off already?"

She sounded disappointed about it. Tom dropped his hand again. "Not yet."

She scooted her desk over so they were sitting right next to each other. Despite himself, Tom felt his hands grow sweaty in his wired gloves.

"Can you believe Elliot Ramirez?" Heather said, tossing her dark hair out of her eyes. "His ego almost explodes out of the screen, doesn't it? I felt like ducking and covering."

"I can't believe you're a real girl and you're not in love with Elliot Ramirez," Tom said appreciatively. Then it occurred to him: she might not even be a real girl. For all he knew, she was a guy with a voice modifier who'd hacked the school feed.

"Let's just say, I feel like I know enough about Elliot not to buy the hype." There was something coy in her voice that made him wonder if he was missing a joke.

"And you really *are* a girl?" Tom couldn't resist asking.

"I am so a girl!"

"Yeah, well, I won't believe it till I see it."

"Is this your way of asking me to video chat?" Heather bantered.

Tom hadn't thought to ask her to do that. He recovered from his surprise quickly. "Yes?"

Heather twirled a lock of her dark hair around her finger.

"So, this *is* an online school," she said coyly. "Is video chatting Rosewood's version of a date?"

Tom opened and closed his mouth. She didn't sound like she hated the idea. He broke into a grin. "Only if you're gonna say yes."

Heather smiled. "What network address will you be at tomorrow, Tom?"

HE WAS ONLY half in the moment as he gave her his network address, as he promised her he'd be right at the same network address tomorrow when they met. He didn't care if they were meeting at an obscenely early hour of the morning. Heather said it was because of the time zone she was in. Tom decided he'd stay up all night if he had to. His brain was whirling. He had a date . . . kind of. With a real, live girl . . . he hoped.

After she logged off, his avatar remained by his desk, his real body sitting stock-still on the couch in the VR parlor, the enormity of asking a girl out for the first time *and* having the girl say yes beating through his brain. He'd thought this would be just another ordinary day. . . .

A throat cleared.

Tom noticed suddenly that he and Ms. Falmouth were the only ones left in the virtual classroom.

"I was just logging off," Tom said quickly, and reached up in the real world to snatch off his visor.

"Not quite yet, Tom," Ms. Falmouth said. "Stay a moment. I think we need to talk."

Oh.

A heaviness settled in Tom's chest, because he'd half expected this, and it wasn't good.

"Let's go to my office." Ms. Falmouth twitched her fingers

to alter the program, and the landscape shifted around them into a private office. She settled at one side of the imposing desk. Tom navigated himself into the seat opposite, and waited for some hint of what she needed to hear before she'd let him off the hook this time.

"Tom," she said, folding her hands on her desk, "I am concerned about this attendance situation."

Tom let out a breath. "I figured."

"You were referred to this institution because your father somehow let you reach age eleven without enrolling you in school. We've worked to catch you up, but I don't feel you're making the same progress as the rest of the class. In fact, considering that you're very rarely *in* class, I am finding this situation outright unmanageable."

"Maybe I need an alternative school," Tom suggested.

"This already *is* an alternative school. This is the end of the line."

"I try."

"No, you don't. And what's more, your father doesn't try, either. Do you realize you missed two quizzes and a history paper last week?"

"It couldn't be helped."

"Russo-Chinese hackers, right?" she said. "Or perhaps you were taken hostage by terrorists again, or washed out to sea and stranded on a desert island without internet access?"

"Not quite." But he'd really get a kick out of using that one sometime in the future.

"Tom, you are not taking this seriously—and that's your problem. This is not some silly game: this is your future and you are throwing it away with both hands. You promised me a month ago that you would never miss class again." Ms. Falmouth's avatar gazed at him with an unnatural, unblinking intensity. "We signed a learning contract, don't you remember?"

Tom didn't point out that she'd demanded that he promise not to miss class again. What had she expected him to tell her, the truth? Should he have outright admitted he probably wasn't going to show up at school? She would've just yelled at him for "being insolent" or something.

"This is not about me," Ms. Falmouth went on. "It's not about your father, even: it is about you, Tom. You realize that whatever actions I take from here, they're for your own good. I cannot sit back and allow a fourteen-year-old boy's entire life to be sabotaged by an irresponsible parent who will not even ensure he gets a proper education."

Tom sat up in both the sim and the VR parlor. "What does that even mean—'whatever actions you take from here'?"

"It means you're under court order to attend school, and you have not been attending. Last week, I reported your absences to Child Protective Services."

Tom slouched back, feeling like he'd just been socked in the stomach. This was not going to end well. Maybe he wasn't reaching great heights of achievement with Neil, but life in foster care wouldn't be a land of hope and opportunity either.

And no way could he stay at his mom's.

No way, no way.

Dalton, her boyfriend, paid for her fancy apartment in New York City. Tom had visited her once, just once, and he'd met him. Dalton Prestwick was this rich, yacht-owning executive at some big multinational company, Dominion Agra. His job was to talk to politicians or something.

Dalton had looked him over like he was something nasty smeared on the bottom of his leather shoes and said, "My attorneys have documented everything of value in this house, punk. The second something goes missing, I'll have you in juvenile hall."

Oh, and Dalton already had a wife. And another girlfriend. Yeah, and Tom's mom.

"I don't have anywhere else to go, Ms. Falmouth. I know that you think you're doing me a favor, but you're not. I promise you."

"You're fourteen, Tom. What do you expect to do with yourself in a few years when you need to make a living? Do you plan to be a roving gambler like your father?"

"No," Tom answered at once.

"A roving gamer?"

He wasn't quite sure how much Ms. Falmouth knew about his gaming, but he didn't say anything. If she'd asked him what he planned to be, he might've said he'd make his living one day the same way he was doing it now.

Hearing it said by her made him think of living like this forever, of going nowhere in life . . . of turning into his father . . .

Suddenly Tom felt kind of fuzzy and clenched up inside like he was getting sick.

Ms. Falmouth leaned back in her seat. "You're competing in a global economy. One out of three Americans is unemployed. You need an education to be an engineer, a programmer, or anything of use to the defense industry. You need an education to be an accountant or a lawyer, and you need connections to go into government or corporate work. Who do you think will hire a young man like you when there are so many high-achieving candidates out there who are desperate for work?"

"It's years away."

"Pretend it's tomorrow. What are you going to do with yourself? What are you good for?"

"I'm good at . . ." He stopped.

"At what?"

He couldn't come up with anything else, so he just said it. "Games."

The word sat on the air between them, and to Tom it suddenly sounded utterly sad.

"So is your father, Tom. And where is *he* now?"

CHAPTER TWO

Back when Tom was little, Neil seemed like a god to him. His dad didn't have a boring job like other people. He was a gambler. He sipped at his martini like James Bond and bluffed his way into winning other people's money. Tom grew up hearing stories about the way his dad used to get flown for free to tournaments for professional poker players, the way he used to get the largest hotel suites on the highest floors and then tip the maids a few thousand dollars. Women always found a reason to talk to him, but Neil waved them away like they were invisible, because he was in love with the most beautiful woman of all.

When Tom was a little kid, he'd believed in the dream. He was sure his dad's glory days would return. Any minute, Neil was going to turn back into that winner he used to be, then they'd stay in one place and his mom would return, and she'd be so sorry she'd left them.

But now, at fourteen, Tom knew his dad didn't even get invited to the same tournaments that used to fly him in for free, and his mother was still gone. They never stayed in the same place for more than a week or two, and they never would. He didn't expect that to change. He was too old to believe in fairy tales.

Tom tucked the wired gloves back in the VR parlor's storage container, his own words resounding in his mind: *I'm good at games.* He drove his hands into his pockets and ignored the fears until they became nothing more than an ache in his gut.

He tried to turn his thoughts toward the other thing that happened today: Heather. His brain buzzed with the memory of her words, the way she'd smiled when she thought he was asking her out. He was still thinking of her later that night when he paid for a double room at the front desk, and he was so wired up with anticipation for the next morning that he didn't manage to fall asleep until well past midnight.

And then his father staggered in.

Neil flipped the light on, blasting the glare through Tom's eyelids. Springs squeaked as he sagged onto the other bed. "Got our room again, Tommy? I can always count on you. You're a real good boy. You're a good kid."

Tom opened his eyes a crack and squinted against the flood of light to see Neil clumsily loosening his tie. "Dad, could you turn the lights back off?"

"Gonna get out of this one day, eh, Tommy?" Neil slurred. "Next big win, s'all done. Finished."

Tom clawed out of the covers and then headed across the room to turn off the lights himself.

"A hundred thou's all I'm asking," Neil rambled on. "Won't squan-squan—lose it all again. Rent an apartment. Bigger than the one that chump Dalton's got your mom living in. Maybe send you ter a real school someday. In a building, y'know?" He smiled sloppily at Tom. With his undone collar, mussed hair, and slack, unshaven face, he looked demented.

Tom flicked the light off. Neil was his family. And his dad had his back, he knew. But ever since those social workers confronted them the first time about the not-going-to-school thing, and Tom saw what the lives of other kids were like, he'd started thinking about stuff.

The truth was, he'd taken it for granted before Rosewood that living like this was normal. He thought that whole idea of houses and schools and dinners at a table were fantasies. Neil always called it "corporate propaganda manufactured to promote lifelong debt servitude."

But it wasn't propaganda. Not really. Sure, a lot of people had it worse. A lot. There were families on the streets, gathered in tent cities, squatting in derelict buildings and abandoned factories. But there were also guys like Serge Leon who'd lived in one place for years on end, and people who knew where they'd be sleeping tomorrow night. Tom couldn't predict anything. All he knew was, he'd be somewhere with Neil. With this.

With *this*.

A nasty, dark feeling descended on him as his father's wet snores saturated the hotel room. Even with the AC on high, the sound thundered in his ears. He shifted, turned, pressed his pillow over his head, trying to muffle it, but it was like ignoring a hurricane. The noise just grew louder and louder.

Finally Tom gave up on sleep and tore off the covers.

He needed to shoot something.

THE VR PARLOR was empty at five thirty in the morning, a lonely lounge of couches and dim screens. Tom settled on the center couch, strapped on a visor, and flipped through the game selection to Die, Zombies, Die. Two hours later, he'd blasted and slashed his way to level nine and upgraded to a bazooka. He was busy blowing a nice hole in the Queen Zombie's torso when the game flickered and went black on him.

"Hey," Tom objected and reached up to slide off his visor, but then it fizzled with another image.

The eyepieces lit with a slash of crimson that expanded into a stark red Martian landscape. Tom gazed around, surprised. It was like he'd unwittingly activated another game within the game.

He went with it.

First thing he did was look at his character's attire and weaponry. He was in a space suit. Obviously his character was humanoid, then. Over the horizon, he caught sight of a tank jerking across the bloodred landscape. An information bubble popped up and informed him that his enemy was in this hydrogen-powered tank and his objective was to kill or be killed.

The cylindrical canon cranked toward him, and his heart leaped. He whipped around as swiftly as his character could move and dove into a ditch just before a bone-jarring blast hurled dust into the air on all sides of him. He crawled through the haze into the nearest artillery pit. Another blast missed him, and he dropped into the makeshift shelter.

There was a rumbling through the thin Martian atmosphere as that tank made its way toward him, the slow harbinger of his death. Thrills of excitement shot through him. He wasn't used to going so blindly into a sim. The tank's targeting would improve once it drew closer, and even this pit wouldn't save him. He had to blow his enemy up before that.

He began to figure out what this was: an incursion.

Incursions happened when gamers hacked into the systems of other gamers to challenge them in a sim. No one had ever incursed him before, and Tom couldn't incurse anyone at all because he didn't know how to do it.

He felt almost delirious with his good fortune. He desperately hoped this was some very awesome gamer, someone spectacular. Someone with a chance of beating him. He'd kill for a real challenge.

He hurled a look around. He was trapped in a gulley, at an utter disadvantage. The only weapon in reach was an iono-sulfuric dispersal rifle planted in the red dirt. He could see the other dugouts in the distance, the symbols etched in their sides telling him one held a batch of grenades, the other C29 antitank guns. According to the information bubble that popped up in the corner of his vision, those were exactly what he needed to take out that tank, but how could he get to them without being blown up?

The ground shook around him with another blast. His gloves vibrated with the rumble. Tom took advantage of the crimson haze and flung himself toward the iono-sulfuric weapon. He seized it and dropped back into the pit. Pretty straightforward rifle, this one, at least according to the next information bubble. Too weak to take out a tank, but it could generate a couple of little blasts, coat his surroundings with a white film, and create a distraction. He needed to fire this, use the haze as cover, and get to the antitank dugout, and then?

The tank rumbled closer, and Tom saw the error in his logic: whoever this gamer was, he probably knew the C29 dugout would be Tom's assured path to victory. If he was the guy in the tank, he'd wait for the sulfuric haze. He'd count on it. He'd get the coordinates for the antitank dugout beforehand, wait a few seconds, and then lay down a line of fire right in the path to it.

No, Tom couldn't play into his hands. He'd have to be trickier than that.

So he made a show of making a fatal error. He fired the iono-sulfuric rifle, coating the atmosphere around the tank in a white haze.

But he didn't go for the antitank guns.

He leaped up out of the ditch and ran straight toward the tank, used his last glimpse of the tank and its velocity to assess position, and swerved to the side before the tank plowed through the haze to run him down. The blast of sound rumbling past him knocked his character over. Tom saw the stark metal through the white haze and charged after it

He leaped forward, fumbling for handholds, and hoisted himself up the back. A few scrabbling grasps with the wired gloves later, and Tom's character was on top of the tank, above the latch. *This* was one thing an iono-sulfuric rifle could handle. He aimed for the lock, blasted it off, and had the hatch open before the guy inside the tank knew his doom was coming through the ceiling.

With an exultant laugh, Tom dropped through the hatch, his feet clanging on the floor. He stalked toward the thrashing body. No space suit. He wasn't meant for the atmosphere. The gases inside him were trying to burst their way out of his skin into the thinner atmosphere of Mars.

"Nice try, buddy," Tom said, and slammed the guy in the head with the butt of his rifle over and over until he went still.

Tom dropped the gun and settled down next to the dead body, waiting for the next level, hoping the incursing gamer wasn't going to tuck tail and run.

But then the body morphed. Tom leaped to his feet and stared, fascinated, as it changed from a man in combat gear to a woman. A girl.

She sat up, tossed her dark brown hair out of her eyes, and gave him a slow, mesmerizing smile. Tom gaped at her, his brain blanking out with disbelief.

"Heather." He realized suddenly that *she* was the incursing gamer. *She'd* been the one to challenge him to a sim. He wondered if the sense of awe and excitement sweeping through him was what it felt like to be in love. "You're a gamer, too!"

"Not exactly, Tom." There was a teasing note in her voice. "Congratulations. You passed."

"Passed what?"

But she vanished and the simulation went black. Tom gazed into the darkness, confused, and then a slow, steady clapping filled his ears.

His *real* ears.

Tom flipped up the visor and shot to his feet to face the other person in the VR parlor.

The newcomer was an older man with graying hair; a long, pale face; bulbous nose; and full-on military fatigues. He rose from the couch across from him, and Tom realized uneasily that the man must've been there for a while just watching him.

"Well," said the old man, "you're everything I expected, Mr. Raines. Most don't even make it into the tank on their first try." He tapped on his ear and said to someone, "I've got visual confirmation that it's Raines. You can log off now. The network address checks out. Fine work, Heather."

The whole transition from virtual Tom to real Tom always made him feel weird and stupid even when he wasn't taken by surprise by some stranger staring at him while he played. "Wait, you know Heather? You two set up that sim?"

"Ms. Akron was scouting you out for me," the old guy said. "I've been looking for you for a month, son. You're a hard fellow to track down. As soon as she secured your network address for today, I hopped on a plane. I wanted to run you through that scenario once before I made up my mind, but I was certain you wouldn't disappoint. And you haven't."

Tom's mind flickered to his dad's constant assertions—*The IRS would love to get their hands on me*—and he edged back. Then again, this could be something to do with Ms. Falmouth's threat yesterday about calling Child Protective Services. Either way . . . "Why have you been looking for me?"

"Let's just say, I've been searching for young people who fit a certain profile, and you top my list. One of my officers discovered you on a gaming network, but you kept moving on to new places before we could make contact. I watched you face off with your opponent here in the lounge last night. Tricky move you pulled in that racing game."

Tom froze. "Oh, you saw that?"

"I've also watched you several other times. Back in Southern California. In New Mexico."

Tom fixed his eyes on the bulbous tip of the man's nose, thinking quickly of some excuse. He hadn't been doing anything illegal. . . . Well, anything illegal *apart* from the underage gambling. Actually, that was very illegal all by itself. What could he say? Maybe he could just deny he was doing it.

"I didn't see you in person," the man assured him. "I was given a feed of some of your old games. You're quite the gamer. I'm impressed."

Tom blinked. "Impressed?" That wasn't what he'd expected. "Um, who are you?"

"My name is General Terry Marsh. As you may know, the government's been monitoring the country for some of our most promising young people to be Combatants in the war."

Tom said nothing. The words did not compute.

Marsh went on, "I'm here because we need someone like

you at the Pentagonal Spire."

The Pentagonal Spire.

The Pentagonal Spire. Where the Combatants for the Intrasolar Forces trained. Where people like Elliot Ramirez lived.

Tom realized what this was. "All right, did someone put you up to this? Because I'm not a total chump. Whatever this is really about, I'm not going for it."

"Sorry to hear that," Marsh noted drily. "Most teenagers would jump at the opportunity to join our Combatants."

Tom spun back to face him, because the old man looked stern, and he was wearing military getup, after all. "You're messing with me, aren't you? You have to be."

Marsh gestured for him to sit down. "Mr. Raines, you've heard of the current war situation. You must have."

Tom stayed where he was. "I don't live in a cave."

"I'll take that as a yes. You see, we used to give programmers control of the Indo-American machines fighting across the solar system. They created programs that determined the actions of those machines. Logical actions. The Russo-Chinese alliance adopted the same strategy, so combat became very predictable. The outcome was predetermined, and oftentimes, an outright stalemate. So we became clever. We inserted a human factor into the behavior of machines."

"Combatants."

"No, first hackers. They tampered with Russo-Chinese software. Russia and China deployed their own hackers, and we stalemated again. But the Russo-Chinese military went a step further, and gave human beings active control over their combat machines. Strategists. Unconventional thinkers. Risk takers. Mavericks. Young ones, because teenagers have certain attributes critical to this type of warfare. So now we, too, have young people on the front lines, young people playing a critical role in the war effort."

"Young people like Elliot Ramirez," Tom pointed out.

In other words, young people who were promising, talented, go-getters. Young people who were nothing like him.

"That's right," the general said, undaunted. "Elliot has a particular set of strengths he brought to our forces. Charisma, charm, and he's an excellent figure skater."

Tom snorted. He couldn't help it, picturing the heroic warrior, Elliot Ramirez, in a sparkly unitard.

Marsh's eyes narrowed. "Make fun all you like, young man, but that kid has golden DNA. He'd have been something spectacular wherever he went. If he hadn't ended up with us, Ramirez would be competing in the Olympics. For us, it's the potential that counts. We look for people who are promising, those who can deploy effective strategies against the Russo-Chinese Combatants. We can train our recruits, we can make them better than they ever imagined, but potential? It's the single quality we can't create. Ramirez brought something unique to the table. And we're hoping you can as well."

That sense of disbelief crept over Tom. This couldn't be happening.

"Do you need to see proof, Tom?"

"Yes," Tom answered at once.

"How about I show you a Challenge Coin?" Marsh slipped out a coin from his pocket. "Members of the Air Force—"

"Show this to each other to prove they're military. I know. I've played about a million military sims." Tom snatched the coin and turned it over in his hands, seeing the Air Force insignia, on the back.

Marsh took it back from him and pressed his fingertip over the logo. "Brigadier General Terry Marsh, United States Air

Force," the old man said. The coin's surface flashed green, verifying his voiceprint, his identity, his fingerprint, and DNA all at once.

Tom looked at Marsh's stubby fingertips, coin clenched between them, trying to figure out ways someone could fake Air Force technology. The very idea this general guy might be here for him was so incredible, he couldn't get his head around it.

"Does that pass your inspection?" Marsh asked him, waving the coin in two fingers.

Tom stared at it, then dragged his gaze up to Marsh's. "You're really here for me? You think *I* could be a Combatant?"

"It's a great opportunity, son. We give trainees an education in strategic theory, and if they're good, we give them a chance to be the Combatants who direct our mechanized intrasolar arsenal. In cases like yours, the cognitive skills and reflexes fostered by these gaming simulations prime you perfectly for operating combat machines."

"That's why you picked me? Because I'm good at games?"

"Because you show a killer instinct in them."

Tom thought suddenly of Ms. Falmouth. Her words rang in his brain: *What are you good for?*

For this, apparently. For saving the country just like Elliot Ramirez.

"Your quick victory in that test scenario?" Marsh went on. "That's my icing on the cake, so to speak. It confirmed everything I suspected. You'd be perfect for us."

Tom closed his eyes and opened them, expecting this to be some glorious dream. But Marsh was there, the VR parlor was real.

Marsh gave a crisp nod at something he saw on his face. "That's right, son. Your country needs you at the Pentagonal Spire. The question is, are you man enough to win a war for us?"

"NOT A CHANCE," Neil said.

Tom sat on the edge of his bed in their hotel room. Neil nursed a drink, since, as he always liked to say, a good screwdriver was the only reliable hangover cure he knew. The very mention of Tom's encounter with General Marsh made every line stand out on his face.

"Dad, I can't pass this up." Tom flipped through the parental consent form Marsh had given him. "They'll train me and I'll be a Combatant. And it's for our country—"

"You won't be fighting a war for this country, Tom." A wave of Neil's hand sent orange juice sloshing over the rim of his glass. "Our military fights to secure first extraplanetary mineral rights for Nobridis, Inc. The Russo-Chinese alliance fights back to secure them for Stronghold Energy. War isn't about countries! Multinationals use taxpayer-funded militaries to fight their private skirmishes, and then they sell the public on paying for it by donning the mantle of patriotism. This is all just a big fight between members of the Coalition to see who will become the richest CEO in the solar system!"

Tom had heard this whole antiestablishment thing many times before. Neil pulled it out every time someone asked him why he hadn't ever held down a job—*Why haven't I jammed my neck in the yoke of corporate servitude, you mean?*—or paid taxes—*I've got better causes to support with my money than stuffing the coffers of Amerika, Inc.!*

So Tom studied the consent form and tuned him out.

"You know how the military treats its people, Tom? They chew them up and spit them out, that's how. You're just another piece of equipment to them. And for what? Not for your country. For the wallet of some business executive you'll never meet in some luxury suite you'll never see!"

Tom looked over his father, with his sloppy morning drink, his rumpled clothes, and unshaven face. "Dad, this is a career. It's a real life. Marsh said I'll even get a salary."

"You have a real life. Don't let that rat general tell you—"

"I don't need him to convince me of anything," Tom burst out. "I'm sick of this. It's the same thing over and over again. You lose all our money, and I miss school and have to deal with Ms. Falmouth. I bet this is why—" He stopped talking.

He'd almost said it. That dark thought, the one he never voiced.

I bet this is why Mom left us.

It took Neil a moment to speak, as though he'd heard the phantom words. "This is not the only way we have to live. If you're tired of this, we'll settle somewhere. You don't have to join them. Next win and I'm done."

Tom closed his eyes, blood beating in his head. There would never be a "next win." And even if there was, it wouldn't be enough, and the next win would be gambled away just as quickly as the other ones. He'd heard this all before. His dad would never give up this life. The promise was worthless. And Tom would be worthless, too, if he didn't get away while he had the chance.

"I don't have to join the military, Dad. I *want* to." He opened his eyes and approached it from his father's perspective. "Is it the money thing? My salary will be in a trust, but I get a living allowance. I can send some along. I can help you out."

Why was Neil looking at him like he'd stabbed him or something? They both knew Tom was the one paying for their rooms lately.

Neil's jaw clenched. "Fine. Fine, Tom. I'll sign whatever blasted form you want. You want to throw your life away? Want to pledge yourself to the corporate war machine?"

"Yes, Dad. I want to pledge myself to the corporate war machine." Tom's voice grew ferocious. "It's my choice."

"It's your mistake."

"Maybe. But it's *mine*."

Neil yanked the consent form from Tom's hands. "This isn't how teenaged rebellion's supposed to go. You're supposed to shock me by doing something scandalous. Not by joining the establishment."

"This is about as scandalous as I'm going to get, Dad. Sign the form."

"I'd rather you got a tattoo."

Neil scrawled his signature on the form and handed custody of Tom over to the US military.

LATER IN THE afternoon, General Marsh returned to collect the contract—and his newest recruit.

"Mr. Raines, you have no need to worry about Tom while he's with us. We'll take good care of your boy." Marsh offered Neil a hand to shake.

Neil stared back at him with stony hatred. He ignored Marsh's hand and instead reached out to envelop Tom in a rough, parting hug.

"Tom"—Neil ruffled his hand in Tom's hair—"whatever happens, you take care of yourself. Got it?"

"Got it."

Tom couldn't help wondering at the look on his dad's face when he walked away. Neil stared after him like he was sure this was the last time they'd ever see each other.

CHAPTER THREE

As the airplane hummed around him, Tom imagined himself as a Combatant, saving America from some devastating Russo-Chinese plot. And maybe then Ms. Falmouth would see him on TV and gasp, realizing her least favorite student had just saved her country. Then everyone at Rosewood would find out, too.

Suddenly he wanted to tell her where he was going. He had this weird need to hear what she'd say. But when he asked about visiting Rosewood one last time, Marsh shook his head.

"As far as your Ms. Falmouth is concerned, you've been moved to a foster home. We keep as quiet as we can about our young recruits, Tom. The only face we put out there publicly is Elliot Ramirez. The rest of you are only known to the public as call signs."

The flight from Arizona seemed to take forever. When they flew over Arlington, Virginia, Tom finally spotted the building he'd been watching for since takeoff: the Pentagonal Spire, military headquarters for the Intrasolar Forces. The massive spire rose from a five-sided pentagonal base and twisted up into a gleaming, chrome point.

Marsh rapped a knobby knuckle on the windowpane. "Used to be, when I was a kid, Tom, this building was a giant, flat pentagon. The place where the Spire is? Right where it's planted, there used to be a courtyard and two inner rings of the Old Pentagon. We called the courtyard ground zero. It got that name way back in the Cold War, when everyone thought that would be the first place the Soviets bombed. A lot of people were upset when the higher-ups decided to build the Spire over that piece of history, but we were just ramping up competition with the Chinese in space, and we needed an edge. The Spire itself is more than a building. It's the most powerful transmitter in the Western Hemisphere."

"What do you do in the old building?" Tom said as the plane rudders tilted up, outside his window. They decelerated as the hybrid plane shifted into helicopter mode.

"We've got some military traditionals stationed in the remaining three rings. Might as well call them the Corps of Engineers nowadays, though. Don't get me wrong, we have combat companies just in case of civil unrest or the emergence of some new, rogue nation, but they'll never see any real action. A shame, because I was a combat guy myself in the day, and we did more than fight. Helped Interpol track down criminals, overthrew corrupt regimes, even distributed humanitarian aid."

"You were a veteran?" Tom had never met a real one before. His stomach gave a great leap as they descended toward the roof of the Old Pentagon. "Did you shoot guns at people?"

"Not that kind of veteran. I started off as a pilot. Flew troops who *did* shoot guns at people in and out of the Middle

East back when there was some fight in the region. Believe it or not, when I was a young officer, violence wasn't a small-scale, isolated matter. There were always several wars going on somewhere in the world, with guns and bombs and insurgencies and everything you've read about."

The plane touched down on the helipad. Tom and General Marsh unbuckled their seat belts and emerged onto the old building's roof, where a line of military traditionals stood at attention. Marsh exchanged salutes with the ranking officer, stood statue stiff for his retina verification scan, then gestured for Tom to accompany him into an elevator. They dropped into the Pentagon, and emerged into a first-floor corridor joining the old Pentagon to the Pentagonal Spire.

In the hallway leading to the Spire, a crisply dressed woman with large, clear eyes and dark skin awaited them. She strode forward as they drew closer to her. "Thomas Raines, I assume?"

Tom glanced at General Marsh, and began a salute like the ones he'd seen moments before.

General Marsh shook his head. "No saluting, Tom. This is Olivia Ossare. She's a civilian."

The woman beamed at him. "It's a pleasure to meet you, Tom. He's right. I'm a civilian—as are you. When the military began requisitioning teenagers four years ago for intrasolar combat operations, the Congressional Defense Committee, which oversees operations here, drafted a document known as the Public Accord."

Tom followed her into the vast lobby of the Pentagonal Spire, General Marsh behind them. The entrance to the Spire was no less daunting than the glittering chrome outside: high marble ceilings, with a golden eagle glaring down upon those at the threshold. A large American flag stood by the door, ringed by the flags of the current US military allies: India, Canada, Britain, and various European and Oceanian states.

Olivia's heels echoed on the floor. "All recruits are subject to child labor laws. Although you are joining the military, you won't serve in the same capacity as traditional soldiers unless you choose to reenlist at eighteen. You will not hold a formal rank. The military may be your custodian while you're here, but according to federal law, your legal guardian is still your father. The military does not own you."

Tom's eyes strayed to a group of uniformed regular soldiers marching past in formation. Olivia's hand on his shoulder urged him forward.

"Like me, Tom, you'll be something of a civilian contractor. You'll be in the employ of the government but on a limited schedule. You'll receive a traditional education—"

Tom winced. He'd hoped he was done with school forever.

"—a stipend, with a regular salary in a trust, and you'll have Calisthenics as well as a minimum of twenty hours of free time per week. You'll have twenty vacation days per year, some at standard holiday intervals, some at times determined by General Marsh. On weekends, the time is entirely yours to fill. You have liberty of movement as long as you ensure you're back at the Spire by ten p.m."

"And as long as you remain within a twenty-mile radius of this installation," Marsh cut in. "This is the designated zone, Mr. Raines, and you don't stray from it without getting approval from me first. If a trainee goes outside the designated zone, we assume the Russo-Chinese alliance is involved, and we go to DEFCON-2."

"DEFCON-2?" Tom said, stunned.

"That's right. Losing a trainee is a national emergency. We mobilize the traditionals for a hostile retrieval. It's happened recently, and that young man who snuck off to see his girlfriend was not happy with the consequences after we found him. He no longer has liberty of movement. He's lucky to still be here at all, considering how much work it took to keep that story off the internet."

They emerged into a vast circular area with sleek black tables.

"This is Patton Hall," Olivia told him. "It's the mess hall for young trainees and the officers who live at this installation." She steered Tom toward the banks of elevators. "This brings us to"—she pointed to a glass door at the end of the hallway beyond the elevators—"my office, Tom."

Tom squinted, and saw the print: OLIVIA OSSARE, LCSW-C.

"As I said, I'm not military. I'm a licensed social worker, and I'm here for you kids. You can speak to me in confidence if any issues arise. I am here to be your advocate, even if your problem is with your military custodians."

General Marsh took over the tour. He showed Tom the Hart Medical Wing and the Lafayette Room. The latter was a massive chamber with rows of benches and a raised stage between a US flag and a flag of the six Indo-American corporate allies on the Coalition of Multinationals: Wyndham Harks; Dominion Agra; Nobridis, Inc.; Obsidian Corp.; Matchett-Reddy; and Epicenter Manufacturing.

Marsh gestured around them. "The trainees have core classes here in the Lafayette Room with civilian instructors. You'll get to know this room quite well. As a first-level recruit—a plebe—your classes are divided between this room and MacArthur Hall on the fifteenth floor."

They took the elevator to the sixth floor and stepped out into a sleek, windowless room with a plush arrangement of couches in rows, gaming consoles, an air hockey table, a

Ping-Pong table, a pool table, and towering bookshelves. Around the room were sliding doors. One had a giant ax painted across the door and the words GENGHIS DIVISION. The next had a feather and the words MACHIAVELLI DIVISION. The next one had a catapult and the words HANNIBAL DIVISION. There was a musket and the words NAPOLEON DIVISION, and then a sword and the words ALEXANDER DIVISION.

"This is the common area for plebes," Marsh informed him. "Those signs? Those are the doors to the five living quarters for trainees, the 'divisions,' all named after prominent figures in military history—generals and a strategist. Five sides to a pentagon, five divisions." He studierd Tom a moment. "Now, it's time you saw the training rooms, Mr. Raines. I think he's ready, if you concur, Ms. Ossare?"

Olivia's face froze. "I concur, General," she said shortly. "Now's the time." She strode past Tom and pressed the button for the elevator.

They rode up to the training simulation rooms on floor thirteen. Marsh glanced at the information dockets by a door, and pressed a finger to his lips. "Come in here."

He opened the door to reveal a vast, dark chamber. Tom's eyes adjusted to the dimness, and then he saw them: a group of a dozen or so teenagers stretched out on cots in a ring, eyes closed.

Tom was thrown by their zombielike silence, by their stillness, by the EKG monitors with jagged lines registering their heart rhythms. What were they even doing? Marsh called it a simulation, but he didn't see any VR visors or gloves or even one of the old-fashioned sensor bars. No one was gesturing or waving. No one was moving at all, in fact. They looked more like they were patients in some coma ward.

General Marsh gestured for him to come back out of the

room. "Those are plebes," he told Tom in the hallway. "They're running a group scrimmage. Before they get into advanced tactical training, plebes are drilled in teamwork exercises. They're also acclimated to the neural processors in their brains interfacing with something other than their own bodies."

It took Tom a few seconds to comprehend the words: *neural processors . . . in their brains . . .*

He stopped walking. "Wait, what?" He swung around to look at the two adults. "What do you mean, processors *in their brains?*"

Neither Marsh nor Olivia reacted. It was as if they'd both expected this.

Marsh said, "To become a trainee here, Mr. Raines, you have to have a neural processor installed in your head. It's a very sophisticated computer that interacts directly with your brain. You're still human afterward, just something extra as well."

Olivia's hand squeezed his shoulder. Tom pulled away from it. "You didn't say anything about—" he began.

"What did you think, son?" General Marsh raised his thin eyebrows. "Our Combatants control machines, and they fight machines. You've got quick synapses yourself. But your brain isn't machine fast. Not yet. Those kids in there? Their brains are."

Tom understood the zombielike stillness of those kids: the computers were inside their heads. The simulation they were using to train was running inside the computers that were inside their brains.

"All the trainees undergo the procedure, Tom. It's safe." Marsh's eyes riveted to Tom's forehead. "What you teenagers have in great supply—and we adults do not—is neural elasticity. Your brain's adaptable. Adults and neural processors don't go together. We tried it, and it turned ugly. Adult brains couldn't adjust to the new hardware. So we use teenagers. By virtue of your youth, your brains are primed for enhancement. The fact is, you can't control Indo-American combat machines in space if you can't interface with them. To become a Combatant, you need to cross some of that distance between human and computer yourself."

Tom gaped at him. "So all of the trainees here, and those combatants on the news, have all got these neural processors? Even *Elliot Ramirez* has a computer in his brain?"

"That's right. Even Elliot has one."

"What about the Russo-Chinese Combatants?"

"They have them, too. This is top secret information. The public doesn't know this, but it's the key to everything. This is how the war's fought. Combatants use the neural processors to interface with the unmanned drones in space, to control them, and wage battle against the drones controlled by the neural processors of Russo-Chinese Combatants."

Tom looked back and forth between the general and the social worker. He remembered that expression on Olivia's face a few minutes ago when Marsh talked about showing him the training room, and his thoughts dwelled upon it. She'd expected his reaction. They'd both expected it. *This* was the catch. And they'd just decided to ambush him with it.

He found himself thinking of Neil and the way he said Elliot Ramirez wasn't a real human. His dad had been right. Elliot was part computer.

Tom regarded them warily. "Does it change people?"

"No," General Marsh said.

Olivia cleared her throat.

"Somewhat," Marsh amended. "But little changes. Undetectable to you. You're still *you* in every important sense of the word. Your frontal lobe, your limbic system, and your hippocampus are all intact." At Tom's blank look, he elaborated, "We don't alter your thought process, emotions, or memories. We don't change the essence of who you are. That would be a human rights violation. But once we install some hardware in your head, you'll think faster. You'll be one of the smartest human beings alive."

"And, Tom, if you have doubts, you can decline," Olivia added.

Marsh gave a crisp nod. "That's right, son. Give me the word, and we'll have you back at the Dusty Squanto with your old man. You signed a confidentiality agreement on the plane, and we'll hold you to keeping what you've seen here to yourself, but I don't think that will be hard for you. What's important is, you come into this with your eyes wide-open."

Tom couldn't speak for a long while. His dad's words returned to him, unbidden: *You know how the military treats its people, Tom? They chew them up and spit them out, that's how. You're just another piece of equipment to them.*

Equipment. A computer was a piece of equipment. He would *be* equipment.

"That's the only way I can do this?" Tom blurted.

"The only way. Without the neural processor, you're useless to us."

And Marsh had waited until now, after Tom had turned on his father, pressured him into signing the consent form, flown across the country, and gotten his hopes up so high he'd been soaring in the stratosphere, to drop this bomb. It was manipulative. Tom didn't need some computer in his head to see that. If there was one thing he hated, it was feeling like a chump.

"Maybe this isn't for me." Tom watched Marsh's face as he spoke, relishing the shock that washed over the old features. The general thought he'd hooked him. Thought he would feel he had no choice anymore. He felt a surge of vindictive satisfaction at proving him wrong.

"Well, son. That's unexpected. That's, well . . ." Marsh seemed to be fumbling for something to say.

"He's made his decision," Olivia said, triumph in her voice. "Take him home, Terry."

The words sent panic skittering through Tom, because he wanted this life at the Pentagonal Spire. He wanted it ferociously. But he couldn't just be some chump tricked into it. He'd never forgive himself. He'd rather gouge out his own eyes than let Marsh get away with manipulating him.

Marsh studied him for a long, tense moment. Then he said, "I'll tell you what, Tom, how about I give you some time to think it over?"

Tom could have laughed. He'd bluffed and won. He'd forced Marsh to give in a bit. The tension eased in his muscles. He hadn't let the general totally snow him. "Fine. I'll think."

Marsh seemed to relax, too. He held out a shiny black keycard, his watery eyes searching Tom's face, trying to gauge how serious he was about resisting the idea of joining up. "Ms. Ossare, why don't you escort Tom down to the mess hall? There are some meal points on this card. Have a bite to eat. On me. When you feel ready to make your decision, click on the pager."

Tom glanced at the keycard and turned it in his hand for effect. "And if I say no, I get to leave?"

"Yes, Raines." Marsh's voice grew gruff.

"He's legally obligated to allow it," Olivia added.

Tom raised his eyes to hers and returned her smile with a quick one of his own. "Fine. I hope there are a lot of credits on this. I'm starved."

Marsh's look of irritation made it all the better.

TOM SETTLED AT a table in the mess hall directly beneath a row of screens in sleep mode and a large oil painting of a man with a plaque that proclaimed him General George S. Patton. He stared up at the gruff face of the general, an empty meal tray sitting on the tabletop before him. He didn't actually feel like taking it over to the serving line and grabbing food. His head began to ache. He found himself wishing his dad was around.

Then again, if Neil had been there when General Marsh pulled that Oh-I-forgot-to-mention-the-computer-in-your-head-earlier thing, he would've exploded. Maybe punched him. And that wouldn't have helped anything.

Tom scrubbed a hand through his hair. What was the matter with him? He couldn't turn this down. And he shouldn't take it personally. Marsh probably had some standard military recruitment playbook: get the kids away from their parents, get them to the Spire, get their hopes up, and then spring the big surprise-brain-surgery thing.

He held up the keycard and idly turned it back and forth, watching it glint in the light. Knowing he was being manipulated didn't make him feel any better about it.

"If you're not going to use those meal credits, can I?"

The voice startled him. Tom's gaze jolted. It took him a long moment to remember the English language and the fact that he was capable of using it.

"So that wasn't an avatar."

"Nope." Heather Akron was impossibly prettier in person, with her dark brown hair escaping its loose ponytail, her yellow-brown eyes like no color he'd seen naturally before. This time, she wore a uniform: camouflage trousers and dark tunic. The bald eagle insignia of the Intrasolar Forces was on her collar, and beneath it were four triangular points stacked on top of one another, like the tips of arrows shooting upward. "Yours isn't an avatar, either," she teased.

"No." It wasn't so funny this time, knowing she was seeing him up close.

"May I?" She gestured to the keycard.

"It's the general's. Go nuts."

Heather's eyes twinkled as she took it. "Thanks. I used up my snack allotment for this week on lattes. It's so bad, but I can't say no to myself sometimes."

"You don't have to. Say no to yourself, I mean. Not about lattes." He stumbled over the words as she leaned in closer—close enough for her breath to brush his skin.

"How about General Marsh buys us both a drink, Tom?"

"That's a great idea." As long as Heather said his name like that while smiling at him like that, he'd agree that jumping in a nuclear reactor was a great idea, too.

Heather winked. "Perfect!" And she swept off to the coffee stand across the mess hall.

He watched her hips sway away and tried to think of witty things to say when she finally returned, even though he knew after that, she'd be gone. Beautiful girls didn't hang around to talk to short, ugly guys with bad acne.

So he was all the more astonished a few moments later when she lowered herself across the table from him and slid a drink his way, her fingers poking out of the holes of what looked like biker gloves or something. He could see the Intrasolar Forces insignia on her palm, too. He knew what that bald eagle insignia looked like with his eyes closed. He'd seen it on the internet, on the news. He'd never even dared to hope he might get a chance to wear it himself. He knew he was crazy, even hesitating like this.

"I know I should cut back," Heather lamented, sipping at her drink, "but I'm *such* a caffeine addict. I just love how wired it leaves me."

"Yeah," Tom agreed, unsure what he was agreeing with, and took an overlarge gulp of the drink she'd given him. The hot liquid singed his tongue.

"So how about it, Tom? Are you going to be a plebe soon?"

He wasn't sure how to answer that.

"Oh, but I saw how you handled that tank simulation," Heather went on. "I bet you won't be a plebe for long. There are promotions twice a year, and I bet you'll move quickly to Middle Company. After that, it's Upper Company, and then, if you can network with the right people and get a corporate sponsor, you'll join the Combatant group."

"Camelot Company," Tom said, awed.

"It's mostly civilians that use the full name. We're called CamCo here."

Tom straightened. *"We?"*

"Uh-huh. I'm in CamCo."

He gaped at her. He'd probably seen her in action, too. Probably seen clips of her on the internet. "What's your call sign? I bet I've heard of you!"

"Well, I'm a newer Combatant, but maybe you have. I go by Enigma."

Enigma. He'd seen her! She was sponsored by Wyndham Harks, and he remembered this time on Jupiter's moon Io . . . Oh, and that time on Saturn's moon Titan, when . . . A half-dozen battles from the last few months flipped through his head. "I can't believe it," Tom marveled. "You're Enigma.

You're one of the best. I remember that time you guys were fighting on Titan, when you—"

Heather laughed, and linked her fingers with his to stop him. The physical contact was something of a shock to Tom, because it was nothing like VR.

"Tom, that's so sweet of you to say, but this isn't about me right now. It's about you. It's about the choice you're going to make today."

"Right. Right." His attention was riveted to the way her thumb stroked across his knuckles.

"I bet I know why you haven't signed up yet. You're freaked out by this, right?" She tapped at her temple, indicating the implanted processor.

"I wouldn't say 'freaked out.' I'm not freaked out."

Her voice grew softer, her touch still tickling along his skin. "You sure? It's okay to tell me. I can answer any questions you have."

And suddenly, Tom knew why *she* just happened to be here, of all possible people in the Pentagonal Spire. He knew.

He pulled his hand back and grabbed his drink. Globs of whipped cream were melting into the light brown liquid. He could see Marsh's invisible hand in this: he'd sent Heather here because he thought a gorgeous girl could talk Tom into getting his skull split open. This was more of Marsh trying to play him for a sucker. Well, his maneuver wouldn't work.

"I know what you must be wondering." Heather paused and bit her bottom lip. Despite himself, Tom stared at the pink flesh, his mouth suddenly dry. "I worried about it, too. I thought maybe after I got the neural processor in my head, the voice in my brain might disappear and get replaced by some robotic thing, like, 'Good morning, Dave.'"

Gorgeous and a science fiction geek. Tom's heart was

beating faster. Okay, maybe Marsh's maneuver was sort of working.

"But I was worrying over nothing, Tom. I'm still me. I'm just a *better* me."

"Look," Tom told her, before she could go on with the pitch, "it's not the computer itself I have a problem with. I'm not even so worried about being a different person. It's just that Marsh didn't mention any of this brain-surgery stuff until after he was pretty sure I was sold on this. It's the way he did it."

Her amber eyes stayed fixed upon his. "You feel manipulated?"

"No," Tom said flatly, "because he hasn't manipulated me. He's just *trying* to manipulate me. I mean, would you be talking to me right now if he hadn't sent you?"

Heather rested her chin in her palm. "Of course he's trying to manipulate you."

Tom blinked, surprised she'd just admitted that.

"General Marsh even ordered me to come here and talk you into it, just as you guessed. Can you blame him? He doesn't want you to turn this down after you've found out the big secret about the neural processors." She tapped a finger thoughtfully on her lips, studying him. "Good thing you won't."

"I won't?" Tom said, feeling out of his depth with her.

"Mmm, no. You won't," Heather said matter-of-factly. "You know exactly what it means if you come here. They stick an expensive, multimillion-dollar computer in your head. They invest tens of millions more training you. Then they give you control of billions of dollars of military machinery and a critical role in the country's war effort. You're valuable. So of course General Marsh has an agenda when it comes to dealing with you. But that's really what you have to put up with if you want to be one of us. The question is, Tom, do you want to be one of us?" She leaned closer, her eyes gripping his. "Do you want to be somebody important?"

And there it was.

There it was.

Tom leaned back in his seat and tipped his drink to Heather—and the man who had just won this match.

Because, more than anything, Tom wanted to *do something*. Something other than move from casino to casino, something other than turn into his dad.

He'd give anything to be important.

CHAPTER FOUR

WHAT SEEMED A timeless period later, *it* realized something was different.

It held *itself* very still and tried to comprehend what was happening.

Its brain was humming at a different frequency somehow, *its* thoughts meaningless yet logical. *It* blinked at the strange yet familiar symbols running through its awareness—the periodic table of elements—and recognized through some hazy curtain the chemical configuration of the medication in *its* system. *Dexmethasone.*

There was a trail of 1s and 0s, data signals moving through wires, and *it* followed them into what seemed an endless maze of electric pulses swapping back and forth. *It* became a security camera in Rio de Janeiro, gazing upon a large Jesus statue with arms flung wide over a vast, rolling city. Infrared sensors alerted the security camera to the presence of organic beings moving around the statue. The 0s and 1s were leaving there, and *it* followed them to an autonav system in a vehicle winding down a highway in Bombay. A flexure of *its* will could send this car off the road, but *it* knew better. The autonav had strict parameters that dictated *its* actions when *it* was this autonav.

And then *it* followed the next stream and settled in the filtration system in a reservoir in Northern California. Through a process of facilitated diffusion, *it* absorbed organic solutes and then bound them into an inactive compound. Water slapped and dashed at osmotic pressure sensors. But this wasn't right, either.

It found the Grand Canyon and managed to stay there in the security network, frightened by the knowledge that this wasn't what *it* was, either. *It* remained there, a sensory ghost analyzing the perimeter and linking on and off like firing neurons with the autonavs of the visitor cars. *It* lurked in the fizzling thermal sensors overlooking the snoring security guard with boots propped up on the desk, watching the creature, analyzing the being's temperature (98.5° F). Strange to regard this mammal with its vast tangle of chemical processes and the steady thump of the heartbeat (76 beats per minute) and the . . .

Human.

That was right.

It was human.

It was human. Why was *it* . . . Why was *he* so confused? Why was *he* drifting like this?

He. He was *it*. *It* was he. He knew who "he" was.

Tom Raines. Tom. Tom. Tom.

Tom clung to this sudden awareness of self, waiting for reality to resolve back into somethng he understood. He remembered things, just for a moment: the sedative he'd swallowed. Feeling woozy in the operating room. His head being shaved and washed, and being told it was an "antiseptic practice to avoid infection." Heather tapping on the glass wall of the surgical suite and giving him a wave good-bye. The way seeing her made him smile as they strapped a mask on his face . . .

The thought connected him with his body, his sensory receptors, and for a frightening moment, he experienced utter numbness. His hand twitched on the metal table, and he heard a voice inside his eardrum, noting the spike in his neural activity.

". . . centered on the orbitofrontal cortex. Is he aware of us?"

"That's not possible," said another voice. "These instruments can be faulty. I've requested new ones out of Denver. Do you remember that delivery girl?"

But there was something else there, too, something with him, something *not* Tom.

0100010001111100101001010000101110110001100001001011111001010100 . . .

A number that seemed to stretch into infinity. So foreign, so alien, he jerked away from it. But then it felt like he'd been caught in a tsunami, because a great wave crashed over him and swept him back into that ocean of machines drowning him in signals. . . .

A sense of vastness pressed in on him. It hummed all around him in a tangle of infinite complexity: the security cameras in Rio and the Grand Canyon and the reservoir filtration system and four billion car autonavs and hundreds of billions of text messages and stray data bits and computers pinging and games swapping signals and machines sending them from space and satellites and security systems of a billion different . . .

"Stop! Stop!" Tom's voice never left his mouth. That body remained still on the table, its lips frozen, its muscles like lead, its hands cold, its head chilled because it was shaved. Voices chattered on, oblivious to it, and that computer in its brain offered logic and order, and kept restructuring, restructuring him . . . and that maelstrom of signals threatened to sweep him away into infinity itself. . . .

AND THEN TOM opened his eyes in the infirmary. He was in Section 1C3 of the Pentagonal Spire. He knew that because the red number glowed in the bottom right corner of his vision for a split second before vanishing. He stared up at the bars of fluorescent light hanging overhead, and then a round, friendly face appeared above his.

"Feeling better today, Mr. Raines?"

Tom blinked, because something strange was happening. He saw the man's face, but he also saw text, scrolling rapidly through his brain.

NAME: Jason Chang
RANK: Lieutenant, BSN
GRADE: USAF 0-3, active duty
SECURITY STATUS: Top Secret LANDLOCK-6

Tom blinked again, and the text was gone.

"Tom," said Jason Chang, drawing his attention back to the present. "Can you tell me your full name?"

"Thomas Andrew Raines."

Lieutenant Chang flashed a penlight in his eyes. "Do you know where you are?"

"The Pentagonal Spire."

"That's right. Do you know why you are here?"

"Surgery. To get a neural processor implanted."

"Tell me, what's my name and security designation?"

Tom remembered the profile information he'd seen in that

fleeting second, every last word of it. "Jason Chang, BSN?" At the nurse's nod, Tom went on. "Your security designation is Top Secret LANDLOCK-6. . . . How did I remember that?"

"You have a photographic memory now, Mr. Raines, and there's a directory in your processor of everyone's names. You'll see a basic information list the first time you look directly at the faces of the other personnel here in the Spire, and once you've seen it, you won't ever forget it. Now, let's test your internal chronometer. What's the time?"

"It's oh five fifty-three," Tom answered immediately. Then he realized that he'd automatically switched to thinking in the military's twenty-four-hour time.

"Well done."

He blinked three times. He watched the lieutenant lifting a bedside conferencer, tapping in 1-380-4198-4885. Chang spoke, "Dr. Gonzales, Mr. Raines is A and O times three. I understand. I'll run him through the standard assessment."

"I feel strange." Tom's voice registered in his brain, lower than he remembered.

"It's natural." Lieutenant Chang slanted him a dark gaze from almond-shaped eyes. "Your brain needs to adjust to the software. You'll have difficulty at first sorting through the influx of data. It will pass."

Tom glanced up at a seventy-watt light glowing overhead. He'd gazed at this light all day. He'd been awake for a while, blinking at fifteen second intervals. Eighteen days, four hours, nine minutes, twenty-six, twenty-seven, twenty-eight seconds . . .

"I've been awake," Tom realized. "My surgery was eighteen days ago."

Chang peeled a blood pressure cuff from Tom's arm. "Your surgery was eighteen days ago, but no, you have not been awake in the traditional sense. Your brain's been undergoing restructuring. The implanted trainees all have to optimize. You've been conscious and unconscious at intervals, but you were unaware. Your mind needed to adjust to the new neural pathways forged by the hardware in your head. Your brain will regain homeostasis now that you're awake. The extra details will disappear. Soon enough, you'll feel like your old self again. Better than your old self, I'd wager."

Even now, Tom felt like he was regaining a sense of normalcy. He raised his hand to touch his scalp. Only the faintest trace of a scar was there. A thin incision of 3.1 centimeters. His hair was back, 0.7 centimeters of it. He'd been lying here long enough for it to grow. His hand roved down to a numb spot on the back of his neck, and he found a flat, metal port there. It was a neural access port. He just knew what it was.

"Now, Plebe, I'm going to run you through a few procedures to test whether we can send you out yet."

"Already?" Tom croaked. "I'm going to combat now?"

Lieutenant Chang's laughter rippled through the stale, cold room. "Not quite yet. You'll need years of training before you become a Combatant."

"Right." Tom closed his eyes, because there was a datastream blasting the answer through his head: *Standard advancement path in the Intrasolar Forces at the Pentagonal Spire: Initial Training as plebe, followed by Middle Company, Upper Company, and in cases where the trainee is found to excel, Camelot Company, the Combatant group. In cases where a trainee is found unsuitable for intrasolar combat, avenues with other government agencies will be considered, including the NSA, the CIA, the State Department, the . . .*

Tom willed the datastream to stop, and it ceased

immediately. So strange. He knew the information was coming from the neural processor, but it had felt like he was thinking it, like it was an ordinary scrap of information that belonged in his mind.

He was distracted when Chang ran him through the basic assessment, checking his pupils, his sensation of touch, his circulation. And then the lieutenant turned on a recording with various musical notes and asked Tom to identify them.

"I don't know anything about music—" Tom began to protest.

But he did know them. With a strange shock, he listed E, C, D, A.

The nurse saw his shocked face, and patted his shoulder. Then he gestured for Tom to sit up. "We upload a few gigs of information to test you out, plus some class assignments so you don't start off behind. You should have a reference database for your first week here, correct?"

Tom's brain called it up. "Yes." There was a file manager in his brain. In it were three files: *Civilian Classes, Calisthenics, Trainee Specific Programs.* And he knew he could just open and peruse the files with a thought. He just knew it.

"And where are you supposed to go right now?" Chang asked him.

"To meet Vikram Ashwan. My new roommate." Tom paused. Again, something he just *knew.* "This is so weird."

The nurse nodded. "You'll get used to it, I'm told. You're dismissed, Plebe."

Tom opened his mouth to tell him he didn't know where to go, but the Pentagonal Spire answered him this time, a mainframe with a careful tracking module following every recruit within its walls, feeding data into Tom's neural processor.

Tom hopped down from the bed. His legs held, and he wasn't even dizzy after lying in bed for three weeks. He started for the door.

"Mr. Raines, don't forget this," Lieutenant Chang called, holding something out in his hand. "It belongs to you now."

Tom reached out and took the metal object. He held it up and realized it was a Challenge Coin just like the one General Marsh owned. The coin was stamped US INTRASOLAR FORCES. It flashed green when he held it, just like the general's coin had.

A strange but awesome feeling shivered through him as he gazed at the bald eagle and realized this was now *his*.

He felt Chang's dark eyes on him. "Welcome to the Pentagonal Spire, Mr. Raines."

CHALLENGE COIN IN pocket, Tom followed the map that loomed in his awareness like some nagging worry. The Spire said Vikram was 8.6 meters northwest of him. He stepped through the door into the first floor hallway, and indeed, Vikram was 8.6 meters away from where he'd been. Tom's neural processor even ticked down the distance as he closed it.

When he clapped eyes on the Indian boy waiting for him, more text planted itself in his vision:

NAME: Vikram Ashwan
RANK: USIF, Grade III Plebe, Alexander Division
ORIGIN: New Delhi, India
ACHIEVEMENTS: Top honors for Youth Innovation at the International Science and Engineering Fair, recipient of the Enterprise India Scholarship
IP: 2053:db7:lj71::338:ll3:6e8
SECURITY STATUS: Top Secret LANDLOCK-3

Tom must've looked shell-shocked, because the kid with dark skin, bushy eyebrows, and a high hairline of bristly hair flashed him a grin. "Weird, right?"

"Weird," Tom agreed.

"Great thing is, you and I don't need introductions, Thomas."

"I guess not, Vikram."

"Call me Vik. Not Vikram."

"Tom. Not Thomas."

Vik studied him as they headed toward the elevators. "That's strange. You have N/A listed under Achievements. Not available?"

Tom realized Vik must be seeing his profile, the way he'd seen Vik's. "More like not applicable," he said honestly.

Vik raised his eyebrows. "Brace yourself. Everyone here has achievements. You're going to get asked that a few million more times."

"Right. Guess I can't change it."

Vik thought about that. "Actually, you could if you wanted to. There's a girl who can stick something in there. I heard she tweaked some profiles for people before the last round of promotions. We'll see her at morning meal formation."

The time for the Spire's formal breakfast popped instantly into Tom's brain. "At oh seven thirty."

"Right, at oh seven thirty, so you've got just enough time to get into your uniform."

Then, information hit: *Uniforms. Dark tunics with an Intrasolar Forces insignia on the collar, division-specific insignia on the sleeve, camouflage fatigues, combat boots, gloves, portable keyboard* . . .

Tom must've stared a bit too long at the sudden images dancing before his eyes, because Vik waved in his face, then jabbed his thumb toward the elevator doors as they slid open. Tom headed inside, and Vik punched the button for floor six.

"That data flow's a pain, right?" Vik eyed him knowingly. "See, neural processors are useful because there's no fixed time of year for new plebes to join the Spire, but then latecomers have to download a lot more material just to catch up with the trainees who have been around longer. It makes a rough transition even worse."

"When did you join?"

Vik shrugged. "Couple months ago. But I remember it like it just happened. I kept noticing all the stupid details about stuff and couldn't tune them out, and the processor kept defining every new term. It took me maybe three hours to start getting my head straight."

Tom touched the scar on his head. "I don't think this is so bad now."

"Really?" Vik wagged his thick eyebrows. "So you're saying you're better at handling a neural processor than I am?"

There was a note of challenge in his voice that made Tom's mouth quirk. "Yeah, sure sounds like it."

Vik had this crazy gleam in his eyes. "So you don't need some more *sy-nap-tic pru-ning*?"

The term slammed Tom—*Synaptic pruning: During the development of infant brains, excess neural connections are culled and destroyed in order for the world to take on a logical representation within the human mind. . . .*

It took Tom several moments to remember himself, to remember how to will off the datastream.

"Maybe you have fantastic *neu-ral e-las-ti-ci-ty*?" Vik added.

That term hit, too: *Neural elasticity: Elasticity refers to the ability of the brain to adapt as a result of new experiences by adding or removing neural connections. The brain is most elastic during periods of youth before* . . .

"Or maybe you've got—"

Tom shoved at Vik's shoulder before he could throw out another term. "Okay, stop!" He laughed. "You got me, okay?"

Vik gave a laugh that sounded like a giggle.

"Funny guy," Tom said.

"I have a great sense of humor," Vik agreed. "It's been called sparkling."

The elevator doors slid open on floor six to reveal the plebe common room that Marsh had shown him on his tour.

Vik waved around them. "On your tour, they probably told you this is the plebe common room? It is. Technically, it is, but we plebes never use it. It's the largest and best equipped, so the upper-level trainees like to spend their free time here and kick out any plebes who try to linger."

"And you guys let them?"

"Sure," Vik said gamely. "We all aspire to one day be upper-level trainees who kick plebes out of their own common room. I know I do."

They stepped through the door marked Alexander Division into an empty corridor with three hallways branching from it.

"Here's Alexander Division, your home while you're here. I'd call it a dorm, but I think the cruddiest dorms are actually nicer than this. Not much to look at, huh? Come on, we're down here."

In the third hallway, toward the far end of the division, they stepped into a small room with two low beds, stark gray carpets, and off-white walls. There was a small window about the size of Tom's head that gazed right onto the roof of the Old Pentagon, one story below.

"Here we are," Vik said. "Bare walls, and forget about posters or photos or anything. You earn more privileges with personalizing your bunk as you move up the ranks."

"It's perfect," Tom said, meaning it, turning in a slow circle to see the room. *His* room. He'd never had a room that belonged to him before, even partially.

"Low standards. Good for you. You'll like it here."

Tom spotted a leg poking out from beyond one of the beds. He strode forward and saw that the leg belonged to an orange-haired kid in a uniform who was sprawled on the floor.

"Your bed's that one," Vik told Tom, indicating the other side of the room.

"There's a dead guy on our floor," Tom pointed out.

"Yeah, that's Beamer, our neighbor." Vik stepped over to Tom's bed, and kicked open a drawer beneath the mattress. He swept down and yanked out a bundle of fabric. "Here's your uniform."

"There's a dead Beamer on our floor," Tom said again.

Vik dumped the uniform on Tom's bed. "Not dead. He's just being Beamer."

The orange-haired kid turned in his sleep, showing that he wasn't dead but more in a stupor. The round, freckled face triggered an information stream in Tom's head.

NAME: Stephen Beamer
RANK: USIF, Grade III Plebe, Alexander Division
ORIGIN: Seattle, WA
ACHIEVEMENTS: Winner of the NFIB Young Entrepreneur Scholarship, member of National Association of Young Business Owners
IP: 2053:db7:lj71::342:ll3:6e8
SECURITY STATUS: Top Secret LANDLOCK-3

"See," Vik explained, "Beamer made this mistake a few months ago where he snuck outside the DZ—the designated zone—to meet up with his girlfriend from back home . . ."

"Marsh said something about that!" Tom exclaimed. "The military went to DEFCON-2, right?"

"Yeah." Vik laughed. "Then they descended on the girlfriend's house with helicopters and tanks and a gunship, I think, and gave her dad a heart attack. Literally. So Beamer's still trying to make it up to his girlfriend. He spends all night talking to her online instead of downloading homework. He's on restricted libs—you know, restriction of liberties—so I don't even know where he goes to do that. It defeats the point of the neural processors, though. We have computerized memory. We can put anything we want in our heads, but all that info's useless if you don't process it. You have to have time for your brain to make sense of all the data you've downloaded."

Tom stepped over Beamer toward the clothes Vik had slung onto his bed.

Vik nudged Beamer's inert leg with his boot, testing how awake he was. "Most people plug in the homework download during their sleep. Beamer crams the homework download into a few hours, so he doesn't understand any of it. Then he comes staggering in here first thing in the morning and passes out on the floor to make sure I either trip on him on the way out, or drag him to morning meal formation."

The inert, orange-haired boy's eyes snapped open. Beamer sat up so quickly, Tom shot back a step, startled.

"I object to this discussion," Beamer informed Tom, his pale face cloudy, making him look for all the world like someone sleep talking. "Vik is casting aspersions on my character.

Catabolic processes oxidize carbon-containing nutrients."

"What?" Tom said, confused.

But Beamer slumped back down to the floor and said nothing more. It took Tom a long moment to realize he was unconscious again.

"Moron," Vik said fondly, his eyes dancing. "No processing, see? All that info in his brain, none of it in context yet."

"Guess not," Tom murmured. He could kind of sympathize with Beamer there. He felt rather information overloaded himself at the moment.

"Now hurry up with that uniform before the Android swings by to get us for morning meal formation."

"An actual android?" Tom asked. He couldn't tell what was real and what was science fiction anymore.

"Nah. That's what we call Beamer's roommate, Yuri. He goes jogging every morning even though we have Calisthenics three times a week, and he's always in a fantastic mood. He'll help you with homework or move heavy things for you, and he's always trying to make friends with this weird girl Wyatt Enslow, because he feels sorry for her. Nicest guy you'll ever meet. Beamer and I have decided he must be an android. An android slash spy."

"Spy?" Tom yanked the dark tunic, with an Alexander Division sword on the arm, the Intrasolar Forces eagle insignia on the collar, and a single triangular point beneath it. He wriggled on the biker-guy type gloves, and then spotted the last item: a flat keypad.

His neural processor told him to clamp the metal prongs on the bottom of the keyboard onto the slots of the glove on his nondominant hand.

"Shove your sleeve over it," Vik instructed him. "You

won't need the keyboard until later."

Tom pressed the keyboard against his forearm, and found it was made of a flexible polymer that bent with his arm. He hooked the ends into the slots on the glove of his left hand, then pulled down his sleeve to keep it in place.

Vik went on, "So anyway, Beamer's roommate, Yuri, is Russian, right? He also comes from a connected family. His dad knows this guy who practically founded the Intrasolar Forces. He got Yuri into the Spire, whether the US military wanted him or not. Since Yuri was born and raised in Russia, a lot of people think he's a spy. The military must think he is, too, since Yuri became a plebe three years ago and he's still never been promoted. Most plebes are promoted after a year or so. All the others who began the program when he did have advanced to Upper Company or gone off to work for another government agency by now."

Tom tugged on the combat boots, did up the laces, and shoved the ends of his camouflage fatigues in them the way he saw Vik wearing his. "Do you think he's a spy?"

"Nah. I told you, man. He's an android."

The doors slid open. In bounded a giant, wavy-haired kid standing at six foot eight, his body a coiled mass of muscle, a good-natured grin on his swarthy, handsome face.

NAME: Yuri Sysevich
RANK: USIF, Grade III Plebe, Alexander Division
ORIGIN: St. Petersburg, Russia
ACHIEVEMENTS: Chris Canning Award for Academic Excellence, Elsevier Woods Award for Young Humanitarian
IP: 2053:db7:lj71::236:ll3:6e8
SECURITY STATUS: Confidential LANDLOCK-1

Tom stared. He really did have a lower security designation than the rest of them.

"Why, hullo, fellows. Are you ready to head to breakfast soon?" Yuri's gaze lit upon Tom. "Ah. And you. You are the new plebe. Timothy Rodale."

Tom opened his mouth to correct him, but Vik caught his eye and mouthed, "Don't ask."

"You got it," Tom said, bewildered.

Yuri bellowed a hearty laugh. "It's very fine to meet you. I'm Yuri—but this you know." He tapped his own temple.

"Yeah, this I know," Tom said.

"I do not see your achievements listed."

"It's a mistake. We're getting that fixed," Vik told Yuri.

"Uh, yeah," Tom agreed.

A ping in his head. *Morning meal formation is in five minutes.* Tom was caught off guard by the sudden notice, plastered there in his brain like one of his own thoughts. The other boys in the room responded to the same notice. They all jumped to their feet. Beamer didn't stay there long. He keeled right over again. Yuri caught him before he hit the ground.

"Ready?" Vik said to Tom.

Tom nodded eagerly, ignoring the butterflies fluttering inside him. "Ready."

Yuri hauled Beamer up from the floor and hoisted him over one broad shoulder for the trudge down Alexander Division's corridor to the elevator. He hummed merrily the whole way.

"I can walk," Beamer protested blearily.

"You said that last time, and then you bopped your head," Yuri told him. "This is no trouble, Stefan."

Beamer raised his bleary head, and squinted back at Tom. "Huh. New guy doesn't have any achievements."

That stupid profile.

Vik sidled up to Tom. "Told you that would get annoying. Want it changed or not?"

"You said there's a girl who can do that?"

"Wyatt Enslow," Vik answered. "It'll take some doing, but I can talk her into it."

"Why does he think I'm Timothy Rodale?" Tom nodded toward Yuri's large back.

Vik spoke in a normal tone of voice as though Yuri couldn't hear them: "Well, there's never been an official explanation for it, but Yuri's scrambled. Something's wrong with his software, and none of the officers want to fix it, which makes us think he's scrambled deliberately. We figure the military thinks Yuri's a spy, and they couldn't keep him out of the Spire because he has family connections, so they admitted him and then planted a worm in his neural processor's software so he can't hear anything classified."

Tom glanced at Yuri's wide back, but Yuri hummed and showed no signs of having heard them. "*His* neural processor distorts the info he hears?"

"Exactly. From what Beamer and I have figured, he seems to understand the basics of the Spire, but not our identities, IPs, strategies, or anything that might compromise the war effort. His processor's rigged so he doesn't hear our real names if someone mentions them. And forget confidential info. I'll show him some code from Programming, for instance, and he'll look at it and know just what it is, then remember it all wrong. You know how we're talking about him right now literally five feet behind him? Yeah, the processor's interpreting it as something else entirely, I bet."

"Seriously?" Tom was both impressed and disturbed. This was one thing he hadn't even thought about. He should have realized having a computer in his brain made him susceptible to misprogramming like a computer. "Vik, if they mess with Yuri's software, how do you know they can't do something with ours?"

Vik shot him a creepy, unsettling grin, and his eyes gleamed like a madman's. "Why, Tom, we don't."

"That's reassuring. Thanks."

"Anytime, pal. It's what I'm here for."

CHAPTER FIVE

T HE PATTON MESS Hall was already crowded. Meal trays sat at each place on the rectangular tables. Tom looked over the crowd, identifying the division insignias on the arms: a quill for Machiavellis, an ax for Genghises, a sword for Alexanders, a musket for Napoleons, and a catapult for Hannibals.

Vik elbowed him, then nodded for him to follow. They headed toward what Tom's neural processor identified as the Hannibal female plebe table. The girls all sat at one end of the table, talking to one another and ignoring a tall, gawky girl with flat brown hair sitting alone at the other end, her shoulders hunched, eyes darting furtively between the other girls and her tray.

"Hey, Enslow!" Vik called.

The girl looked up, her eyebrows drawn closely together in a solemn, oval-shaped face. Tom's processor identified her as

NAME: Wyatt Enslow
RANK: USIF, Grade III Plebe, Hannibal Division
ORIGIN: Darien, Connecticut
ACHIEVEMENTS: Mathlete of the Year, Riven Middle
School; twice annual winner, Scholar Mathlete
Award; Gold Medalist, International Mathematical
Olympiad; first place James Lowell Putnam
Competition
IP: 2053:db7:lj71::335:ll3:6e8
SECURITY STATUS: Top Secret LANDLOCK-3

"You still helping out with profiles?" Vik asked her.

Wyatt's lips compressed. "Feel free to shout louder, Vik.
I don't think Lieutenant Blackburn heard you on the officer's
floor. And *no,* I'm not doing that anymore. I almost got caught
last time."

"Come on, Enslow," Vik urged. "Help Tom out. Yuri wants
you to."

"So why isn't Yuri asking me himself?"

"He's busy ambulating Beamer."

"What do you guys want changed?" Her gaze settled on
Tom. "Oh, that."

"Yeah, that," Vik said. "Someone forgot to program in
Tom's vast number of achievements."

Tom glanced at him, fighting back a snigger. Yeah, his many
great achievements. He beat lots of video games and even ate
two pizzas in the space of five hours once.

"Tom here's kind of embarrassed about looking so
unaccomplished," Vik said, jabbing his thumb at Tom.

"That would be embarrassing," Wyatt said solemnly.
"People might assume you've done nothing to earn your place

here. Well, I'll change that if Yuri wants me to, but you have to cover for me if Blackburn notices. You have to swear it!"

"I swear, I'll cover for you," Tom assured her.

She bit her lip, then yanked back her sleeve to expose the portable keyboard strapped around her right forearm. "What do you need me to put in, then?"

Vik raised an eyebrow at Tom. "Well?"

Tom wasn't sure what accomplishment he should make up about himself. "Champion lawn bowler?" he tried.

Wyatt scowled at him. "Lawn bowling?"

"Oh yeah," Vik agreed. "If there was a lawn bowling Olympics, Tom would've gotten a gold medal. He's also a national spelling bee champion."

Wyatt nodded crisply, obviously considering *that* a respectable accomplishment. "Many people can't spell. It's rather sad."

Hoping to shock her, Tom added, "I'm also a founding contributor to the world's largest ball of . . ."

"Twine?" Vik suggested.

"Why, no, Vikram," Tom said. "Earwax."

Wyatt lowered her keyboard an inch. "Are you making these up?"

"Of course he isn't," Vik said.

"I'll put in the spelling bee stuff, but I am not sticking an earwax ball in your profile. *Or* lawn bowling. I don't even know what that is."

"Not everyone can be a math genius. Don't mock Tom's grand achievements," Vik said.

"Yeah, it's not nice," Tom said.

"Fine, I'll put in the lawn bowling, okay?" Wyatt typed briskly on her keyboard.

Tom found himself staring at her left hand as her fingers

danced over the keys. She had broad palms and long fingers. They looked too large for the rest of her.

"There," Wyatt announced.

"It's done?" Tom said, surprised.

"Yes, it's done." She stared at him flatly like he'd just missed something very obvious. "And tell Yuri this is the last time I'm doing this. Lieutenant Blackburn is still looking for the person who hacked the personnel database last promotion round. He'll murder me."

"Enslow, he won't murder you," Vik said. "He'll just report you to General Marsh."

Wyatt's eyes widened.

"Thanks," Tom said hastily.

"Don't thank me," Wyatt said earnestly, hugging her arm to her chest. "Just go away and don't talk to me again. Both of you."

The strange thing was, she didn't say it viciously. It was more like she had no idea how rude it was. Tom and Vik went away and didn't talk to her again.

"She's friendly," he said to Vik as they threaded through the crowd.

"That's just Enslow. Man name, man-sized hands, but no real sense of humor. Also, she's got this complete inability to relate to other people on a normal human level. There's a reason Yuri's the only one in the Spire who hangs out with her. I guess he feels sorry for her. But that hacking she just did? It takes her thirty seconds to do something anyone else would need hours to do. She's that good."

They reached the Alexander male plebe table, where Beamer was holding himself up on a chair, and Yuri loomed over his own spot. He greeted Tom with a friendly wave, his teeth so perfectly straight and white, his brown hair in such neat waves over his handsome, symmetrical features, that he really did resemble some android for a moment.

"Yuri, we took advantage of Wyatt Enslow and said you sent us," Vik informed Yuri. "I think she's annoyed at you now. You should go apologize."

Yuri closed his eyes and sighed. "You are not very nice to Wanda, Viktor."

"I'm fine with Man Hands," Vik protested. "She just wouldn't do it if I asked her. And do you really want poor Tom here to feel all embarrassed and unaccomplished?" He gestured to Tom.

"I wasn't embarrassed," Tom protested. He was just unaccomplished.

But Yuri was busy viewing Tom's profile again. "Ah, a spelling bee champion. This is impressive."

"Yeah, I spell things while lawn bowling," Tom said. "You know. Words like 'lawn.' And 'bowling.'"

He started to dip into a seat, but Vik waved him back up. "Don't sit yet. We have to stand at attention until Major Cromwell puts us at ease. It's a pain, but it's only at breakfast and at formal dinners."

There was a ping in Tom's brain: *Morning meal formation has now commenced.*

Silence descended upon the room, and every trainee in the room straightened and snapped to attention. A group of trainees marched inside the room, unfolded a US flag, and hoisted it up a pole for the day. Then they formed two lines by the door.

Tom glanced around, trying to see if he was standing the right way. The computer in his brain was instructing him to relax his shoulders, puff out his chest, pull in his abdomen, keep his hands to his sides, and ensure his body was in perfect alignment.

A whippet-thin, tired-looking woman in an overlarge set of fatigues headed through the door. The woman halted there, looking around at them, her face set with heavy lines and her faded auburn hair streaked with gray, a hard, downward twist to her lips. Tom's neural processor spun out her information:

NAME: Isabel Cromwell
RANK: Major
GRADE: USMC 0-4, active duty
SECURITY STATUS: Top Secret LANDLOCK-8

"At ease," she said gruffly.

The bodies on all sides of Tom relaxed, and after Major Cromwell assumed her lone seat at the officer's table in the corner, the trainees sank down in a massive black wave to their tables.

Tom took his seat. Around him, people lifted the metal lids from the food trays to reveal a standard breakfast of eggs, toast, bacon, and orange juice. Tom followed suit, but he only found two Snickers bars resting on his plate.

Vik, munching on his toast, noticed his puzzled expression. "Oh, yeah. You've gotta eat those."

"Snickers? For breakfast?"

"Actually, Tom, that's a meal bar. You've gotta eat about ten of those a day for a while. When you first get the neural processor implanted, your hormones go crazy. You get a spike in hGH."

Tom's neural processor identified that at once. "Human growth hormone?"

"Yeah. Major growth spurt comes next. It'll go away on its own once you've finished your natural growth cycle. They give you the nutrient bars to help with the process."

"But this is a candy bar. How does this help?"

"That's what you *see*." Vik took a hearty gulp of his orange juice. "Your neural processor's configured to feed you sensory info for foods that you like. It looks like a candy bar, but it's really a high-energy-density nutrient bar. When you look at the nutrient bars and see them the way they appear in real life, that's when you know your hGH is done spiking."

"What do these really look like, then?"

"They look like high-energy-density nutrient bars. You don't want any more details than that. Trust me."

Tom unwrapped the first Snickers and devoured it. It tasted like a normal candy bar. How odd to think his brain was fooling him. His eyes fell on the real food the others were eating. The sausages looked so delicious he could almost taste them. When he reached for the second Snickers, he saw with a start that the nutrient bar now resembled a greasy sausage link. Tom bit, and sausage exploded on his tongue. Intrigued, he turned the picture in his brain to a banana, even though he didn't like bananas, and when he looked down, the nutrient bar was a banana.

"This is so cool," Tom murmured.

He saved a bite of his banana/meal bar/Snickers thing to marvel at on the way to Calisthenics. He turned it into a dumpling, into spaghetti, into that French snail dish, escargot. He couldn't believe his brain could be manipulated this easily. He was looking at one thing and *seeing something else* just because the computer in his head told him it looked like something it wasn't.

Vik filled him in on the way. "Calisthenics is pretty straightforward. You work out. You get in shape. The first few times are pretty intense, but you'll get used to it."

"Oh. Great," Tom said, pretending he meant it. He stuffed

the last of the nutrient bar in his mouth and instantly regretted not turning it back from escargot into something else. He just barely choked it down.

"Calisthenics can be a bit intense right after three weeks in bed," Vik warned, "but adrenaline will get you through it. Believe me."

Tom followed him into a vast room, where the other plebes from various divisions waited. When he glanced at the sign overhead proclaiming it the Stonewall Calisthenics Arena, a blueprint unfolded in his vision, telling him the vast arena encircled the interiors of the second, third, and fourth floors. His eyes lit upon the various obstacles they'd have to overcome—ditches to leap across; sets of ladders and rocky walls to climb over; sand pits; water pits; long stretches of plain old running track with fake grass that twisted around and vanished from his sight with the curve in the Spire; stairs to looping, open platforms that featured more obstacles.

And then the landscape transformed around him. They weren't in the arena anymore. They were in a vast, rolling green field.

Tom blinked, and blinked again. The field was still there, stark and clear as day. "What just happened?"

"You've got a neural processor now," Vik answered. "Get it? The computer has direct control of the signals from your optic nerve."

Then Tom understood: his brain was being fed a false image like with the nutrient bars at breakfast.

"So none of this is here," Tom said, scuffing the heel of his boot experimentally on the grass. He even *smelled* it!

"The arena you saw? That's real. This field is just the processor fooling your eyes. The sounds you hear, the wind you feel? All fake," Vik said. "Basically, this is an attempt to make exercise more of an educational activity. Most of the exercise scenarios are based on real battles. You learn some things about military history without them needing to actually teach you."

A chill breeze cut across Tom's skin, rippled through his hair. The grass squished beneath his boots, and the milky morning sun seared into his eyes. Tom began to smell the acrid smoke that was floating in dark wisps from over the distant horizon. He could even hear the murmurs of voices from somewhere across the field and feel the ground vibrating with the thumping of thousands of footsteps.

He strained his eyes, trying to see the real arena through the illusion, but he couldn't. "If we can't see the real world, how do we avoid bumping into stuff?"

"The illusion adapts to the actual arena," Vik said. "A river in place of the pool. Boulders in place of low walls, cliffs in place of the climbing walls, that sort of thing. By the way, you'll want to stretch and then start jogging while you can. Calisthenics always starts with the cardiovascular component for phase one."

Tom glanced around at the rest of the plebes, dispersing from the main body, spreading out across the battlefield. They were all stretching and darting anxious looks over their shoulders. Tom glanced back toward the rolling hillside, wondering what they were waiting for.

"What happens next?" he asked Vik.

"Incentive to start sprinting."

Tom stretched, wind ripping against his cheeks, his heart picking up several beats. The distant welter of voices rose. He saw the plebes quit stretching abruptly and break into a flat run.

Screams filled the air. Tom looked back toward the

hillside, and his breath caught as he saw the "incentive to start sprinting." Thousands of men in tartans were spilling over the hillside, shouting a ferocious battle cry, swords flashing in fists.

This is so cool, Tom thought for one dazzled moment.

A spear whizzed by his face, and his survival instincts kicked in and reminded him he was unarmed in front of a raging horde of medieval Scotsmen. He broke into a run, the screams behind him splintering his ears. Another spear whizzed past him and careened with a solid *thunk* in the grass. Tom swerved around it, his heart pounding, and he reminded himself that this wasn't real. He wasn't in danger. This was an illusion.

He forgot that when he heard a shrill scream. Tom glanced back in time to see that Beamer had fallen behind into the clasp of the Scottish warriors. A Scotsman drove a sword through his gut.

"Aaah!" Beamer screamed, thrashing on the ground. "The pain. The terrible pain!"

"Oh God, no, Beamer," Vik cried, anguished. He grabbed Tom by the collar. "For God's sake, run faster. Run faster or that will be your fate, too!"

Tom's easy assurance this wasn't dangerous evaporated into real fear. Vik was panicking, Beamer had screamed like he was being killed. Was something wrong with the simulation? This wasn't supposed to be like real battle with people being killed, was it?

He was heaving for breath by the time he skidded to a stop before a solid rock wall with ladders attached to it. That's when the scenery shifted around him, and he saw Beamer again, standing at the base of a wall, doubled over in laughter.

"Vik, did you see new guy's face?" Beamer crowed.

Vik bellowed a laugh and socked Tom's shoulder. "Poor Tom. You really thought he got gutted, huh? Nah, Beamer just bailed on the workout and let them kill him. He's lazy that way."

Beamer nodded proudly.

Yuri had skipped the ladders and chosen to scale the rock wall itself. He was already halfway up, but he paused to look down at them and shook his head. "That was not a nice prank to play on Tim."

Tom understood then: the battlefield really was just a sensory illusion. You couldn't actually feel anything in an illusion. Beamer had faked the agonized death, and Vik had gone along with it.

"You're still a funny guy," Tom told him.

Vik began to hoist himself up the wall. "This is phase two, interval training. You going to die again, Beamer?"

"No way am I climbing up that," Beamer grumbled, surveying the looming stone wall.

"See you in the next life—or rather, the strength training segment. Come on, Tom."

Tom followed Vik up the ladders, leaving Beamer behind to the angry Scotsmen. In the real world, this was one of those climbing walls he'd seen. Here in the simulation, it resembled the wall of a castle of sorts. Tom scrambled up the rungs of the ladder, engaging a new set of muscles, and found himself jerking up toward medieval English soldiers waiting at the top, cursing them for being "scurvy barbarian invaders."

When they reached the top of one wall, another wall presented itself. Behind him, Tom heard more battle cries. He looked back and saw that the massive army of angry Scotsmen was climbing up the walls, too, still chasing them. Beamer got—or rather, let himself be—impaled again. He didn't fake scream this time. He dropped onto the ground and waved lazily up at Tom and Vik.

Up and down the ladders they were chased, until Tom was heaving for breath. The Scotsmen pursued relentlessly. And then Tom met the rest of the plebes in a four-walled armory. He followed them, seized a sword off the wall, and nearly dropped it. It was unexpectedly heavy.

"How do you fight with this?" Tom asked Vik, hoisting it up with two hands.

"You don't fight, really. Lifting it. That's the point of phase three: strength training."

Screams pierced the air. Tom braced himself for whatever was coming next.

Japanese ronins rushed into the room.

Tom started laughing. It made *no* sense having Japanese ronins in a medieval English castle under siege by Scotsmen, but he didn't care. He hurled himself into fighting with the heavy sword. He ignored the fact that blocking the blows from the ronin invariably began to resemble lifting weights in a gym, since the illusion of the fight made it so much better. He saw Vik dodge a sword and spotted Beamer in the corner, getting impaled for a third time. Yuri leaped forward to avenge Beamer and then threw himself gloriously into the battle with two ronins at once, wielding a sword in each hand. Then he heroically stepped between Wyatt and the ronin besieging her and began fighting three ronins, all at once.

"Yuri, stop showing off!" Wyatt snapped at him, shoving him out of her way and taking on the ronin herself again.

And then the ronins faded away, the dank castle walls vanished, and Tom found himself standing in the middle of the arena, heaving for frantic breaths, a thick iron weight clutched in his grip. Yuri had a weight in each of his hands, and he set them on the floor with a plunk. He didn't even look like he'd broken a sweat.

Vik turned to Tom, his tunic plastered to his chest. "So what do you think?"

Tom managed a breathless reply, "Beats . . . running . . . laps."

IN THE LOCKER room, Tom's body shook with exhaustion as he stood beneath the hot jets of the shower, steam curling up around him. His mind swam with the images of angry Scotsmen, charging ronins, and furious English soldiers. He had to remind himself this was not a dream or a hallucination, this was his reality now. His hands scrubbed through his short hair, and over his face. . . .

Tom froze, startled by smooth skin.

He pressed his fingers over his cheekbones, his forehead, his chin. Not a single bump. It felt as if . . .

He yanked his towel down from the curtain rod, wrapped it around his torso, and scrambled over to the mirrors outside the stall. One swipe of his palm cleared the steam, and for the first time since he was ten years old, he looked at his own face without seeing skin disfigured by acne.

Tom stared at his face, a strange feeling welling up inside him. This was him. This guy, he wasn't so ugly. Not Elliot Ramirez, yeah, but this guy could walk into a high school—a real, building one—and he'd actually fit in there.

Tom had taken it for granted he'd always be that ugly kid. He knew that even if the acne cleared up, his face would be so scarred it might as well still be there. But he looked like a normal guy now. A normal teenager surrounded by other normal teenagers, with possibility and a future ahead of him. He even had a profile that proclaimed him a national spelling bee champion, not a homeless loser who couldn't even make it at a reform school. His brain ached, but in a good way. There was this feeling inside him that for the first time in his life, he'd become a real person.

"Mirror, mirror on the wall," Vik said, emerging from the steam behind him.

Tom stepped back.

"What's up, man?" Vik's dark eyes flicked to the mirror. "You've been staring at yourself for, like, twenty seconds. Now, if you looked like me, I'd understand being awestruck by your own beauty."

"I was thinking about something. I didn't realize they changed stuff about you when they did the surgery. Physically."

"Oh, you mean the way you don't get facial hair anymore?" Vik rubbed his smooth chin.

Tom nodded like that was what he'd meant.

"Yeah, it's a pain, but the processor pretty much shuts off anything it deems extraneous like the function of hair follicles on your face when you have to be clean-shaven for the military, anyway. And I had this fantastic scar over my eyebrow that was all healed when my surgery was done, too. It's too bad. It made me look tough."

"I can't believe that."

"No, I really had a scar." Vik pointed to his eyebrow.

"Yeah, I believe that. I just can't picture you looking tough."

He dodged Vik's towel before he got snapped with it.

TOM FOUND TWO more nutrient bars in his locker. He imagined them as bacon and devoured them on the way to classes. Information popped up in his head. He examined the data, and realized it was his class schedule. He waited for that thing Vik called data comprehension to come along with the information. The schedule looked odd.

Mondays, Wednesdays, and Fridays consisted of Calisthenics from 0800 to 0930, and then math, but only from 1000 to 1020. That wasn't right, was it? How could a math class be twenty minutes long?

But all the other standard classes appeared to be a mere twenty minutes: English from 1025 to 1045, US History from 1050 to 1110, Physical Science from 1115 to 1135, World Languages from 1140 to 1200. After that? Just lunch and an entire afternoon dedicated to Applied Simulations.

The normal high school classes didn't appear on the Tuesday/Thursday schedules, either. Programming from 0800 to 1130, and the entire afternoon was Level I Tactics.

Tom followed the other plebes to the Lafayette Room, the lecture hall he'd seen on his tour. He tailed Vik to a bench and slid onto the wooden seat. For his part, Yuri parted ways with them and settled down next to Wyatt. Before him, the plebes flipped back their sleeves to expose their forearm keyboards.

A ping in Tom's brain: *Morning class has now commenced.* Silence descended upon the room as a small, gray-haired man mounted the stage in front of the room. Tom's brain scrolled through his profile.

NAME: Isaac Lichtenstein
AFFILIATION: George Washington University
SECURITY STATUS: Confidential LANDLOCK-2

"Good day, trainees," said the professor. "Please put away any extraneous materials for our exam."

"Exam?" Tom asked Vik sharply.

"Yeah," Vik said. "Hard-core math exam. Better pass it, Tom, or you're out of the program."

Tom didn't think he'd be out of the program now that the military had gone to the trouble of installing a processor in his head, but the words horrified him.

Then the test sequence began. A question blasted itself in front of Tom's vision. He began to read, *Estimate graphically all the local maxima and minima of* . . .

Tom had no idea how to do this. He'd never learned this. And yet as he stared at the numbers the strangest thing happened, like a series of sequential, ordered thoughts. A visual formed in his head of a cube with slices, and the values took on a new shape in his head.

Something this difficult shouldn't make such perfect, logical sense—but it did. Tom began typing on his own keyboard. He worked through the problem, the calculations flashing through his brain like *he* had turned into a calculator. He submitted his answer with a tap to his forearm keyboard. The next problem was just as straightforward, and the next.

He submitted his exam, and his vision center flashed *100 percent*. He stared at the number, disbelieving. He'd answered eighteen calculus questions in seven minutes. He'd never taken calculus before. He'd never even passed algebra.

At his side, Vik, who'd finished a few minutes earlier, glanced sidelong at him and waggled his caterpillar-like eyebrows, as if to say, *Ha-ha, freaked you out again.*

Tom fought the urge to break into peals of laughter, because this was unbelievable. How strange to think about this—to realize that something that had always been so frustrating like math could be so easy once his brain was supplemented with a computer.

Dr. Lichtenstein's voice came from the front of the room again. "Excellent." He was looking over the results on his own screen. "I see our lowest score was an eighty-nine."

Beamer snorted. Tom suspected suddenly that he'd scored the 89.

"And it looks like number eleven tripped a good many of you up. Perhaps I should have clarified that concept in your homework feed. As we have four minutes left to class, we'll go over that together."

Four minutes later, their math lesson was done. Dr. Lichtenstein told them their assigned downloads for the Wednesday exam were already in the system and bade them farewell. It was 1020 hours on the dot. Tom watched him leave, disbelieving. The schedule wasn't a mistake. Math class was only twenty minutes long.

The rest of the morning's classes proceeded the same way, the plebes seated in the room, the teachers changing three times in an hour. Tom had learned more in the weeks while his brain was being resequenced than he had in four years at Rosewood Reformatory. In English, his grammar was impeccable, and his reading comprehension on his exam 100 percent. In US History, he readily filled out all the dates and names and historical implications of the major political events surrounding the French and Indian War. In Physical Science, he correctly identified quantum entanglement as the concept behind the military's intrasolar communications grid. When the day's World Languages teacher strolled in speaking Japanese, Tom understood her before he knew he understood her. He spoke into the microphone on the computer during the oral examination, and the processor recorded his voice patterns. His accent matched that of a native Okinawan.

At noon, he staggered out with Vik at his side, his brain buzzing like he'd received an electric jolt. "Wow." Tom spoke half to himself, trying to get his head around it. "I speak Japanese."

"Sure you do."

"What else do I speak?"

"Depends on what language we'll get tested on Friday."

"And what else can I do? Create a nuke? Build a starship? Do I know kung fu?"

Vik answered, "If you're scheduled to kung fu fight in Applied Simulations later, you got it in your homework download."

Tom understood it finally: he could do anything now. The entire world was his.

AN HOUR LATER in the mess hall, Tom carried his tray toward the conveyer belt by the door and toyed with a fantasy: dropping in on Rosewood Reformatory with his fluent Japanese and telling them all about some starship he'd built single-handedly and won the war with. He didn't notice the large kid with a Genghis ax on his sleeve until the guy had elbowed past him. Tom stumbled to the side, caught off guard by the sudden explosion of muscular impulses from the processor in his head, trying to balance him. His drink slipped from his tray. He watched it launch on a collision course with the dark-haired girl in front of him. . . .

But she whipped around like a striking snake and caught the glass before the dark liquid sloshed over the rim.

"Nice reflexes," Tom said, impressed. He glanced up at her face—and caught his breath.

NAME: Heather Akron
RANK: USIF, Grade VI, Camelot Company, Machiavelli Division
CALL SIGN: Enigma
ORIGIN: Omaha, NE

ACHIEVEMENTS: Member of the Young Social Innovators, recipient of the RAIA Fearson Scholarship, Junior Miss Nebraska two years running
IP: 2053:db7:lj71::212:ll3:6e8
SECURITY STATUS: Top Secret LANDLOCK-6

Heather gazed back for a searching moment, then her yellow-brown eyes widened. "Oh, Tom, you're here!"

She sounded so happy to see him that his stomach flipped. "Yeah, I'm here."

"I barely recognized you without the . . ." She trailed off, eyes scanning his face. Then she said brightly, "I've been waiting for weeks for you to pop out of the surgery suite. I thought you'd changed your mind on us."

Tom didn't know what to say to that, staring into the gorgeous face of a girl who he'd thought would never give a guy like him the time of day.

Back when he wasn't smart.

Back when his skin was messed up.

Back when he was homeless and had nothing going for him.

The thoughts fired in his brain all at once. A sense of having been reborn as a new person overcame him. He wondered at his own daring when he leaned closer, held her eyes, and said, "Sorry. I'd never keep *you* waiting."

He was rewarded by Heather's giggle. "Aw, you're still cute, Tom."

"Cute?" Tom tried to puzzle that one out. Was that flattering or unmanly?

A rich laugh broke in between them. A tall, handsome guy shoved his tray onto the conveyer belt, then casually propped his elbow on Heather's shoulder. "I see the H-bomb has claimed another victim."

Tom didn't need the neural processor to tell him who *this* was. He'd know Elliot Ramirez anywhere. The text scrolled over his vision center nonetheless.

NAME: Elliot Ramirez
CALL SIGN: Ares
RANK: USIF, Grade VI, Camelot Company, Napoleon Division
ORIGIN: Los Angeles, CA
ACHIEVEMENTS: Recipient of the Taco Bell Teen Hero Award, first place World Junior Figure Skating Championship, founder of the Shoot for the Stars Inspiration Forum for Children, *Teen People*'s Young Heartthrob of the Year, winner of the Latin American Achievement Award
IP: 2053:db7:lj71::209:ll3:6e8
SECURITY STATUS: Top Secret LANDLOCK-6

Laughter tinged Elliot's voice. "You've gotta live up to that wily reputation, don't you, H? Toying with the affections of poor, innocent plebes."

Heather shrugged her shoulder so Elliot's arm slipped off. "I like poor, innocent plebes. And I'll have you know, *I* helped General Marsh find Tom's network address, and *I* helped run him through Marsh's experimental screening scenario."

"So what did you get for that?" Elliot teased. "Is the next slot for Camelot Company guaranteed to someone in Machiavelli Division?"

"Don't listen to a word Elliot says, Tom," Heather said sternly.

Elliot raised an eyebrow. "Actually, Raines, you'll have to listen to what I say. You're in my Applied Simulations group."

"I am?" Tom said.

"Yes," Elliot confirmed, his dark eyes flicking over some information he could see, scrolling through some manifest in his head. "Thomas Raines, my newbie."

"Oh." Heather pouted. "That's too bad. I hoped I'd have you, Tom."

Tom fervently wished she had him, too.

Elliot clapped his shoulder. "Hey, you lucked out." He winked. "Trust me, the people back home will go nuts when you tell them I'm the one training you."

Tom thought of Neil's reaction if he ever found out his kid would be taking orders from Elliot Ramirez, of all people.

"Yeah," Tom agreed. "My dad would definitely go nuts."

0 0 1 0 1 0 1 0 1 1 0 0 0 0 0 0 1 0 0 1 1 1 0 0 0 0 0 1 0 1 1 0 1 0 0
0 0 0 0 1 1 1 1 1 0 1 0 0 1 1 1 1 0 0 1 1 0 1 1 0 0 1 1 0 1 0 0 0 1 0 0
1 0 1 1 0 0 1 1 1 1 1 1 1 0 0 1 1 1 0 1 0 1 1 0 0 0 0 0 0 0 1 0 0 1 1 1
1 0 0 0 1 1 0 1 1 0 1 1 1 0 0 1 1 1 1 0 0 0 0 0 0 0 0 1 0 1 1 0 1 0 0 1
1 1 0 1 0 0 0 0 1 1 1 1 0 0 1 0 0 1 0 1 1 1 0 0 1 1 1 0 1 1 0 0 1 0 1
1 0 1 0 1 0 0 0 1 1 0 1 1 0 0 0 0 1 1 0 1 0 0 1 1 0 0 0 1 0 1 1 1 1 0 0
1 0 1 1 0 0 1 1 0 1 0 0 0 0 0 1 0 1 1 1 0 1 1 0 0 0 0 0 0 1 0 1 1 0 0
1 1 0 0 0 1 1 0 0 0 0 1 1 1 0 1 1 0 1 1 0 1 0 0 0 0 0 1 0 0 1 1 1 0
1 1 1 1 0 0 1 0 1 0 1 1 0 1 1 1 0 1 0 1 0 1 1 1 1 0 1 0 1 1 0 1 1 0
0 1 0 0 1 1 1 1 1 1 0 1 1 0 0 0 0 1 1 1 0 1 1 0 1 1 0 1 1 1 0 0 0
0 0 1 1 0 1 1 0 0 1 1 0 1 0 0 1 0 0 1 0 0 0 1 0 0 1 0 0 0 0 1 0 0 1 0
1 1 0 0 0 1 0 0 1 1 0 0 1 0 0 1 0 1 1 0 1 0 1 0 1 1 1 0 0 0 0 1 0 1 1 0
1 0 0 0 0 0 0 0 1 1 1 1 0 1 1 0 0 1 1 0 1 1 0 0 0 0 0 0 0 0 0 1 0 0
0 0 1 1 1 0 1 1 0 1 0 1 1 0 1 0 0 1 1 0 0 1 1 0 0 1 1 1 0 0 1 0 0 0
1 0 0 1 0 0 0 0 0 1 1 1 0 1 0 0 0 1 0 0 1 0 0 0 0 0 1 0 0 1 1 1 1 0 0

CHAPTER SIX

Vᴵᴷ ꜱᴀᴵᴅ Aᴘᴘʟᴵᴇᴅ Simulations were groups of plebes battling simulated enemies together under the leadership of members of Camelot Company. Vik really liked his group because it was led by Heather, who was apparently very hands-on, the thought of which made Tom wild with envy. Yuri, on the other hand, didn't care for his. He was in a group led by a Combatant named Karl Marsters, who always chose the goriest, bloodiest simulations available for his plebes. Apparently, Karl especially loved assuming the role of his division's namesake, Genghis Khan, and ordering his plebes to pile up the heads of villagers.

Tom and Beamer entered a thirteenth floor training room. It resembled the one Marsh and Olivia had showed him on his tour: vast and dim, with a series of cots in a circle, EKG monitors at the ends.

"Do we need to put on electrodes or something?" Tom asked Beamer, pointing to the EKGs.

"No. There's a neural wire under the cot, and it goes in

your brain stem access port."

Tom's hand flew back to his neck, to the round port he'd felt earlier.

"It's how you hook into the simulations and get downloads, too," Beamer added. "Just stick the wire in, and the neural processor will do the rest."

They settled on empty beds. Tom spotted Wyatt Enslow already perched on one of them, her long legs curled up in front of her.

Tom said, "Hey."

She replied, "Shh."

Nice to see you, too, Tom thought.

Plebes continued to shuffle in, and then Elliot Ramirez came and slid onto the edge of the last empty cot. The EKG monitor bathed his black hair in a faint green glow. "Good to see you're all on time." He beamed at Tom. "Now, let's give a warm welcome to our newest member."

Awkward clapping followed. Tom felt for a strange moment like he'd accidentally wandered into a support group.

"You see, Tom," Elliot went on, "I don't like to throw my plebes into a simulation like a lot of other instructors do. It's important we all have a chance to chat first, get out some of our emotions, decompress from the tensions of the day. I like to get my group thinking about self-empowering topics. Today, we're going to discuss something very important. And that thing is perhaps the most important concept of all: self-actualization."

Elliot was silent a moment to let the lofty words sink in. Then he launched into a tedious description of something called Maslow's hierarchy of needs. He related those needs to anecdotes from his own life, and other moving tales of triumph over adversity he'd read in letters from his many adoring fans.

Then he veered into a discussion about the triumph of the human spirit.

Tom grew so restless with the talk about self-empowerment that he almost shifted his weight right off the cot. He knew—just knew—that Heather and even that Genghis Division guy, Karl Marsters, had been running their own groups through fantastic simulations for over a half hour while Elliot perched in that preschooler circle with them, delighting himself with the sound of his own voice.

After what seemed like an eternity, Elliot gave a start. "Wow. Has it been thirty minutes? Time sure zipped by, didn't it?"

Tom laughed. He muffled it behind his hand and pretended it was a cough. Elliot flicked him a glance but bought it. Wyatt shot him a ferocious scowl, and Beamer gave a not-so-subtle conspiratorial grin.

"Let's get started with the simulation, everyone," Elliot called. "Hook yourselves in."

A shuffling sound filled the chamber as the plebes around him leaned down to grab neural wires from beneath the cots, then they connected them to their brain stem ports and stretched out on their cots. Tom heard clicks throughout the room, and he reached down to grab his own wire. He was so excited suddenly that his hands shook as he unwound it.

"Hold on there, Hot-to-Trot."

It took Elliot's grip on his shoulder to make Tom realize he was the one being addressed.

Elliot raised a finger. He seated himself at the foot of Tom's cot, waiting out the others. Within moments, they were as good as alone. The rest of the plebes had lapsed into silence and utter stillness. The EKG monitors registered the steady electric lines of their heartbeats.

"Is something wrong?" Tom blurted.

"Tom, I realize we're not military regulars, but I'm your superior, and you need to address me as sir."

"Right."

Elliot waited.

"Right, *sir.*"

Elliot removed the coil of wire from Tom's grasp and began unwinding it with a graceful, fluid twirl of his hands. "Now, Tom, do you know much about Applied Simulations?"

"I know enough," Tom said. "We enter a group simulation, we work as a team, we carry out some objective. It's all in the brain, like Calisthenics without the workout."

"Not quite. You see, in Calisthenics, you're presented with false images, but you're still aware of your own body. In Applied Sims, you are literally receiving sensory info directly from your neural processor according to the simulation's parameters. Applied Sims is designed to mimic the way we use neural processors to interface with machines in combat. Hooking in feels like *being inside* a new body. You may not remember yourself; you may only know what your character knows, depending on the parameters of the program. Some people find it frightening the first few times because it's a total immersion experience. The emphasis is on teamwork."

"Sounds great."

"You say that, but I bet you're nervous."

"I'm really not."

"Oh, sure you're not." Elliot gave him a knowing look Tom did not appreciate at all. "Now, Tom, the first time hooking in can be scary. I like to take my plebes through it personally."

"I'll be okay. Sir."

But Elliot strode around to the other side of the cot. "Lean forward."

Tom braced his hands on the edge of the mattress and dipped his head. A hand clasped his shoulder to anchor him in place. Tom clenched his jaw. Elliot was so close that he could feel hot breath on his neck.

"You can let me know if you get frightened or un-comfortable. It's pretty common—"

"I'll be fine," Tom cut in. Then, "Sir."

The wire clicked into his brain stem and the world tunneled into blackness. All sensation seeped from his limbs with a horrifying abruptness.

"That happened faster than I . . ." Tom's voice blurred away mid-sentence.

The last glimpse he had through his own eyes was of the world flying downward as he keeled over.

AND THEN TOM was not Tom.

Blinding whiteness on all sides of him. An icy tundra crushed beneath a thick gray sky. Chill wind stung at his eyes, his skin, yet it felt perfect to him, bracing.

A strange feeling pulsed through him, his muscles, his tendons. Blood, vitality, life. He bounded forward, his paws treading over the cold, hard snow, and the scents tearing at his nostrils overwhelmed him. His vision became a dim afterthought and all he could do was stand there, experiencing the tastes on the wind.

The earthy scent of friends.

A hot, rich taste of prey.

That distracted him. He thrust his muzzle up into the wind and inhaled it, the teasing, taunting scent calling to him. But there was something else.

Danger.

He thrust his muzzle against the icy ground and checked

on it. An image in his head: the stale white fur of a predator, blood-crusted paws, a low roar.

Danger gone for some time now. A massive predator. Stalking across the snow. Gone now.

He followed more scents, entranced. *Ice . . . metal . . . dirt . . . man . . .*

Howling.

The call of his friends split the air. He hurled himself toward them without deciding to, tearing across the snowy plain, driven by an insatiable need to add to that sound. The scent of family grew stronger and richer in his nostrils and then he was among the other wolves of his pack and throwing back his head, the sound rising from deep in his throat. The wail seemed to pierce the sky above them and spread over the valley, a sense of union like he'd never known before welling inside him.

The largest and the strongest wolf charged into their midst. The tails of the other wolves flopped down submissively. Ferocious barking from the alpha, and then the alpha whipped around and charged toward that scent on the wind, toward the sweetness of prey with its fresh, pulsing blood and tender flesh. The pack became a gray surge tearing over the plains, tails straight and tense, following their leader.

The warm, rich scent of prey mounted on the air, its gathering power the single measure of time. They stayed with the winds, icy blasts of it carrying the scent toward them while concealing their approach from the target.

Then they were upon their prey. The moose raised its massive head. It knew they were closing in on it. It bounded forward and tried to run, but the alpha snarled and cut off its retreat. The prey knew it could not outrun them. As the alpha tore toward the beast, it turned and ducked its massive horns, ready to impale him. The alpha leaped clear by instinct.

The rest of the pack enveloped the creature, leaping forward, nipping, gnashing at it with teeth. Barks and growls filled the air along with the bellows of the massive creature. Hooves swiped down and the bloody scent of the first wolf killed—*Beamer*—roused something human in Tom.

Two more went down, victims to those massive horns, yet the alpha wolf kept circling, leaving tiny, gashing injuries on the magnificent creature too powerful to be toppled by such a pitiful attack.

So Tom hung back.

Tom ignored the call of instinct, demanding he join the fruitless attack, the subroutines trying to force him in line with the alpha's plan. He instead watched, like Tom the boy in the VR parlors used to, and he saw his opening. He didn't hesitate. He sprang into the fray, flying right over the heads of the others, and faster than any human could ever move, lashed forward to clamp his teeth around the moose's throat. In one smooth movement, he tore at cartilage and flesh while propelling himself away. Hot blood spurted over him, and he was out of reach before the lethal hooves could dash his brains out.

It was finished. The creature staggered, dark blood gushing from its gaping neck wound. It sagged to its knees, then heaved up, but now other wolves tore at its tendons; its hindquarters; its soft, vulnerable abdomen. Tom licked at the fresh blood on his lips, feeling so alive and dangerous in that instant he never wanted the simulation to end.

Then he heard a low rumble. Danger swelled on the icy air.

Tom grew aware of Elliot stalking toward him, legs ramrod stiff, tail curled forward, ears slanted, jagged teeth on full display. Responding to his defiance. A warning note of instinct thrilled through Tom and he knew what Elliot was trying to do with those narrowed eyes fixed on him, with that fur bristling. Tom did not move. A ferocious bark tore from Elliot's throat.

Tom understood the order. The instinct and parameters in his brain urged him to obey the alpha, but the blood was sweet on his lips, and to the depths of his being he rebelled against the very notion of rolling over and baring his belly, his throat, accepting a position of subservience to this one even if he was torn apart for it. Power and a sense of possibility ripped through him. He could defeat the alpha, he was sure of it. Claim the pack, make it his. He felt a prickling as fur bristled up all over his body, and his lips curled back to bare his own teeth, the growl mounting in his throat.

The other wolf rose to its hind legs and lifted a paw above its head in a completely human gesture. And in that way, Elliot ended the simulation.

Tom OPENED HIS eyes and gazed up at the slashing green line of the EKG, blazing through a standard rhythm. He grew aware of a hollow ache inside him as the sense of union, of belonging, faded away into nothing. He sat up fast enough to make his vision darken for an instant. Around him, everyone else was rousing as well.

Except for the dead ones. Beamer was already up, his elbows perched on his knees. He shrugged. "Death by moose."

Inside Tom's head, the neural processor registered that more than two hours had passed. Time held a very different meaning as a wolf.

"Wow," Tom whispered, his mind blown.

Elliot sat up, tucked his wire back beneath his cot, and told them all to sit again for post-conference. He sighed loudly, focused his attention on Tom, and folded his arms over his chest. "So tell me, what did you do wrong, Tom?"

"What?"

"Tell me what you did wrong."

Tom glanced at the faces around him, carefully neutral, and back at Elliot. "I did something wrong?"

"The point of Applied Sims," Elliot said, pointing toward the back of his own neck, "is not just getting you used to the idea of mentally detaching from your body and interfacing with another form using the neural processor. The point is to practice teamwork."

"I know that. You said so earlier."

"Clearly, no, you don't know that. The scenario was about emotional attunement: a pack of wolves working as one to take down a moose. You should've helped the pack kill the prey. Instead, you broke with the team and worked all by yourself. And then you tried to challenge my leadership of the pack. That indicates to me, Tom, that you don't feel like being a team player. You didn't feel like going with the team strategy. That concerns me."

"But the team strategy sucked. Three of us were already dead."

"Tell me, then, Tom, what do you call a lone wolf that doesn't work with others?"

Tom thought about that, a bit puzzled. There was a trick question in here, right? "Uh, you call it a lone wolf."

Elliot's mouth bobbed noiselessly open and closed—like he was caught off guard because he hadn't even thought of that—and then he shook his head. "No, Tom. It's called a coyote."

Silence filled the room.

Wyatt raised her hand and waited for Elliot to acknowledge her, as if they were all sitting together in a classroom. When he waved graciously for her to speak, she blurted exactly what

Tom was thinking: "Coyotes aren't a type of wolf. Coyotes and wolves are two entirely different species."

But if Elliot caught the implication that he'd just said something astoundingly stupid, he didn't show it. Instead, he nodded, like Wyatt had made his point for him. "Exactly, Wyatt. Exactly." He turned back to Tom. "Think about what she said, Tom. Wolves and coyotes are entirely different species. Think about that long and hard."

CHAPTER SEVEN

T HE NEXT DAY, Tom opened his eyes, wide-awake, when the
neural processor informed him, *Consciousness initiated.
The time is now 0630.*

Vik sat up at the same time and mumbled that he was
going to go check and see whether Beamer was "capable of
ambulating today," or whether he'd binge downloaded all his
homework after yet another long night with his girlfriend.

Tom tossed off the covers and stretched. Sore muscles and
tendons objected all over his body. He wasn't used to exercise.

He also wasn't used to growing 0.86 of an inch in the
course of a night.

Tom registered the height change with a shock. But the
neural processor informed him of it. He leaped to his feet, and
found that his eyes were definitely looking down from a greater
height than on the day before.

Vik hadn't been kidding at breakfast when he'd told him

about the nutrient bar. Tom was having a serious growth spurt.

He loved being pseudomachine.

PROGRAMMING CLASS ALSO met in the Lafayette Room, only this time there were Plebes, Middles, Uppers, and CamCos present. It was the only class they shared with all levels of the Spire. Vik told him it was because Programming was the hardest class, and most everyone sucked at it equally.

Tom settled with Vik, Yuri, and Beamer on the same bench they'd grabbed the day before during civilian classes. "So Programming's that bad, huh?"

"That's one way of putting it." Vik slung his boots up on the back of the bench in front of him. "We're not allowed to use the neural processor to do the work for us. The processor will do some stuff, sure, like memorize the rules of syntax and semantics for you, but you actually have to sit down and piece it all together. You have to use your brain and write the code yourself. It's tedious and awful."

"Speak for yourself, Viktor. I am happy to use my—" Yuri grew limp and keeled over onto Tom's side.

Vik flicked Tom an amused glance as he struggled to dislodge the dead weight. "The Zorten II computer language is Indo-American neural processor-specific. It's classified, so Yuri's neural processor sends him into shutdown mode."

Between Tom and Beamer, they were able to prop Yuri up on the bench in a way that stopped him from crushing either of them.

"What does he remember happening during Programming?" Tom asked Vik.

"I asked him once what he thought of this class, and he started rambling about 'munchkins' and 'fractals.' I think he just gets so scrambled, he doesn't even realize he's scrambled later."

The door to the lecture hall slid open, and chattering voices died away. Tom looked up, and saw an imposing man with close-cropped brown hair and a hawkish face stride up to assume the podium. His profile said he was:

NAME: James Blackburn
RANK: Lieutenant
GRADE: 0-3, USAF, Active Duty
IP: 2053:db7:lj71::008:ll3:6e8
SECURITY STATUS: Top Secret LANDLOCK-10

He greeted them with, "Well, folks, I had a big laugh after your class prank."

Then a ping in Tom's brain: *Morning classes have now commenced.*

"I had to look over your firewall programs twice just to be sure." Blackburn leaned his elbows on the podium, his broad shoulders stretching his fatigues. "At first, I honest to god thought those were the real programs. But then I remembered that these are the best and the brightest young people in the USA even without neural processors, so they couldn't possibly be serious about such laughable, poorly written code. Well done, trainees! You had me. Now where are the real programs? Feel free to submit them now."

Blackburn began drumming his fingers on his podium, waiting. Despite his easy words, there was a grim, almost angry set to his features. Tom glanced around for some cue about what was going on. All the faces he saw were fixed in varying degrees of tense expectation, like they knew the mildness of their instructor's tone was deceptive.

After a time, Blackburn glanced up into space. "That's funny. Looks like I got . . . nothing. Do you mean to tell me those were your real programs? In that case, we need to talk about some fundamentals here for a minute, children. In fact, let's start with fundamental number one. Are you listening? Here it is: there are computers in your brains."

He let those words hang there and looked over the room.

"Do I need to repeat myself?" This time, he jabbed his finger at his temple with each word. "There are *computers* in your *brains*. Do you know why I am wasting my breath trying to teach you to program? No, it's not so I can spend precious hours looking at this sea of happy, shiny faces. It's so *you* can learn to control your own neural processors." The mild tone vanished from his voice—his irritation seeping through. "Mastery of programming is mastery of self, and if you can't take that seriously, then the joke's not on me, it's on you. What, Ms. Akron?"

Heather's hand dropped. Her voice rang out, "If it's really so important we learn this, sir, then it would make much more sense to just put everything we need in the download streams."

Blackburn puffed out his cheeks and released his breath very slowly. "I've said this before," he replied, "and I'll say it again: those neural processors can't manipulate computer languages the way they do human languages, and there's a very simple reason for that—it's illegal. We have federal laws in this country. One such law prohibits self-programming computers. Your neural processor, as a computer, falls under this law. Your brain, as an organ in your skull, does not. If you have a problem with this, then you can take it up with the good folks at Obsidian Corp. who lobbied your congressmen for that legislation. You see, they built the neural processors, so it makes sense for *them* to keep the military dependent on their programmers. That's why you folks are all so very lucky I'm here, and I, unlike you, realized how important it was to control the computer in my brain, even if it meant I had to sit down and teach myself the Zorten II computer language the hard way."

Tom stared at Blackburn, still stuck on those words "The computer in my brain . . ." How could Blackburn have a neural processor? He had to be forty, at least. General Marsh said adults couldn't handle neural processors. But he remembered seeing an IP address in Blackburn's profile. That must be his.

"But, sir," Heather pressed, "some of us are Combatants. We're fighting the war. You had more time to learn the regular way, since you were just . . ." She trailed off.

She didn't seem able to say it, so Blackburn gave a short, harsh laugh. "I was just . . . locked in a mental institution?"

"He was in a mental institution?" Tom whispered to Vik.

"First test group was sixteen years ago," Vik replied softly, "three hundred adult soldiers. The military didn't know yet what neural processors do to adult brains."

"They *all* went insane?"

"Only the lucky ones. The rest died."

Tom took a moment to absorb that as Blackburn went on, "No need to dance around my mental illness, Ms. Akron. I've never tried to hide it from you. If there's one monstrous representation of a neural processor's destructive potential, you can see it standing right here. That computer in your head is a weapon, but it is a double-edged sword. Don't ever forget that."

"He doesn't seem all that crazy," Tom whispered to Vik.

"He taught himself how to reprogram his neural processor and fixed his own brain."

"There's this attitude," Blackburn was saying, "and I find it in trainees again and again. The first few months with a neural processor, it's all amazement and awe. And then? You start taking it for granted. Don't. Never take a neural processor for granted. There is nothing natural about having a computer in your head. So while you have a point, Ms. Akron, about having a time crunch, you also fail to see the forest for the trees. Yes, I was a paranoid schizophrenic with nothing better to do than figure out how to program, but *you*, as an actual fighter in this war, have a much more critical reason to learn programming for yourself. Let's start with point one: you're fighting a war. What is the basic definition of war? I don't need anything deep, just a quick, one-sentence answer."

Silence. Then, a Middle Company trainee Tom's processor identified as Lisa Sanchez answered, "War is a violent conflict to resolve a dispute."

"That's right, Ms. Sanchez. This war springs from a disagreement over ownership of the solar system. Each side has laid claim to it, and each is trying to enforce that claim using violence. Point two: why do you think your identities are classified? Anyone?"

An Alexander Division Combatant Tom's processor identified as Emefa Austerley raised her dark hand. "Security, sir."

"Why?"

"To protect us."

"From what?"

No answer this time. Tom glanced around, wondering about it himself. It wasn't like they'd be killed if their identities were in the open. That didn't happen now.

"To protect you from violence," Blackburn supplied. "And I know what you're all thinking: no one kills in this war. We've evolved beyond that, right? Even you Combatants aren't putting your lives on the line to fight since the battle is taking place thousands of miles from you. . . . So why protect you from violence? Nigel Harrison, you seem to have something to add."

A slim, dark-haired boy said, "War evolves over time. It's better to say, 'No one kills in this war yet.'"

Blackburn snapped his fingers and pointed at him. "Give the boy a gold star. No one kills in this war *yet*. Violence hasn't reached you *yet*. Let's face it, why would the Russians and Chinese try to kill you? They know if they kill one of our Combatants, we'll set out to kill one of their Combatants. And then the two companies sponsoring those Combatants will have wasted a whole lot of money on some dead kids. There are what, forty something Combatants in the entire world? You're valuable. It's not worth it financially to bring death into the equation. But what happens a few years down the road when some discount neural processors hit the market and there are four hundred of you? What about four thousand? Here's a hint, trainees: your stock goes down. You become expendable."

In the front row, Elliot Ramirez must've said something too quietly for Tom to hear. Blackburn whipped around toward him. "What's that, Ramirez? Say it louder."

"I said that's very cynical, sir," Elliot said.

Blackburn chuckled drily. He dropped down onto the edge of the stage, legs sprawled, eyes fixed on Elliot. "Did you know that back in the nineteen fifties in the early days of nuclear technology, the military stationed soldiers close to an atomic bomb testing site? The soldiers received massive doses of radiation. So did the civilian population that lived downwind of the site. Was this done in ignorance? No, Mr. Ramirez. It was deliberate—so we could learn about radiation poisoning. Same story with mustard gas, dioxin, PCP, nerve gas, LSD— you name it, some unwitting group of nobodies got a dose of it because some bigwig deemed them expendable. Same story with me—one of three hundred soldiers who received neural processors sixteen years ago, who either died or lost their minds. People are expendable. Period. The only difference between the nineteen fifties and today is that there are billions more of us expendable human beings. If you think you have any true value beyond your impact on someone's bottom line, you need to wake up from your dreamworld."

A thick silence hung on the air. Blackburn let those words sit there for a long moment, and then he jounced to his feet.

"I know that from birth you've been taught to trust in institutions, laws, systems. But I'm here to tell you, the only person you can trust to protect you is *you*. It's your responsibility to defend yourself with every weapon in your arsenal, and one of those is knowledge—knowledge of programming. If you willfully choose to reject that knowledge, then I will have no pity for you when you wake up with an enemy surgeon cutting into your head to extract that neural processor, and you can't move a muscle because they've hit you with a paralysis program you couldn't defend against. I warned you, and you chose to delude yourself with the illusion someone else would save you. Helplessness can only be excused in children and fools. You gave up your right to be children the day you came here, and the last thing this world needs is to shelter its fools."

Tom stared at him, surprised by the words. Everything else at the Spire so far had encouraged camaraderie, teamwork, adhering to the regulations of the place. Blackburn's words sounded more like . . .

Well, something Neil might say.

Maybe Blackburn realized he'd taken his spiel too far, because he let out an exasperated breath. "All right, pick your jaws up off the floor and go take a five-minute break. No one's hacking your heads open today. When you return, I'm going to call someone up here to test a firewall." When no one reacted, he grew impatient. "Four minutes, fifty-nine seconds, fifty-eight, fifty-seven . . . *Go!*" He turned his attention to his forearm keyboard. A tap of his finger lowered a screen over the stage.

The mass of people in front of Tom reacted. Many trainees raised their forearm keyboards and dove into frantic work on last-minute tweaks to their firewalls. A couple, like Vik, just surrendered themselves to the possibility of facing Blackburn with shoddy firewalls, and rose from their seats.

"Wanna grab something in the mess hall?" Vik asked him.

"Sure," Tom said, thinking of turning the nutrient bar in his pocket into a burger. He rose to follow Vik from the room, but then several words popped up in his vision center.

Mr. Raines, get up here.

Tom turned, confused—and saw Blackburn beckoning to him impatiently from the stage. Apprehension squirmed in him. "Vik, I've gotta—" He gestured to Blackburn.

Vik glanced back and forth between Tom and Blackburn. "It's probably nothing," he assured him.

"Yeah, sure." Tom hoped so. He headed up to the stage where Blackburn was waiting, elbow propped against the podium. As he neared, Tom made out the frown lines on the man's face and the pair of thin scars down his cheek.

"Sir, I don't have a firewall," Tom blurted.

"Of course you don't, Raines. This is your first day here," Blackburn said, kneeling down at the edge of the stage. "It may take you weeks or even months to catch up in this class. I don't expect that of you. What I do expect is an explanation from you about something." His eyes were fixed on Tom's, gray and intent. "Yesterday, someone hacked into one of the Spire's classified personnel databases. Can you guess whose profile they changed while they were there?"

Tom's heart plunged. Oh. *Oh*. This was about the favor Wyatt did him.

"That's right, you're suddenly a national spelling bee champion," Blackburn noted. "I don't care what background you want to make up for yourself, Raines. Not my problem. The reason I called you up here is because that hacker committed a security breach. I want you to tell me that hacker's name."

Tom drew a sharp breath. He'd made a promise to Wyatt. He couldn't go back on that.

Blackburn studied him. "This is probably your first time living away from home, isn't it? Trust me, you don't want to start your time here by getting on my bad side. You won't be getting anyone in trouble if you tell me who did it. I only want to speak to the hacker."

Tom had ripped off enough people in VR parlors to know threats when he heard them. And he didn't believe for a second that Blackburn just wanted a friendly chat with a hacker breaking into secure databases. He held Blackburn's gaze, his heart picking up a beat. "I've forgotten, sir."

"No, you haven't. You just don't want to tell me. Fine. If you don't want to talk, then I'm drafting you to be the subject for my demonstration today."

Tom glanced uneasily up at the screen, where some lines of code were now displayed. "What do I do?"

Blackburn shook his head. "You'll do nothing but stand on the stage and receive the computer viruses I'm going to feed into your processor. The code will manipulate your brain."

Tom's stomach flipped. "Uh, manipulate it how?"

"Anything your brain can do, I might make it do. Get up here."

Tom mounted the steps on the side of the stage, his legs

suddenly shaky. That was not reassuring.

As soon as everyone had returned to the room, Blackburn jerked his head, summoning Tom over from where he'd been hovering uneasily by the steps.

Blackburn announced to the class, "Let's talk computer viruses. The process of infecting a neural processor works in much the same way it would on a computer at home. If Raines here were physically connected to a computer via a neural wire, I could infect him with a virus from anywhere if I also had an internet connection and the ability to hack through the firewall protecting him. But he's not physically connected to the internet; he's connected to the Spire's server via his internal transmitter. So I'm going to feed him a virus from my transmitter to his."

Blackburn began jabbing at a keyboard strapped to his thick forearm. Tom looked back, and saw Blackburn's code dancing across the massive screen, allowing all the trainees to see what he typed.

"A virus like this gets into a system by piggybacking itself on an existing program in the target's active applications. For the final step, I stick in my target's IP address. You can target more than one IP. Now here"—he typed something more—"I code the initiation sequence. The malicious program will trigger as soon as it's in his processor. Then the self-termination sequence to ensure the program stops itself in five minutes." He clapped his heavy hand on Tom's shoulder, jostling him. "Are you ready, Raines?"

"Does it matter if I'm not?"

"No, that was a courtesy. So is this: name the part of your brain you want me to tamper with first."

Tom felt himself tense. "How about none?"

"No preference? Fine. First target: the hypothalamus."

Blackburn began typing, and then text scrolled across Tom's vision: *Datastream received: program Insatiable Appetite initiated.*

Tom cringed, expecting something horrible. But nothing happened.

Nothing except . . .

Except . . .

His stomach growled. Tom realized suddenly he was starving—absolutely starving. The painful ache in his gut consumed him. His entire brain riveted to the idea of food, delicious food. He'd kill for fries. He could eat a horse. He could eat a hundred nutrient bars. Wait, he had a nutrient bar!

He dug into his pocket frantically, so desperate for food that he didn't care about all the eyes on him. He'd quite forgotten what he was supposed to be doing up here, anyway. He tore open the packaging of the nutrient bar with his teeth. He devoured half the bar in one bite, not even bothering to form a mental image of some food he liked.

"The neurons in your brain communicate through a series of electrical signals," Blackburn told the class. "The neural processor mimics and interprets these signals. I can stimulate almost any part of the brain with the right program. The mind is everything. Manipulate a mind, and you manipulate the entire world as far as that person's concerned. This is how your Applied Sims programs convince you you're an animal, or trick you into thinking you're in an artificial landscape. "

Text flashed across Tom's vision as the program ended. He noticed for the first time the lumpy, grayish-green appearance of the nutrient bar, and dropped it, revolted. Without a mental image of a food he liked, it just looked the way it really did: like something someone had digested and then puked up again.

Blackburn, meanwhile, was calling Karl Marsters to the

stage. The large, jowled Genghis mounted the stairs, and Blackburn said something in a low voice to him, then typed on his forearm keyboard. Another line of text flashed across Tom's vision: *Datastream received: program Fight-or-Flight initiated.*

Suddenly, Tom was at his wit's end. He wasn't going to stick around to see what Blackburn hit him with next. He tried to bolt out of the room, but Karl Marsters was waiting for this, and he caught him. Fury exploded through Tom. He had to *kill this guy*! He punched Karl across the jaw, hard. Karl bellowed out, and raised his massive fist to punch him back. Blackburn stepped in and caught his arm.

"Knock that off." He shoved Karl back. Then, with a few strokes on his keyboard, he ended the program.

Karl glowered at Tom menacingly and rubbed his jaw.

More programs followed. A manipulation of his limbic cortex, and Tom fell in madly love with Blackburn's podium. Just as he threw his arms around it and pledged his eternal devotion, Blackburn targeted his hippocampus, and Tom lurched back away from the podium, utterly perplexed. He'd forgotten everything from the last year. He started demanding explanations as to why he was in this strange room with these strange people, and where was his father? A program targeting the amygdala made him react to the podium again, but this time, he was deathly terrified of it. Karl grabbed him and tried forcing him to get closer to it, so Tom drove his elbow back into Karl's stomach, doubling him over. Karl roared out and started after him again, but Blackburn stepped in his path.

He must've terminated the virus, too, because Tom's head cleared. He found himself staring at the decidedly unmenacing podium, his heart pounding, his breath coming in ragged gasps. He spun around and saw Blackburn warning Karl, "Get a hold of that temper, Marsters."

Karl's face was bright red, his massive fists clenched at his sides. "But, sir, he—"

"Is half your size and under the influence of malware, and he still got the slip on you. Twice. That's *your* problem, not his. Sit down."

Karl threw Tom a look of death and stalked from the stage.

Blackburn turned and surveyed Tom, where he was trying to regain his bearings. "Holding up there, Raines?"

Tom glanced at the audience, where some trainees were trying to smother their laughter. His cheeks burned. He deliberately stepped closer to the stupid podium, just to show that he really wasn't afraid of it—but not too close, because he wasn't in love with it, either. "I'm great, sir." He wasn't going to plead for this to stop, if that's what Blackburn was hoping for.

"Thatta boy." Blackburn turned back to the class and typed again. "One last virus, then. This targets the cerebral cortex: higher cognition and sense of self." The program hit. *Datastream received: program Agitated Canine initiated.*

Tom spent the last five minutes of class convinced he was a dog. He barked and crawled across the stage. In front of everyone. With 137 trainees laughing at him. The firm belief he was a dog stayed with him even after class ended, when a couple of the older trainees were determining what to do with him.

"Blackburn said it'd only be a few minutes more. I've got time to wait it out. Try scratching behind his ears. My dog Buckley always liked that," Elliot Ramirez was saying.

Tom realized himself suddenly: he was sitting on the ground between Elliot and Heather, and Elliot was patting his head. He leaped to his feet, his cheeks burning.

"Two legs again?" Elliot observed. "Feeling better, or is this your way of asking for a treat?" He chuckled at his own joke.

Tom flushed. He was aware of Heather giggling, and felt distinctly unmanly. To his mortification, she rose to her feet, reached out, and rubbed his shoulder. "Aw, that's a good boy."

"Thanks," Tom said drily. "Thanks a lot, Heather."

"Don't be embarrassed, Tom," Heather said sweetly, while Elliot just kept chuckling good-naturedly behind her. "You really did make an adorable puppy." She leaned a little closer. "And you should probably stay clear of Karl for a few days if you can help it."

Tom's cheeks still burned as he stalked down the aisle, and just as he reached the door, he met Blackburn coming back into the room.

The lieutenant slowed, his gaze sweeping over him. "Still holding up?"

"Why wouldn't I be? Sir?" Tom said shortly.

"A fine show of bravado." Blackburn considered him thoughtfully. "You know, Raines, if a rogue hacker gets away with minor security breaches on my watch, it calls into question whether they can get away with major security breaches, too. Likewise, if a plebe gets away with hiding that hacker's identity from me, it encourages him to continue defying my authority in the future."

"You've made your point."

"I hope so. Well, Raines, misguided as it was, I still respect your commitment to protecting a fellow trainee. That took stones. Now shoo, get out of my sight."

TOM WAS ALMOST mollified by Blackburn's parting words. At least, he was until he stepped into the mess hall and laughter greeted him. That's when he began cursing Blackburn with all his heart. Then Karl offered him a slice of bacon. "Here,

Lassie," with a menacing gleam in his eyes like he was just hungry for an excuse to pummel him.

Now that Tom really had a chance to look at him, Karl's profile flashed before his eyes:

NAME: Karl Marsters
CALL SIGN: Vanquisher
RANK: USIF, Grade VI, Camelot Company, Genghis Division
ORIGIN: Chicago, IL
ACHIEVEMENTS: Two-year winner of Mr. Illinois Heavyweight Wrestling title, John Schultz Heavyweight Wrestling Excellence Award, Terminator World Championship first runner-up
IP: 2053:db7:lj71::231:ll3:6e8
SECURITY STATUS: Top Secret LANDLOCK-6

At least I got to punch him, Tom thought venomously, and forced himself onward instead of jamming the bacon down Karl's throat. He arrived at the Alexander male plebe table, and found Yuri standing with Wyatt, trying to coax her into sitting down with them.

"You are always sitting alone," Yuri said. "There is no need. You can join us."

She shook her head, arms crossed over her chest. "It's not my table. I should sit with my division."

"Why?" Vik called back to them, mouth full. "No one in Hannibal Division talks to you."

Wyatt glared at his back.

Yuri was more diplomatic. "This is not morning meal formation. No one cares about assigned seating."

Wyatt made no effort to lower her voice. "But, Yuri, *Vik* sits with you. I don't like Vik."

"Hey," Vik protested, looking over his shoulder, "Vik is two feet away from you."

"You call me Man Hands."

"I only point out the obvious facts, such as the manliness of your hands and the way your division—" Vik stopped mid-sentence when he spotted Tom, hanging back with his tray. Wyatt's dark eyes moved to him, too, and widened. She closed her mouth tightly, as if biting back whatever she wanted to say.

"Timothy," Yuri said softly, "you look troubled."

"Really? Why would that be?" Tom sniped. "Maybe something to do with Programming?" He realized only after dropping into his seat that Yuri couldn't know what happened. Already, he was zoning out, staring into space, his face cloudy.

Awkward silence hung on the air. Then Wyatt blurted, "How was being a dog?"

Tom scowled. "Great, Wyatt. Really great. I love looking like a moron in front of hundreds of people."

Vik and Wyatt watched him with grim expressions. And then, Vik's lips twitched. And twitched more.

"And I can't figure out why he kept programming me to obsess over his stupid podium," Tom ranted on. "Maybe *he's* fixated on the podium, huh?"

Vik's entire face spasmed.

"And thanks for leaving me there, by the way, you guys. I got to wake up to Elliot Ramirez stroking my hair! You know what I want to wake up to? Gosh. How about anything other than some guy stroking my hair?"

"Look on the bright side," Vik said, his voice choked. "At least Blackburn didn't add an algorithm to make you start humping anyone's legs, or, you know, the podium." He might've been trying for something genuinely consoling, saying that broke his self-control. He burst into laughter.

Wyatt pressed her palm over her lips, too.

"Glad this is funny to you people," Tom said.

But Vik was doubled over, and Wyatt's shoulders were shaking, and suddenly Tom's black mood broke, and he found his lips pulling up in a grin. Just like that, it was funny to him, too.

Because yeah, they were laughing at him. They were laughing with him, too.

Tom had never stayed in one place long enough to make a friend before. But he began to understand suddenly what friends were for: they reminded you that things weren't so bad after all. Reminded you never to stop laughing at yourself. He might've felt for a minute there like he'd turned back into Tom the Loser, but he hadn't. This was never going to be Rosewood.

CHAPTER EIGHT

TACTICS WAS A different beast from Programming. Located on the very top floor of the Spire, the MacArthur Hall was a vast planetarium. A screen curved over their heads, and the diagrams in Tom's head informed him the roof and screen were capable of retracting. CamCo held postmission briefings here to analyze their battles and see where they went wrong.

Here the plebes got to analyze CamCo's past battles, too.

Here they learned about real war.

Tom watched Major Cromwell assume the podium at the front of the room. "Sit down."

Her hoarse voice flooded the room without her raising it. The last stragglers were in their seats before the ping could even say, *Afternoon classes have now commenced.*

"You've downloaded this information," Cromwell said briskly, "so let's make sure you understand it. We've been examining the evolution of combat, weaponry, and tactics. History has shown one simple fact: people are people. Period.

All the technology and progress in the world can't change the fundamentals of human nature. There will always be war as long as human beings are capable of envy, hatred, and fear."

Cromwell typed something into a keyboard attached to her podium. An image of an oil painting depicting a bloody battle plastered itself across the vast screen. "Combat itself has taken new forms over time. In the ancient times, whole armies descended upon nations, fighting in the names of kings, of religions. Over the years, the scope of violence narrowed. Technology improved targeting to the point where we could destroy certain individuals rather than whole communities, attacking by air rather than by planting armies."

Tom heard a rustling next to him. He looked over and saw Beamer slouching down in his seat. Greenish light flickered over his pale features, and Tom glanced back at the grainy image on the screen—a target locked on a flat, rectangular building from somewhere above it.

"Wars were fought over oil, over territory. And now, the last engagement on Earth thirty-three years ago saw us destroying people and leaving buildings and infrastructure intact, all on behalf of private business, in the name of patents. Your generation may take for granted that countries go to war on behalf of private rather than public interests, but this wasn't always considered an acceptable reason for violent conflict. Let's trace the changes that led to this."

"Let's not," Beamer murmured.

Vik elbowed him but kept his dark gaze on the front screen.

"Early in the century," she said, "globalization was uniting countries across the traditional bounds of cultures, languages, and borders. Old boundaries became virtually obsolete. As a result, a corporate class emerged, with executives who identified not with any nationality but rather with the business interests that bound companies to one another. Without national loyalties of their own, large businesses moved jobs from country to country whenever labor was more affordable. This depressed wages worldwide. Most businesses were left without a consumer base, and this led to the Great Global Collapse. The companies that survived were the ones with control over vital resources. There are two prominent examples. The first one is Dominion Agra."

Tom stiffened. Dominion. Where his mother's boyfriend, Dalton, worked.

"As you know, when a company creates life, they own the patent to it. Over the last century, Dominion Agra's genetically engineered plants and animals cross-pollinated and cross-bred with the natural food supply. There are no consumables today without some trace of Dominion's patented genetic material. The dominance of their genetic strains led to their total ownership of the food supply. This leads to the other monopoly you've heard of: Harbinger Incorporated, with their patent on Nobriathene, an industrial by-product that, over time, leeched into the water supply all over the world. It's completely nonreactive in a human body, but to this day, no one has developed an effective filter for it. If you drink water, use water, irrigate your crops with water, you're making use of their patented chemical. That's why your families pay a usage fee every year to Harbinger along with their water bills. Whatever the global situation, the elements of basic subsistence are always in demand. Dominion and Harbinger have both thrived in this post-Collapse world."

Tom had heard all this from Neil. Even though they were on opposite sides of the World War III conflict, Dominion Agra backed Harbinger's patent, and Harbinger backed Dominion Agra's patent. It was only natural, his dad claimed. Dominion

Agra could brush off criticisms of its monopoly on food by pointing to the other culprit—the company with a monopoly on water. They justified each other's existences. And besides, it wasn't like anyone in a position of power in the world actually wanted to break their monopolies. Every politician hoped to get a job in a Coalition company once they were through with public office.

"And now," Cromwell said, "this brings us to what happened in the Middle East thirty-three years ago. This conflict had been coming for a long time. It was the last show of mass resistance against the centralization of global authority. As influence in the rest of the world became more concentrated in the hands of a worldwide business community, it went the opposite direction in the Middle East. Traditional authoritarian leaders were being replaced by representative governments. These societies resisted the idea of respecting the patents of either Dominion Agra or Harbinger. Because the resistance was at the street level—a societal refusal to play by the same rules as the rest of the world—it was determined that we would address the problem at the street level. With neutron bombs."

Tom knew the rest. It was the last time United States and Chinese militaries worked together on anything. They carpet bombed most of the Middle East with neutron bombs, weapons of mass death that killed people but left buildings. Every regional resource remained intact, available, ready to be purchased on the free market. The Coalition companies had already divided the resources up among themselves. They cleared the 1.3 billion dead bodies ruining the view. Rumor had it, Dominion Agra and Harbinger were the first companies to open new offices in the region.

There were protests, Neil told him, but they simply were

ignored or forcibly dispersed. And most people reacted to the genocide with a dull outrage that soon turned to apathy and finger pointing. Everyone blamed someone else. The few people in public office who suggested Dominion Agra and Harbinger had spurred their countries into committing a crime against humanity were quickly replaced by better-funded politicians willing to look the other way.

It was another thing everybody seemed to feel angry about, but no one lifted a finger to act upon. His dad used to bring it up in his angry rants at the morning commuter crowd, usually while people scurried past him and tried to avoid him. Tom wondered suddenly where Neil had been sleeping this last month or whether he'd managed to win a few games in the last weeks. It occurred to him suddenly, for the first time, that he really had no way of finding out.

"We're not here to discuss ethics," Major Cromwell went on. "That's not our job here. We're discussing tactics, and I ask you to examine the bombing in purely tactical terms: the resistance came from the ordinary people, and neutron bombs targeted ordinary people. The weapons were suited to the nature of the conflict, and they destroyed none of the infrastructure that would hinder the repopulation of the region. One of the founding goals of the Coalition of Multinationals, in fact, was to see the Middle East revived as a region."

Tom slouched down in his seat. All he knew was, the Coalition of Multinationals—the twelve most powerful companies in the world, including Dominion Agra and Harbinger—united their power after the neutron bombing campaign. They did it, or so they claimed, to serve as a "privatized" version of the UN and prevent more neutron bomb–type incidents. But Neil always said they really did it because they'd just gotten away with something so horrendous, it convinced them they could get away with almost anything, as long as they united their power and held financial sway over every major government in the world. Together, the twelve multinationals had the money and the influence to do just that. Between them, they could buy and sell every country on the planet.

"After that bombing campaign, the Coalition assumed a foremost role in global governance," Cromwell said, "which lasted until the famous splintering of their alliance. One lingering consequence of the Global Collapse was the devaluation of currencies worldwide. Precious metals soared in value, and the Earth's reserves had been mined to near exhaustion. Nobridis Incorporated was the first company to turn eyes toward space. They wanted official backing from our government so they could receive taxpayer funding, so they petitioned our Congress for the first bid to the territory. This insulted the Chinese, who argued that the United States didn't possess the unilateral authority to grant a claim to a territory in space. When our Congress granted Nobridis that claim, China retaliated by awarding the exact same territory to Stronghold Energy. It was a symbolic gesture, but it started everything."

She flipped to an image of the asteroid belt between Jupiter and Mars. It was relatively close to Earth and one of the most potent, resource-laden areas of the solar system, which meant it was the most fiercely contested. Tom had seen so many news clips of skirmishes in the asteroid belt that they all blurred together.

"Various companies in the Coalition sided with Nobridis and the United States, while others sided with Stronghold and China. Soon the Coalition itself was split down the middle, every company on one side or another of the Nobridis-Stronghold conflict. Whereas before, these multinational conglomerates spread their influence throughout the world, a new trend arose when they began concentrating on holding financial sway over certain governments and not others. Our allied multinationals stopped sending funds to China or Russia and concentrated instead on sending them to India and America. The other half of the Coalition did the reverse. In this way, a fight between Nobridis and Stronghold turned first into a struggle between two halves of the Coalition and then into a new space race between the Indo-American and Russo-Chinese alliances—and soon into World War III."

She flipped to an image of a shipyard in space. "Within a decade, territory was claimed throughout the solar system when one side or the other established a physical presence. Establishing 'a presence' means introducing a mining facility, a shipyard, sometimes just a single satellite. But the conflict mounted when the Chinese seized an Indo-American–affiliated platinum mine in the asteroid belt. After this, the conflict evolved into a true war. Not a war in any classical sense, of course. There are no civilian casualties, no bombs, no deaths. Authority over our planet isn't even in dispute, since the warring companies of the Coalition still work together to shape the global agenda for governments worldwide. But out in space, all bets are off."

She flipped to an image of a traditional pilot boarding a jet plane. "The first fighters were pilots in the Air Force who remotely controlled the ships in space. They couldn't keep up with the preprogrammed maneuvers of the Russo-Chinese machines, so they were phased out. Many believed combat had evolved beyond the participation of human soldiers. Both sides switched to fully automated attack fleets. These automated arsenals waged the war until the first Intrasolar Combatants appeared on the Russo-Chinese side. With the advent of neural processors, human beings could finally hold their own against mechanized forces. The presence of human fighters had another benefit, because they added a personal element to the war, and this was exactly what the American public needed to remain invested in the fight."

Tom thought of all the cereal boxes with Elliot's face and the way all the girls at Rosewood loved him so much. He wasn't sure if those girls really supported the fight. They definitely supported Elliot, though.

"For most of the public," Cromwell said, "this war is a spectator sport. The average American knows they are helping to finance this, but they also know they're not seeing the winnings. Their only reward is the entertainment they receive from following the battles, and in the last three years of Combatant-driven combat, a sense of national pride when an American wins new territory. It's important you never take public support for granted. There's a reason we're always sending Elliot Ramirez out there for the cameras. He gives the war a face. If exposure weren't a safety issue, all the Combatants would be public figures just like him. A Combatant is a PR asset, a means of personalizing the war for the general public. People form attachments, even if a Combatant is known only by his or her call sign. One of a Combatant's most vital roles is to keep the public on our side. But that's not your most important duty."

Tom sat up straighter in his seat, sensing that she was about to get into the fighting itself.

"America has only had Intrasolar Combatants in the field for three years. That means those of you in this room destined to advance to Camelot Company may be the tactical pioneers in this new era. Every age has seen a transformation of the ideal soldier. Basil Liddell Hart said, 'Loss of hope, rather than loss of life, is the factor that decides wars, battles, and even the smallest combats.' And what destroys an enemy's hope? In ages long past, the mighty Achilles was the most fearsome warrior in the world. His very presence made armies tremble. In subsequent ages, the famous generals took the glory. And now? What is the name that destroys hope in our time? Who is the greatest Intrasolar Combatant? Who is this moment's Achilles?"

Tom braced himself for the words "Elliot Ramirez."

But Cromwell pounded out something on the keyboard fixed to the podium, and turned to face the curved wall. Tom's eyes riveted to the massive screen curving over them. A view of the black expanse of space flared to life on all sides of him. The image focused upon the planet Venus, then Cromwell zoomed into a Russo-Chinese fighter whose call sign Tom knew from the news.

He'd heard about this fighter. Just a bit, because this Combatant was sponsored by the state of China itself. No sponsoring corporation meant no airtime. But rumors on the internet said this was the best fighter of all of them. This Combatant never lost.

"Today," Cromwell said, "we call the ultimate warrior Medusa."

Dead silence penetrated the air as every plebe watched the battle, and the Russo-Chinese ships controlled by Medusa danced around the Indo-American forces and maneuvered them into obliteration.

Chills moved down Tom's spine. He'd seen clips of battles on the internet, but edited ones, whatever the military wanted the public to witness of the war effort. Any clips favorable to Russo-Chinese forces were censored, and he was sure it worked the same way in reverse in their countries. So Tom had never seen a full engagement, never had a chance to marvel at how incredible this Medusa person was.

Major Cromwell's voice rang out in the darkness. "In the last six months, this single Combatant has changed the course of the war against us. How do we know it's Medusa alone doing this? Watch. An acute student of tactics can identify an opponent just by watching them in action. You'll begin to recognize the mind working behind the maneuver."

And when Cromwell flipped to a recording of a past engagement on Jupiter's moon Io, Tom knew which Russo-Chinese fighters were controlled by Medusa. He just knew them. They anticipated the moves of opponents. They fired missiles in space moments before opponents blundered into them. They reacted to hazards the other ships seemed oblivious to.

"One Intrasolar Combatant can do this," Cromwell told them. "This is the first age in history when a single fighter has the capacity to sway whole battles."

Next, the screen showed a battle on Mercury, where the Indo-American fighters spiraled away after Medusa's trickery ripped them out of orbit and knocked them into the sun's gravity. Then the screen showed an intensive skirmish in the asteroid belt, where ships were torn to pieces by the asteroids that Medusa used like virtual missiles. The last battle they viewed took place on Saturn's moon Titan. Medusa blasted a hole straight through the ice layers, spouting liquid methane into space, knocking the Indo-American ships into a lethal plunge to the moon's surface.

This, Tom thought. This was why he was here. His skin prickled with goose bumps as he watched it all, his eyes fixed on Medusa's machines every time. Medusa. Medusa. Here was a king. Here was a god.

He wanted to face Medusa more than life itself.

If he could be that person, the one who defeated this giant among warriors, *then* he'd be somebody.

When the lights brightened around them and Medusa faded from the overhead screens, Cromwell sent them away for the afternoon. And Tom strode out of the room feeling dazzled like he'd drifted into some strange dream, his lips pulled into a grin that went from ear to ear.

Medusa.

IN CALISTHENICS THE next day, Medusa filled Tom's thoughts. He couldn't tear his mind from the Russo-Chinese Combatant even though the Battle of Stalingrad raged around him.

"I looked up the Medusa myth on the internet," Tom said breathlessly. He ran beside Vik through the bombed-out streets, both Soviet and Nazi soldiers blasting at them. He'd learned it was a Greek myth about a female monster so hideous to behold, any man who saw her face turned to stone. "Do you think Medusa's a girl?"

Vik dodged some shrapnel. Dust whipped into their eyes. "Nah!" he shouted over the sound of gunfire. "Medusa's a call sign. You can't tell whether you're dealing with a guy or a girl from a call sign, especially if we're talking a Russian fighter. Think about it: Sasha is a guy's name over there, okay? The person probably went with Medusa because if you end up face-to-face with her, then bam—you're dead. You saw Medusa fight. It's appropriate, huh?"

"Oh yeah," Tom said, awestruck. He followed Vik into a demolished building, explosions rattling his bones. He'd heard the Russo-Chinese Combatants took on call signs for the same reason the Indo-Americans did: they picked their own when they were promoted to active combat status. It was for the general public. Tom had seen his own share of news snippets about Enigma, Firestorm, Vanquisher, Condor, and the rest of Camelot Company. Of course, now he knew the names behind those call signs: Heather Akron, Lea Styron of Hannibal Division, Karl Marsters, and Alec Tarsus of Alexander Division.

The building rattled, and they dodged falling plaster as they stumbled into an armory, where they found a solid wall of nunchakus. Tom hoisted down a set. "So what happens next? Ronins again?"

"Don't be ridiculous. No ronins in Stalingrad." Vik led Tom through the doorway into the burning building's courtyard where some plebes were already in the thick of fighting Nazi ninjas.

Tom made it five minutes into the strength training session before he paused to wipe away some sweat, and a Nazi ninja swept forward and impaled him through the abdomen. Text flashed across his eyes: *Session expired. Immobility sequence initiated.* All feeling seeped out of his body from the chest on down, and he dropped to the ground, sword still jammed in his abdomen.

"Got killed, huh?" Vik called, from where he was still fighting his Nazi ninja.

"Looks like it." Tom tried to sit up, but even though he could move his arms, they kept collapsing beneath him.

"Don't bother trying to sit up," Vik said, noticing his efforts. "You're supposed to stay where you were killed until the next phase of the workout. You can move your upper body, but you can't bear your own weight or drag yourself anywhere."

Tom gave up on moving and linked his fingers together behind his head. "Why don't people get killed all the time if relaxing is the big punishment?" he said idly.

"Because," Vik answered breathlessly, flashing him a grin before turning back to his duel, "it's about pride."

Pride.

Tom resolved not to get killed again. For now, though, he

contented himself with relaxing beneath the smoky Stalingrad sky, the clank of swords, the rattle of bullets, and the roars of explosions thundering in his ears.

His muscles were still aching from the exercise after lunch, but his mood was soaring thanks to acing all of his subjects for the second time in his life in the civilian classes. Elliot spent the first twenty minutes of Applied Sims giving a speech about the power of positive thinking, and then they all hooked into the program for the afternoon.

Tom snapped into the character of Gawain, a knight of the Round Table from the Camelot legend. A castle fizzed into existence around them. Elliot mounted his throne, playing King Arthur, and announced that the first thing they were going to do was a ritual of fealty.

Tom watched the other plebes—all playing various knights of the Round Table—kneel down before Elliot, kiss his hand, and receive his sword pats to their shoulders. It made Tom's skin crawl. They were practically groveling.

Elliot held out a hand for Tom to kiss, and Tom didn't move a step closer. He wasn't going to kneel down and kiss Elliot Ramirez's hand. He just wasn't.

"You're not swearing fealty to me, Tom?" Elliot asked him.

"You want my fealty, I'll swear it. Without kneeling and kissing your hand. Sir."

"This ritual fosters team cohesion."

"I just don't want to bow, okay? It feels un-American to me. Sorry."

Elliot sighed. "I'm sorry. I'm sorry you don't understand the value of working with others. But if you really don't want to play along like everyone else, I suppose I can give you a role in the sim other than Gawain."

Tom's hopes soared. Maybe Elliot would assign him to play a Saxon barbarian. He'd love that.

Elliot raised his hand skyward, modifying the sim.

Tom's body shifted into Guinevere's.

He stood there, frozen, gaping down at his floor-length dress, the wavy brown hair flowing down to his waist, and, well, his *boobs*. He was still gaping down at those when the company of knights trundled to the courtyard for the ride out to fight the Saxons. Tom stumbled over his skirt, following them, confused by the way his legs felt like they were slanting at a strange angle.

"Wait," Tom called. His voice came out so high, so girly to his ears, that he jumped. It took him a moment to recover from that shock and remember what he was going to say. "My armor disappeared!"

"No, Gawain's armor disappeared," Elliot said. "As my beloved wife, Guinevere doesn't fight in the sim. She provides moral support. She waves us good-bye and waits for our return."

"I don't get to fight?" Tom blurted.

"Only people who swear fealty get to fight."

Elliot raised an eyebrow, waiting. Tom knew what he wanted: for Tom to apologize, crawl over, and kiss his hand. But he couldn't. He didn't crawl to people or bow to them, and he didn't kiss hands.

"Fine."

"Fine." There was suppressed laughter in Elliot's voice. "We'll tell you how the battle went."

Tom stood there in the courtyard, listening to the hoofbeats thump away. Then he felt a tentative tug at his sleeve. One of the queen's attendants spoke: "Your Highness, we were embroidering. Will you join us?"

The instructions for embroidering wove into his brain.

Guinevere liked embroidering. Since Tom was Guinevere, he also liked . . .

He shook it off, aghast. "I don't embroider!" he cried, and bolted away from the virtual woman.

Wild thoughts about what he could do for the next three hours and twenty-eight minutes of the sim ran through his head. He decided to head out anyway, on foot, and fight as Guinevere. But as it turned out, he couldn't even cross the drawbridge. The simulation informed him, *No parameters in place for this action.*

The Guinevere character was restricted to the castle. And her fingers were itching with the need to embroider something. Tom found it all very horrifying. He was *not* going to let Elliot come back after some awesome battle and find him doing embroidery.

So he decided to be proactive. He wielded candlesticks and challenged random guards to duels. The guards just shook their heads and declined to do anything so unchivalrous as fight a lady, which about drove him to madness. So he bashed them over the heads anyway, and they shouted at him that he'd gone mad. Despite this, none dared raise a hand to their psychotic queen.

That gave him a brilliant idea.

He relayed some orders to the castle's guard and dispatched a messenger boy. Then it became a matter of biding his time. Tom avoided the embroidering ladies by exploring the castle's corridors. He found a heavy ceremonial sword the Guinevere character could barely lift, but it was better than nothing. The metal scraped over the stone floors as he hoisted it down the flickering, torchlit corridors, searching for a good, defensible spot.

He wandered into a vast library and beheld an armed

knight looming over a stack of scrolls. Perfect. He'd kill this guy, and take his armor and sword.

"Avast, ye scurvy knave!" Tom cried, getting into character and hoisting up his ceremonial sword. "Prepare to meet yer maker!"

The knight sighed, then turned around and folded his arms over his broad chest.

It was Wyatt's character, Lancelot.

"This is Arthurian England, Tom," she reproved, the note of irritation the only familiar thing about her now-manly voice. "It's not a pirate ship."

"Codswallop," Tom cursed, lowering the sword, the blade clanging on the ground. "What are you doing here, anyway? Lancelot is supposed to be riding out with Arthur to fight the Saxons."

"I told Elliot I wanted to defend the castle in case they got around us, and he thought it was a good idea."

"Yeah, you're defending it, all right," Tom said, nodding to her scrolls. "Are you reading?"

"I'm playing a more erudite Lancelot who prefers to sit here and defend it with his mind."

"He's not supposed to defend stuff with his mind like he's Yoda or something. He's supposed to be Lancelot. He's a knight. He fights barbarians. It's fun."

"Feel free to go fight them yourself, then. I'm not stopping you."

"The sim's stopping me. I'm stuck in the castle."

"Well, feel free to just go somewhere else, then."

Tom ignored her and hoisted himself up onto the table. It was a bit tricky, since he wasn't used to Guinevere's body, the way the hips seemed unbalanced, the weight pressed down at different spots than he was used to.

"Look, Wyatt, Blackburn did that whole dog demonstration on me because I wouldn't tell him who changed my profile. The least you can do is tolerate my presence for a bit."

Wyatt's hand flew to her open mouth, a gesture that looked distinctly girly in Lancelot's body. "Blackburn asked you about me?"

"About the person hacking the profiles, yeah. I didn't tell, though, so don't worry." He shifted back and forth, trying to figure out the best way to position himself. "Man, this girl stuff is throwing me off." He settled with leaning back with his legs slung wide. It earned him a scandalized look from Wyatt, but he was comfortable, so he stayed that way. "A wolf is a completely different body, so you expect to move all differently, but a girl's close enough that I keep trying to move the way I do normally."

"You won't notice after a few more sims."

Tom became distracted by the sight of his own boobs. He reached down to grab them. Wyatt cleared her throat.

"What?" Tom said defensively. "They're mine."

"You aren't seriously planning to just sit here groping yourself in front of me, are you? That's kind of rude."

Tom dropped his hand, a bit sheepish. "What, come on. You've got some new equipment, too. You're not curious?"

Wyatt's armor clanked as she shifted awkwardly in her seat. "It's not like I haven't played sims as men before."

"Right." Tom grinned. "So you've already done the groping thing."

"That's not what I said," she protested. Her cheeks flamed so red, Tom began to enjoy himself.

"You have to have wondered—"

"I am not having this discussion!" She gathered up her scroll and pointedly moved to another table in the empty library.

Tom was just getting started, though. He hopped down to follow her to the new table, hoping to annoy her some more, but a low rumbling saturated the air. Screams drifted into the library's open window, and he knew what must be happening.

Finally. Tom started for the door, thrumming with excitement.

"Wait," Wyatt called after him. "What's happening?"

Tom wheeled back around and remembered she had a sword resting forgotten in her scabbard. He closed the distance between them and drew it before she seemed to realize what he was doing.

"Look, Wyatt, if you want to be a bookworm Lancelot, that's fine. Just lock the door to the library and maybe slide a table in front of it. I'm stealing your sword if you're not fighting, though."

"What are you going to do with it? You said Guinevere can't leave the castle."

"She can't. But *Queen* Guinevere can lower the drawbridge and order the castle sentries to stand down. Just like this Queen Guinevere did about ten minutes ago. Oh, and she can also send a messenger to the Saxon king to let him know Camelot's defenseless."

Wyatt gaped at him. "That sound outside is the Saxon army, isn't it?"

"Yuri's right. You really are smart." Tom heard the screams starting, and started for the sound with a bounce in his step.

"Tom!"

He paused in the doorway, saw Wyatt running her fingers up and down the desk next to her. "Thanks for not telling Blackburn. I'm sorry I got you turned into a dog."

"Hey, I was a dog for you, and now you've given a glorious instrument of death to me"—he waved the sword—"so I'd say we're even."

CHAPTER NINE

SATURDAY MORNING, TOM woke up and wished he hadn't. Everything hurt. Everything. His joints, his bones, his brain. He pressed his face into his pillow and lay there. His thoughts reached back to the day before when Applied Sims ended. Elliot returned to the castle after King Arthur and his knights realized the Saxons weren't showing up at the battlefield. He strode into the throne room and found Tom lounging on Arthur's throne, his gown soaked in blood, and the Saxon king's head mounted on a pike beside him.

He'd offered Elliot the head as fealty, but Elliot didn't take it. He just gave Tom a stern, you've-disappointed-me-young-one look and ended the simulation.

On the bright side, he hadn't given Tom a long speech about teamwork this time.

"Get up." Vik swatted him. "We're going to Toddery's Chicken Barn and then maybe downtown."

"Toddery's Chicken Barn?" Tom mumbled into his pillow.

"They don't just serve chicken. It's way better than it sounds."

"It would have to be. Look, it's too early."

"Come on, man. People with neural processors don't need to sleep in."

"I do," Tom said, even though that technically wasn't true. He was wide-awake, and in pain. Each breath sent pinpricks racing through his rib cage, each movement an electric current down his limbs, like someone was holding a live wire to his joints.

He gritted his teeth and crammed his pillow over his head. He'd try to get more sleep and hope that helped. Maybe he'd been beaten up by someone and gotten hit in the head so hard he'd forgotten it? No. He sorted through his memories of the previous night. He couldn't seem to find any gaps. The neural processor had even helpfully time-stamped his recent memories with the date and hour, so he was certain he'd never been throttled and subsequently forgotten it.

When another shift sent pain prickling through him, his neural processor kicked into scanning mode.

"Huh?" Tom mumbled into his pillow.

A series of statistics flashed through his brain: pH, CO_2, HCO_3, WBC, RBC, RDW, HR, RR . . . Tom pulled the pillow tighter about his head, hoping to smother himself to make the scanning mode stop.

And then one number flashed before his eyes that shocked him to his core.

He was 4.2 inches taller than he'd been on Wednesday.

Tom rolled over onto his back, and pain shot through him in a blinding jolt. He ignored it and looked down at his legs. They actually looked longer. He wiggled his toes, just making sure he really was in his own body. His toes even looked longer. His feet were bigger.

Tom raised his hands before his face, curled and uncurled his fingers, and marveled at the broadness of his palms. "Man hands," he murmured.

"What about Enslow?" Vik said, from the other side of the room.

"Not her. Ignore me."

Tom flopped his head back and decided it was okay that he was aching all over. After all, things couldn't be so bad if he now had large, manly hands.

IGNORING THE PAIN grew trickier after Vik, Yuri, and Beamer headed out. At first, moving slowly was enough to keep it at bay. But soon, Tom found himself sitting on his bed, using his forearm keyboard and his vision center as the monitor, surfing the internet—and still clenching his jaw at the sensation like glass grinding into his joints.

The only thing that seemed to tear his mind from his physical discomfort was the thought of Medusa, the Russo-Chinese fighter. Tom had downloaded every last recording of Medusa's engagements with Indo-American forces. He'd spent a couple hours last night with his eyes closed, accessing those files in his neural processor and playing them in his brain.

Now he started watching a few more: Medusa blasting through the rings of Saturn and shifting the course of a comet to send it crashing into an Indo-American drilling platform on Titan. In another battle, Medusa evaded a trap that got the other ships, then dodged the weapons fire from a dozen ships, all focused on him, and still managed to lure the Indo-American forces to Venus. There, Medusa planted his vessel straight into a wind current that buffeted him back into the high atmosphere, while the pursuing Indo-Americans were forced down toward the surface, hulls melted and then crushed.

Tom was so caught up in replaying that one that he barely registered the knock on his door. He jumped when the door slid open.

A girl's voice rang out: "Are you deaf or something? You didn't hear me knock?"

Tom cracked open his eyes, and saw Wyatt standing tall and gangly in the doorway with her customary frown.

"Nice of you to just come in anyway. Ever occur to you that maybe I was ignoring it?"

Her eyebrows sank down. "You could've taken two seconds to tell me to go away, then."

He felt like he'd just kicked a puppy. "I was caught up in something, or I'd have let you in." He mentally ordered the files to stop playback, and the images of Medusa's vessel vanished from his vision center. "Why are you around the Spire on a Saturday? You didn't go out with Vik and the others?"

"Yuri didn't ask me this time. He's the only one who ever wants me to go anywhere with him."

Tom thought about that. "Do you remember telling me to go away and never talk to you again the first time we met? Do you say stuff like that a lot? Because people generally assume you mean it."

Wyatt considered that. "Oh."

"Just a thought."

"Well, I came to ask if everything was okay yesterday. Did Elliot end up yelling at you for the Saxon thing?"

"Yelling's not his style. He's more about the power of disapproving looks." He gave a heavy sigh and shook his head, mock regretfully, to imitate Elliot for her.

Wyatt's lips pulled up in a quick smile. She was still hanging back in the doorway, shifting her weight awkwardly like she didn't know the rules of conduct for entering someone's room.

"You can come in," Tom told her.

She took a few tentative steps inside. After several moments of her just standing there near his doorway, staring at him and him just staring back, he searched for a distraction. "Hey, you play any games?"

Then he regretted saying it. She might stick around longer now, and then more awkward staring would ensue.

But Wyatt just frowned, like the words did not compute. "Games?"

"VR games," Tom said, exasperated. "You know. Role-playing games. Strategy games. First-person shooters."

"I don't like fighting."

"Strategy, then." Actually, that worked for him, too. He didn't have to move much to play most strategy games, and he could pick a game they only needed keyboards for. He flipped through the Spire's database and found Privateers.

Privateers largely involved trading and negotiating. It wasn't his favorite game, but it was more for brainy people, and he figured she'd be into it.

Wyatt was. She wasn't so great at negotiating, but she plotted courses like a pro.

"You're good at this," Tom told her, when she reached the Polynesian Islands before he did.

"It's just math."

"Right. Math's your thing, huh? The reason you got recruited."

She was sitting with her back against the leg of Vik's bed, her arms curled over her bent knees, tapping halfheartedly at her forearm keyboard. "I was good at it. My parents were always entering me into competitions, and if I'd wanted to, I could've gone to college early. Of course, since everyone here has a neural processor, it's not like being good at math means anything now." Her eyes flickered over to him. "I guess it's the same for you, with the spelling bee thing. Everyone can spell as well as you now that they have neural processors."

A laugh rose in Tom's throat. He couldn't help it. "Yeah, it drives me nuts knowing everyone else can spell correctly now. It really cheapens my talent."

"Well"—Wyatt smoothed her hair back behind her ear—"at least I found something else. I don't see why so many people don't understand programming. I think they just don't know how to work anymore. They're too used to just downloading something and understanding it, so it seems like too much effort actually connecting the dots and writing out a program."

"Blackburn seems to think that," Tom said, remembering the stuff he'd said to Heather in class. "Too bad he's hunting you. You'd probably have some great meeting-of-minds thing going on."

Wyatt pressed her lips together.

"Or not?"

"I hacked the profiles my first week here to help a couple people who were hoping to get promoted," Wyatt said flatly. "It was a dumb thing to do, and ever since, I've had to mess up my own code before I turn it in so Blackburn doesn't realize I'm the one who did it. And the people I did that for? None of them have even talked to me since."

"You didn't do it to make friends or something, did you?"

She didn't answer that.

"Look, Wyatt, they sound like jerks. Why would it make so much of a difference when it comes to promotions, anyway? The profile achievements are all in the past."

"Coalition companies have more interest in sponsoring people with great backgrounds. One of the people whose profile I changed got into Camelot Company a month later.

She probably would've gotten sponsored anyway, but her new profile helped her get the company she wanted."

"Who was that?"

"It doesn't matter," Wyatt insisted, and focused her attention back on the game. "It's all over and done now, anyway."

ON SUNDAY, TOM was six inches taller than when he first arrived at the Spire, and something strange was happening. His neural processor ran scans constantly, one after the other. A message began blinking in his vision center: *CA 7.3 (8.9–10.3).*

"Vik." Tom said to his roommate, who was sprawled on the other bed, playing a game with wired gloves he'd smuggled out of the ground floor VR parlor. "What's CA seven point three?"

"CA . . . California?"

"I don't think so." After a moment, Tom admitted, "My bones are kind of killing me. It's kind of hard to move." And his lips and fingers were tingling like he had bugs crawling below his skin.

Vik studied him. "I don't think that's normal."

"Really?"

"Go ask about it at the infirmary."

Tom groaned inwardly. That was all the way on the ground floor.

But now that he thought about it, he was starting to wonder if something was very wrong with him, after all. He'd actually brought it up with Wyatt the day before, and she'd listed about twenty different fatal diseases he might have. That really didn't reassure him. Vik's words finally motivated him to grit his teeth and stagger down the hallway.

He made it as far as the plebe common room.

There, he found a group of Genghises playing pool. A familiar voice bellowed out, "Hey look, it's Fido!"

Tom sighed inwardly. It was Karl Marsters. The massive, jowl-faced Genghis straightened up from the shot he'd just made, the cords standing out on his thick neck, a grin on his face.

"What do you want?" Tom asked him.

Karl's stepped forward to block his path when he made for the elevator. "He's not very polite, is he? Not a good doggie."

Tom tried to shove past him, but one meaty blow to the chest sent him reeling back. He caught himself against the wall, then yanked himself upright, his heart thudding.

"I hear you're giving my boy Elliot a hard time," Karl said.

"*Your boy* Elliot? Why do *you* care?"

Karl looked at his buddies, three large guys and a muscular blond girl. "You're a spelling bee champ, aren't you, White Fang? How do you spell 'If I don't learn to speak to my betters with more respect, I'm going to get my face smashed in'?"

Tom laughed, unable to resist: "That one's easy. It's K-A-R-L."

In a flash, Karl's fist flew toward his face. Tom ducked just in time. An ugly crack split the air as Karl's knuckles met the wall. Karl screamed out, and Tom didn't need any warning message to flash across his vision center this time. He knew this was trouble. He hurled himself past the large Genghis and made for the elevator. But it would never arrive in time, so he swerved around it, hoping he could duck into one of the other divisions.

Luck was on his side. The first door he reached slid open. He stumbled through and locked it behind him. Thumps against the door, bodies crashing against it, people who'd pursued him coming to their sudden halt.

Tom laughed, breathless, elated, the weird pain in his

joints all but forgotten in the surge of adrenaline. He heard soft footfalls on the floor behind him, and then a familiar voice, "Take a wrong turn?"

Tom jumped. He whirled around to catch gazes with a familiar pair of yellow-brown eyes. "Heather."

She leaned against the wall of the corridor, her dark hair loose about her shoulders. "You realize this is Machiavelli Division, don't you?"

Fists drummed against the door behind him. Tom jabbed his thumb toward it. "Any way to seek asylum? I'm being chased."

"Who's chasing you?"

"Genghises. Large, angry Genghises."

Heather propped a hand on her hip and made a tsking sound. There was a playful twinkle in her eyes. "Did you do something bad, Tom?"

"No, I swear, I barely even know Karl Marsters. He got all in my face about me messing with Elliot."

"Oh, of course." Heather swayed forward, then looped her arm through his and led him down the hallway to a living room area with a circular arrangement of chairs. "It's because Elliot's a Napoleon. Napoleons and Genghises are allies. They always look out for each other. You should've gone to Hannibal Division. They're aligned with the Alexanders. They'd protect you."

She was pressed close up against him, her warmth seeping into his arm. "Huh," Tom said, trying not to get too distracted by it. "It's funny. I didn't even think divisions mattered that much."

"Right now, for you, they're just dorms. It's really later on when it comes to potential corporate sponsors that divisions matter at all. Alexanders and Hannibals will introduce you to their company reps—those are the people in each Coalition company who determine which Combatants they want to sponsor. They pay for a Combatant's airtime, supply ships for them to use in combat, and basically make it financially viable for the military to use them in space battles."

"So people aren't CamCo because they're good."

"Being good helps. But this isn't a pure meritocracy, no. It's also about knowing people."

"I thought this place was all about war. I didn't expect it to be political."

She bumped him with her hip. "Tom, haven't you heard that phrase—'Politics is just war by other means'?"

"What about Machiavellis?" Tom said, his eyes dropping to the quill on her shoulder. "Who are you guys aligned with?"

"We Machiavellis shun permanent alliances. We're free agents."

"Freedom's good. I'm all for freedom." He was all for Heather's hands all over him like this, too.

She tugged him around by the arm, then pressed on his chest. Tom moved back at her urging until his legs met the soft cushion of a chair. He dropped back into it.

"Well," Heather said, dropping back into her own chair and crossing her legs, "freedom has disadvantages. I'm the only Machiavelli in CamCo because the alliances stick with their own when they're introducing potential Combatants to their sponsors. Alexanders and Hannibals introduce each other, and Napoleons and Genghises introduce each other. It's all about influence. When you have more people from your division in CamCo, you're able to get more people from your division in CamCo. That's why it was so hard for me to get in."

"Hard for *you*?" Tom said, disbelieving. Someone who could fly like her, and looked like her, and she didn't have companies falling over each other to sponsor her?

"I got in the program in the first place because I actually earned it. I didn't have a rich uncle to connect me with Matchett-Reddy like Lea Styron, or a dad who used to work for Dominion Agra like Karl Marsters." She tapped her fingers on the armrest of her chair. "Actually, it's why I'm visiting the plebe floor. It has the biggest common area, and we've been plotting how to get another Machiavelli into CamCo. General Marsh agreed to approach the Defense Committee and nominate an Upper from our division, so now I have to figure out how to get a company behind him."

"Why don't you just use your sponsor?"

"I tried, but I can't get Wyndham Harks onboard. So we have to look somewhere else and figure out how to get someone from another division to help."

Tom thought of the other two Camelot Company members sponsored by Wyndham Harks: Yosef Saide of Genghis Division, and Snowden Gainey of Napoleon. They were both clean-cut, symmetrical-featured guys with ready grins. Between them and Heather, Tom figured there was one specific criteria Wyndham Harks cared about in their Combatants: looks.

"Who are you putting forward?" Tom asked her.

Heather's nodded to someone in the hallway behind him. "Nigel."

Tom turned, saw a weedy guy lingering in the hallway beyond. He was skinny and delicate, with full lips, a tiny nose, and a face that looked almost girlish.

NAME: Nigel Harrison
RANK: USIF, Grade V Upper, Machiavelli Division
ORIGIN: Cambridge, England

ACHIEVEMENTS: Winner of the International Linguistics Olympiad, member of the British Association for Computational Linguistics

IP: 2053:db7:lj71::262:ll3:6e8

SECURITY STATUS: Top Secret LANDLOCK-5

"I guess you've been listening. Did you hear about Tom's situation?" Heather asked him.

"Yes. Those are Genghises trying to break in here, are they?" Nigel's voice had a crisp British accent. Everything about the kid was smooth, from his gelled hair to the way he walked so lightly Tom couldn't hear his footsteps. He had a strange tic going on with his face. It was this low, continuous spasm around his right eye, like he wasn't quite in control of it.

"Yeah." Tom tried not to stare at his twitching face. "Sorry about the door pounding."

"It's fine. It makes me wonder about something. You?" Nigel looked at Heather.

Heather cupped her chin in her palm. "Maybe."

"Yes," Nigel said, in a voice so low Tom almost didn't hear it.

"Fine," Heather said.

If Tom didn't know better, he'd wonder if they were having half this conversation telepathically.

"Tom," Heather said abruptly, "can you wait in one of the bunks while Nigel and I finish here? I'll be there soon, and we'll figure out how to get you out of here. Of course"—she winked—"if you're okay with waiting it out, I suppose I could come keep you company."

Good. God. That smile of hers could seriously crash planes.

"Yeah. Yeah, I'll go wait." He headed into the nearest empty bunk, bumping into the doorframe in his haste.

Tom laughed once he was inside the empty bunk. That girl even made his neural processor malfunction.

He winced at the pain in his knees as he settled onto the edge of an empty bed, his hand tapping an impatient beat on his thigh. As time stretched on, he closed his eyes and began sorting through a schematic of the Spire, trying to figure out how to get past the Genghises waiting for him. That CA number blinking in his vision center kept getting lower, and now that he thought about it, his lips and fingertips were tingling again. . . .

The door slid open. Heavy footsteps thumped toward him.

Too heavy for Nigel or Heather.

Tom's eyes snapped open, and he experienced an electric jolt of terror.

Karl Marsters loomed above him, bruised and bloody. His fist descended into Tom's face.

HE ROUSED AS Karl hauled him into the Machiavelli hallway, Nigel and Heather watching from a few feet away. Tom choked on the blood in his nose and struggled against the massive arm locked around his neck but couldn't budge it.

"Thanks. Thanks, guys," Karl was telling them.

"Did you punch him?" Heather demanded. "That's not part of our deal, Karl."

"Sorry, I couldn't resist. I know the agreement. I wasn't supposed to punch him in Machiavelli. Whoops."

Tom struggled against the headlock. Now he understood it: Heather hadn't been flirting, sending him off into the bunk. She'd been getting him out of the way so she could sell him out. The realization settled like something sour in his gut as Karl jerked him forward one reluctant step after another.

Nigel drew near, his eyes bright. "Remember the important part. You're committed."

"Yeah, yeah. I'll remember." Karl hauled Tom another few jerky steps. "You gave me the little punk, so once Marsh nominates you to the Defense Committee, I'll take you to meet my Dominion Agra reps to see whether they'll sponsor your bid."

Heather smiled at Tom as though she could charm him even while a large Genghis was practically suffocating him thanks to her treachery. It just made him feel like more of an idiot, knowing he was stuck here in a headlock with a bloody nose, totally suckered by her. "Sorry, Tom, you have to understand: we need more Machiavellis in CamCo, and I promised Nigel I'd try my best."

Tom kicked back, trying to wrench out of Karl's grip again, but he wasn't some heavyweight wrestling champ for nothing. A large hand clasped Tom's wrists behind his back and twisted them up hard enough to make him keel over just to keep his arms in their sockets.

Karl clamped his hand over Tom's head, pressing it down, walking him forward in that undignified way. "That's it. Keep going, Lassie."

Tom couldn't resist the steady march into the common room where a crowd of Genghises were gathered. His face throbbed. He was in serious trouble here.

Karl's voice boomed across the common room: "Now, ladies and gentlemen, sometimes we get a plebe who needs to be taught humility."

Tom tried to jerk up again, but Karl yanked his arms higher and the pain grew so much worse, like his arms were matches about to be snapped. He dropped down again, unable to help it, and was stuck watching his own blood drip onto the carpet.

"Do you want to apologize to us, Old Yeller?" Karl's hand jerked Tom's head in a nod. "I bet you do. Make it loud and clear so everyone can hear you."

Tom gritted his teeth. "No."

Karl wrenched Tom's arms toward his shoulders, and he gasped in pain.

"This doesn't feel very nice, does it?" Karl's big hand tugged Tom's head back and forth to shake it. "You don't like this, do you? Want it to stop? Then bark for us, Fido. Bark."

Tom couldn't help the pained sound that escaped his lips when Karl shoved his arms higher. But he'd never bark. He didn't care how much it hurt. He'd rather tear out his own intestines than do anything Karl wanted.

"Do it now or I'll rip your arms out of the sockets, Benji."

"Do it! Do it, then, 'cause I'm not going to bark!"

"Fine, you think I'm bluffing? I'll show you a bluff!"

Tom yelped out when his arms were shoved beyond their limits, and then a strange sound filled the room. Like a bunch of people making clucking noises. He heard Karl exclaim, "What the—"

And then Karl released him, staggered back, and knelt on the floor.

"Bock," Karl said.

Tom stumbled away from him, swiping his sleeve at his stinging nose. "What?"

"Bock, bock," Karl replied, and began pressing at the carpet with his nose. "Bock, bock, bock."

Tom clutched his sleeve to his face, utterly bewildered. He looked at the other Genghises, saw them all kneeling, pressing their noses rhythmically into the carpet, all bocking.

"Well, I'd say that worked."

Wyatt Enslow's voice startled him. He whirled around to see her emerging from the open doors of the elevator, her forearm keyboard bared.

"What's going on?" Tom asked her, baffled. "What are they doing?"

"They're chickens," Wyatt answered.

And sure enough, when Tom watched them, he realized they were all pecking at the carpet just like chickens.

"I based it on Blackburn's dog program," Wyatt remarked. "I saw you were in trouble, so I figured now was a good time to try it."

Tom turned to her, regarding her with new eyes. "Wyatt, you seriously helped me out there. Thanks, I owe you big-time."

"I just wanted to try the program. It's not like I went out of my way to save you."

Tom laughed and pressed his sleeve against his face a bit harder. "This is where you say, 'You're welcome.' It's okay to take credit."

Her cheeks flushed. "Oh. Right."

"And you pump your fists in the air and say something about how awesome you are. That's how it works."

"Isn't that gloating?"

"Of course it's gloating. When you do something awesome, you get to gloat—" Tom fell silent, because the door to Machiavelli slid open, and Heather strode out.

She halted, looked over the situation, then giggled. "Oh, good. I guess I don't need to call your friends to come rescue you."

Tom stared at her, completely aware of the blood drying on his face. She didn't look the least bit guilty, or even aware that she'd done something wrong just now.

"You're telling me you were planning to call them?" he said cynically. "Doesn't that defeat the purpose of selling me out?"

She flipped her hair back over her shoulder. "It's not like that, Tom. Did you really think I was going to let Karl beat you up? Karl and I had a deal: I'd let him take you out of Machiavelli, and in return, he agreed to help us get Nigel into Camelot Company." Her eyes glinted with a wicked light. "I only agreed to let him haul you out of Machiavelli. I never said a word about not calling someone here to help you. And I was just checking to see what was happening, to see if you really needed it."

Tom wanted to believe her. He took another step back, considering it. "You could've let me in on it beforehand."

She bit her lip. "Aw, but you had to look all hurt and betrayed for Karl to trust me. I didn't know how good of an actor you are."

When her eyes were wide and imploring, like she wanted nothing more than for him to believe her, Tom found it so hard to remember there was any reason to be angry. She hadn't meant for him to get punched.

And then Wyatt cut in, "That's so easy to say now that it's all over. But if you were going to call one of Tom's friends to tell them he needed help, why didn't you do it at the same time you called Karl so they'd be ready to come help him? For all you knew, they weren't even in the Spire today."

Heather blinked at Wyatt like she'd just noticed she was there. "I'm sorry, but I don't really know you. . . . Wyatt, isn't it?"

"That's weird. You knew my name a few months ago when I helped with your profile," Wyatt said flatly.

Tom's gaze shot to Heather's. *That was her?*

Heather opened and closed her mouth, caught off guard. She recovered quickly. "Well, Wyatt, it's still a little presumptuous for you to say what I should've done when you don't understand the whole situation."

Wyatt crossed her arms. "I thought I was just pointing out the obvious."

"Tom is fine, so this argument is pointless." Heather wasn't so gorgeous with that gray color in her cheeks, and there was something very narrow and calculating in her expression, like she was sizing Wyatt up as an enemy.

"I thought I brought up a good point, and you haven't even addressed it—"

"Wyatt, it's okay," Tom broke in, stepping between them.

Wyatt scowled at him now, and then muttered, "Fine. It doesn't make a difference to *me*." She took a few jerky steps toward the door to Hannibal Division, then spun around, and awkwardly raised her arms up in the air.

Tom gazed at her, perplexed, wondering why she was making claws like she was pretending to be a monster.

"I am awesome," she said.

And he laughed, realizing she was gloating just like he'd told her to. Wyatt nodded, then abruptly whirled around and scrambled from the room.

Heather was gaping after her, like she'd just encountered an alien. "It's true what everyone says. She has, like, no social skills."

"She's blunt," Tom agreed.

If Heather caught that he was telling her Wyatt was painfully honest, unlike some other girl he knew, then she didn't show it.

"You remember, don't you, that I made Karl promise not to hit you in Machiavelli?"

Tom hit the button to the elevator several times. "Sure, I remember you saying that. Look, I've gotta go to the infirmary."

He began remembering the way Heather and Nigel looked at each other in Machiavelli Division when he told them he was being chased by Karl, and the way Heather sent him off so they could talk alone, but really so she could call Karl to offer him up.

Heather's hand slid up the back of his arm and rested there near his shoulder. Goose bumps prickled up his skin. She whispered in his ear, "I'll come see you later, just to be sure you're okay."

She usually made his brain feel like it was dissolving, but he felt now like they were surrounded by a fog of sorts, muting whatever it was she did to him. Maybe his face was just throbbing too much from being punched for her to have the usual effect.

He shifted so her hand dropped from him, and stepped into the elevator. "You don't need to," he said. "I'm doing great." And then before she could say another word, the doors slid shut between them.

Tom FINALLY MADE it to the infirmary a full half hour after leaving Alexander Division. After Nurse Chang packed his bleeding nose with gauze, Tom told him about the CA thing, which sent a flicker of alarm across the man's face.

"What?" Tom said, aghast. "What is it?"

"Nothing, nothing," Nurse Chang said hastily, paging Dr. Gonzales. "Let's look at those shoulders."

Tom's joints had been hurting even before Karl kindly twisted his arms nearly out of their sockets. By the time Chang tested Tom's range of motion, he couldn't even raise his arms past his shoulders. Chang gave him some Percocet, which took care of the pain. Tom was almost able to forget why he'd come a few minutes later as he lay in a conical machine that was testing his bone density. He'd just yanked the bloody gauze out of his nose when Olivia Ossare's voice startled him.

"Tom, how are you?"

He peered over at her, surprised. He hadn't realized she worked weekends. His neural processor flashed:

NAME: Olivia Ossare
AFFILIATION: United States Social Services
SECURITY STATUS: Confidential LANDLOCK-3

He hadn't spoken to Olivia since his first day at the Spire, but he'd heard about her from the other trainees. She'd told him she was there for the kids, there to be their moral support and stuff, but Tom had learned enough to realize no one actually went to her. Or if anyone did, they definitely didn't talk about it.

It was more of a joke to the trainees, a way to ridicule people who seemed like wimps: *oh, if you don't like it here, why don't you go cry to the social worker, Plebe?*

It embarrassed him, seeing Olivia there, concern on her face. He balled up the gauze in his hand and glanced toward the door, hoping no one passed by and thought she was there because he needed to talk to her.

"Fine. I'm having some bone density issues or something, but it's no big deal."

Her black eyebrows drew together. "The nurse told me you tore some ligaments. What happened?"

"Oh. Yeah. I tripped. This is nothing, really."

"That neural processor's supposed to help your balance."

"It didn't this time."

He hoped the words would end the questions, but she pressed on. "Has everything been okay so far?"

"Everything's fine," Tom said.

"No, it's not," a voice broke in. Dr. Gonzales walked over, studying his lab reports.

NAME: Alberto Gonzales
RANK: Lieutenant, MD
GRADE: USAF 0-3, Active Duty
SECURITY STATUS: Top Secret LANDLOCK-8

Tom blinked away the text as the doctor informed him, "You're showing signs of strain upon your joints and low density in your bones. There's a low serum calcium level, too—you must feel some tingling in your extremities. This growth spurt's overtaxing your body."

Tom went cold. "I told you, I fell. That's why I got hurt."

Dr. Gonzales shook his head. "Your injury's secondary to the overall strain on your body. It's a result, not a cause. Your system doesn't have the resources to support this bone expansion. I'm going to have to access your neural processor and shut off the hGH spike."

"But you can turn it back on later, right? When I have more, uh, resources?"

"There'd be no point."

"What do you mean, no point?"

But Dr. Gonzales strode from the room without answering him. Tom sat up, gritting his teeth at the grinding sensation in his joints. "What does he mean, there'd be no point?" he asked Nurse Chang, who was typing something into a computer.

Chang came over and joined Olivia at his bedside. "Tom, the neural processor takes over some of the natural functions of the human brain. The brain's a use-it-or-lose-it organ. The areas of the brain that become unnecessary begin to atrophy.

155

Some areas that regulate growth are among them. That's why we have the processors spike your hGH when you first get here. We want to make sure you don't miss out on those growth spurts you'd normally have over the next five years."

"So if I don't get taller now, it'll be too late," Tom concluded. "Fine, I get that you have to turn it off—but can't you wait just a few days? Until I'm six feet, or maybe six two?"

Dr. Gonzales reentered the room and moved to the computer, not even looking at him. "No. I can't wait an hour. You should've come to me the moment the pain flared up. Your body has a finite number of resources to support bone growth. We try to aid the process with nutritional supplementation, but nothing can make up for fourteen years of poor eating habits. For instance, I can tell from the plaque buildup in your arteries that you were raised on a steady diet of junk food and have never seen a vegetable in your life."

"That's not true." He ate French fries all the time.

"Plug this in for me." Dr. Gonzales offered him a neural wire.

Tom didn't take it. "I want to wait."

"Sure, you can wait, Mr. Raines," Dr. Gonzales said drily. "And after you've decalcified your bones and contracted osteoporosis in your mid-thirties, you can sue me for malpractice."

Mid-thirties? That was *years* away. "I won't sue. I swear it."

Dr. Gonzales scoffed. "The decision's not yours to make. Lieutenant Chang, plug it in."

Nurse Chang plugged in the wire. Tom slumped down to the bed, feeling the numbness of a neural connection seeping through his muscles. "I don't see why it's your decision, though. It's my body. My osteoporosis. The military doesn't own me."

"No, but it owns the neural processor in your head

regulating your pituitary gland."

Tom felt Olivia's hand on his wrist. "You'll thank him for this one day."

Resentment boiled through Tom as he listened to Dr. Gonzales's keyboard tapping, tapping away, switching off the growth hormone. He wouldn't be grateful for this. Not ever. He'd have to go through his life as a short guy.

Well, not so short anymore. But not the guy he'd wanted to be. A big guy. A huge guy Karl Marsters would never mess with. He didn't understand why someone else was allowed to make this choice for him. Yes, it was their processor, but it was *his brain.*

He closed his eyes and tried to shut out the phantom echo of his father's words: *You're just a piece of equipment to them . . .*

CHAPTER TEN

LIFE AT THE Pentagonal Spire brought something new into Tom's life. He'd never quite experienced it before.

Routine.

There was a code of conduct in his neural processor, there to inform him of what he could and could not do. He knew he had to be in the Spire by 2000 every weeknight, 2300 on weekends. He knew a GPS signal tracked his movements to ensure he stayed within the Designated Zone twenty miles around the Spire. Even the design of the Spire was careful and predictable. Each fifth of the Spire was divided by the letters A, B, C, D, E, and each room numbered from lowest to highest the farther outward he wandered from the elevators in the center.

Every weekday at breakfast, there was morning meal formation at 0700. Twice a month, male Alexander plebes were assigned to be the ones who rose an hour earlier than usual, formed up at the door to the mess hall, and shouted out the time at five-minute intervals until the start of Morning Meal Formation. Nights were dreamless times filled with downloading all the material needed for the following day's classes.

The only real free time came in the evenings, and it was filled with Vik, Yuri, and Beamer, and increasingly with Wyatt Enslow.

When Tom's shoulders healed, he got back into playing VR sims. As time passed, though, he spent fewer and fewer hours diving into video games. The world of the Spire was consuming him, one where the shooting would one day be real, where the victories would actually mean something. A new favorite activity began to take up his free time: he started watching Medusa's battles over and over again.

It didn't matter that he had basically memorized the Russo-Chinese fighter's every move. He still marveled at each of the files he'd downloaded to his neural processor, enjoying the ultimate warrior in action all over again like it was the very first time he'd seen the Achilles of the modern era. When he got bored in class with the civilian instructors, he accessed the Medusa clips then, too. When Elliot gave long speeches, he didn't have to pretend to be entertained, because he was tuned into Medusa. He was sure that if he could dream with his neural processor, he'd see the battles in his sleep.

The rest of his life at the Spire was shaping up nicely as well. For a while after the Genghis chicken debacle, the threat of Karl hung over Tom's head, but Karl never moved, almost as though he was leery of risking another humiliation.

Elliot Ramirez never moved openly against Tom, either, though there was always an air of disapproval whenever he spoke to him. Tom had wondered for a while whether Elliot sent Karl after him, but quickly decided against it. Elliot wasn't a revenge type of guy. The worst Elliot ever did was make pointed comments about *some* people not being team players.

As for Wyatt Enslow, she accessed the Spire's internal cameras to edit herself out in case any of the Genghises carried the story of their mysterious computer virus to Blackburn. But she couldn't resist the urge to save a short video clip of the Genghis chickens, which was edited so no one else appeared in the picture with them. She showed it to Vik and Yuri, and then Vik got a brilliant idea and planted Karl's finest moment ever in the homework feed.

Wyatt was so angry, she refused to talk to Vik for a whole week. Vik told Tom it was his greatest week ever, but Tom couldn't help noticing the way Vik bugged Wyatt more and more, trying to get her to say something to him. And he was in a great mood the night he finally needled her so much, she snapped back at him.

But Wyatt had more reason to be upset soon enough, because the clip reached Blackburn. He surprised them all by playing it in class one Tuesday.

"This, right here, is an incredible program." He gave some mock applause and encompassed the audience with a deceptively lazy sweep of his eyes. Only the intensity in his voice betrayed him when he asked, "Who wants to take credit? Don't be shy."

Tom could see that Wyatt wasn't fooled by his mild tone. She shrank down a bit farther in her seat. Today, it wasn't as easy to hide as usual. The rows of benches in front of hers looked sparse, even though the Lafayette Room was only missing the twelve Combatants in Camelot Company.

Tom had puzzled over their absence earlier at Morning Meal Formation. Then everyone received a message in their processors to apprise them that the Russo-Chinese forces had launched a surprise attack on the Indo-American shipyards near Neptune. If they destroyed them, it would be a massive setback to Indo-America. It took so long to get machinery to the outer solar system, much less to establish shipyards there, and that arsenal formed part of the access corridor to the mineral-rich Kuiper Belt. The CamCos had all been summoned to the Helix, the area between the ninth and tenth floors with neural interfaces that directly controlled ships in space. As the minutes dragged by in Programming, Tom grew more and more aware there was some awesome battle going on in space, and he had no way of knowing who was winning.

If Blackburn had heard any news of the latest battle, he showed no sign of it. He was too busy studying the coding of Wyatt's program and firing questions at Karl's friends, the Genghises who had been turned into chickens.

"Where was the programmer standing? . . . Did you hear a voice? . . . What did you do when you first recovered?"

The muscular blond Genghis, Lyla Martin, finally grew tired of it. "I'm telling you, sir, we don't know who did it. I can't help you."

Blackburn's lips pulled into a flat smile. "Oh, you can help me, Ms. Martin. If you don't have a name for me, I'll think of something else for you to help me with today."

Everyone knew what that meant: it meant he'd be selecting her for his next demonstration.

Lyla grew desperate. "Ask Tom Raines!"

Oh no. Tom slouched down in his seat.

"He was there. He saw it all. He probably knows!"

Blackburn's gaze crawled to Tom's. "Is that so, Mr. Raines?"

"No, I didn't see anything," Tom said quickly.

"But you were there."

"I wasn't . . ." Tom looked at Lyla, and the other Genghises who'd been *chickened*. They'd all argue against him. He sighed. "I was there, yes."

"And you have no name for me, I presume."

"No, sir," Tom said, knowing Blackburn wasn't going to let him get away with this, especially not with everyone watching.

"Fine, Raines. *You* can be my volunteer today. Get up here."

Tom gave Vik and Beamer a mock salute, then rose to his feet and plodded down the aisle. His gaze darted to the device Blackburn had brought into class. The metallic instrument that looked like an upside-down claw. He hoped this wasn't going to be too awful.

"Today," Blackburn announced to the class, "we're discussing Klondike. I am not referring to an ice-cream bar. Like Zorten II, Klondike is a neural processor–specific computer language. It's used in two areas: it helps a neural processor communicate with technologies in the intrasolar arsenal, and it tweaks the brain in certain ways Zorten II can't, specifically when it comes to indexed memories."

Tom mounted the stage. Blackburn gestured him over, then jabbed his index finger toward the screen over the stage.

"Focus on that, Raines."

Tom heard faint sniggers as he neared the podium. People still remembered him falling in love with it. His cheeks burned and he tried to focus on the screen, but it was hard. Blackburn was preparing the clawlike device, positioning it right over his head. With a flick of a button, Blackburn sent thin beams of blue light from the claw tips into Tom's temples. He flinched reflexively, but he felt nothing other than a tingling against his skin.

"This won't be painful," Blackburn assured him, typing at his forearm keyboard. "Just keep staring at the screen."

Tom focused on the wriggling line on the screen. It was wavering. It reminded him of a snake or a spider or something. Apprehension bloomed through him, hearing Blackburn typing, typing away on his forearm keyboard, but Tom kept his eyes fixed on the line. A memory drifted into his head—*that weekend Neil spent in the hospital and Tom had to stay at his buddy Eddie's house. He opened a closet and found a bunch of scorpions. Eddie screamed, but Tom laughed and stamped on them and—*

"There you are," Blackburn said triumphantly.

Tom jumped, startled from the memory.

Blackburn twirled his finger, telling him to face the class again. "This contraption is called a census device. For the majority of the people in this room who can't ever hope to understand how to use something like this, it's a large, shiny object to admire. For the few of you who might one day master Zorten II and Klondike, it's a potent psychological weapon. Your neural processor indexes all your memories, new and old. This device accesses those memories. And once you can access memories, there are worlds of applications. I'm going to show you one right now."

More typing as he spoke.

Tom's eyes remained fixed on the waving line that suddenly looked like a scorpion, and his memory drifted back to him of *the time when he opened that closet and the scorpions came scuttling out. They'd climbed up into his jeans and stung his skin along his legs. He shrieked and shrieked in pain and ended up in the emergency room, and he remembered the smell of antiseptic in the hospital, and the pain, and the venom that had burned like fire all over his calves. . . .*

Blackburn's voice yanked Tom from the memory. "Now, hold out your hand, Raines."

Tom eyed him. "Why?"

"Do it."

Tom raised his left hand.

"Thatta boy. Now palm down."

Tom turned his palm down, and Blackburn placed something on his skin.

He felt it before he saw it. Felt the tiny, pointed little legs, the exoskeleton. He was aware of the blood draining from his cheeks, the sickness churning up in him, the coldness seeping into his shaking limbs. His heart pounded faster and faster in his ears and he didn't feel he was breathing, he was suffocating. His vision focused with horrified clarity upon the scorpion nestled on top of his hand.

"Don't move." Blackburn settled back to watch his face.

"Wh—what—"

"Stand very still or it might sting you."

Tom gasped for breath, cold sweat pricking over his skin. He couldn't move. Couldn't. It would sting him like that time, that time they all scuttled out of that closet, and he remembered shrieking, and even though he'd been a little kid back then, he felt the panic clawing up inside him again. His vision tunneled, his head spun. He couldn't take this. He was going to scream. This was so much worse than the virus that made him fear the podium. *It was standing there right on his hand!* He was going to dissolve right here in front of everyone—faint or something—and he'd get laughed at, laughed at.

"Why don't you tell the class how you feel, Raines?" Blackburn suggested. "Be honest."

Tom glared at Blackburn, fury seething through him. He knew what Blackburn wanted. Well, he wasn't going to look like a weak, pathetic person in front of all his friends. He *wasn't*. He'd rather gouge out his own eyes.

164

So he seized the scorpion in his right hand, squeezed the body as hard as he could in his fist, then raised it to his mouth and ripped the head off with his teeth. The bitter taste of triumph flooded his mouth. He spat out the head, and realized with a strange sense of shock he hadn't even been stung.

Blackburn stared at him, stunned into silence. Then, "Mr. Raines, if that had been a real scorpion rather than a nutrient bar your neural processor projected as a scorpion, you'd be poisoned right now. Do you realize that?"

Tom looked at the headless remains of the scorpion in his hand, and realized that it was, indeed, a grayish mass with lumpy green clumps. A nutrient bar. He'd bitten into a nutrient bar.

"I didn't think that through," Tom admitted.

Blackburn rubbed a hand over his mouth, eyeing Tom, then he plucked the remains of the nutrient bar from Tom's hand and tossed it into a waste receptacle by the podium. "There's a difference between bravery and rash stupidity. Learn it." He tapped his keyboard. "Get back to your seat, Plebe."

Tom headed back to his usual bench, his whole body shaking, sweat plastering his uniform to his body. He found himself thinking about the scorpions again, the way they'd scuttled out of the closet. It was the same weekend Neil had gone to the emergency room, not him. Tom had never even been stung by one scorpion, much less a whole bunch of them. Blackburn had changed the memory somehow.

Blackburn spoke, "I exposed Raines to a trigger designed to mimic a small, crawling creature. It brought a memory related to that to the forefront of his brain. The census device retrieved it and allowed me to see the recollection of scorpions. Using the Klondike computer language, I rewrote it, and then I stuck it back in his brain. This new version of the memory created a phobia, and if I hadn't chosen to demonstrate on this particular plebe, then maybe you would've seen a natural panic reaction. Instead, you saw Mr. Raines trying to show us all what a big, tough man he is."

Tom slouched down on his bench, ignoring the laughter bubbling up around him.

Blackburn's gaze moved to the Genghis Division trainees, laughing louder than the rest. "Another demonstration is in order. Lyla Martin, come up here so we can do this properly."

Lyla stopped laughing. Once Blackburn changed her memory of squashing a black widow into a memory of being stung by one, he got the proper fear reaction out of her—she shrieked and bolted from the room. Blackburn sent them from class early, and started off after her to undo the program.

As soon as Tom walked out of class, Vik turned to him and said, "I thought that was awesome. He wanted you to get all shrieky, and you were like—grrr!" He mimed biting something in a feral, animalistic way.

Beamer sniggered and put in, "Yeah, he was just annoyed you didn't wet yourself up there."

Tom shoved his hands in his pockets, instantly cheerful. He spotted Wyatt Enslow through the crowd, and she gave him a quick, grateful smile since he'd covered for her again. Beside her, Yuri looked mildly confused the way he always did after Programming, but he gave Tom a friendly wave. A warm feeling spread in Tom's chest, a sense of rightness soaking down to his very bones, like he was home for the first time in his life.

And then Vik said something that knocked that feeling away. "Your parents coming this weekend?"

Tom's heart jerked. He'd heard there was a Parents'

Weekend here. He hadn't realized it was coming so soon. "My parents? Uh, no."

At least, he hoped not. He really, really hoped not. Neil and the Pentagonal Spire? It was like mixing two volatile chemicals. Odds were, nothing good would come of it.

"Mine are," Beamer said. "My sister, too. You, Vik?"

"Mom's flying in from India." Vik scrubbed his palm over his hair, now growing out in lumpy, uneven clumps. "Last video chat, she threatened to come all this way just to give me a new haircut. She said I'm starting to look like an animal died on my head."

Beamer cackled away at that, and began speculating about what type of animal Vik's hair resembled. Tom laughed along with them, even though he wasn't really listening now. He was still worrying over what his dad might do if he came here. He knew one thing: Neil wouldn't march into the stronghold of what he called "the war cartel" just to give him a haircut.

LATER IN THE evening, the CamCos all trickled back into the mess hall to wolf down some dinner, shoulders slumped, exhaustion on their faces. News of their latest defeat spread quickly. The Russo-Chinese Combatants had demolished the shipyards and all the ships the CamCos sent after them, mostly due to Medusa, who had somehow uncovered the hidden Indo-American satellites in the area and blinded most them midway through the battle. The CamCos had to rely upon the limited sensors of the vessels themselves. Without satellite support, they were practically fighting blind—and easy pickings.

"Man, this would all be a different game without Medusa," Vik remarked as they strolled toward the Lafayette Room.

"Yeah," Tom agreed, "completely different." It wouldn't be nearly so exciting. He couldn't wait to download a recording of the battle and see more of Medusa in action.

They'd all been summoned to hear a speech by General Marsh. He wasn't actively present in day-to-day life at the Spire, but he always came by after CamCo battles for the postmission briefing. He'd clearly decided to kill two birds with one stone and address the upcoming Parents' Weekend, too. The trainees all settled on the benches. Even though they'd already downloaded the rules, General Marsh mounted the stage and lectured them about what information they could reveal to their parents, what they couldn't. What areas of the Spire were permitted for parental access, what areas were not.

Tom flicked away Marsh's profile when it popped up in his vision.

NAME: Terry Marsh
RANK: Brigadier General
GRADE: USAF 0-7, Active Duty
SECURITY STATUS: Top Secret LANDLOCK-16

"They need to wear a badge at all times," Marsh said, "and you must remain with them. You are not to reveal the names of your classmates. I don't care how many times they ask about your friends. You do not answer them. If they somehow sneak in a camera, you are to take it away. You are also accountable for any acts of espionage or sabotage your parents commit while they're here." Marsh didn't look pleased at the sniggers that greeted this. "Countries have been betrayed by attitudes like that! You're lucky you have a Parents' Weekend at all. Were it up to me, and not the Congressional Defense Committee, we'd have you on lockdown. And we'd have much better security for it."

Tom couldn't seem to muster a snigger at Marsh's worry about parental sabotage of the Spire. He wouldn't put it past

Neil to do something like that. He couldn't predict anything when it came to his dad.

After the briefing, Olivia halted him in the hallway. "Tom, I've been compiling a list of visiting parents. I haven't been able to get in touch with your father to issue an invitation."

Tom's shoulders relaxed. Profound relief surged through him, edged with a strange sense of disappointment. "You won't. He moves around a lot. No number, doesn't even use VR. There's no chance you'll find him."

"Do you have any idea—?"

"You're wasting your time looking for him. He wouldn't want to come, anyway."

WHEN THE DAY finally came, he settled on his bed for a long afternoon of watching Medusa fight and maybe video gaming a bit. So it shocked him when he was just getting ready to replay Medusa's battle on Titan, and he received a ping: *Report to the lobby to serve as parental escort.*

Tom lay there on the bed, staring at the ceiling, utterly stunned. No way. No way, no way. Could Neil have found out somehow? Had he come? How was it possible?

Report to the lobby to serve as parental escort, came a follow-up ping.

Tom leaped up from his bed, shoved his hair into something resembling a decent state, and then headed for the elevators. Neil was really here? He smoothed down his hair again, his every nerve jumping inside him.

It occurred to Tom after the elevator was sweeping downward that it might not be his father.

It might be his mother.

No. Impossible. It wasn't something she did. He'd visited her that time Neil was sentenced to sixty days in jail. She'd stared at him, amazed, as though she couldn't believe such an ugly creature came from her. She hadn't hugged him—and he hadn't hugged her. They'd probably said three words to each other.

And then her boyfriend, Dalton, showed up with a rent-a-cop toting a retina scanner, and demanded, "Are you all right, Delilah?" As though Tom would travel all the way across the country just to hurt his own mother.

Even after the scanner verified Tom's identity, Dalton planted himself in the apartment, watching Tom's every move suspiciously, like he was certain Tom'd only visited so he could burn the building down. His mother sent her maid out to rent a VR set for him, and then left somewhere with Dalton, and didn't return again. Tom didn't bother waiting for her when Neil got an early release. He left her a note and headed back to his only real family—his dad.

He felt like he was in a strange dream when he emerged, threading through the masses of parents. He spotted Vik and his sari-wearing mother, and trailed to a halt, fighting the absurd impulse to enlist backup.

And then he really saw Vik, and noticed the way Vik's mother was smoothing down the shoulders of his uniform and saying in Hindi, ". . . still don't know why you wanted to come all the way overseas when you could have trained in Bombay."

"I've told you a hundred times," Vik replied, "I have a much better chance of being a Combatant if I train in America. There's a lot more funding over here."

"Are they feeding you enough, Vikram? You look skinny!" She switched to heavily accented English: "I should have brought you a home-cooked meal. Are you still having tummy troubles?"

"Mom!" Vik cried.

She switched back to Hindi. "I just want to— Is that boy laughing at us?"

Tom fought to smother his laughter. Vik's eyes narrowed. "Of course not. He doesn't speak Hindi, so he doesn't understand us."

Tom was getting a real kick out of Vik's torment. When Vik's mother wasn't looking, Vik made a strangling motion and mouthed, "Kill you." Tom patted his stomach and mouthed, "Tummy troubles," back at him. Then he darted farther into the crowd before Vik's mom could notice him again.

He passed Beamer with his parents and his loudmouthed little redheaded sister.

"Show us guns, Stephen!"

"It's not allowed, Crissy, I told you . . ."

He also spotted Yuri at the edge of the crowd with a tall, light-haired man with such pale eyebrows, they blended into his forehead. Tom guessed that was his father. They weren't moving at all, just standing at a careful distance from each other, speaking too quietly for any words to reach Tom's ears.

In a back corner beneath the dip of the eagle's wings, Tom passed Wyatt, sitting ramrod stiff, her arms folded across her torso. Her mother, a toothpick-thin woman with tumbling dark curls, was hanging back at several feet's distance looking her over like a piece of artwork she didn't want to buy. ". . . just can't get over how tall you are now. I thought for sure you were done growing. Look at her! She's taller than you, George."

Her husband, a squat man lounging indolently in a nearby chair, glanced over and gave a hearty laugh. "First glance, I wondered if I should call you 'my son,' Wyatt. What's with all these muscles, anyway?" He grabbed her bicep and shook her arm jokingly. "Guess you came here to be some girl Rambo?"

Wyatt reclaimed her arm and hugged it to her chest.

"Physical fitness is part of being here. I can't help it if I'm getting muscles."

And just beyond Wyatt's parents, Tom picked out a lone man gazing up toward the eagle. Then it all made sense. This was his visitor.

Of course. *Of course.* What had he really expected?

Tom smirked, feeling like an idiot. He closed the distance, eager to get this over with.

"This is for family only. What are you doing here, Dalton?"

Like the last time Tom saw him, Dalton Prestwick had gelled hair, a smarmy smirk, and a crisp suit. He spotted Tom and tilted his chin a bit so Tom had to look higher to meet his eyes. He wished he'd hit six feet so this guy could never look down on him again.

"I was in the area, and your mother signed a waiver for me to be your guest instead of her," Dalton informed him. "Quite a place you've got here. How you holding up, sport?"

Tom's hands curled into fists. He was honestly tempted to laugh, because he felt so stupid for even thinking one of his parents might visit him. "Just tell me what you want."

Dalton's eyes narrowed, the pretense of civility dropping off his face. "That's no way to talk to me, little punk."

There it was. That was the real Dalton.

Dalton sighed and looked away from him. "I'm here with some colleagues of mine. Joseph Vengerov, over there"—he nodded toward the man with Yuri. *Not* Yuri's father, then. "I used to work for him. The other's off in the crowd somewhere. Mike Marsters. A retired coworker. His son's here. The boy's named Karl."

Tom laughed. He couldn't help it. It figured that a business partner of Dalton's would father a great guy like Karl.

"They were coming here, so I thought I'd swing by and

check on you. It about knocked my socks off when I heard you were here. Never thought you'd make something of yourself."

"I know what this is about. You're playing nice with me so you can get a good look at the Spire. And if you think I'm going to be your ticket inside, forget it." Tom turned to leave.

"Uh-uh."

A hand grabbed his shoulder. Tom threw it off and whirled around. "What?"

Dalton's voice dropped to an intent whisper. "Listen up, kid. I don't think you understand the politics of this place. Who do you think has a chance of making it here? Of joining Camelot Company?"

Tom regarded him intently, wondering if Dalton knew something he did not.

"You need sponsors. Corporate sponsors to back your bid."

"I know that."

"Well, who do you think put the nail in the coffin of that Nigel Harrison kid's bid for Camelot Company? I did, on behalf of Dominion Agra."

"*You* nixed Nigel?"

But it made sense. It must have been Dalton. Trainee identities were classified. The process of advancing to CamCo was classified. There was no other way Dalton could know about how Nigel got nominated for Camelot Company, then shot down in a matter of days when it became clear he was never going to find any sponsors from the Coalition to back up his bid. Rumor had it, various company reps wrote to the Defense Committee and deemed him "flat, charmless, and uninspiring." None of the companies wanted him affiliated with them.

Dalton straightened up, brushing some invisible lint off his designer suit. "Of course I did. I'm with Dominion Agra, and

Dominion is one of the main funders of the war effort. I could point out a half-dozen members of Camelot Company we talk to. We even sponsor Karl, specify him as our Combatant of choice for certain conflicts, and supply him with combat machines. That's how sponsorship works. It's not just about giving certain Combatants more airtime than others. It's about helping out the military financially on behalf of that Combatant. That's how you get influence around here."

This time when Dalton leaned closer, Tom didn't back away.

"But we're looking for more, Tom. More Combatants to represent Dominion. The right ones. You were useless to me before, but you could be something here. We could be of use to each other in the long run, you and me. If Dominion sponsors you, it's your ticket straight into CamCo."

"So what do you get out of it?"

"In the short term? Two years from now, you'll be a Combatant, and we'll have another call sign affiliated with Dominion. In the long run? You kids don't seem to realize, Elliot Ramirez isn't the only walking brand among you. People want to know all about the other Combatants. Enigma, Matador, Firestorm, Stinger. They have fan followings, blogs devoted to them. Mystique. A market. One day, if we have our way on this, the Combatants will all become public, and you'll all be as valuable as Ramirez. And the sponsors attached to you? They'll profit from it, too. You could represent Dominion one day, Tom. It's always good to have a nice, wholesome kid attached to our image."

"Wholesome?" Tom echoed.

"And it helps that you're not so runty now. I see they got that stuff off your face, too. You're not a bad looking kid. Certainly not a mouthy little eyesore like that Nigel Mctwitchy kid."

Tom thought of Nigel, with his perpetual tic, and tasted something sour in his mouth. If he ever helped out Dalton Prestwick with anything, he knew, he'd be betraying his father. And *himself*. He wanted nothing more than to laugh in Dalton's face and see that look of smug superiority disappear. But he couldn't treat Dalton like he counted for nothing. Not if he wanted to go anywhere here.

Not if he wanted to be in Camelot Company one day.

"Yeah, well, even if I make it to CamCo, it's still a long way away," Tom told him. "I'm not even thinking that far ahead."

"Well, start." Dalton tapped his temple beneath his gelled hair. "Prove to the world that you're smarter than your old man."

Tom drove his balled-up fists into his pockets. It was that or drive them into Dalton's face.

Nearby in the crowd, Tom saw that the man Vengerov had parted ways with Yuri and was walking toward them. Vengerov snapped his fingers at Dalton as he strode past him. Dalton jumped and began straightening his tie. "I have to go, Tom, but think it over. You'll hear from me again soon."

Tom stood there, rooted in place, taking several deep breaths as Dalton's footsteps echoed their way across the marble floor. His fists throbbed from the effort of keeping them jammed in his pockets.

He didn't relax until he was sure Dalton Prestwick was gone. If he'd said one more thing about Neil, just one . . .

Well, Tom wouldn't have a chance of making CamCo after punching a Dominion Agra exec right in the face.

CHAPTER ELEVEN

ONE FRIDAY IN Applied Simulations, Elliot ran them through a meditation exercise where they visualized a white light interacting with what he called their "chakras." Then he sat them in a circle.

"Now, we've focused in past simulations on playing offense. Hungry wolves attacking a moose. The Greek gods attacking the Norse gods. Terminators hunting Predators. But today we're going to have a change of pace. The trickiest space battles don't happen when we're on the offensive. Our most important focus is on retaining the parts of the solar system we've already secured. There are mining platforms to defend, satellite hubs to protect, and shipyards to patrol, so we're going to practice teamwork as a defensive measure. So I want you to prepare yourselves for being the attacked, the targets of aggression."

The simulation cranked to life around them, and Tom found himself standing with a shield and a sword, guarding a massive walled city. The information stream in his neural processor outlined the scenario: this was the ancient city of Troy; they were in the middle of the Trojan War, defending themselves from the Greek army. The massive collection of enemy soldiers sprawled across the sandy ground beyond the city's walls and crawling over the distant beaches like ants.

Tom's first impulse was to climb down and engage outside the walls, but Elliot knew him by now, and anticipated it. "Tom. Defense. Remember?"

Tom's eyes flipped over the sea of gleaming helmets, flashing swords, clanking armor, positioned at a careful distance. "But they're not attacking. How do we play defense if there's no offense?"

"This was a nine-year-long war," Elliot countered. "The Trojans didn't engage the Greeks every single day."

"So we're just going to stand here for three hours?"

"Consider it a lesson in patience."

Elliot had cast himself as Hector, the greatest Trojan warrior, a prince who could move throughout the city at will. He'd made Tom a sentry and in that way confined him to the walls. Beamer was a sentry, too.

This was his revenge, Tom figured, for their Wednesday simulation. They'd been a school of piranhas. Beamer had decided to attract a nearby crocodile. He'd waggled his tail in hopes of getting eaten. ("Never died by croc before," he told Tom afterward.) Tom saw Beamer eaten and decided to take a bite out of the croc's vulnerable eye, and in the process of maneuvering, led it straight to Elliot. The older boy got gobbled in one bite.

On the bright side, Tom had managed to tear out one of the croc's eyes and devour it before he got eaten, too.

Beamer shuffled his way over to Tom, his character soaked in sweat. "I'm so bored." He dropped his heavy bronze shield with a mighty clang. "Want to commit suicide with me? We could stab each other on the count of three."

"Nah. Mutual suicide's too *Romeo and Juliet* for me. I'm going to wait until Elliot's not looking and jump down to fight the Greeks." Tom glanced over his shoulder, but Elliot—as Prince Hector—was watching them like a hawk from his chair in the shade.

Below, the Greek army had shifted. Tom leaned forward, intrigued, and watched a small detachment of men break away. They scurried to the wall and dodged spears and arrows as they piled some sacks at the base of the wall. He elbowed Beamer. "Look, they're doing something down there. I think they're going to attack."

Beamer looked down with disinterest, then drew his sword. "Nah, looks more like they're having a picnic in the shade. I'm going to off myself."

"Don't do it. *Don't.* You have so much to live for," Tom cried dramatically.

"I have to! Tell my girlfriend I love her!" Beamer cried, playing along. He raised his sword, blade flashing in the sunlight.

Tom waved. "Later, man."

Beamer drove his sword into his own gut. His face changed. He grew deathly pale, his eyes boggled out, and he gave a shrill scream.

Tom watched his dramatics with a smirk. Sims weren't like Calisthenics because it hurt dying in Applied Sims, but only a little, about as much as did a dull headache, just enough to give them a reason to try not to die. Not enough to stop Beamer from dying every chance he got. And certainly not *this* much.

"Oh, oh, OH GOD!" Beamer screamed, thrashing back to the ground. "OH GOD! This hurts!"

"Yeah," Tom said lazily. "I'm not falling for it, Beamer."

"Oh God, oh God, this hurts! It hurts, Tom!"

"Overdoing it, aren't you, buddy?"

But Beamer was convulsing, blood blossoming out around his punctured gut. "Tom, Tom, help me!" He was sobbing. "Help me. Make it stop! This hurts!"

The smile died off Tom's lips as Beamer wept. Cold tingles of uneasiness moved down Tom's spine, because it dawned on him that Beamer wasn't faking this. A fatal wound kicked you out of a simulation. Instantly. He wasn't supposed to thrash. He was supposed to heal or vanish.

"Beamer, hey, you okay?"

It was a stupid question, he knew, but Tom wasn't sure what to say when he dropped to the other boy's side. Slick blood bubbled over the stones around his armored legs, and Beamer's frantic eyes moved up to his. He tried speaking, gurgled something like "help," and then doubled over with racking coughs. Blood splattered from his mouth.

Tom knelt there, frozen, his heart thumping in his ears. He couldn't seem to move, like an icy hand clutched him in place. Footsteps clattered toward him, and a firm pair of dark hands grappled with Beamer's thrashing body.

"What's wrong?" Elliot demanded, taking charge.

"I don't—we don't know," Tom stuttered.

"Beamer?" Elliot called, pinning Beamer's shoulders. "Beamer? Stephen?"

Tom felt Beamer's blood drying on his hands and watched Elliot asking Beamer what was the matter as though it wasn't obvious. He heard Beamer gurgling, whimpering, and watched him twisting back and forth, trying escape the pain, escape the hands on him.

Then Elliot raised his gauntleted hand and waved his arm

in a sequence—up and down, up and down, left and right, up and down. It was a series of muscular impulses designed to signal the neural processor and terminate any active simulations. Elliot's brow furrowed, and he tried it again with his other arm. He dropped them both to his side, baffled. "I can't turn off the sim."

Beamer shrieked, and kept shrieking, and Tom looked between Elliot and Beamer. Elliot was waving both arms now like he was in a surreal dance, and Beamer kept giving these gurgling cries of pain, and the sim kept on going.

"I've got it," Tom called. Of course! This would boot Beamer right out of the sim. He unsheathed his sword, and hacked off Beamer's head.

Elliot scuttled to his feet with a shout, dark blood splashing over the stones around them.

"There," Tom said, pleased with himself for the quick thinking.

Elliot stared at him, openmouthed.

The look on his face and the uncertainty of the moment flooded Tom with horror. He suddenly remembered some movie he'd seen where people died in a video game and then died in real life. It was just like this. He'd just killed Beamer in their malfunctioning sim, and what if it was a serious malfunction and he was dead in the training room, too?

"Oh God, he was really feeling pain," Tom cried, the enormity of his mistake crashing over him. "You don't think he really died, too, do you?"

"No," Elliot said at once.

"I killed him. I killed Beamer!"

"Tom, the program messes up every few months. I've seen it happen a dozen times. People never die from sims."

Tom stood there, breathless in the hot Trojan sun, gazing

down at the headless body of his friend, still thinking of that movie. He couldn't remember the name. He didn't know why it mattered so much, but he couldn't stop wondering what the name was. His whole body was shaking.

Elliot clasped his shoulder. "It's fine. Beamer's out of the sim and he's fine. You did the right thing. You did not kill him. I'll stop this sim, and you'll see." He waved his arm again, trying to end it, his brow furrowed.

"You're really sure he's not dead out there?" Tom asked again.

"Tom, I'm positive," Elliot said with a laugh. "He's okay."

Tom just gazed up into the blue sky overhead, feeling the wind flapping through his hair. Relief crashed through him. He found himself laughing. "Wow. You know, I really freaked out for a second there," he told Elliot, even though Elliot seemed to be preoccupied with the issue of the sim not responding to his command and turning itself off. "I seriously thought it. I seriously thought for a second that I'd killed Beam—"

And then the world exploded around them.

Tom felt like he was hurling through space, weightless. He couldn't hear his own scream over the crashing in his ears. Stone scraped his hand, so he grasped whatever he could—and it tore off the skin of his fingers as he dragged himself to a halt. Black dust blotted out the sky, stung his lungs. It thinned just enough to reveal the broken walls of the city and Elliot coughing where he clung to the wall above him.

Tom's arms stung as he slipped farther, and a glance below told him his legs were dangling down toward the flat plains. A firm hand gripped under his arm, and he knew it was Elliot. "Come on!"

Tom grabbed Elliot's arm, and managed to hoist himself back up onto the remains of the wall. Shouts filled the air. The

Greek army below them surged forward through the blown-out chunk of wall to claim Troy.

Elliot stared down, naked disbelief on his face. "That is *not* supposed to happen. There's supposed to be a Trojan Horse, not an explosion."

And then came the ping in both their brains: *Program integrity externally breached.*

Comprehension flooded Elliot's face. "It's an incursion."

An incursion!

Suddenly it all made sense.

Suddenly it wasn't scary. Tom looked down through the dust, blinking it out of his eyes as it stung his pupils, his brain suddenly thrumming with excitement. An *incursion*!

He'd heard of the Spire version of incursions. They'd happened more often three years ago, when the first batch of trainees joined the Intrasolar Forces. The Russo-Chinese hackers couldn't penetrate too deeply into the Spire's systems, but they could get into superficial, less secure areas such as the Applied Sims feeds. Russo-Chinese Combatants sometimes hacked into the American Applied Simulations channel and pranked them by playing the part of the enemy, even switching on the Indo-American pain receptors, because that was really the worst damage they could wreak.

In the first year of the program, it apparently happened every few months. None of the Indo-American trainees knew how to hack, so there was no reciprocation, and the Obsidian Corp. software consultants couldn't write code for answering attacks due to private business agreements with the Russo-Chinese neural processor manufacturer, LM Lymer Fleet. That was one thing that changed once Blackburn arrived. The first incursion attempt on his watch, he sent something back, and no one knew what it was. He also upgraded the firewall.

The incursions had stopped . . . until now. Maybe the Russo-Chinese victory near Neptune convinced them to try it again.

"There has to be a way to end this program," Elliot insisted, still waving his arm in the command gesture.

But Tom didn't want this to end. He gazed transfixed down at the field, knowing those weren't virtual opponents. Those were real enemies. Enemies who had tampered with the program to make it as real as possible. Kept the pain sensations on. Blocked their escape.

If Russo-Chinese Combatants were here . . .

Medusa might be here.

The greatest warrior in the world could be in the same simulation as Tom. Right in reach of him. And he was just standing here, a useless sentry, removed from the fighting.

"Yes! I'm getting the exit option now!" Elliot gave a relieved laugh. He turned to Tom. "Is the exit sequence working for you, or do I need to unplug you once I'm out?"

"Wait." Tom turned on him, electric with determination. "Don't go yet. Let's fight them, Elliot. Come on. You and me. Hector and random sentry person. Let's take on the Greeks. Let's take on the Russo-Chinese."

"You want to stay?" Elliot stared at him. He obviously hadn't even considered that option. "The pain receptors are on full, Tom. You saw Stephen. Getting stabbed here feels like getting stabbed."

"I'll risk it! Elliot, come on already. This could be incredible! Let's show 'em Americans aren't cowards!"

Below them, the people in the city were screaming as they were cut down by the invading army.

"Come on, Elliot," Tom said. "This is my only chance. You get to fight these people all the time. I may never be CamCo. I may never get to fight them in real life."

"This means that much to you?"

"Look, come on. I'll do anything. I'll pay fealty. You want fealty? You'll get all the fealty you can handle. Just don't unplug me!"

Elliot shook his head, exasperated and, Tom would swear, amused. "You were born in the wrong era, Tom. You should've been a berserker. Fine. I won't unplug you. But go as a combat character." And with a wave of his hand, Tom's body transformed.

He was about to murder Elliot for turning him into a girl again, but he realized that this girl character was the best warrior yet unclaimed in the sim: Penthesilea, queen of the Amazons.

Elliot saluted him. "Don't embarrass your country, Plebe."

"No, sir!"

"And I didn't even have to wrangle that 'sir' out of you, huh? Well, that'll do for fealty," Elliot said with a grin and vanished from the sim.

And so it was left to Tom, the lone, nonvirtual defender of Troy, against the entire Greek army. He whirled around, the grandeur of the moment sweeping over him. He didn't care that he was probably going to be skewered and end up as miserable as Beamer. He didn't even care that it was going to hurt. This was his time of glory.

He watched the attackers and waited for that one. That one person to show up, the fighter he'd know anywhere.

And when he spotted him through the churning mass of the army, the clouds of dust, and the rippling waves of heat, Tom knew him at once.

Medusa was playing *Achilles*. The mightiest warrior in the world of today was fighting as the most fearsome warrior of the ancient world.

It was so fitting Tom could've cheered.

But instead, he caught sight of a stray horse, riderless, panicked with flight, galloping across the dusty ground below him. He timed his leap, and landed right on its back. It was easy in Penthesilea's battle-hardened body. Using her powerful legs, Tom steered the horse's massive body, launched them toward the battle. He kicked its haunches and plunged them into the bloodshed.

Tom ignored the warriors boiling about him. They were mere obstacles blocking his way to Medusa. He needed to attract Medusa's attention, so he tried to pick out the other Russo-Chinese Combatants among the virtual soldiers.

He recognized Rusalka, known as Svetlana Moriakova, the Russian answer to Elliot Ramirez and the only public Russo-Chinese Combatant. She was playing Agamemnon, and she betrayed herself in the way she hung back and tried to ensure others took the brunt of the fighting. Tom had seen enough past CamCo battles to recognize the tactic on sight. He raised his bow and arrow, caught her eye, and winked. Just as the surprise washed over her face, his arrow impaled her throat.

He found Red Terror next, playing Odysseus, a guy who betrayed his identity by the way he cut down the strays, the stragglers, the weakest. Just like Red Terror when he fought in space, who always attacked the soft spot first. Tom clutched his bow in his left hand, drew his sword with his right, and hacked off Red Terror's head as he careened past him.

Then he saw the Combatant Kalashnikov, playing Patrocles, recognizable by the way he played dirty and killed Tom's horse beneath him. Tom leaped clear of the screaming, thrashing creature, rolled to his feet, and drove his sword through Kalashnikov's eye.

That's when Medusa saw Tom.

Medusa charged through the armies in his chariot. With a jerk of the reins, Medusa brought the chariot to a halt just meters away, dust swirling up in a great cloud around his gleaming armor.

Tom just stood there, sword in hand, a huge grin on his lips. He stared at Medusa and Medusa stared at him, and in this moment that made his dreams come true, Tom could only think of one thing to say.

"How's it going?"

As soon as he spoke, he regretted how stupid he must've sounded.

Medusa's eyes raked over him. "You didn't run with the others."

"I'd never run from you."

"I'd call you courageous," Medusa said, "but I suspect you may just be a moron."

Tom laughed, feeling almost giddy, because this was really happening. "Got me in one guess . . . Medusa."

Medusa jerked a bit. "You know me."

"I'd know you anywhere," Tom confessed. "I think about you all the time." He knew how creepy and stalkerish that had to sound, but he didn't care.

"You seem a bit deranged," Medusa remarked.

"That's fair."

And then Medusa charged.

Tom knew he didn't stand a chance in the open. He scrambled into the midst of the massing armies to buy some time. He cast his eyes around for some advantage, then spotted the concave shield of a dead Greek, aware of Medusa fighting through the Trojan army to get him like some relentless angel of death. As the rumbling of the wheels mounted to a roar in his ears, and the shadow of the chariot blotted out the sun around him, Tom twisted around, angled the shield, raising his sword above it—and blared sunlight right into Medusa's eyes.

Medusa was blinded just as he flung his javelin. His wild throw sent it whizzing by Tom's ear.

Tom hurled the shield at Medusa, unbalancing him. He leaped forward, lashed out with his sword and drove it through the neck of one of the chariot's horses. Red Terror wasn't the only one who could play dirty.

The horse tumbled to the earth with a scream. It thrashed to the dusty ground, toppling the second horse and careening the chariot onto its side. Tom leaped clear of the vehicle, saw Medusa doing the same—hurling himself clear of the wreckage. With a whoop of triumph, Tom tore after the struggling warrior, ready to impale Medusa before he could regain his sword.

Medusa resorted to using the only weapon in reach: a cloud of sand that stung Tom's eyes, blinding him in that critical second. Tom's sword sank into the ground, and a kick to his stomach reeled him back to the ground, knocking the breath from his body.

And then Medusa was on his feet, blade flashing toward Tom's head. Tom rolled out of the way, thankful for Penthesilea's agility. He scrambled back up and blocked Medusa's next blow with his sword. And then the next. But Medusa pressed relentlessly, with the raw strength of Achilles overwhelming Penthesilea. Tom's arms buckled beneath the bone-jarring clang, and he twisted out of the way of the blade just in time. When Medusa's next blow came, Tom let his arms give out entirely beneath the power of it and used the momentum to spin himself around. He drew a bloody gash on Medusa's back, and then leaped back before Medusa's blade could swivel around and gut him.

They faced each other, fighting for breath. And then Medusa whirled away from him. Just as Tom moved to pursue, Medusa whipped back around and tossed something into the air. Tom felt a tickling around his legs, and looked down to see the chariot's reins twined in a loop around his limbs.

He slashed downward with his sword to cut the makeshift lasso, but it was too late—Medusa jerked the reins to tighten them, tumbling Tom to the ground. Then Medusa leaped onto the remaining horse and kicked it into a gallop, the reins dragging Tom across the ground behind it. Sand scorched a raw path down his side. A wild slash of his sword finally severed the rope, and he thumped down to the earth, breathless.

Medusa galloped a distance, and swung back around. Sunlight gleamed off his steel helmet and armor.

Tom raised himself to his shaky legs, kicking away the remains of the reins, his sword aloft, waiting. Waiting. His strength was wearing thin, his breath ragged, his body on fire where his skin had been torn off by scraping across the ground. This couldn't last much longer.

And then Medusa charged. His horse galloped faster and faster, grunting with the speed. Tom readied himself for the assault as the clattering hooves filled his ears and the dust blotted out his vision, and then at the last moment, Medusa leaped off the horse. The animal careened into Tom in an explosion of thrashing hooves and muscle. A blow to his ribs, to his torso. Acid burned through him when something ruptured.

Tom dragged himself clear. Fire burned inside him, and each gasp at air felt like a dagger stabbing him. One of his lungs had collapsed. His breaths were gurgles as the shadow of Achilles strode over the sand toward him. He saw the shadowy sword rise and then arc down into him.

It didn't hurt at first. At first. And then Medusa tore out the bloody blade, kicked Tom over onto his back, and loomed above him, a black figure in a halo of sunlight. A nuclear meltdown was happening in his torso. Tom's scream was a gurgle as molten agony consumed him, radiating to his limbs, tearing at every nerve. He couldn't breathe, couldn't breathe. . . .

Medusa knelt down next to him. "I'm sure you now wish you'd left with the others."

Tom's vision darkened around the edges, his body arcing in pain in a futile fight for oxygen, and the plume of Medusa's helmet grew larger and darker as he leaned even closer to watch him die. Tom was half aware of Medusa's hand lifting the back of his leaden head, sliding his helmet off to let his bloody hair spill out—Achilles taking a moment to gaze down at the dying Penthesilea. And as Tom's consciousness tunneled away, he thought he saw Medusa's lips curl into a slow smile. Through his agony, he twisted his lips into a bloody grin of his own.

You're everything I dreamed you'd be.

The last thing he felt was Medusa's hands cupping his head, cradling it until he slipped away into the darkness.

TOM'S EYES SNAPPED open in the simulation chamber.

Elliot was seated at the end of his cot, arms folded. The rest of the simulation group was gathered around behind him, staring down at Tom like he was some weird science project. When Tom tried to sit up, a bunch of hands helped him.

He groped at his aching head. Elliot hopped down and strode over, dark eyebrows raised. "Your heart rate went a bit crazy there toward the end. We were worried. How'd it go?"

"Took out Kalashnikov, Red Terror, and Rusalka."

Elliot laughed. "Rusalka, taken out by a plebe. I'm going

to rub that in Svetlana's face next time we're at the same PR event."

"Then Medusa got me."

Elliot shocked him by clapping his shoulder. "Good job, Tom."

Tom found himself grinning back. Elliot had let him stay, had given him a chance to face Medusa. He was amazed. Somehow he couldn't imagine thinking of Elliot as Dorkmirez ever again.

The crowd around him cleared as everyone tucked away the wires in the simulation chamber. Tom didn't move right away. He felt like he was buzzing all over with the thrill of what had happened. When he did move, it was only to make his way across the room where Beamer was sitting on his cot, legs drawn up to his chest, arms wrapped around them. He looked paler than his character in the sim, his freckles a stark contrast against his white skin.

Tom waved his hand in front of his eyes. Beamer flinched back from him and scrambled off the cot, gasping for breath. "Get back!"

"Tom, leave him alone," Elliot ordered gently, watching from over Tom's shoulder.

"We're friends."

Elliot drew him back with a firm grip. "Try to think: you just killed him."

"Come on." Tom turned to Beamer incredulously. "I didn't *kill* kill you. And hey, I died, too. Sword to the gut." He clutched his abdomen and imitated his own gurgling from a minute before, then collapsed theatrically to the floor. But when he jounced back to his feet, Beamer wasn't looking at him.

Tom grew exasperated. Beamer died all the time. So this one death hadn't worked out for him. He was fine now. Tom had died, too, and he'd never felt this alive or pumped up in his life.

"Come on, Beamer! I beheaded you for your own good."

Beamer sent him a cloudy look, like he didn't really see him. Elliot stepped between them, drawing that foggy gaze to his. "Stephen, would you like me to call the social worker for you?"

"Yeah, that'll make him feel better," Tom said. "Call the guy a wimp."

Beamer's eyes flipped back to him over Elliot's shoulder. He stared at Tom for a long moment, and then bolted from the room.

Elliot sighed and turned to Tom. "I think sometime we'll need to have a discussion about showing emotional sensitivity."

Tom returned to his cot, perplexed by the whole thing. He tucked his wire into its slot and rose to his full height again, then noticed Wyatt standing by his cot, waiting for him.

"*I* think you're emotionally sensitive, Tom."

Tom met her earnest eyes. "Thanks, Wyatt."

She nodded crisply, satisfied her work was done, and left him there.

Tom gazed after her, bemused. Nice of her to say, but then again, she wasn't exactly the authority on emotional sensitivity, either.

1 1 1 1 1 0 0 0 1 0 0 0 0 1 1 0 1 0 1 0 1 0 1 0 0 1 0 0 1 0 0 1 1 0 1 0 1 0 0 1 0 0
0 0 1 0 1 0 1 1 0 1 1 0 0 0 0 0 0 1 0 0 1 1 1 0 0 0 0 0 1 0 1 1 0 1 0 0
0 0 0 0 0 1 1 1 1 1 0 1 0 1 0 0 1 1 1 1 1 0 1 1 0 0 1 1 0 1 0 0 0 1 0 1 0 0
1 0 1 1 0 0 1 1 1 1 1 1 0 0 1 1 1 0 1 0 1 1 0 0 0 0 0 1 0 0 1 1 1
1 0 0 0 1 1 0 1 1 0 1 1 1 0 0 1 1 1 0 0 0 0 0 0 0 1 0 1 1 0 1 0 0 1
1 1 0 1 0 0 0 0 0 1 1 1 1 0 0 1 0 0 1 0 1 1 1 0 0 1 1 1 0 1 1 0 0 1 0 1
1 0 1 0 1 0 0 0 1 1 0 1 1 0 0 0 0 1 1 0 1 0 0 1 1 0 0 0 1 0 1 1 1 1 0 0
1 0 1 1 0 0 1 1 0 1 0 0 0 0 0 1 0 1 1 1 0 1 1 0 0 0 0 0 0 1 0 1 1 0 0
1 1 0 0 0 1 1 0 0 0 0 0 1 1 1 0 1 1 0 1 1 0 1 0 0 0 0 1 0 0 1 1 1 0
1 1 1 1 1 0 0 1 0 1 0 1 1 1 0 1 1 1 0 1 0 1 0 1 1 1 1 0 1 0 1 1 0 1 1 0
0 1 0 0 1 1 1 1 1 1 0 1 1 0 0 0 0 1 1 1 0 1 1 0 1 1 1 0 1 1 1 0 0 0
0 0 1 1 0 1 1 0 0 1 1 0 1 0 0 1 0 0 0 1 0 1 0 1 0 0 1 0 0 0 0 1 0 0 1 0
1 1 0 0 0 1 0 0 1 0 0 1 1 0 0 1 0 0 1 1 0 1 0 1 0 1 1 1 0 0 0 0 1 0 1 1 0
1 0 0 0 0 0 0 1 1 1 1 0 1 1 0 1 1 0 1 1 0 0 0 0 0 1 0 0 0 0 1 0 0
0 0 1 1 0 0 1 1 0 0 1 1 1 0 0 1 0 0 0 0
1 0 0 0 0 1 1 1 0 0 0 0 1 0 1 1 1 1 0 0
0 0 1 0 1 1 0 0 0 0 0 0 0 1 0 0 1 1 1 0 0
1 1 0 1 1 1 0 0 0 1 1 1 0 0 1 1 1 0 0 0 1 1 0 1 1 0 1 0 1 1 1 1
1 0 1 0 0 0 1 0 1 0 1 1 0 0 0 1 0 1 0 0 1 0 0 1 0 0 0 1 0 0 0 1 1 1 0 1
1 0 1 0 0 1 1 0 0 0 0 0 1 0 1 0 0 1 0 0 1 0 0 0 1 0 0 0 0

CHAPTER TWELVE

Tom THOUGHT THE response to the incursion was a ridiculous overreaction. Every member of Elliot's simulation group was escorted to the basement floor into a secured cell next to the Census Chamber, the private room that normally housed the census device. Blackburn plugged them into his census device one by one to retrieve their memories of the incident. Marsh, Cromwell, and Blackburn all watched the incidents play out on the screen.

Tom, as the one who'd remained in the simulation, was stuck waiting after everyone else was examined. He sat beneath the census device, the streams of light blaring against his temples, his memory on the screens overhead.

"Real bright move staying behind, Raines," Blackburn remarked. "Did you honestly think you'd win that battle alone?"

Tom bristled. "I figured I'd try. Better than running away like a coward."

"We have rules of engagement, Mr. Raines." General

Marsh spoke up. "They're in your neural processor. You knew you were supposed to quit the simulation."

Despite the old man's words, Tom couldn't help but suspect Marsh approved of what he'd done.

So did Major Cromwell. She regarded Tom with a gleam of speculation. "We compared the suspected IPs of Russo-Chinese Combatants with the IPs that connected with our servers. You ID'd the real Combatants among the virtual characters."

"I just had to watch a bit."

"Did you figure out their call signs as well?" Cromwell said, gesturing to the screen. "Any guesses?"

"Is this really the time—" Blackburn began.

"Give it a shot, Raines," Cromwell said, silencing Blackburn by simply ignoring him. She flipped through the Combatants he faced.

Tom named them. "Rusalka, Red Terror, Kalashnikov . . ."

Cromwell's lips quirked, and he knew she'd guessed the same ones. "And Medusa," she finished for him, pausing it on a frame of Achilles.

And Medusa. That was the best part of all.

After Cromwell left, Tom answered a few more questions. Then he sank back into his recollection of the fight, replaying it in his head as Marsh and Blackburn began arguing over the security breach.

". . . clearly forgotten the last time. I'll get something ready to send back to them—"

"No, you won't," Marsh interrupted sharply. "The focus right now is on your firewall, Lieutenant, not retaliation. Obsidian Corp. has been arguing for months to the Defense Committee that one man can't handle this entire installation, and after this—"

"Funny you should speak of Obsidian Corp. I was just thinking of them. Have any of their consultants been around the Spire recently, sir?" Blackburn must've seen the answer on Marsh's face, because he gave a harsh laugh. "They have, haven't they?"

"Senator Bixby requested a tour and brought some guests from the company. I could hardly refuse—"

"Then with all respect, General, I'm merely surprised this didn't happen sooner. They only needed to slip away from their escort for ten, twenty seconds. That would be enough time to upload a little something into the system."

"That's a serious accusation, Lieutenant," Marsh warned. "I suggest you keep it to yourself. I'm going to have difficulty explaining this to the Defense Committee as is. They're going to pressure me to get you a support team—"

"We've played this game, General, and you know we always lose. They'll get a nice, long look at my software, and then Joseph Vengerov will hire them away."

"Then use a trainee. You said that Harrison boy is competent."

"But not trustworthy. I need . . . There's a . . ." Blackburn trailed off, and spun around to see Tom still there. "What are you waiting for, Raines? Get out of here."

"Dismissed," Marsh corrected, eyes on Blackburn.

Tom was glad to leave them to it. He slid out of the chair and strode from the room, still mentally replaying the memory of that slow smile dawning on Medusa's face as he died. He remembered those hands, cradling his head, and found himself wondering again if Medusa was a girl. He couldn't imagine a guy doing that, not even if his avatar was a woman. He'd face Medusa again and figure it out. And next time, Tom would win. He'd come so close. It was that horse that got him. But next time it would be different.

There had to be a next time.

Tom was still mulling it over later in the Lafayette Room at 1800 when all trainees were called together to discuss the incursion. Most of the plebes had arrived with their Applied Sims groups, so Tom settled next to Wyatt.

They still had a few minutes before Marsh was due to assume the stage, so Tom took a chance. He nudged her, and asked, "Is there a way to contact someone's computer with yours?"

"Yes. It's called email," Wyatt replied.

"No. I mean, if all you know is someone's IP," Tom said, thinking about what Cromwell said about the Spire logging the Russo-Chinese IPs, "can you leave a message for them on their computer even if they don't grant you access to it beforehand?"

"Is it someone in the Spire? If so, you can use net-send." She was silent a moment, tapping her fingers on her keyboard. Then:

See?

Tom jumped. The word had just popped up in his vision.

He spent a few minutes working out how she'd managed it, with Wyatt pointing out his mistakes, then he typed on his own keyboard. *Like this?* he sent back.

That's it. You're not stupid at all!

Tom laughed. "Thanks. I guess that's a huge shock." He typed out the next words, sent them to her processor. *So why doesn't everyone do this?*

Because people are lazy. They don't bother figuring out stuff that takes time to learn, like all the functions of the neural processor. She gave a quick nod after sending that, utter confidence in her eyes.

Tom shrugged. He supposed he should be offended on

behalf of lazy people but he wasn't. *How secure is it?* he typed.

She typed again: *I've encrypted this conversation. I'll teach you the code, if you think you can learn it.*

I do learn some things occasionally. So I have a quick, unrelated question: what if I want to send something like this to the IP of a computer that's not in the Spire?

She peered at him, trying to figure out what he was getting at.

Tom avoided her eyes. He really just wanted to get in touch with Medusa, maybe see if the guy—or girl—would fight him online sometime. But someone who didn't know better might think he was doing something wrong. Medusa was the enemy after all.

"The reason I'm asking is because Beamer could try it," Tom said. "See how he's not even here?"

Wyatt glanced around the room. "I think he went back to his bunk."

"Yeah." Tom began picking at a large splinter on the back of the bench in front of theirs. "He looked really wrecked. Maybe he'll cheer up if there's a way for him to contact his girlfriend. Without having to sneak wherever he's been sneaking at night."

"He's been taking a big risk."

Tom's hand stilled on the bench. "You know where he does it?"

The eleventh floor, she messaged. *He sneaks into the officers' lounge, or even Blackburn's office.*

"Seriously?" Tom said, so impressed by Beamer's daring that he couldn't manage anything else.

It's reckless. I don't know how he's avoided getting caught this long. He asks me to hide his GPS signal. I set up a router. His GPS sends the signal to the router, and then the router sends it on to the internal tracking system so it records the router's location as his location. It looks like he's just sitting on the toilet for three hours.

Tom laughed out loud. "Wonder what Dr. Gonzalez makes of that?"

"What are you two even talking about?" Vik crowed from several rows in front of them, where he was hanging over the back of his bench.

I hate Vik, Wyatt messaged him.

"Wyatt hates you," Tom called to Vik.

Vik bellowed a laugh. "There's a thin line between love and hate, Enslow." He held up his fingers and pinched them close together to make his point. "Thin, thin, thin."

She bristled at Vik's laughter when he turned back to the stage. Then she turned her glare on Tom. "I told you that privately."

"But everyone knows you hate Vik."

"That's not the point."

"So Beamer," Tom pressed. "Can he use the IP to net-send a message to her computer?"

"It depends. There are probably thousands of computers out there with the same IP address. You'd need more than that. You need the network address. And once you get that, it really depends on how strong the firewall is on her server, unless she knew beforehand he was going to try contacting her."

"Beamer would have to hack through her firewall, then."

"Basically."

"Great." Tom slumped back in his seat, deflated. The Spire may have logged Medusa's IP, but that IP would be on the server in the Sun Tzu Citadel in the Forbidden City, China, a place with one of the most secure firewalls in the solar system. No way was Tom going to be able to hack into that.

At the front of the Lafayette Room, Marsh mounted the

stage. Silence descended over them. The general stood there and surveyed them solemnly. "As you might have heard, there was a very serious security breach today. Some Russo-Chinese Combatants managed to break through our firewall and enter a simulation. They were only here to wreak some havoc with a group of plebes, but this represents a severe internal security breach. Not merely because they penetrated our firewall and not merely because one of our plebes did not respond according to regulations by disengaging . . ."

Tom slouched down in his seat when eyes moved his way. Come on. He'd held his ground. That's what people were supposed to do if they weren't total wimps.

". . . But also because the lot of you did not possess the offensive and defensive programming skills to counter this cyberattack. I see now that we'll have to urge you to make more progress with your programming, and step it up a notch. I am including a second information pack regarding the rules of engagement in tomorrow's download stream; a new list of penalties for noncompliance; and, of course, I am agreeing to one of Lieutenant Blackburn's requests for further training measures."

Tom caught sight of a gleeful look on Blackburn's face, which immediately set him on edge.

Marsh leaned over the podium. "Trainees, Combatants, it's time for some war games."

BLACKBURN OUTLINED THE rules in class the next morning. "For the next five days, we'll wage this Spirewide brawl fought purely on a programming level, which means the vast majority of you are out of luck unless you get your acts together. You can use Zorten II, or even Klondike if you can manage it. Write a virus and inflict it on anyone you'd like, and then enjoy the carnage. I know I will."

Bodies stirred throughout the room. Tom could barely stay in his seat. He hated Programming, but the idea of an all-out war sent thrills of anticipation bolting through him. Maybe he could really work hard and learn a couple of lethal programs just for this.

"General Marsh, of course, wants you to enjoy this, so we'll make this a competition between the five divisions. The division that pulls off the greatest number of successful attacks will be the official winner. Let me note here that no one in the same division can use the same virus twice. If you're thinking about just passing around one set of codes and racking up points that way? Forget it. If, however, someone from another division uses a virus on you? Feel free to steal shamelessly and deploy it on somebody else. That's fair."

Heather raised her hand. "What do we get if we win, sir?"

"Nothing," Blackburn answered.

There was a moment of silence, then Heather raised her hand again. "So why would we go to war with each other if we don't get anything for winning? What's in it for us, sir?"

Blackburn chuckled. "A born mercenary, aren't you, Ms. Akron? And here I was, thinking there are hundreds of teenagers living in close quarters. What, do you all get along so very well you can't imagine doing this?" He looked around at them. "Aren't there any grudges, rivalries, vendettas, or simply a good old-fashioned need for one-upmanship? Well, here it is, right here—the one opportunity you have to act on them. And yes, I know what some of you are thinking. You're thinking, 'I'll just sit this out and no one will attack me.' Guess what?" He cupped a hand to his mouth and stage-whispered to the microphone, "The world doesn't work that way, and neither does the Spire. You try and sit this out, and I can guarantee you that someone from another division will find you easy pickings."

Tom found himself meeting Karl's gaze all of a sudden. Karl drew a finger across his throat. Tom made a shooting gesture with his thumb and forefinger.

Game on, Tom thought gleefully.

"So here are some rules. Whenever you launch a program at someone, you'd better send me the code immediately afterward. If it's a pathetic program that does something like display 'Hello, world' in their vision center? No points. In fact, negative points for wasting my time. It has to be a good program to score. I'm thinking Genghis chicken caliber."

Tom heard sniggering throughout the room from everyone but Karl and his friends. He used net-send and asked Wyatt, *How's it feel being the gold standard?*

She glanced back at him briefly and messaged back, *What difference does it make? It's not like I can claim credit.*

At the front, Alec Tarsus raised his hand. "It sounds kind of arbitrary, sir. You just get to decide if we score points?"

"Thatta boy, Mr. Tarsus. You see how it works. This is all me, and I am the god of this conflict. When I choose, I giveth or taketh away as I please. Here are some more rules: anything you program has to self-terminate within an hour. It can't leave permanent changes to your victim's neural processor. No lasting injuries to the physical body or the software. No attacks involving biological functions that might get you—and us—sued for inflicting psychological trauma. Use your common sense. I hope I'm not making a leap here assuming you have some. And I want to emphasize this: I don't want to see a single virus that will physically damage a neural processor. One of those is worth more than the lot of you put together."

Karl's shoulders slouched. He looked frighteningly sorry to

hear he couldn't permanently damage people. Tom supposed that should worry him, but it just made him feel even more eager to get started.

Vik elbowed him. "You and me, Tom."

"You and me," Tom agreed.

"The Duo of Death."

Tom clenched his fist before him. "The Dealers of Destruction."

"The Doctors of Doom."

Tom thought about that one. "Isn't there already a Doctor of Doom?"

"No, that's Doctor Doom from the *Fantastic Four.* We're plural, with an 'of.' Doctors *of* Doom."

Tom thought about that, then whispered, "Okay, I'll go for that. We have PhDs in the art of Doom."

"Nah, nah. MDs of Doom. See, PhDs mean we're university professors on the side. MD means we practice medicine."

"Why would Doctors of Doom practice medicine?"

"Fine," Vik said. "You be PhD. I'm MD. We both get the title 'Doctor.'"

"Of DOOM!" Tom said, too loudly.

Tom and Vik both jumped with a sudden feeling like an electric jolt. Text flashed across their vision: *Datastream received: program Shut Up So the Rest of Us Can Hear initiated.*

And Wyatt Enslow was glaring over at them, keyboard raised.

Vik made a strangling gesture at her, and Tom aimed his fake gun.

"You know what she can do," Tom said out of the side of his mouth to Vik. "Do we really want to make an enemy of her?"

"She'll probably try to sit out. She can't go all out."

"Right." They were free to posture all they wanted.

As class concluded, someone asked Blackburn when the war games began. He paused before striding from the podium. "When do they start? Well, I'd say you're open to attack as soon as you're in the hallway."

Stunned silence followed that.

Blackburn's unpleasant chuckle trailed him out of the Lafayette Room. He left the entire class sitting there, erupting in frantic whispers. Tom saw the sea of dipping heads, division members plotting their escape.

"Ten bucks says Blackburn's watching a security feed of this and laughing," Tom muttered to Vik.

"I'm not betting against that."

Tom waited. Still, no one rose. Everyone was waiting to see what would happen to the first people out—if they'd get attacked, if someone in their midst had already cobbled together a program.

"Want to run the gauntlet, Doctor?" He glanced at Vik, feeling antsy like he was ready to burst out of his seat.

Vik nodded. "We should, Doctor. One, two . . ."

"Three!" They both jolted to their feet.

Every eye in the room swung toward them. Tom ignored them and shoved his way across the bench to the aisle. The silence loomed in his ears, pressing in around them, as they walked toward the doors. It seemed to take forever.

Vik burst into laughter. He hurled triumphant fists into the air and kept walking, as though daring anyone to attack. Tom smiled at his back, but his grin faded when he detected movement out of the corner of his eye.

Karl Marsters was rising to his feet.

Tom slammed Vik's back with his palm. "Move!"

He didn't need to tell Vik twice. Vik leaped forward,

sprinting toward the entrance, Tom right behind him.

Tom's last glimpse of the classroom was of Karl and a handful of Genghises shoving their way down the aisles after them.

THEY RAN SO fast, their breath came in ragged pants. It was like Calisthenics on speed. They reached the empty mess hall before it occurred to them that this would probably be one of the easiest places for Karl to attack them. An open space, more than one entrance . . .

"Come on, let's find a place we can defend ourselves!" Tom fumbled through the video games he'd played, and came up with a fitting reference: "This is our Alamo."

"Didn't Davy Crockett die at the Alamo?"

"Okay, we're the attacking cyborgs, then."

"There weren't any cyborgs at the Alamo."

"Yeah, there were, Vik."

"I'm confused. Are you talking about the game Alamo or the actual event?"

"Wait, the Alamo really happened?"

Vik whapped the back of Tom's head. "I'm not even from your country and I know that."

They charged past the painting of General Patton and locked themselves into one of the mess hall's private meeting rooms. Tom sprawled on the floor, back against the wall, and propped his arm up to type in Zorten II code, readying an attack virus for the inevitable moment when the Genghises caught up to them.

Vik stared down at him. "What are you doing?"

"Virus."

"But you're a terrible programmer, Tom."

"You do it, then."

"I will." Vik dropped down next to him, and started typing at his own forearm keyboard.

"So what do I do?" Tom asked him.

"Stand between me and anyone else long enough for me to finish coding."

"You want me to be a *human shield*?"

"You can do it, Tom. I believe in you."

"I'm not questioning whether I can do it, I just—"

Suddenly, the room's locks were overridden, and the door slid open. Karl filled the doorway. Vik shrieked in a very un-Doctor of Doom–like manner, and Tom felt a thrill of sheer terror.

Karl leered at them. Then raised his forearm and began tapping at his own keyboard, forehead furrowed, thick fingers banging away.

It was anticlimactic, the way the Genghises trickled in, and yanked Karl's arm back and forth between them, manipulating the keyboard on his forearm.

"That's not how you do it," Tom said, seeing Vik mistype a segment of source code that he remembered seeing once before. He grabbed Vik's arm and took over.

Then Vik said, "That's not it, either. Back to your station, human shield!" He yanked his arm away and shoved Tom into position between him and the Genghises.

Tom looked nervously at the Genghises, expecting to be slammed by a virus from Karl and company any minute. They, meanwhile, were arguing over Zorten II themselves.

"You dunce, this isn't working," Karl snarled at someone.

"Wait, how do you do that error checker program?"

"Why's this value null? What's a null?"

"Give me my arm back! 'Null' means it's not working, idiot."

Tom leaned back against the wall, the room filled with

the tapping of keys. The sense of menace and excitement was steadily draining away. Tom heard Vik curse quietly as he messed up the program yet again. Karl, meanwhile, was threatening to clobber them with his keyboard rather than let them type on it.

After some time, Wyatt wandered in and looked back and forth between them. "You guys have been in here for twenty minutes. You still haven't written one program yet? That's kind of pathetic."

"Stop distracting me, Man Hands," Vik ordered. "It's not like I see you racking up the victories."

Wyatt flushed.

"Man Hands," Karl repeated with a snigger from across the room, typing at his own keyboard. "Hear that?" he said to one of his friends. "'Man Hands.'"

Wyatt glared at Vik. "Thanks for spreading that nickname around. You know what? I hope Karl gets you first." With that, she stalked from the room.

Another five minutes crawled by. Tom had given up playing human shield. He was pretty sure now it wouldn't be necessary. "Karl, Vik, everyone, stop!" he called out.

To his surprise, they did.

"This is so stupid," Tom exclaimed. "We're all lousy programmers."

The Genghises exchanged uneasy glances. It was true.

"We've been at it for a half hour and none of us has managed a program yet."

"What do you suggest, then, Plebe?" Karl folded his beefy arms.

"We go our separate ways, program on our own time, come up with some great attacks, and then meet again later."

Karl's eyes narrowed. "Like a duel."

"Yeah, like a duel. Tomorrow night. In the plebe common room."

Karl stroked his chin, as if he had an invisible beard there. "Okay, I'd go for that. But night after that instead."

"Night after?"

"Yeah, you have a problem with that? I said the night after tomorrow, 'cause tomorrow night, I'm scheduled to go get a haircut. I can't cancel without twenty-four hours' notice."

"Night after, then." Tom was fine with it. More time to program.

Karl gave a satisfied nod. "I don't know anyone who can cobble together a program on the run, anyway."

And then the doors slid open, and Tom glanced over carelessly to see Wyatt standing there again, her keyboard out this time.

"If you came to see Karl get us, you're out of luck," Vik informed her.

"That's not why I'm here," Wyatt replied. "I decided not to sit this one out."

Vik blinked. "Seriously? Why?"

"You changed my mind, Vik." She typed something on her keyboard, and immediately Karl and the Genghis trainees dropped onto their hands and knees and began baaing.

Tom whirled toward the Genghises, watching them all nuzzling their noses at the carpet as sheep. "You sure about this?" he asked her.

"Very sure."

"Huh," Vik said. "Well, guess we can have three Doctors of Doom, then."

But Wyatt still had her keyboard up, a ruthless gleam in her eyes. "Why, Vik, we're in different divisions, remember?"

Vik's eyes widened. "Human shield, save me!" he cried,

grabbing Tom by the shoulders.

"Oh, don't worry," Wyatt assured him, smiling. "I have enough for both of you."

A flick of the button on her keyboard targeted both their IP addresses at the same time and sent text flashing across Tom's vision center: *Datastream received: program Bleating Sheep initiated.*

TOM CAME TO himself, munching on a plant in the arboretum behind the mess hall. He wasn't the only one. Far from it. Wyatt had left carnage all over the first floor. Some trainees were sheep, the way Vik still was. Some were gathered in a crowd, speaking together frantically in a cycling roster of languages, unable to remember English, and others were stumbling over their legs over and over again like they'd forgotten how to walk. She'd taken out a good thirty people luckless enough to cross her path.

"Ugh." Tom swiped his sleeve over his mouth, scrubbing off the taste of tomato vine, and ignored the frantic *baaaa*s of people he passed, hunched on all fours, being sheep.

Tom found Vik and nudged him with his foot, ignoring his *baa*s of anger, until Vik snapped out of it. "What—what—"

Tom reached out and hoisted him up. "Wyatt went on a rampage. The Doctors of Doom can't let this insult stand."

TOM AND VIK decided to confront Yuri that night over whether he planned to unite with his fellow Alexanders to help take Wyatt Enslow down. Their tentative questions over dinner convinced them he understood just enough of what was going on to be of use to them, unless he planned to be a dirty, rotten traitor. But Yuri wasn't in his bunk.

Beamer was.

Vik strode inside. "Hey, man, have you seen the Android?"

Beamer just lay there in bed and didn't say a word. Tom and Vik exchanged an uneasy glance. Beamer hadn't been at classes today. He must have spent the whole day in bed.

"What's going on with you, Beamer?" Vik asked him. "Why are you being such a pansy today?"

It was worse than Tom would've done. He jabbed his thumb toward the door. Vik raised his arms and left him to it.

Tom took over his spot at Beamer's side, then realized he had no idea what to say, either.

"Look, I'm sorry I beheaded you, okay?"

Beamer opened his eyes. "God, Tom, you are so selfish! This is not about you."

"Then what? I don't get it. I don't. Do you need the social worker?"

Beamer shook his head, staring at the ceiling.

"Look, I'm not trying to make fun of you. I can get her to come up here." He braced himself, because this was about as self-sacrificing as he could ever remember being. "I will even say it's for me if you're embarrassed."

Please say no, Tom added mentally.

"No," Beamer said.

Tom's shoulders slumped in relief.

"Don't you see, Tom? Don't you see what my problem is?"

"Yeah, you thought something was wrong with the program and you were gonna die. So you got freaked out."

"No. Yes, but not just that. I thought I was going to die. And afterward, it made me think. Really think. About this." He tapped his head with a pale finger. "About what I've done. I thought this would be fun, Tom, okay? Coming to the Spire, messing around with machines. But I didn't think it through. I didn't think about whether this is what I want. What if I die?"

"You're not gonna die anytime soon. You're fourteen."

"How can you know that?" Beamer sat up in bed, red spots on his cheeks. "We don't even know what this stuff in our heads is. Are there any eighty-year-olds walking around with neural processors?"

"They didn't have this tech back then. But look at Blackburn. He got it sixteen years ago. Other than the acute psychotic break, he's fine."

Beamer rolled his eyes and slumped back down. Tom could admit that "other than the acute psychotic break" was a pretty stupid thing to say, but he didn't know why Beamer would be so touchy about the details right now.

"It's not even that. Don't you get it? We never get these out. Never. We signed up for a few years in the Spire, but this stuff in our heads ties us to the military for life. Do you realize that? They own it. They own *us*."

Tom found his thoughts turning back to his night in the infirmary, the way Dr. Gonzales had a final say over his hGH and not him. But he just said, "What does it matter? They need us. They're not going to do anything bad to us."

"We will always be the front line. The military gets first dibs on us for the rest of our lives, whatever we do from here—don't you see that? Who's going to repair the processor when it breaks, otherwise? And what happens if the Russo-Chinese programmers come up with some great new computer virus to vaporize our brains? . . . If Russia and China ever have a chance to really take down America, we're the first ones they'll kill!"

Tom laughed at that. It sounded so ridiculous. "Come on. No one kills in war anymore."

"It's war, Tom. War. That used to mean stuff like the Battle of Stalingrad, get it? And one day, it might again. Someone might remember one day. Someone might remember this is World War III. Blackburn said it—don't you remember? He said they want to cut open our heads and look at the coding inside!"

"That's Blackburn trying to scare us. Look, I get it, Beamer. I was actually worried about some of this stuff, too, back before I got the neural processor."

"*You*. Worried."

Tom shrugged, trying to remember his conversation with Heather back when he was making up his mind about whether to enlist. It was funny how much murkier his memories before the neural processor felt—not time-stamped at all, not perfectly detailed. Like a different person had those experiences.

"Yeah, I was worried. About the brain surgery being a surprise and the way the military was—well, just some of the same stuff you mentioned. But . . . come on. Come on, Beamer. Look around you. Who else gets to do what we do? Who else gets to be what we are? We're important. We can learn any skill with a download. We can speak any language we want. We're faster and smarter than regular people. We can do anything now."

Beamer rolled onto his back and stared up at the ceiling. "I could've done anything before if I'd tried really hard. I started a business, you know. I figured out how to make some things, so I sold water filters and grills at tent cities. I mean, ever seen one of those places? They're not completely poor. A lot of them have jobs, but they just can't afford a real place."

"Yeah, I've seen a few." Neil always pointed them out to him. He said they were the only alternative to moving from casino to casino.

"Well, people bought my stuff there. I made money. I was doing just fine before the neural processor. You could've done anything before the processor, too. You won spelling bees, remember? That must've taken a lot of work."

Tom didn't say anything. He knew he hadn't won spelling bees before, or even contributed to the world's largest ball of earwax. The old Tom Raines couldn't even make it at a reform school.

"I see you, Vik, and even Yuri, who doesn't have a chance here and *has* to know it," Beamer said. "You guys are just devoted to this thing. And I came here, and I wanted to do well, but I just don't care about it anymore. Ever since that thing happened with my girlfriend and I got stuck on restricted libs, it's like it's all gone into perspective. I keep wondering why I'm still here. I don't want to be Camelot Company. I hate it here. I keep thinking about high school and all those movies I saw about it, and wondering if I'm missing out on something. I want to get older and go to college. And buy a house. And have kids and marry some woman and have block parties and barbecues."

"Barbecue?"—Tom latched on to that—"Beamer, you and me, we can go have a barbecue right now, okay? Forget restricted libs. We'll reroute your GPS signal to the bathroom, then we'll go outside and barbecue anything you want."

Beamer gave a pained sigh. "You don't understand, Tom. You can't."

He turned around to face the wall and buried his head in the covers.

Tom realized it, then: he didn't understand. He couldn't. Beamer wanted to be normal. Tom couldn't imagine ever wanting to be nothing.

Tom would never willingly give up what he had here. He would never willingly lose the neural processor, the life full of possibilities.

He couldn't bear to be worthless again. He'd rather be dead.

CHAPTER THIRTEEN

MOST OF THE viruses on the second full day of the war games came courtesy of Wyatt, but there were a few exceptions. Franco Holbein of Hannibal Division wrote one called Icy Night that caught a few Machiavellis when they hooked into neural access ports in their bunks. They spent all of lunch huddled together, teeth chattering, bellowing out demands for someone to turn up the Spire's thermostat. Then Nigel Harrison pulled off a virus called Food Face that caused people sitting in the mess hall to smash their own faces into their meal trays. By the end of the day, Britt Schmeiser of Napoleon Division had retaliated with a Trojan named Nigel Harrison that triggered whenever an infected trainee's vision center registered that Nigel Harrison was nearby.

The Trojan infiltrated the homework feed overnight and managed to infect most of the Spire. On the third day of the war games, Nigel strode into the mess hall for lunch, and the Trojan triggered in almost a hundred trainees at the same time. A sea of faces began twitching just like his face always did.

Nigel stared around the room, looking like he'd entered some surreal nightmare, and then he lost it. "Stop it," he shrieked. "Stop it!"

But getting upset made his face twitch harder, and his facial twitch triggered their facial twitches. And a whole debacle ensued where Nigel began threatening to hit people with his meal tray. Eventually, he fled the room in tears of rage, pursued by laughter and shouts of "Go cry to the social worker!"

Tom and Vik missed the incident, though they both passed Nigel Harrison outside the Lafayette Room, and therefore spent the next hour irritated by continual facial twitches. They skipped lunch altogether, too busy putting together their program for the duel with Karl. It was beautiful. They called it Frequent Noisome Farts.

"You ready for this, Doctor?" Vik asked Tom.

"I'm ready, Doctor. Let's go."

They marched out into the plebe common room at 2000 to face Karl. From the fiendish pleasure emanating from Karl's jowled face beneath his new haircut, he had something nasty ready, too.

"On three." Vik's eyes were locked on those of Karl's companion Lyla Martin. It was the first time Tom had really seen her up close, and her profile flashed before him.

NAME: Lyla Martin
RANK: USIF, Grade IV Middle, Genghis Division
ORIGIN: West Palm Beach, FL
ACHIEVEMENTS: Amateur flyweight winner of six world and national boxing championships
IP: 2053:db7:lj71::275:ll3:6e8
SECURITY STATUS: Top Secret LANDLOCK-4

"One-two-three," Lyla shouted all in a jumble, and Tom was too startled to react right away.

Karl cried, "Ha!" and struck first.

Nothing happened. *Datastream received: program Rabid Fido initiated. Value null,* flashed across Tom's vision center.

"Nice try, buddy boy." Tom launched Frequent Noisome Farts.

Karl waited. And waited. Then laughed. "Value null, Plebe."

"Secret Indian ninja attack!" Vik raised the portable keyboard he'd snuck behind his back and unleashed their supersecret, superexperimental backup program.

"Ka-pow!" Tom cried triumphantly.

Karl and Lyla looked back at them questioningly.

Lyla scratched her nose. "My nose itches. Does your nose itch?" she asked Karl.

Karl shook his head. "Nah."

"Secret Indian Ninja Attack doesn't make your nose itch," Vik said.

"Okay," she said. "That's all I'm noticing. The itchy nose."

"Another null, Plebes," Karl announced.

They all looked at one another for a long time. Karl pounded one first into a meaty hand, visibly longing for a chance to pummel them the old-fashioned way. Then they headed off their separate ways.

"Worst duel ever," Tom decided.

"Tom," Vik said as they entered their bunk, "we suck so much it's depressing."

UNFORTUNATELY, BLACKBURN AGREED with them. The next day, he played their duel on the overhead screens for the class, and even he had to smother his palm over his mouth to fight his laughter.

Tom decided he hated the census device. After they'd transmitted their source code to Blackburn, he ordered all four of them down for memory viewing just for this. Blackburn had played a vast number of humiliating programming failures for their entertainment and capped it all off with Tom and Karl's epic duel.

"The last three days have confirmed it," Blackburn said. "The vast majority of you, to put it gently, are pathetic. Hannibal Division is winning, with Machiavelli at a distant second. This appears to be solely due to the efforts of Nigel Harrison and, to my endless surprise, Wyatt Enslow."

Cheers and whoops from the other Hannibals and Machiavellis rang through the Lafayette Room. Tom looked over and saw that Wyatt's cheeks had grown bright red. She wasn't used to being the center of attention—and certainly not accustomed to being celebrated by the other members of a division that mostly ignored her.

"What's your secret, Enslow?" Blackburn said, leaning on the podium, gray eyes fixed on hers. "How did you turn into a prodigy on me?"

Tom saw Wyatt duck her head, letting her dark hair swing in her face. "I just really wanted to attack people before they attacked me, sir."

Blackburn let her off with that, but Tom noticed Blackburn glancing at her from time to time even after he moved on with the lecture. "Now, I've caught word of a few attacks on Mr. Ramirez. General Marsh doesn't want him to be in this conflict."

Elliot rose to his feet. "Sir, I'm fine with—"

"Mr. Ramirez, you have a summit at the Capitol Building coming up. As you'll *appear* to be representing the Indo-American forces, no one wants to risk messing up your software. And, let's face it, you're hardly a coding genius whose absence will have a devastating impact on this conflict. I think we'll survive your nonparticipation."

Tom could have sworn that Elliot looked embarrassed as he dropped back down.

"Ramirez is out, everyone. As for the rest of you"—Blackburn waved his finger in a circle, indicating the whole room—"you have one more day. I know this is asking a lot, but try to stop humiliating yourselves."

As VIK AND Tom headed up in the elevator to the sixth floor, Tom asked him, "What did Blackburn mean about Elliot 'appearing' to represent Indo-America?"

"Well, you know what the Capitol Summit's *really* about," Vik said. "Dominion Agra is allied with India and America, and it controls the patents on the food supply. Harbinger, Inc. is allied with Russia and China, and it controls the patents on the water supply. So this is the time of year when the Coalition of Multinationals meets and agrees that even if they're at war in space, they'll still enforce each other's patents here on Earth. It's also a big show for the public to keep them engaged in the war. Our best Combatant faces the best Russo-Chinese Combatant."

"But Elliot's the one who fights there," Tom pointed out. "And he's not the best one in CamCo."

The doors slid open and they strode into the plebe common room, heading toward Alexander Division. "But we call him our best. And from the outside, it'll look like Elliot and Svetlana are the ones fighting because they've got the pretty faces and the stage presence. So they go through the gestures of facing off for the cameras, while behind the scenes, proxies do the actual fighting. Elliot sure does, and everyone assumes Svetlana does, too."

Tom sputtered a laugh. "Wait. Wait. So he just goes there and pretends to fight?"

"Yeah," Vik said. "It's kind of funny. See, the public doesn't know about neural processors, so Elliot and Svetlana even have a wheel, a throttle, and controllers like they're steering ships in space, while somewhere else their proxies are hooked in and actually navigating the ships."

"Who's the proxy?"

"Last year it was Alec Tarsus. But since Svetlana is sure to be proxied by Medusa this year, and Alec always gets stomped by her in space, I'm not sure who they'll use this time around. I'm guessing Heather Akron or that Genghis Division guy Yosef Saide maybe? He won't beat Medusa, but you've seen Yosef in action. He's big on mass destruction. He might pull off something insane that'll make them both lose."

They passed Beamer as he left his bunk for the bathroom. "Hey," Tom called, "who do you think will . . ."

But Beamer walked past them like they weren't even there. A cold fist seemed to curl in Tom's stomach, and it wasn't until Vik tugged on his shoulder that he headed on his way again.

Once they were inside their bunk, Vik accessed the Spire's internal processor and ran a cursory virus scan to try locating the other malicious attacks planted in neural interfaces. He pulled back with some shock when he was done and showed Tom the results: Wyatt Enslow had sabotaged everything. *Everything.* She'd planted attacks in the homework feeds, in the databases. She'd even manufactured firewalls that blocked other people's viruses from infiltrating the feeds.

Vik sat back on his heels, blown away. "Doctor, you realize Man Hands has stomped everyone."

"She needs a proper supervillain name. Man Hands isn't doing it for me."

"You're right. How about 'Evil Wench from the Darkest Reaches of Mordor'?"

"Too wordy."

"Just Evil Wench, then. Look, I refuse to concede defeat here."

"Every villain has a weak spot. What's hers?"

Vik rubbed at his chin and frowned at the wall. Tom flopped down on his bed and propped his head up on his elbow, concentrating on the carpet.

Wyatt didn't play games. They couldn't sneak something into a VR sim. She liked reading, but Tom couldn't think of any way to sneak her a Trojan in a book. She never hooked into those, so the text would just get memorized by the processor. She just read them word by word like a regular person without a neural processor did.

"Training room neural interface sockets?"

"How do you know what cot she'll pick?" Vik pointed out.

"You'll have to plant some virus in all of them."

"You'll get it, too."

Tom waved that off. "I'll take it just to score a point against her."

"And Elliot will get it."

"Oh." Tom's hopes faded. They couldn't risk hitting Elliot. "Well, there's gotta be some other . . ." And then, suddenly, he knew what Wyatt's weakness was: "Vik, what about Yuri?"

Vik's eyes shot to his. "The Android. Of course. He's been her best friend since she got here. She trusts him."

"So we get him to sneak her a virus," Tom said. "He doesn't

have to understand any of it. We just tell him to show her something and send a file."

Vik grinned. "She'll get curious and look!"

It was perfect.

There was just one catch: Yuri was horrified at the very idea of helping them take Wyatt down. "I cannot do that."

"You don't have to do much of anything," Vik protested. "Just ask her to take a look at a program of yours, have her hook in."

"And bam. She's in virus town," Tom finished.

"It is too deceitful," Yuri said.

Vik threw up his hands. "Come on. Where's your patriotism? You're an Alexander, for God's sake!"

"But I do not like this idea of attacking Wanda."

"It's not like the Evil Wench is gonna ditch you for all her other friends—"

"I will not lose her trust."

"We get that you feel pity for her or whatever—" Tom began.

Yuri rose to his full height. "Why should I pity her? She is magnificent. She is so intelligent and honest, and her eyes are lovely." He stopped, maybe because Tom and Vik were both staring at him like he was a madman, or maybe because he could feel how pink he was turning.

It hit Tom like a lightning bolt. He turned to Vik, aghast. "He likes her."

"Yuri, no!" Vik said.

Yuri turned redder, confirming it.

"Yuri, come on, man," Tom cried.

Yuri gave a helpless shrug. "Divisions cannot divide human hearts."

"Oh God," Vik cried, clapping hands over his ears. "He's

even spouting cheesy lines now. Make him stop, Tom!"

"I can't," Tom told him. "My ears . . . They're bleeding. Bleeding!"

"It's a brain hemorrhage! He's murdered us!" Vik said.

"Murderer!" Tom cried, fake collapsing onto the ground.

Yuri shook his head. "This is not very mature."

But they were both on the ground now, pretending to writhe with spontaneous brain hemorrhages. Yuri sighed and stepped over them to get out the door.

THAT NIGHT, VIK devoted himself to staying up and putting together the ultimate program to take Wyatt down. Tom wasn't going to sleep while his partner in doom did the bulk of the programming, so he stayed awake in a show of solidarity, occasionally offering suggestions. One idea came to him very late in the night. He jumped to his feet in a flash of inspiration.

"Vik, what if we use an outside transmitter?"

"What? I was concentrating, Tom."

"Listen. Maybe we don't need some elaborate virus. Maybe we just need to hit her from somewhere she doesn't expect. We know her IP. And we have the authorization to allow us through the Spire's firewall. So we find a transmitter powerful enough to send it to her from a distance, hack into that, and use it to slam her with something."

"What kind of transmitter?"

Tom leaned forward eagerly, because this was where he was sure he was being visionary. "A satellite."

"How do you expect to use a satellite? I don't know a thing about how those are controlled."

"We hook in. Just like satellites hook into ships in space, we hook into the satellite."

"The ships in space are designed for a neural interface,"

Vik informed him. "Satellites aren't."

Tom rubbed at his head, fumbling with scraps of his memory—from the first day his neural processor was installed. "We can do it. I swear, it's possible. Remember when you first got your neural processor installed, and you were getting configured for the internet? I remember when I kept hooking into random places, and one of them was a satellite. It was just like a neural interface. I was inside it. We've just gotta do something like that on purpose."

Vik stared at him like he was crazy.

"Come on, don't you remember your installation?" Tom demanded, recalling the vast sequences of 0s and 1s, and the way his brain felt tugged in an infinite number of directions. "Your brain first gets on the network and it starts jumping around a bit . . ."

Vik considered him, his fingers drumming on the edge of his forearm keypad. "Tom, I'm not saying that didn't happen, but, uh, I'm going to work on this. This program. If you have something else you think might work, give it a shot, but I wouldn't count on it, buddy. That thing you're talking about? It's just not possible. There is no neural processor in the world that can interface with just any machine at will. Machines have to be built for a neural processor, or it doesn't work. You probably just dreamed it. Anesthesia does weird stuff like that to some people. My dad's a doctor. I know."

Tom knew he hadn't imagined that. "I'm going to hook into a neural interface and show you, Vik. Just wait."

"You hook into the internet, you're going to catch one of Wyatt's viruses," Vik warned him. "She's got this whole place rigged up."

"I'm not using the trainee server."

▲▼▲

As SOON AS Tom reached floor eleven, a warning flashed in his head: *Restricted area.* He ignored it. He headed down the empty hallway, located the officers' lounge, and then settled into a chair.

There was a neural access port in the middle of the table, all ready for Blackburn. Tom pulled out a neural wire, hooked it into the port, then plugged it into the back of his neck.

The internet server for officers popped up, and Tom navigated a bit aimlessly, getting the feel of using just his brain to move through the internet, to click links. The images popped before his eyes, much more vivid and encompassing than they appeared with just a pair of VR visors.

He wasn't sure how he'd managed to interface with the satellite right after his neural processor installation, but he knew it had something to do with following one connection to the next.

He tried focusing on his neural processor. He barely noticed the computer in his brain now, but he remembered how early on he'd been so aware of it. It used to feel so alien. If he concentrated just enough, he could still detect it, still feel the machine buzzing in his brain like another entity entirely, sending electrical impulses to something else, to the hub in the Spire.

And then like he'd received an electric jolt, Tom suddenly found himself jerked out of his body. His limbs felt cold and distant and his brain melded to the Spire, a massive charged source of energy, a building doubling as a transmitter with a hybrid fission/fusion core, sending signals into space that—

The signal tore Tom farther from himself, thrusting him into the satellites ringing Earth with their electrical impulses transmitting data, a vast ring of 0s and 1s that seemed like so much nonsense when it was flooding his brain like this, and suddenly he felt like an *it* again, gazing through electromagnetic sensors—

And then another stream tore him away, and he was connected to those vessels near the dark side of Mercury, the surface registering in the infrared sensors of the Russo-Chinese automated machines, floating in orbit, exchanging signals with Stronghold Energy's palladium mines that connected back to—

The central server in the Sun Tzu Citadel in the Forbidden City, with two hundred and seven neural processors registering on the internal network, IPs flickering through Tom's brain—

He slammed back into his neural processor, into his own body so abruptly it felt like he'd been swatted by some vast, cosmic hand. He sat there, his eyes closed, hand gripping the table, heaving in frantic breaths. He hadn't imagined it the first time. He really had seen out of satellites. But his assurances to Vik seemed laughable suddenly. He hadn't just seen satellites. He'd glimpsed inside the server of the Sun Tzu Citadel . . . where the Chinese Combatants trained. That was . . . that was something big. He wasn't sure what to even make of it. Was that supposed to happen?

He returned to their bunk, still a bit in shock. Vik glanced up from his keyboard. "So?"

Tom hesitated, debating what to say for a long moment, remembering Vik's words: *There is* no *neural processor in the world that can interface with just any machine at will.*

But he'd done it. He knew now for sure that he'd done it.

But whatever it was that he'd done, it was too much for some tiny skirmish in the Spire. He wasn't even sure what it *was* that he'd done yet.

Tom shook his head. "You were right. I guess I imagined it."

CHAPTER FOURTEEN

TOM AND VIK binge-downloaded the night's homework and then tried to walk out the door of their bunk. Neither of them made it. They collapsed in a stupor on the floor. Tom roused only when Vik cried, "Wake up! We missed Calisthenics!"

Tom jolted to his feet, feeling stupid and strange. He fell behind when Vik rushed off to Math class. Flashes of the night's homework kept plaguing him, appearing before his eyes, confusing him, drawing his attention to irrelevant facts his processor hadn't yet sorted out. It took him a full minute to remember how to press the button to summon the elevator.

When he finally made it inside, he found Karl Marsters already in there. The two boys froze, shocked for a full second.

Like that, Tom's brain snapped into gear. He tore back his sleeve to bare his forearm keyboard and frantically typed. He heard Karl doing the same thing.

"Aha!" Karl cried.

Tom launched Walk Only Right as Karl launched Exorcist.

Exorcist had been floating around ever since Alec Tarsus wrote it, so Tom opened his mouth to taunt him, "You couldn't come up with your own?" even though Vik had practically rewritten all his code for Walk Only Right. But creepy Latin-sounding words spouted out instead.

"Gotcha," Karl exulted, but he wasn't laughing for long. When he tried to step out of the elevator, he turned right. When he tried to go left, he went right. He bellowed and tried to change direction, and he turned right again.

Tom had planned to say, "Don't get too dizzy" to rub it in a bit, but instead heard himself shriek, "I'll spit on your grave!" He covered his mouth and left Karl turning in endless circles in the middle of the elevator.

He arrived at the Lafayette Room several minutes late. Vik glanced up as Tom slid onto the bench next to him. "Have your head on straight yet?"

"Oladae holovii inuladus," Tom answered.

"Ooh. Got Exorcisted, huh?"

Out of habit, Tom tried to say yes. Instead, he shrieked, "I'll eat your soul!"

At the front of the room, Dr. Lichtenstein jerked, startled by the noise. Vik muffled his laughter, and Tom just covered his mouth to stop it from chanting more pseudo-Latin or homicidal phrases.

"The program's all compiled. We're on for taking down the Evil Wench tonight?" Vik said in a low voice.

Tom nodded, hand still over his mouth.

"Are you sure? That was a reluctant nod. I'll really feel a lot more confident if I hear you say yes or no. Just say it out loud for me."

Tom glared at him, knowing he just wanted him to Exorcist

a little more, and gave him a nonverbal reply. It only required one finger, too.

NIGHT CAME, AND Tom and Vik made their first move: they tricked Yuri into getting locked in the Census Chamber so he couldn't stop them. Then they began stalking Wyatt like stealthy hunters. The Evil Wench settled in the arboretum, probably to read the way she did sometimes. They waited until the last five minutes of the war games to spring their trap, just so she wouldn't have a chance to strike back.

At 1855, Tom gave Vik a thumbs-up. "It's time. I'm going in, Doctor."

Tom was the decoy. In a minute, Vik would pop out of the shadows and unleash their devastating program, a combination of Exorcist, Nigel Harrison, Walk Only Right, Secret Indian Ninja Attack, and of course, Frequent Noisome Farts.

"Good luck, Doctor."

"You, too, Doctor." He waited for Vik to slip away, then began whistling and strode forward toward Wyatt.

He made sure to give a cry of startled horror when he came upon her, sitting by a fern and reading a book. She closed her novel and raised her keyboard.

"Wait, wait." Tom raised his hands, and ducked behind one of the plants. "I didn't even realize you were here."

Wyatt held her distance as she emerged from behind the leafy canopy. "You didn't?"

"No, I only came here to hide out the last minutes of the war games." Tom shoved his hands in his pockets. "Can we play it cool?"

Wyatt lowered her arm. "You're tired of fighting all the time?"

"Oh, yeah. Always being on guard against attacks . . . It's

exhausting." Tom saw Vik sneaking out from behind her and fought his smile.

Wyatt's brow furrowed. "Can you tell me something, Tom? Something important?"

Tom hesitated, didn't give Vik the signal yet. "What?"

"I just really need to know—how stupid do you think I am?"

"Uh, what?"

"How stupid? Just tell me. On a scale of one to ten."

"Is ten very stupid or very smart?"

"You love fighting. You'd do it all the time if you could. The way I figure it, you're probably just distracting me so Vik can sneak up behind me and send me a virus."

Vik froze in place behind her. Tom felt a thrill of foreboding. They'd blocked Vik's GPS signal from the Spire's tracking system. Obviously not well enough.

"Of course"—Wyatt set her book aside— "what you didn't realize was that I lured you here for our final showdown."

Vik mouthed the words disbelievingly as Tom said them: "A final showdown?"

This was not going to plan. It was supposed to be their ambush of her, not her ambush of them.

Wyatt nodded grimly. "You see, Tom, when you stumbled right into my fiendish scheme, I knew you'd try to go out by facing me. I counted on it. In fact, I even instigated the circumstances that drew you here. I know you're wondering how I did all this, so I'll explain in detail." She'd barely launched into her detailed explanation when disaster struck.

Time is 1900. War games are now concluded.

Tom didn't believe the ping in his brain. He stood there, in shock.

Vik stumbled forward. "What—what . . ."

When Tom looked at Wyatt again, he realized she was grinning ear to ear. "I got you guys."

"You did not," Tom protested. "You were about to spring a diabolical trap. You said so. You ran out of time."

"You really thought I lured you here? Wow. No. Yuri warned me over net-send that you guys had trapped him in the Census Chamber, so I figured you were coming for me next. I didn't even have a decent program ready, so I decided to talk to you until the time ended."

"Wait, what?" Tom said. "We squandered our ultimate program?"

"Pretty much. You know what this calls for?" Wyatt raised her arms up and held her hands on either side of her head, fingers bent like monster claws.

"A bear attack?" Vik guessed.

Wyatt dropped her hands. "I'm gloating."

"It looks more like you're a bear." Vik nodded at Tom, hoping he'd back him up.

"You should clench your fists and make sure they're high over your head next time," Tom explained. "Then you say the whole I-am-awesome thing. That's a proper fist pump."

"How about this instead," Wyatt said. She put her hands on her waist, cleared her throat, then said, "I have to ask you guys something. Something important." Her words sounded stilted, like something she'd practiced in front of the mirror several times.

Vik clamped a hand over his eyes. "Must we subject ourselves to this indignity, Doctor?"

"She won, man," Tom said.

Vik dropped his hand with a sigh, turned to Wyatt, and played along. "What do you want to ask us, Wyatt?"

"How does defeat taste?" Wyatt said, with flourish. "Is

it bitter? See, I am curious because I wouldn't know from personal experience, and you would."

She let that sink in, and Tom winced. "Yeah, that's gloating. Face rubbing, actually."

Vik shook his head regretfully. "The day's officially yours, Evil Wench."

And then a voice spoke, "I'm disappointed."

Tom jumped so high, he nearly careened back into a tomato vine. Vik gave a yelp. Wyatt just froze like an animal caught in the glare of headlights, staring at Lieutenant Blackburn as he emerged into the clearing.

"Here I was," Blackburn said, rubbing his hands together, "waiting with anticipation for whatever nasty program you were going to unleash on them, but it ended with a whimper, not a bang. Well, there's one consolation: at least I can now announce the winner of this competition."

Vik's shoulders slumped. "Hannibal Division, right?"

"Wrong, Mr. Ashwan." There was a gleeful smile on his face. He jabbed both his thumbs at his chest. "Me. *I* won. There is one very simple reason I wanted war games: I wanted my rogue hacker to out herself."

Wyatt froze.

"And you sure didn't disappoint, Ms. Enslow. After all that time, playing it so careful, what was it that changed your mind? Caught up in the competitive spirit? Maybe goaded by your peers? I hoped you would be."

"It's not her—" Tom tried.

"Tom, it's okay," Wyatt said suddenly. She gave a resigned shrug. "I was tired of it, okay? You're right. It was me all along, sir. So what happens now?"

"Well, let's see." He folded his arms and seemed to think about it. "Hacking a classified database, not to mention altering the content . . . I'm fairly sure one or both of those are illegal. I could report it to General Marsh and have charges drawn up. They'd certainly have to remove your neural processor if you were convicted, since there's no room in this program for felons. You've had the processor long enough, so its removal may damage some of your intellectual faculties, but you'll recover most of them in time. I'm sure the prison sentence won't be so severe, given your youth. You were simply messing around, hardly committing treason, so it won't be a nasty confinement facility either. And your record will be expunged once you turn eighteen."

Wyatt had grown completely pale, her eyes bugging out. Tom felt like there was a fire in his chest. He fought the urge to charge over and punch Blackburn's smug face.

"Or alternatively," Blackburn said, "you could be removed from Programming class, which isn't moving at the advanced pace you require anyway, and spend that time instead performing some minor software updates around this place as I deem fit."

Wyatt's mouth moved without making a sound. She looked like she'd forgotten how to speak.

"Your choice, Ms. Enslow," Blackburn added.

"Well, the second one," she cried. "I would've done that anyway, even without choice number one."

"Yes," he said, "and I would have offered it anyway, even if, say, *someone* had given me your identity on his very first day here." His eyes found Tom. "It infuriates me seeing such skill go to waste."

Tom just stared at him. He couldn't get his head around to the fact that he'd been protecting Wyatt from Blackburn for *no* reason.

"Go to my office, Enslow. We'll draw up a schedule."

"Sure. Okay. Sure." Wyatt scurried past him. She broke into a flat run for the door.

Blackburn waited until she was out of the arboretum and then he turned on Tom and Vik. They both remained rooted in place. Vik gazed after Wyatt, like he wanted to flee, too, but couldn't make himself move.

"Mr. Raines, if I were a lesser man, I'd rub this moment in your face." He considered that. "Actually, I am a lesser man. This must be a very bitter moment of realization for you. You could've avoided that entire ordeal your first day in class. Couldn't he have, Mr. Ashwan?"

Vik snapped to attention. "Sir, yes, sir!"

Tom gaped at Vik. The traitor.

"Thatta boy, Ashwan." Blackburn leaned toward Tom and pointed at Vik. "That's a smart kid who's going to go somewhere. Learn from him." With that, Blackburn turned and left them in the arboretum.

As soon as he was gone, Tom shoved his hands into his pockets and turned on Vik. "'*Sir, yes, sir*'?" He imitated Vik's earlier words. "Why didn't you offer to clean his office while you were at it?"

Vik shrugged, not the least bit embarrassed. "At the end of the day, he's our superior officer, and I wanna be a Combatant someday. Admit it, Tom, so do you, too." He reached out and clapped his shoulder. "It's over. He won. Just think: no more covering for Wyatt. Life's going to be easier."

TOM SPENT A few days deeply suspicious that Blackburn was just luring Wyatt into a false sense of safety before springing some nasty surprise on her. But soon it became apparent that all his trouble to protect Wyatt's secret had truly been for nothing.

Wyatt began working in Blackburn's office three days

a week, reformatting old neural processors, then she began spending dinners telling them every painfully tedious detail about it.

"It's interesting to actually use Zorten II on a processor," she told them while they ate. "I can see why it would get overwhelming, reformatting all the neural processors on his own. They design the processors so you have to reformat directory by directory to erase all the info on them—"

"What do you mean, you're reformatting old neural processors?" Vik cut in, digging into his chicken pot pie.

"They're from all those adults who died in that first test group. After they died, the processors were cut out of their heads"—Vik began choking on his food—"and then they get reformatted and stuck back in our heads."

"They use refurbished neural processors on us?" Vik sputtered, when he caught his breath.

"Yes," she said, blinking at him, as though she couldn't grasp why he was horrified. She picked up her glass of water and weighed it thoughtfully in her hand. "But it's really okay. They've been completely wiped clean. Can you imagine if they hadn't been? You'd get a neural processor with someone else's personality stored there."

Tom looked up from where he'd been wolfing down his meat loaf. "That can happen?"

Wyatt nodded. "Once you get the neural processor, your memories start getting stored on there instead of inside your brain. So I guess a part of you actually gets stored in the neural processor. Blackburn told me it's how they scramble Yuri." She darted a quick glance at Yuri where he was zoning out over his salad. "They have some malware in him that downloads scraps of memory from other neural processors and jumbles what he's hearing with them. That's why he understands some things, but not others."

Tom glanced at Yuri, with his glazed eyes, a bit disturbed even thinking about what was going on in his head.

"Blackburn showed me one of the brains, too," Wyatt went on. "It was one of the adults who survived almost three years with the processor because they gave him a bunch of epilepsy drugs. Once you look past the frontal lobe and the limbic cortex, you see the rest of the brain's atrophied. It looks like a shriveled husk."

There was such a look of horror on Vik's face that Tom started sniggering.

"Wyatt, food," Vik said, gesturing to the punctured crust in front of him, trying to get her to stop talking about this while he was eating.

"Tummy troubles?" Tom asked.

"Die slowly, Tom." Vik glared at him as he shoved a forkful of pot pie in his mouth.

Wyatt waited for Vik to start chewing again. "Maybe not a shriveled husk. More like ground-up shiitake mushrooms."

Vik choked again.

"Actually," Wyatt added, "I think the brain belonged to the person who used to have *your* processor, Vik."

Vik spat out his food.

Wyatt smirked. "Just kidding."

"You're an Eviler Wench every day," Vik accused her, tossing his napkin down on his meal, giving up on eating.

Yuri roused from his stupor as Vik said that. "That she is," he said adoringly.

Ever since he'd admitted to liking Wyatt, Yuri had begun sounding her out, trying to gauge her feelings for him, and repeatedly hinting about his crush. Tom and Vik found the whole thing comically fascinating, seeing Yuri try to yawn and put his arm around her in class, and clueless Wyatt then complaining that he was taking up her space. Yuri tried to ask her to a movie, and Wyatt told him the movie he suggested sounded dreadful.

It took Yuri a whole week to score one victory: he finally managed to convince her to go out with him to a museum. Unfortunately, Wyatt didn't even seem to get that it was a date, because she asked Tom and Vik if they were going, too.

"Sure, we're going," Tom told her, just grinning shamelessly at Vik's warning look. They'd made a bet about when Yuri would finally manage to get somewhere with Wyatt, and Tom was going to lose if it happened this soon.

So when the following Saturday came, they were tailing a few steps behind Yuri and Wyatt in the Smithsonian.

"It doesn't count if you sabotage them," Vik informed Tom as they passed the caveman exhibit.

"Come on. They sabotage themselves."

"He's going in," Vik proclaimed, grabbing Tom's arm to halt him.

They ducked behind a mock saber-toothed tiger, out of sight of the two. Wyatt was staring fixedly at a woolly mammoth skeleton, and Yuri was staring fixedly at her. Resolve filled Yuri's face. He leaned down, reaching out to draw her into his arms, and Wyatt turned at the same time and smacked her forehead into his.

Tom burst out laughing. Vik's hand clamped over his mouth to muffle the sound.

Wyatt's voice rang in the air. "Ow! Why'd you have to head butt me?"

Tom fell down, laughing so hard he was suffocating. He couldn't get to his feet. He couldn't. He was going to die, going to choke to death on smothered laughter. Vik hauled him from the room and let Tom fall down again. Then he staggered away, waving for him to stop laughing. Then he fell down, too.

"That was so"—Vik gasped, when he could manage it—"It was just so *Enslow*."

Tom clutched his ribs where they were starting to hurt. "Just pay up now, Vik. Save your dignity."

Museum visitors were starting to stare at them. Vik hoisted himself to his feet. Tom lurched to his feet, too, his sides aching.

"I am not surrendering, Raines. Yuri might go for it again. Double or nothing, the Android gets his hands on Man Hands by tonight."

"You seriously wanna pay me double? The only base Yuri's getting to is—" Tom stopped talking.

Wyatt was standing just in the doorway, staring at them, her face deathly pale. The smile dropped from Vik's face, and Tom suddenly felt like the biggest jerk in the world.

She cast a stiff look back toward where Yuri was and then looked back at them.

"I get it," she said. "I suspected something when you guys started inviting me places and telling me to sit with you in the mess hall. I get it now. I suppose this is some real funny joke, isn't it?"

Tom blinked. Wait, she thought they were *all* having her on?

Yuri emerged from the room behind her. "Wyatt? I must explain myself."

Wyatt spun around and shoved him back. "Go away!"

Yuri's face filled with hurt.

"Find someone else to make fun of with your friends!" She turned around and stormed from the room.

Tom stood there frozen for a moment, and Yuri rubbed at his bruised forehead, staring helplessly after her. Vik looked at

Tom, then mouthed, "You?"

Tom let out a breath. "I've got it." He turned around and headed out after Enslow.

HE CAUGHT UP to Wyatt outside the museum, where she stood on the sidewalk, reaching up to scrub her sleeve across her face. Tom would never have imagined her as the crying type, and he really felt like the scum of the earth.

"Hey, come on, Wyatt. Don't cry."

She jumped. "I am not crying! I have allergies." She started for the Metro stop, and Tom tailed after her.

"You can't just leave, okay?"

"I'm not stupid." She tore around to glare at him. "I know people don't like me. I just thought Yuri . . . I just thought *you* were different."

"Yuri is different. He's a good guy. And me, I don't . . . I'm not . . . Come on, okay? Vik and I are just jerks. We didn't mean anything by the bet thing. We were just messing around. Yuri's got no idea, okay? It's not like we were all setting you up. You've gotta know he's into you."

"Me," she echoed flatly.

"Yeah. You've gotta see it. He wouldn't even help us go after you in the war games."

"I don't believe you. Yuri doesn't see me that way. Even Vik calls me Man Hands."

"That's just a thing we humans call a joke. Vik gives most everyone nicknames. Again: me, Vik—jerks, got it? It doesn't mean every guy in the world thinks the same thing. You're supposed to turn it around on us, anyway. Like, maybe tell Vik he only thinks that because his hands are delicate and girly. That's how it works. Anyway, I've never heard Yuri say

236

it. I bet he thinks you have girl hands. I mean, have you seen that guy's?" He raised his palms. "They could envelop people's heads."

She finally stopped walking, seeming to consider it. "So what am I supposed to do now?"

"Just go back and, I dunno. Talk to Yuri. And don't hit him? Or something?"

"What about your bet?"

Tom rubbed the back of his neck. "Do you like Yuri? If it's no, you might as well break it to him. If it's yes, well, I'm out thirty bucks. No big deal."

She shifted her weight and took a few deep breaths, like she was bracing herself for something. Then her dark eyes moved up to Tom's. "Do you think I should be with him?"

"I can't tell you that."

"But you can. Do you think that he's really the one I should go out with? You bet against it. Was there a reason for that?" She was looking at him with an odd intensity. Tom stared back, bemused, and her cheeks grew pink. "I don't want to make a mistake, that's all," she mumbled, looking at the ground. "I just don't want to do the wrong thing here."

"Wyatt," Tom said with a laugh, and he reached out to poke her shoulder. "It's not like you're marrying the guy."

She turned very red, and jerked back from him. "Fine. Fine, I'll just go tell him yes, then. Okay?"

Tom watched her hurry away, wondering why she looked so sulky about a guy wanting to ask her out. If he ever found out some girl liked him, he'd be all over her.

CHAPTER FIFTEEN

TOM DIDN'T HEAD back to the museum. He figured it would be better to give Wyatt and Yuri a chance to do whatever they were going to do. If he knew Vik, he would probably stick around just long enough to make sure he'd won, and then head out to find Tom and rub his victory in his face.

So Tom loitered on the curb, chin propped on his hands, elbows on his thighs, waiting for Vik. He was caught off guard when a limo slid to a halt in front of him and a voice called from its plush depths: "Tom! Tom Raines. Hi, there!"

Ugh. He knew that voice.

He raised his head up. "What are you doing here, Dalton?"

"I heard you were in the area. I've been waiting for you. Now get in here." Dalton gestured Tom into the limo.

"I'm busy."

"No, you're not. I've been waiting for you too long already. Come on."

"What do you want?"

"Don't be rude. I went to the trouble of having Karl Marsters check the location of your GPS signal," Dalton answered. "I really wanted a chance to talk to you. Now get in."

The driver circled around to open the door. Tom reminded himself that Dalton was with Dominion Agra. He couldn't blow him off.

He glanced toward the museum—no sign of Vik yet—and then dropped into the backseat and slouched down, hands in his pockets. "I can't go far."

"Not a problem." Dalton nodded to the driver, and soon they were heading off down the busy Washington, DC, streets. He poured himself some brownish liquid, then offered Tom the bottle. "Scotch?"

Tom shook his head. "Not allowed."

"You think they'd kick you out of the Spire for this? I know they've got rules, but one word from me to them, and they'll look the other way."

"I don't like alcohol." Even the smell of it made him nauseous.

Dalton eyed him knowingly. "Reminds you of that old man of yours?"

Tom's hands curled into such tight fists his fingers throbbed. He imagined breaking that glass over Dalton's head.

"Well," Dalton said, waving as though to move them on from the subject, "we've already had a chance to speak once, Tom, about the possibility of Dominion Agra sponsorship down the road."

"Yeah, and I don't get it," Tom cut in. "I'm a plebe. Not even a Middle. I'm nowhere near CamCo level yet."

"These things start earlier than you think. Dominion has dawdled with courting Combatants in the past, and regretted it when the other companies jumped all over them. We've decided to start securing the bonds of loyalty earlier in the process."

Tom suddenly understood it. He laughed. "So let me get this straight: once someone's about to be a Combatant, and they have a choice of sponsor, they don't tend to choose you guys, do they? Huh. What do you think turns them off, Dalton? You as Dominion's sales guy, or the whole genocide thing?"

Dalton's hand clenched tightly around his glass. "Believe me, we could have more Combatants tomorrow if we wanted, Tom—but we want the *right* ones. The ones who wow us. If we started working with someone while he was a plebe, for instance"—this was spoken pointedly—"we would have more than enough time to groom him into the refined, polished Combatant we're looking for."

"Refined and polished. Like Karl Marsters."

Dalton actually winced. "Karl is another issue entirely. And as for that other *charge* you made . . ."

"You mean the genocide thing?"

"What happened in the Middle East was hardly genocide."

"Last I checked, killing a billion people's genocide."

"Genocide is the systematic destruction of another group of people because of their nationality or their race. It's malicious. What we did was not. The entire region was engaged in the willful and repeated theft of our property—because, like it or not, if you eat it, it's our property, and the farmers in those countries were never going to agree to pay a licensing fee. If one region of the world gets away with that, then everyone begins to think they can get away with it, and soon we have no company. There was no malice in what we did. It was simply a business decision to keep Dominion Agra viable."

"I'm sure the dead people are glad they weren't killed maliciously."

"And we even acknowledge that it was a terrible tragedy. We regret that they made it necessary even to this day. But think of what came from it: that area of the world was so contentious, there never would have been peace on this planet if it hadn't been for those bombs. We haven't lost a single human life in war since we neutralized that region. Those neutron bombs made today's world possible."

"Yeah, of course no one goes to war anymore," Tom exclaimed. "There's no alternative when the Coalition owns everyone in power. And no one's going to take you on if they're just going to be wiped off the planet."

"That sounds like your father talking."

"No, it's me. It's me saying—" Tom realized it suddenly. "It's me saying no. No way. I would never, ever help Dominion Agra. Even if it was the only chance I had to be CamCo, I wouldn't do it." He looked at the city street sliding past, realizing that some things were just too profoundly wrong. He also realized they were farther from the museum than he'd expected. "Let me out, Dalton. The answer's no, and it's final. We're done here."

"Don't be ridiculous, Tom. I'm not here to ask you to decide today."

"Yeah, well, I've decided today."

"Fine." Dalton raised his drink to him. "You've decided today. But this meeting isn't about what you can do for us. It's about what we can do for you."

"There is nothing in the world you can do to change my mind."

"Of course. Of course. Just take a look at something. That's all I'm asking."

The limo slid to a stop. Dalton waited for the driver to come back, as though opening a car door was too lowly a task for him. Tom jerked open the door himself and clambered out. Dalton rose behind him, then left the door open for the driver to close. They were standing on a shaded street, the humid air clinging to the lush trees around them. Tom could see the dome of the Capitol Building looming in the distance.

There was an unmarked door to a derelict building. It had a sign hanging on it: SECURITY ON PREMISES.

"Come on, Tom." Dalton tapped the sign. "This means it's open today. When Beware of Dog is up, it's closed. Very suburban middle-class, eh? Our private joke."

Ugh. That was it. He wanted to be gone.

Dalton dipped into the stairwell and his footsteps echoed down. Tom looked around the street, but he didn't see a Metro stop or even a taxi. He let out a breath and slogged down the stairs after him. He'd take one look at whatever Dalton wanted to show him, then he'd get a ride straight back to his friends.

The farther downward they walked into the guts of the building, the more doors they passed through and the nicer the stairs became. They went from creaky old wood to marble, the doors from scuffed plaster to carved oak. At the bottom of the staircase, Dalton leaned in for a retina scan. The wall panel lit up, and a steel portcullis creaked up to let them into the room beyond.

They emerged into a vast chamber with a polished glass bar, a vast screen on the ceiling and walls projecting an image of a sprawling green landscape, and scattered tables with privacy alcoves encircling them, the shadowy forms of people conferring within them.

Dalton encompassed it all with a wave of his hand. "This is the Beringer Club, Tom. This is where the elite come to relax in Washington, DC. The political class, members of the Coalition when they're in town, foreign ambassadors, and those world power players you may not have even heard of. Essentially, the top one percent of the top one percent. And you're welcome to come here now. As a recruit for the Spire, you have a Challenge Coin, don't you?"

Tom delved into his pocket and pulled out the coin stamped with US Intrasolar Forces.

Dalton tapped it with an elegant finger. "This is your access pass here. Whenever you want to come here, you can feel free. Anything you want here, you can ask them to secure and I'll foot the bill. It's on me. Consider this the first of many chances to mingle with the right people."

"I'm more of a wrong-people type of guy," Tom remarked, glancing around. Signs directed people toward luxuries offered by the place: a sauna, tennis courts, a spa, and other stuff Tom was not the least bit interested in.

He turned to tell Dalton this, but then caught sight of the VR panel on a distant wall.

Dalton chuckled. "Ah, and that, of course. Those are for children of US congressmen. We get a few from the Spire here sometimes. That's why there are private rooms with VR access. Even neural processor ports."

"What? I can hook in here?"

"Some of Camelot Company come here all the time. They like the privacy. Every transmission in the Spire is monitored. Rather cramps your style if you're, say, meeting a girlfriend or exploring certain sims." He leaned closer, leering. "I remember being a teenage boy, after all."

Tom got the implication and didn't appreciate the seedy smile on Dalton's face. *This is the guy dating my mother,* he thought, disgusted.

"And you're setting me up with this out of the goodness of your heart?"

"That's right," Dalton answered. "I like to think an act of generosity begets another."

In other words, he wanted Tom to come here, rack up a debt, and feel obligated to pay it back, probably with interest. Tom glanced back toward the access port room. He supposed it might be useful having some nonmonitored means of hooking himself into the internet, but he didn't know. Something about this place gave him the creeps. Between the lack of windows, the shadowed forms speaking in muted voices within the privacy alcoves, and the steel bars of the portcullis, it struck him as something much more malevolent than a club for rich guys.

"All right, thanks for showing me. I'm gonna head back up now."

But Dalton waved down one of the large employees of the joint, a guy with a crew cut and huge neck. "Hayden, can you show Mr. Raines the private neural access port? Then he'll want a ride back to the Pentagon."

The man, Hayden, nodded.

Tom, irritated, followed the large man. "I don't need a ride. I can find the Metro."

The big man stepped aside so Tom could go into the private neural access parlor. Tom gave it a cursory glance. Yeah, it was nice. Nicer than the Spire with its makeshift cots—here they were reclining loungers that he'd bet cost a regular guy's yearly salary.

"It's great. Now I'd better—"

But Hayden was moving forward, his sheer bulk making Tom stumble into the room. He was like a walking wall or something. And when Tom tried to shove away from him, he found himself being manhandled toward the recliner.

"Wait, wait," Tom bellowed at the man, fighting his grip. "What are you doing? Let me go!"

Dalton appeared in the doorway over his shoulder. "Do you need another pair of arms, Hayden? I can call someone over."

"I've got him." Hayden squashed Tom into the recliner so hard he couldn't breathe. And then a meaty grip bruised his chin before Tom could jerk his head away. Tom kicked out at Hayden and it felt like kicking a wall for all the effect it had. Something familiar poked at the back of his neck. Then the wire clicked into his brain stem.

Tom's vision tunneled, sensation drained out of his limbs. It was like hooking in during applied sims, but Tom didn't sink into some other world. There was no sim running to slip into. The familiar paralyzing of his muscles, the dimming of his senses. Hayden flipped him onto his back. Terror clawed inside Tom's chest. What were they doing to him?

Hayden released him. Tom forced his eyelids open. "What's—what's . . ."

"Should I begin, sir?" Hayden's voice was low and rumbling.

"Get it ready," Dalton said. "The boy's being uncooperative, so work on that first. Some behavior modification to start." He leaned forward to see what Hayden was typing. "Yes, the primer. That one. That'll be about four hours?"

"Approximately. And that's all I'd recommend installing for now. You don't want him to disappear for too long."

"Fine. We can upload more when he's back in the Spire. I have someone I can use there. And be sure to plant a compulsion to return next week for another package of software."

Tom felt a spike of panic and tried to move, tried to lash out. He couldn't. "Dalton, what are you doing to me?"

Dalton pulled a cigar out of his pocket. "You always call me 'Dalton.' It betrays a lack of respect. From now on, it'll be 'Mr. Prestwick.'"

"Let me go, *Dalton*, or I'll kill you!"

Dalton lit the cigar, the point of light cutting through the dimness. Wheels squeaked over to Tom's side, someone rolling in a chair for Dalton. He settled down by Tom's side and crossed his legs. "No need to panic. This won't hurt." A negligent shrug. "Or so I'm told."

"Why are you doing this?" Tom strained to see Hayden where he was typing something in. Something that was going to end up in his brain. The thought made him ill. What were they going to stick in him?

Dalton chuckled. The smell of his cigar seeped through the air. "Come on, son. Did you think I was giving you a choice here? Did you really? Are you so naive?"

Fury boiled through Tom. He'd murder Dalton. He would. As soon as he could move. "Let me go or I'll jam that cigar down your throat!"

"You'll be let go. You'll be released very soon. And you'll be a much better boy when you are. You've got a lot that needs changing if you're going to work with us."

"I am not working with you!"

"Quiet, Tom. And I assure you, you are. It's very lucky you've become a valuable asset. And I know there's someone in the Spire advancing your interests, because General Marsh has already put your name before the Defense Committee as a promising trainee to keep an eye on."

Tom was too stunned for a moment to remember he was terrified.

"Now, we'd never ask you to represent Dominion Agra with those qualms you have about our company." Dalton tapped on Tom's forehead. "So Hayden's going to install some data to correct a few of the misguided views you inherited from your old man. After that, you and I, Tom? We're going to be good pals when this is done."

"No, we're not."

"Oh, we are. And hey"—a light, teasing punch to his arm—"if we're behind you, you're guaranteed to be Camelot Company, and we'll make sure it happens fast. You'll get to be a real hero. Think of the girls. You've never had a girlfriend, have you? They'll be crawling all over you."

"Shut up. Just shut up."

"The first batch is ready, Mr. Prestwick," Hayden said.

No, Tom thought, real fear mounting in him. *No, no, no.*

Dalton chuckled. "Give our boy his lesson."

And then the information poured into Tom's brain. Dalton lounged in his chair, smoking that cigar, watching Tom's face as the programming interfaced with the neural processor, then began implanting the data into Tom's brain. Tom fought it. Gritted his teeth and fought it, rejected it. At first. At first.

And then he couldn't tell what was supposed to be there and what wasn't. And he didn't know what was his and what wasn't. The terror receded over the horizon and his fight died away. His gaze drifted up to the ceiling, the gentle wash of commands and code sweeping over him again and again, and he couldn't remember why he'd been so afraid a minute ago. He lay there feeling his brain being reworked.

Dalton watched him the whole time, gazing at his face as Tom shifted into another person.

After an hour of it, Hayden spoke. "The first layer's installed."

Dalton rose to his feet. "Is it? Good work. And that's a good boy, Tom. We're going to be real friends soon, you and me. Aren't we?"

Tom answered him, "Yes." He was confused about what was going on but pretty certain that Dalton was right.

"It's Mr. Prestwick."

"Mr. Prestwick."

"That's my boy." Mr. Prestwick patted Tom's cheek. "I'll see you next Saturday."

TOM WASN'T SURE why Hayden had shown him the neural access port. He stood there by himself, in the middle of the empty room in the Beringer Club, staring at the access port. There was something he was missing. Something he couldn't put his finger upon.

"Mr. Raines, sir?" Hayden peeked his big head inside. "Your car is waiting outside whenever you're ready."

"Oh. Okay." Tom felt dumb. He didn't even know where Mr. Prestwick had gone. He must've left after telling Hayden to show him this place. And the internal clock in his head said it was 1700. Had that much time passed?

Something inside him shut down the line of thought.

Restricted Access.

The thought resounded in his brain, forbidding.

Restricted Access. Restricted Access.

A hollow formed in his chest as his thoughts slammed into that phrase, as he realized he couldn't access a segment of his own brain. But even as he struggled to fight his way around it, his short-term memory faded and he couldn't quite recall what put the cold feeling in his chest.

He emerged up the staircase into the wash of sunlight, and found himself thinking of Mr. Prestwick again as he headed to the private car. Maybe he hadn't been fair to him all this time. He'd mindlessly hated him, and Tom couldn't think of why.

He remembered the smell of Mr. Prestwick's cigar. . . .

Restricted Access.

What? The words were like an electric jolt, something

foreign inside his own brain. He stared inward, aghast.

Tom's fears faded along with the recollection, and his brain was again wrapped around a harmless thought. Neil always talked like Dominion Agra set out to destroy every natural-growing crop with their genetically engineered, self-terminating strains. But they hadn't. It was an accident. It happened because Dominion Agra's crops were better. It was an accident that they ended up owning the entire human food supply. Simple cross-pollination. Sure, they may have played a role in the neutron bombings, but didn't they save billions on a daily basis by feeding them? And maybe they forced everyone to pay a yearly usage fee to grow crops, but wasn't that good business?

Tom was giddy with the beautiful sense he could suddenly make of so much he'd once hated about the world. He settled in the private car with the blacked-out windows. The Beringer Club was really something. The driver already knew he'd be returning the following week, as though the guy had psychic powers or something, and Tom found himself agreeing to get picked up at the Spire the following Saturday at 1100.

Tom settled back into the comfortable leather seat and spent the whole ride back to the Spire marveling at the idea that maybe, maybe Dalton Prestwick was a great guy after all.

CHAPTER SIXTEEN

WHEN TOM RETURNED to Alexander Division, he found that Vik had already been to their bunk and left a note on Tom's bed: *I suppose you fled to avoid the shame of defeat, but you're going to pay up, sucker! Victory parade will be downstairs.*

Tom braced himself for the face rubbing soon to follow and swung by Beamer's room to see if he could get him out of bed for dinner.

"Beamer, want to—" Tom stopped.

Beamer's bed had been stripped of covers. Right now, Olivia Ossare was packing up Beamer's belongings in a suitcase: a couple journals, a picture of his girlfriend, some civilian clothes.

"Where's Beamer?" Tom blurted.

"Hello, Tom."

"Where is he?"

Olivia folded her hands and settled on the edge of Beamer's bed. "Do you want to sit down?"

"No." Tom stayed where he was. This was change. He'd just gotten used to the idea that things could stay the same for weeks on end, and now it was all going to get messed up again. He realized suddenly that he didn't like change.

"Stephen's having a very difficult time right now. He's going to be evaluated for a few days to see whether he needs help."

"So why are you packing up his stuff?"

Her eyes flickered. "It's probably going to be more than a few days."

"Is he as crazy as Blackburn now?"

Olivia made a sound, like she'd almost laughed and caught herself. "No. Stephen's suffering from some anxiety. We've given him time, but he's just been getting worse and worse. It's time he left here and got some real help."

"So what's going to happen? Can't they do that thing where they grow some new brain matter for him? Wouldn't that fix him? I read about that somewhere."

Olivia zipped up the suitcase. "Tom, neural grafting is only used sometimes, when for some reason brain matter is deficient in the frontal lobe at birth. It's for sociopaths, psychopaths, the brain damaged. Beamer doesn't need that." She propped the suitcase up on its side. "I can't guarantee you he'll be back here, but I don't think you should worry about him. He hasn't had the neural processor for very long. Worst case scenario, he'll have a phased removal and go back to his old life."

Tom stepped back into the hallway of Alexander Division, feeling like a hole had opened up inside him. There really was nothing firm, nothing certain. Even here, even at this place where he thought he'd found something permanent, everything could change in a day. Everything could be lost so quickly.

He found Vik, Yuri, and Wyatt downstairs and broke the news to them.

Yuri was too intent on holding Wyatt's hand, and Wyatt on enduring the hand-holding to really give thought to Beamer. Only Vik seemed to hear Tom's bombshell. He nodded, unsurprised.

"Guess it was inevitable. What did you think when he started skipping classes?" Vik pointed out. "You can't do that and get away with it."

"They're not punishing him, Vik. They think he's crazy."

"Look, Tom." Vik scraped his hand through his hair. "Beamer's a great guy. He is. He's funny and he's laid-back, but sometimes that's a problem, too. He came here, and what did he do? People would cut off their arms to be here. Literally would cut off their arms if they could get the chance to do what we do. And what did Beamer do with it? He went online to meet his girlfriend. He binge downloaded. He died as soon as he could in sims, in Calisthenics."

Tom stared at Vik, feeling like he didn't know him. "You're acting like he deserved this."

"I'm saying, maybe he wasn't supposed to be here in the first place. Maybe he was a lousy fit. You remember all those psych test we had to do, all those screenings before coming here?"

Tom looked at Vik, Yuri, and Wyatt. What tests? Why were they all nodding like they knew what tests these were?

"Beamer should've realized then that this was serious business," Vik went on. "Maybe he finally realized it."

The words didn't make Tom feel any better.

A STRANGE SENSE of wrongness nagged at Tom throughout the following days. He couldn't put his finger on it, but he felt out of place. Sometimes something—a puff of smoke in Applied Sims, the steam in the shower room—triggered a memory of the Beringer Club, but always, those words popped up,

Restricted Access, followed by the dissolution of the memory from his consciousness.

But the sense of something missing remained. He found himself retreating more often to his bunk, watching Medusa in the latest battles of the war. They were the only things that kept the sense of strangeness away. He thought often of their fight outside the walls of Troy and Medusa's strange smile as he died, and just wondered what would happen the next time they met.

It could be years until he was Camelot Company, if he ever made it. It could be years until he faced Medusa in a real fight.

Tom decided it: he couldn't wait years.

So he snuck onto the officers' floor. He was clever about it. Wyatt told them at lunch that she and Blackburn were going to spend the evening in the basement with the Spire's primary processor, configuring the reformatted neural processors for the network.

"How long does that take?" Tom asked her, making sure to sound offhand.

"Three hours. Maybe four."

Three hours was more than enough time for what Tom wanted to do. When Wyatt disappeared down to the basement with Blackburn, Tom set his GPS signal to the router he'd gotten from Wyatt, left the router in the bathroom, and then headed upstairs to the officers' floor. This time he didn't go to the staff room, since anyone could come in there.

Only one person could interrupt him in Blackburn's office, and Tom already knew where he'd be for the next several hours.

He hooked himself into the neural access port on Blackburn's desk and tried to ignore the way his heart was suddenly slamming against his rib cage. He could do this. He'd done it twice.

He focused upon the neural processor, the buzz in his brain, the connection to the Spire, and it happened again. He jerked out of himself, fused to the Spire's network. He let himself drift that way, his brain melding first to the satellites and then to those ships near Mercury and then to Stronghold Energy's palladium mines. And back, he caught onto that stream of data leading to the Sun Tzu Citadel in the Forbidden City.

Through his consciousness, they flickered, the IPs of neural processors hooked into that network. He flipped through the directories, taking it all very deliberately, reminding himself every few seconds that he was a *he* not an *it*, a person and not one of those vast streams of 0s and 1s pressing in on all sides of him. . . .

And then that IP registered, the same one the Spire's databases logged as belonging to the Combatant Medusa: 2049:st9:i71f::088:201:4e1.

He flashed between his own body—that cold, numb thing slumped in a chair—and his consciousness in the foreign network. The net-send function in his neural processor triggered with a thought, and he locked onto Medusa's IP just as it buzzed in his consciousness. Then he took the biggest risk of his life:

You dragged me through the dirt and killed me. I seek to avenge myself. Yours, the Deranged One. He enclosed the URL for his favorite VR sim dueling site and deposited it right there in Medusa's neural processor.

Tom snapped back to himself, his body tingling all over with shock at the audacity of what he'd done. His hands were slick with sweat, his heart still pounding wildly in his chest. Had it worked? Had she received it?

There was only one way to find out.

He logged onto the internet and went to that URL, preparing himself for what might be a long, futile wait. His vision changed. Stone walls resolved into life around him, nooks set with rippling torches. Someone had already set up a duel, which meant Medusa was already here.

Tom started laughing, giddiness washing through him.

This was really happening. This was happening.

He shifted, and felt with surprise the rippling muscles across his skin. The neural processor was taking the ordinary parameters of the video game and interpreting it in three dimension for him. He looked down at his body. An information bubble registered the identity of his character: *Siegfried, a legendary hero with unbeatable strength.*

"I think you have a question to answer."

The woman's voice was deep, resonant. Tom whirled around to face her. The tall, muscular blond woman stood on the other side of the vast stone chamber, a curved basin with a fire between them. Her pale face flickered in the leaping flames, an information bubble identifying her for him: *Brunhilde, a legendary Valkyrie who was forced out of Valhalla. She was queen of Iceland and the mightiest warrior in the world, apart from Siegfried, her true love and the one man capable of beating her.*

Tom laughed. He couldn't help it, because no guy would pick these two characters. "I knew you were a girl in real life. I knew it."

She didn't take the bait. "How did you slip a message into my neural processor?" she demanded, prowling toward him.

"Net-send function. Your neural processor's got it, too, or you wouldn't have received it. It's kind of cool. You can type something out or even *think it out* and it'll get sent along. Typing's way easier, though." He'd tried the thought interface to send a message to Vik, but a bunch of stray, unrelated things that passed through his mind completely garbled the message. He dared not risk that with Medusa.

She considered that. "So you directly accessed that program in my neural processor. That doesn't answer my other question. How did you get past our firewall?"

"Maybe I'm just that awesome," Tom suggested.

"That's no answer."

"I'd die before telling you." He hoped the words would get her in a fighting mood.

They did. "Oh, you'll die," Medusa agreed. "Again."

Tom gave an exultant laugh, bared his character's pikestaff, and charged. Siegfried was powerful enough to leap clear over the flames in the fire pit. He hurtled down toward the blond woman. As soon as his pikestaff met her sword, both weapons blazed into twin columns of flame.

Tom reared back a step and lifted his pike to admire it. "Fire weapons. Awesome."

"I use this site a lot. I programmed the add-on."

"It's great."

"Thanks." Medusa slashed at his throat.

It was the reverse of their other fight: he was stronger, she was more agile. He managed to swat her sword right out of her hand, but the power behind his blow unbalanced him—and she hiked herself up on his shoulder and used him to vault clear across the fire pit.

"Nice, Medusa." Then Tom kicked the basin toward her, upending the burning sparks.

To his delight, the flames caught on a tapestry, and Medusa seized it and hurled it at him as he closed in again. The pain stole his breath, and it was followed by a dagger thrust to the ribs. He caught her before she could escape and twisted at her neck, trying to snap it. He saw her hands scrabbling on the castle's table, beneath the burning wall, and then close upon a candleholder. Tom tried to wrench her neck again, and she slammed the candlestick between his legs.

The pain was terrible. Tom doubled over, gagging. He felt it like it was really happening. He suddenly wondered if hooking in to face her was a mistake.

Medusa danced out of arm's reach as he collapsed to his knees.

His voice came out choked. "You . . . are . . . a girl."

Her sword flashed in the firelight. He could hear her cackling laughter.

"You have to be. No guy would resort to that!" Tom added.

"Never denied it." Medusa was haloed by flames climbing up the wall behind her. They were beginning to sting his throat. He heaved in frantic breaths and tried to reach for his pikestaff—but she kicked it out of reach, and her sword pressed against his throat.

"Why did you really message me?" Medusa asked him, eyeing him over the blade.

"For this."

"Just so I could kill you again?"

Tom gave her a slow smile. "No, so I could kill you." He kicked her legs out from under her, pinned down her sword arm, and was halted by a dagger to his throat.

"The next time you have a death wish, don't hack my processor," Medusa told him. "Someone might track you."

"I'd risk it," he pledged.

"I wouldn't. I'll send you a URL for a gaming message board. It's safer that way. I'll keep an eye on it, so if you post something there, I'll be happy to come kill you."

Tom imagined the post. *"Deranged one seeks fearsome warrior?"*

"Try, 'Hideous beast,'" she finished for him.

Tom regarded her over the point of her dagger, wishing he could see her real face, wishing he could tell if she was really going to follow through on this. "You sure you'll check?"

"I'll check," she assured him. Then she slashed his throat.

TOM OPENED HIS eyes in Blackburn's office, blown away. She'd agreed to meet him again. She'd actually agreed. He rubbed at his throat, where the skin stung with the memory of that sword slash.

He became aware of a blinking in his neural processor, and his blood froze.

He'd set the alarm to track Blackburn's GPS signal in the Spire, and to go off if Blackburn returned to the eleventh floor. He'd been too immersed in the fight to notice it. His heart jolted in his throat, because Blackburn was stepping out of the elevator now, and Tom didn't have time to flee down the hallway.

He hurled himself under the desk just as the door slid open.

". . . and you'll want to try any new programs on a simulated neural processor first." Blackburn's heavy footsteps moved into the room, followed by Wyatt's lighter ones, and the doors slid shut behind them. Tom felt sweat break out on his forehead. He pressed back as far as he could under the desk, his heart hammering. This was not good. Not good at all.

Blackburn circled around so Tom could see his boots less than two feet away. The desk rumbled as a drawer was yanked open. If Blackburn stepped back just a bit, or leaned over to root through another drawer, he'd see Tom.

He heard Blackburn shuffling through the drawer. And then he must've found what he was looking for, because the desk rumbled as the drawer slid shut again.

"Here, work with this one, Enslow. Initiate a program just like you would normally. It'll give you all the information you need about how the person's processor and physiology would be reacting to your coding. It's a safe way to experiment so you don't have to use other trainees as guinea pigs. Oh, and here's something else that might help."

There was a loud smack on the desk that made Tom jump. He looked upward, wondering what it was.

"A *cognitive science* textbook?" Wyatt's voice rang out.

"Yes, yes, I know it's a bother having to read the pages one by one—"

"I don't mind that."

"No, you don't, do you?" There was an appreciative note in his voice. "Well, the military sees no need to offer this in your upload feed, however much I've tried to convince them people with computers in their brains should learn something about those brains, not just the computers. Some of the research in here is outdated, so I crossed those sections out. But read it. This book got me started. It's a clear, understandable primer. If you want to learn to program the way I do, you have to start by learning the human brain."

Blackburn settled into his chair, his knees at level with Tom's head. Tom flattened himself against the back of the desk and scrunched his legs up to his chest to avoid Blackburn's boots kicking him. The air was split by the crackling sound of old textbook pages being turned.

"'The dopamine hypothesis of schizophrenia,'" Wyatt read. She was quiet a second, then said defensively, "It flipped right to this page. I didn't mean to open it to that."

"It opened right there because I looked at that chapter almost every day for a year. That's where I started. The first time I reprogrammed my processor, I was trying to control the dopamine. It turned out, I needed to do a lot more than that, but it was a first step."

"You just experimented with your own brain like that?"

"I had nothing to lose. My mind was gone, my career was over, my wife—" He stopped abruptly.

Silence hung on the air. Tom could practically sense Wyatt working herself up to asking something. He knew her that well by now.

"What's being crazy like?" Wyatt blurted.

Wyatt, don't, Tom thought, wincing, certain Blackburn was going to make her sorry.

Blackburn didn't answer her for a drawn-out second. Tom could hear his fingers begin drumming on the desk. "It really depends, Enslow. What's being tactless and completely inappropriate like?"

The question seemed to catch Wyatt off guard. "Oh. Oh! I'm sorry." Her footsteps thumped over, and there was a squeak as she settled in the other chair. Tom hoped they weren't getting ready for a long conversation. "I don't try to be rude," she said. "My mom flew in her old pageant coach to live with us one summer and teach me all about how to talk to people but eventually, she just told me I should try not to talk when anyone's around."

Blackburn gave a reluctant chuckle. "Fair enough." His legs stretched out, his boots settling an inch from Tom's hip. Tom leaned awkwardly to the side, away from them. "'What is being crazy like?' At the time, it felt like I was having one long moment of insight."

"Like when you get the neural processor and you just *know* some things you didn't before?"

"Much more powerful than that. I felt like my thoughts could burrow right through the layers of reality and see the way everything was truly interlinked. At the time, I thought it was the processor giving me this understanding of the world. I tried sharing this new perspective, but people disregarded me. It was the most frustrating thing you can imagine. I began to suspect they were willfully ignorant. Then I grew convinced they were plotting against me. I was delusional, but I believed I was the single sane one in a world gone to madness. I began to see everything I'd once believed in, as they say, 'through a glass, darkly.' And even now, even after all this time . . . there are things that can't be unseen."

A heavy silence settled in the air.

"Any more awkward questions you want to get out of the way?" Blackburn prompted. "Let's do this now. I told you that trust is the most essential thing I ask of you—and I'll make every effort to return it. Better to ask me now than ask someone else later."

"Um, well, with your face . . . People say you tried to claw it off when you were crazy."

He laughed.

"I figured that wasn't the reason you have those scars," Wyatt went on.

"These were just my ex-wife bidding me a fond farewell. With her fingernails."

"Oh."

"Is that it?" His voice was tense. After a moment of silence, "Good. And with that, Enslow, caring-sharing hour is officially over." He rose from his seat, and Tom was finally able to stop hugging his knees to his chest. He heard Wyatt's chair squeak as she got up, too.

"I actually do know better than to ask about something like that," Wyatt blurted out.

They were moving toward the door. Tom leaned his head back against the wood behind him, relief swamping him. He'd get out of here unseen, after all.

"Then maybe there's some hope for you yet. Come on, now. Those processors aren't going to configure themselves." The door slid open and closed again.

Tom waited a minute to rise from beneath the desk, until he was sure Blackburn's GPS signal was back in the basement. Then he bolted safely out of the office and back into the elevator.

Consciousness initiated. The time is now 0000.

Tom had been asleep for two hours when his eyes snapped open. This never happened. He never woke up in the middle of the night.

He gazed into the darkness, confused, wondering why he was awake. He heard Vik's heavy breathing on the other side of the bunk. He threw off his covers and rose from the bed without quite knowing why he did it. His brain pulsed with the need to get out, get out into the hallway.

Tom followed it, but once he was in the hallway there was no relief from the restless feeling. He needed to leave Alexander Division, and that was off-limits after 2300, but Tom did it, anyway. He emerged right into the common room and stood there in the darkness.

What am I doing here? What am I doing? he wondered.

And then a door slid open to another division. Karl Marsters filled the doorway to Genghis. "Come on," he said, and didn't wait for Tom to plod over before heading into the hallway.

Tom scrambled after him to make it through the door before it slid back closed, even though his brain was exploding with disbelief. What was he doing? What was this?

Karl headed up the stairs to the upper-level floors of Genghis Division. He opened the door to an unoccupied bunk and Tom followed.

"All right, come on, already, Fido." Karl snapped open a case and pulled out a portable data chip attached to a neural wire.

Tom looked around. "I don't know why I'm here."

"Yeah, I got that. Take the bed. Facedown."

Tom's heart pounded harder and harder. He stretched out on his stomach, even though every instinct he had railed against the idea of this. Karl could beat him up if he wanted to, and Tom had no grounds for explaining why he was in Genghis Division on the wrong floor after lights-out.

"I was pretty mad when they said you, of all people, were gonna work with Dominion," Karl said. "That's my gig, right? But I've gotta say, it cracked me up when I found out you said no. I'm gonna love watching them neuter you, Fido. You think you're such a tough guy, don't you? Yeah, we're gonna see once you've got all these programs crammed in your brain. A few weeks from now, you'll be a vegetable."

From where he was sprawled on the mattress, Tom gritted his teeth. He'd never hated Karl so much.

"I don't want that," Tom managed when Karl approached with the wire.

"Too bad. Nighty night, Lassie." Karl clicked the wire into his brain stem.

CHAPTER SEVENTEEN

SATURDAY MORNING, THE private car arrived at 1100 and took Tom to the Beringer Club. The sign read SECURITY ON PREMISES today. Tom headed down the stairs, pressed his Challenge Coin against the retina scanner, and headed inside.

The big guy, Hayden, was there. He led Tom to a table where Dal—*Mr. Prestwick* was already nursing a scotch. The man surveyed him, gestured him into a seat. "Go ahead and order lunch, Tom. We're going to meet a few others with the company."

The menu blurred before Tom's eyes. He couldn't concentrate on it.

"Did Karl give you the update?" Mr. Prestwick asked.

"Oh, I sure gave it to him." Karl slouched down into the seat across from Tom's and planted his elbows on the tablecloth. "You buying us both lunch, Dalton? I was surprised you hadn't invited me. I had to pay for my own taxi. I think you owe me one."

Mr. Prestwick eyed the newcomer with what Tom would swear was distaste. "I was going to show Tom to a few of our people. I think our behavioral modifications have really made a difference."

"I'll say!" Karl laughed and snapped his big fingers in Tom's face. Tom jumped, but nothing leaped to his lips. "Got nothing clever to say right now, do you, White Fang?"

Exasperation stole into Mr. Prestwick's voice. "Karl, please."

"Yeah, sorry." Karl grinned viciously at Mr. Prestwick. "I just wanna say, whatever you're sticking in him, I like it."

"We're trying to cultivate a suitable public persona for the Combatants we sponsor. Dignified, respectful, polite." Mr. Prestwick spoke this pointedly, but from the oblivious smirk on Karl's face, the large boy didn't seem to realize Mr. Prestwick was speaking of him, too. "*Tom* seems to be responding very well to the reprogramming."

Reprogramming. They'd been reprogramming him. The vague, murky wrongness of the last several days began to take form in his head, began to make sense. Tom suddenly understood just what was happening, yet he couldn't seem to translate the thought into action. He found himself staring at the portcullis, the steel bars that could be jammed into the ground like a cage. He could get up and walk out, close that behind him. Then they couldn't catch him. He needed to use his arms and legs and do it. And his brain needed to agree to let him do it. He could escape, and tell someone. . . .

His brain halted him with a thought, utterly foreign: *That wouldn't be a good idea. Mr. Prestwick's generously given me his time and attention. Why would I leave?*

And Tom couldn't escape. Couldn't budge. Mr. Prestwick smiled at him and he smiled back. But the two impulses—escape and compliance—warred in his brain. He still hadn't managed to tear his thoughts from the conflict by the time the waiter came by, so Mr. Prestwick put in an order for him. Salmon.

Karl jabbed his thumb at Tom. "He's got a huge problem with authority. That's why he didn't order something the way you told him to."

Mr. Prestwick brushed him off. "It will be fine, Karl. We have this under control."

After lunch, Mr. Prestwick took Tom around the room and introduced him over and over as "our newest acquisition" to various executives with Dominion Agra and its partner companies. And Tom shook the hands, and spoke when spoken to, because he couldn't seem to ignore the urge to conduct himself in a way that would do credit to those who had taken the time to invest in him.

One man Tom recognized as Yuri's visitor in the Spire. Mr. Prestwick halted Tom with a hand to the shoulder and whispered hastily in his ear, "That man is Joseph Vengerov. He's the founder and majority shareholder of Obsidian Corp. That makes him a very important person. Show him your utmost respect."

If Tom could've, he would've done everything he could to disrespect Vengerov, simply to spite Dal—Mr. Prestwick. But instead he stayed silent as the light-haired man with pale eyebrows looked him over, then remarked in an accent that sounded like upper-crust British mixed with something else, "And how is this project coming?"

"Very well," Mr. Prestwick assured him. "The software's taking well. It's everything you said it would be. I think we'll be sending much more business your way in the near future. I'm sure we'll find other trainees who'll suit us."

"As long as you do your research. What of this one? You're certain you thoroughly combed his background before the install? I told you, there will be a marked personality change, and I'd rather avoid a public lawsuit."

Mr. Prestwick shrugged negligently. "Karl assures me that Raines's contact with most of the officers is so limited, it's nonexistent. No one will notice. As for that fellow who works on their software there—"

"James Blackburn, yes."

"Outright adversarial."

Vengerov shook his head. "Blackburn was never my concern. He's quite easy to neutralize, if you push the right buttons, and the boy's programmed to do exactly that, if necessary. What I want to know about is the family situation. I know about the mother, naturally. What about the father? Will he make trouble for us over this?"

Mr. Prestwick laughed. "It's what, mid-afternoon on the West Coast? His old man's still lying in a pool of last night's vomit somewhere. Isn't that right, son?" He clapped Tom's back.

Tom looked at him. A mental image of gouging out Mr. Prestwick's eyes passed through his brain, then the repressive voice in his head: *Mr. Prestwick is my friend. Mr. Prestwick is always right. Public displays of temper don't become me.*

Mr. Prestwick's hand squeezed on his shoulder. "Isn't it right?"

Agree with Mr. Prestwick.

Tom choked back the words that wanted to come up. Never. He would *never* say them.

"Well before, he was—" Mr. Prestwick began.

Vengerov held up a finger, eyes like a hawk's on Tom. "This is a critical test of the software. Make him agree with you."

Mr. Prestwick turned back to Tom, grabbed his shoulder again. "Isn't it right, Tom?"

Tom's teeth ground together so hard his jaw ached. Vengerov and Mr. Prestwick both watched him closely, and that voice in his head commanded, *Agree with Mr. Prestwick.* He felt like something was squeezing his skull, crushing it.

"Isn't it right?" Mr. Prestwick said, voice hard.

AGREE WITH MR. PRESTWICK.

"Yes, he probably is," Tom said. Then he felt a sudden, insane relief like a vise had stopped squeezing his head.

Vengerov nodded crisply, then shook Mr. Prestwick's hand. "My people will call yours with the bill."

"Always a pleasure to do business with you."

Soon after that, Tom was sent back to the private neural interface for his next packet of software. He passed right by the portcullis, mere feet away, and couldn't seem to tear his gaze from it as he headed to the private neural access room. Then he hooked himself in to receive more and more programming in his brain.

THE NEXT FEW times Tom met Medusa, he did it in free hours using a VR parlor in the Pentagon City Mall. He couldn't bring himself to sneak into Blackburn's office or the officers' lounge again, because for some reason, there was this voice in the back of his head warning him, *Don't draw attention to yourself. Don't attract Blackburn's attention. Don't break rules.*

It was foreign, and sometimes made him feel a bit ill whenever he heard it, but he couldn't seem to ignore it without that feeling like his head was about to be crushed. And as soon as he thought about something else, he couldn't even remember the voice was there.

So he didn't hook in. He just logged in from a VR parlor

and faced her in regular video games, missing the full fighting experience. But he stopped caring as they fought in one sim after another. She always beat him. It was always close, too— there was one move she made that he didn't, one moment she was faster than he was.

Medusa wasn't a big talker, and Tom liked fighting more than talking, so they didn't get much use out of the computerized voices the first couple of times. But then they began using voice chat, and the taunts started. Tom never won the games, so he started rubbing his small victories in her face. ("Aw, look at that! You thought you were going to shoot me. But hey, at least you killed that frightened villager, instead.") She started rubbing her large victories in his face. ("Oh no, where did your head go? Maybe it got tired of not being used?") Sometimes they lingered after the battles, talking about what had happened. ("If I'd just ducked, I'd have had you. I had a dragonslayer ax." "No, because I was waiting for you to duck, and I had a dagger ready.") Then sometimes, the talk strayed to the real-life battles Medusa fought.

At one point, when Tom started rambling about Medusa's victory on Titan, Medusa asked Tom whether he was stalking her.

"I am," Tom admitted. He even owned up to watching her battles 394 times.

Strangely enough, his honest admission that he was unhealthily obsessed with her made her like him more, and let her own guard down. She started speaking in her real voice, so he started responding in his real voice.

And Medusa? Yeah. She was definitely a girl.

"What time is it there?" he asked her one Saturday morning, just so he could hear her speak again.

"Five in the morning, obviously."

Tom knew that was a stupid question. They knew each other's time zones. He didn't care. "When do you sleep?"

"When I'm not stomping you and your country."

Tom laughed. He was suddenly certain she was the most awesome person he'd ever encountered. "I had a six-year winning streak until I met you." He adjusted the microphone so she could hear him over the background buzz in the public VR parlor. His avatar was a muscular blue ogre with a samurai sword that doubled as a phase gun.

Medusa's avatar was an Egyptian goddess with retracted, batlike wings and eyes that shot fire. "I had an eight-year winning streak when I met you. And I still have an eight-year winning streak!"

Their characters were idling in the exploratory phase of their RPG. She'd been pestering him to make up a call sign, since his avatar's name, Murgatroid, wasn't doing it for her. Neither was the nickname he suggested, "the Troid."

"I've got one," Tom told her. "Merlin."

Medusa didn't like that. Her Egyptian queen turned into a large bat that flapped across the room, like she was going to leave. Tom's ogre leaped up to block the window and stop her escape. She transmitted a sound wave of loud booing and shot some fire from her eyes.

Tom's ogre threw up his beefy arms to shield his face. "What's wrong with Merlin?"

"Too Camelot Company. You said you're not in Camelot Company."

"What, you want me to come up with a name that's anti-Camelot? That's treasonous, isn't it? It's betraying my country to be anti-Camelot."

The bat fluttered around his head. "Isn't this treason right now? You're meeting with the enemy."

"It's not like I'm giving you confidential info. And besides, we're both meeting with the enemy here."

"Well, look, it's not that bad. It's not like we're going to go fight in real life tomorrow."

"Why don't you tell me what my fake call sign should be, then? It's not like it counts for anything."

Medusa transmitted the booing again. "You have to come up with your own call sign."

"I've got a great one. Lord JOOSTMEISTER," Tom joked. "All in caps."

Fire blasted from Medusa's eyes. She didn't like that one.

Tom leaned back in the chair to avoid the flames. "How about Sir Roostag the Mighty and Free?"

She considered that one a second. Then, booing.

"Okay, okay. Serious one. Exabelldon."

Medusa zinged his ogre with the fire from her eyes. Tom's ogre bellowed, and Tom laughed.

"Now you're trying to make up the worst names imaginable," Medusa said.

"Fine, fine." Tom had been trying to do just that. "How about . . . Mordred? He destroyed the real Camelot."

Applause answered him. Medusa poofed back into an Egyptian queen and stopped trying to fly out the window or zing him with flames.

"Fine," Tom said. "Mordred it is."

Her Egyptian queen fluttered her long black eyelashes. "Mordred is a sexy name."

Tom's cheeks grew hot, like there really was some girl in the room teasing him. "You think so?"

"I know so."

Tom was still remembering that exchange, when he headed back to the Spire that night. She'd called him sexy. He felt like an idiot, standing there in the middle of the mess hall, grinning about something said by a girl whose name he didn't even know. And then he found himself meeting Karl's gaze across the crowded room, and the massive Genghis nodded his head toward the elevator.

Karl disappeared into it but held out his hand to keep it open. Tom followed without deciding to. A sense of doom crashed over him during those few, agonizing steps to the elevator. Even though he knew something was very wrong here, he couldn't stop himself from going inside and then walking behind Karl to an empty bunk in Genghis Division.

"We've done this before," Tom realized as the door slid shut behind them.

"We sure have. More than once. And this?" Karl waved a neural chip tauntingly. "Is your last personality update, Benji."

"And then?"

"Then some of the software that's already been installed gets triggered, and bam, you're gone, Lassie. The little punk I know and hate is wiped. The best part is, I get to be the one to do it. I owe Dalton for this big-time."

Tom stood there in the middle of the bunk, watching Karl set up a video camera, and felt like he was going to be sick. He wished suddenly that Vik or Wyatt or Yuri were nearby— anyone to stop this. He'd even take Blackburn.

Karl flipped the camera on, trained it on Tom, and then settled back in a chair. "Any last words, Fido?"

Tom's blood pulsed up in his ears. "Drop dead, Karl."

"That's not very nice. Kind of hurts my feelings, Raines. How about you make it up to me? I know. You can get on all fours like a good little dog, and bark."

Tom closed his eyes. *Listen to Karl and get your update* warred with *Disembowel him. Disembowel him now.* The vise around his head was back because Karl was telling him something and he was trying his hardest not to listen.

"Drop. Dead. Karl," Tom choked out, fighting everything inside him trying to force him down.

"No, get on your hands and knees, and bark. Do it, Raines. Do it right now so I can film it." Karl leered at him over the camera, his jowled face shadowed in lamplight. "You think I don't get you? You wanna be the big man in charge here. You think you're the alpha dog. But you're not. *I* am. So you're going to do this right now before I eradicate you."

"I hate you." Tom's limbs trembled with the dual effort of trying to force himself back out the door while something else tried to force him down on all fours.

"I hate you, too," Karl said. "Now hands. Knees. Bark. Consider it an order."

Something about that sequence of words did it, and then Tom was on the ground, barking, while Karl's laughter filled the air around him. By the time the wire clicked into his brain stem, that second voice in his head had already fallen silent from the sheer horror of it all.

CHAPTER EIGHTEEN

"**W**HAT IS WITH you?"

"What do you mean?" Tom said to Vik. He was gazing into his new mirror in his bunk, very intent on gelling his hair before morning meal formation. It was long enough now that he could do something with it. Mr. Prestwick had given him a credit card and instructions to go clean up, starting with a two-hundred-dollar bottle of hair styling cream so he wouldn't look like a street rat anymore.

He was trying very hard to ignore the way Vik was gaping at him, like he'd just walked naked into morning meal formation. "You realize you've been preening in front of the mirror for half an hour."

Tom frowned, then stopped, knowing frowns made people wrinkle, and it was important he protect his youthful good looks. "You've told me a dozen times you're hoping to make Camelot Company one day. Well, I hate to break it to you, but appearances matter if you want to get somewhere in life, Vik."

"Gosh, I'm sorry, Tom. Did you displace your Y chromosome somewhere? I hope it's not on the floor where someone might step on it." Vik made a show of looking around.

"I'm sorry you don't understand the value of presenting yourself in the right manner." Tom felt bad for him.

A few weeks ago, he'd have told the world Vik was his best friend. But Vik was getting weirder by the day. He kept treating Tom like he was a freak of some sort. He sniggered when Tom started exercising in the mornings before classes or when he was the first to raise his hand with the civilian instructors or when he volunteered to escort a committee of senators and business leaders on a tour of the Spire.

Tom didn't get what Vik's problem was. This was how a guy got ahead in life. He connected with the right people, conducted himself well enough to give a good impression, kept up his appearance, and leaped upon opportunities as they neared. That's what Mr. Prestwick said, and everything Mr. Prestwick said was true.

"I DON'T UNDERSTAND him anymore, Mr. Prestwick," Tom told him Wednesday night, when Mr. Prestwick took him to get fitted for an eleven-thousand-dollar Italian suit. Dominion Agra executives were holding a soiree on the following Saturday night at the Beringer Club, and after a month of downloads, Tom had been deemed ready to be introduced to everyone.

The tailor stepped out of the dressing room, and Mr. Prestwick occupied himself by flipping through a rack of designer ties. "Perhaps it's time you had new friends, Tom. They don't sound like the type of people we want around you."

"I like my friends."

"We'll see if you feel that way in a download or two."

"I don't want to lose them."

Mr. Prestwick strolled over to him. "Now, Tom, everything we're doing is for your own good."

"I know." Tom didn't know why he knew that, but he was sure of it. A strange giddiness washed through him with that certainty.

"Then you know better than to question me. Try this on."

Tom took the tie. He looked it over. He could call up references to sixty different types of knots, but there was nothing in his neural processor about tying a tie.

"Ah, of course. Never bought a suit with your old man, I wager. Here we go." Mr. Prestwick looped it around his neck, then tied it into place, standing in a way so Tom could follow his movements in the mirror. He stepped back and surveyed it. "There. I think that's a good choice for you. Makes you look like you're worth something. Put it on your credit card."

They don't sound like the type of people we want around you. . . .

The words echoed in his head later, when Mr. Prestwick sent him a leather case with his next software update. He sat with the closed case in the mess hall, baffled by the strange urge not to hook it into his brain. He'd been updating himself for a couple weeks now. The new updates were small: manners, etiquette, suggestions for self-improvement. He knew it was a privilege that Mr. Prestwick allowed him to participate in his reeducation. He'd be abusing Mr. Prestwick's trust if he didn't download this.

Still.

He watched Vik and Yuri, in animated conversation with Wyatt near the entrance to the mess hall. He trusted Mr. Prestwick. Mr. Prestwick was always right. But his stomach churned at the very possibility he'd plug this in and eradicate everything that mattered so much to him a month ago. His first real friends. He felt sick at the very thought of losing them, but Mr. Prestwick had as good as told him that was about to happen.

A heavy footstep behind him. A hand clasped the back of his neck, and someone leaned down and whispered in his ear: "Go upstairs and use that, Old Yeller."

Tom sighed. "Yes, sir."

Karl strode off. Tom closed the case with infinite care, then rose to obey the command. Two pairs of hands on his shoulders shoved him back into his seat. Yuri and Vik slid dropped down onto the bench on either side of him, and Wyatt took the seat across from him.

"What was that?" Vik cried.

Tom frowned. "What was what?"

"You called Karl sir!"

"So?"

"Thomas Raines," Wyatt said, folding her hands on the table, very formal. "We feel it is imperative we discuss your recent conduct with you."

"Come on, Evil Wench," Vik snapped, "this is an intervention, not an excuse to start talking like a robot."

"Well, it's not an excuse for you to have such delicate, tiny hands, either," Wyatt retorted, glaring at Vik.

"What?" Vik said, confused. "What about my—" Then he shook it off. "Look, Tom, we've discussed this at length and concluded that in recent weeks, you've become an embarrassment to manhood."

"Not just to manhood," Wyatt said. "I'm embarrassed for you, too, Tom."

"All right, I'm not—" Tom said, shrugging off Vik's grip. He tried to rise, but Yuri shoved him back down.

"Sorry, Tim," Yuri said, regret in his voice. "Normally I would not push you around, but I must because you have become such a pansy."

"A pansy?" Tom cried.

"The Tom Raines I know," Vik said, "is not supposed to spend a half hour primping his hair. You're not supposed to call Karl Marsters 'sir.' And you haven't even been giving Elliot Ramirez crap in Applied Sims. He actually came up to me today and asked me whether you're depressed and need the social worker. Come on, Tom. *Elliot* of all people has remarked on the conspicuous absence of your spine!"

"Elliot's misreading the situation, and so are you—HEY!" He saw Yuri examining the leather case that held the neural chip, and snatched it from his grasp. "That's mine. You should respect other people's property! And as for Karl"—he turned on Vik—"it may have escaped your notice, Vik, but he's a member of CamCo. He outranks us. He deserves our respect. That's why I call him 'sir.' If I remember correctly, you talked to me about this exact same thing the last day of the war games."

"I was talking about Lieutenant Blackburn, not Karl!"

"Do you even hear yourself, Tom?" Wyatt said. "You're being weird and very creepy."

"I am not being weird or creepy. And you are *no one* to lecture me about being weird and creepy!"

Yuri gripped the back of Tom's neck so suddenly, Tom gasped.

"You do not talk to her like that," Yuri warned him, and Tom was suddenly aware of how much larger the Russian guy was than him.

"Yuri, it's okay," Wyatt said.

Yuri released Tom.

Tom rubbed the back of his neck, trying to gauge his chances of escape.

"I think Lieutenant Blackburn should give you a system scan," Wyatt said. "There might be some worm in your processor, messing up your personality."

Tom clutched the case closer. "Ludicrous. Absolutely ludicrous."

"Ludicrous" wasn't a word he'd ever used in his life, but it was among an array of eleven possible responses that jumped into his brain as responses to any accusation regarding neural tampering. The next action his processor suggested was flight, removing himself from the situation.

Tom rose to do just that. "I think I've heard more than enough," he began, but Yuri shoved him back down with a murmured apology about the "pansy" thing. "What is wrong with you people? You can't keep me here against my will. This is assault! Consult the regulations in your neural processors if you don't believe me."

"That's it," Vik announced. "New approach."

He whapped Tom across the back of the head hard enough to jolt his vision.

"Hey!" Tom cried, rubbing his head. "What are you doing?"

Vik nodded. "You need another." He raised his arm to hit him again.

Yuri grabbed Vik's wrist. "I do not like this approach."

"He needs a clobbering!" Vik ripped his arm from Yuri's grip. "Maybe it'll jar him out of this!"

"Maybe you—" Tom stopped before he could threaten, "need a clobbering." Because public displays of temper did not become him.

"Maybe I what? Maybe I what?" Vik spread his arms, the crazy-eyed look back, his grin gigantic, challenging.

Tom glanced around at the other trainees in the mess hall. "Maybe you should calm down. You're drawing a lot of attention to us."

Vik groaned. "Ugh. That's pathetic, Tom."

Tom looked between the two guys flanking him, at the girl perched across from him, and saw exactly why Mr. Prestwick thought they were a bad influence. They were all wrong. Dead wrong. They didn't understand that nothing was the matter with him. He was learning, that was all. He was *improving*.

And if they didn't understand that, then Mr. Prestwick was definitely right about them. He needed to be done with them forever.

Tom remained jumpy long after his intervention. He kept opening and closing the case with the neural chip, knowing this was the one thing that could fix him, that could prevent him from caring what they thought of him ever again. But whenever he looked at it, a feeling settled inside him—a low, churning sickness. The case burned in his grip and he wanted nothing more than to smash it for an absurd instant.

He was contemplating it again when someone overrode the lock on his bunk.

Vik! Tom stashed the neural chip under his pillow, and tore to his feet, ready for a confrontation. The door slid open.

It was Wyatt.

"How did you get in here?" Tom said, wondering how she'd busted through his lock. His voice died in his throat, because Lieutenant Blackburn filled the doorway, right behind her.

"Mr. Raines," he announced, pulling a neural wire from his pocket. "You're in luck. Ms. Enslow here wants to learn how to perform a system scan, and she volunteered you to be her guinea pig."

Tom's eyes flew to Wyatt's. She bit her lip, obviously a bit guilty about siccing Blackburn on him. He knew what this was about. She was using Blackburn to try to search his processor for that worm she'd accused him of having.

"Sit down, Raines. This won't take long. To start a scan, Enslow, you first open the—"

Tom interrupted him, "Sir, I don't want to be the guinea pig. I'd rather you chose someone else."

Blackburn gave a short laugh. "It's strange you think you have a choice here. Now be a good guinea pig and stop talking." He stuck the neural wire into the access port on the wall, the same one that always gave Tom his homework downloads, then gestured Wyatt closer to see what he was typing into his keyboard. "Start with the program I sent you . . ."

A warning beacon flashed in Tom's vision over and over again as they talked. This was an emergency. This was a disaster. He was supposed to avoid Blackburn's notice first and foremost. He had to stop this somehow.

". . . and you need to select the directories to include . . ."

"Wait!" Tom protested, interrupting Blackburn again. "You have to use someone else as a test subject. I've got somewhere to be."

"Where, exactly?" Blackburn said.

Tom tried to think of a place he might urgently need to be, but couldn't seem to come up with one.

"Oh, that must be urgent," Blackburn said sarcastically when he remained silent. "Well, you can afford to wait for twenty minutes more. The more you fight me, the longer this will take."

"I am not fighting you, sir."

"That's exactly what you're doing. Stop. Now."

Tom knew it suddenly: he couldn't win this. There was no avoiding the scan.

And maybe that realization was what triggered it, what activated something in the recesses of his brain. A backup algorithm written just for this situation.

He closed his eyes and found that there weren't eleven possible responses this time, not like there'd been at lunch. Only one word popped into his brain. Just one, but Tom knew—he just knew, somehow—that this was the only weapon he needed.

He opened his eyes again, armed and ready.

"I am not battling you, sir," Tom said to Blackburn's back, watching the lieutenant turn back toward him, irritated. "You see, if I was trying to fight you, you'd know it. I'd probably throw something out there about, I don't know, *Roanoke*?"

And there it was. The word sat on the air between them, and it had a strange effect on Blackburn. His face grew completely still and blank like he'd been carved into granite.

Tom waited, his heart pounding, uncertain what he'd done. He could see Wyatt's brow furrow, too.

And then Blackburn closed the distance between them so suddenly, Tom knew he was going to hit him. He threw his hands up over his face and backed up until he hit the wall. He opened his eyes to find Blackburn just inches away, gray eyes burning—his face inhuman with rage. He planted large, shaking fists against the wall over Tom's head.

"Digging in my personnel files, were you, Raines? *Were you, Raines?*"

Tom stared back at that twisted face so transformed by fury, it was unrecognizable. He managed, "No, not me."

Blackburn caught the implication right away. His eyes widened, and the realization seemed to wash all color from his face. Tom stayed there, plastered back against the wall, as Blackburn retreated one step, then another. He turned to Wyatt.

"*You*," Blackburn breathed. "It was you, wasn't it?"

Wyatt put the pieces together right away. "What? No! I never looked in your personnel files."

"You broke into that exact database," Blackburn said quietly. "Twice."

"But—"

"Tell me, was it a fun read? It must have been, if you spread it around to the other trainees."

"I wouldn't do that!"

"Then how does he know about Roanoke? I suppose he hacked the file himself"—fury filled his voice—"*with his astounding hacking skills*?"

"Please, I don't know how he got it," Wyatt insisted. "I don't even know what you're talking about."

"I've told you, Enslow, trust is everything. The day you start lying to me is the day I wash my hands of you."

"I am not lying! Please, sir, I'm not."

Blackburn stared at her for a long moment. The rage disappeared from his face, replaced with a strange, resigned look like he was closing some door on her. He left them without another word.

Wyatt stared after him, shell-shocked. Her arms were hugged around her body, and Tom could see from across the room that she was shaking. A wave of crazed relief flooded him. He'd come so close to disaster, thanks to her.

He turned to his mirror and smoothed his uniform back down, absolutely certain he'd averted something terrible, even if he didn't understand what it was.

"Why did he react like that, Tom?" Wyatt asked shakily. "What's Roanoke?"

Tom didn't have an answer for that. It didn't really matter, either. "I'd say it's the reason you never should have messed with me," he said coldly, looking at her in the mirror. "Now get out of my room."

1 1 1 1 1 0 0 0 1 0 0 0 0 1 1 0 1 0 1 0 1 0 1 0 0 1 0 0 1 1 0 1 1 0 0 1 0 0
0 0 1 0 1 0 1 1 0 1 1 0 0 0 0 0 1 0 0 1 1 1 0 0 0 0 0 1 0 1 1 0 1 0 0
0 0 0 0 0 1 1 1 1 1 0 1 0 1 1 1 1 1 0 1 1 0 0 1 1 0 1 0 0 0 1 0 1 0 0
1 0 1 1 0 0 1 1 1 1 1 1 0 0 1 1 0 1 0 1 1 0 0 0 0 0 0 1 0 0 1 1 1
1 0 0 0 1 1 0 1 1 0 1 1 1 0 0 1 1 1 0 0 0 0 0 0 0 1 0 1 1 0 1 0 0 1
1 1 0 1 0 0 0 0 0 1 1 1 0 0 1 0 0 1 0 1 0 1 1 0 0 1 1 0 1 1 0 0 1 0 1
1 0 1 0 1 0 0 1 1 0 1 1 0 0 0 1 0 1 1 0 1 0 0 1 1 0 0 0 1 0 1 1 1 1 0 0
1 0 1 1 0 0 1 1 0 0 0 0 1 0 1 1 1 0 1 1 0 0 0 0 1 0 0 1 0 1 1 0 0
1 1 0 0 0 1 1 0 0 0 0 0 1 1 1 1 0 1 1 0 1 1 0 1 0 0 0 0 1 0 0 1 1 1 0
1 1 1 1 1 0 0 1 0 1 0 1 1 1 0 1 1 1 0 1 0 1 0 1 1 1 1 0 1 0 1 1 0 1 1 0
0 1 0 0 1 1 1 1 1 1 1 0 1 1 0 0 0 0 1 1 1 0 1 1 0 1 1 1 0 1 1 1 1 0 0 0
0 0 1 1 0 1 1 0 0 1 1 0 1 0 0 1 0 0 0 1 0 1 0 1 0 0 1 0 0 0 0 1 0 0 1 0
1 1 0 0 0 1 0 0 1 0 1 1 0 0 1 1 0 1 0 1 0 1 0 1 1 0 0 0 0 1 0 1 0
1 0 0 0 0 0 0 1 1 1 1 0 1 1 0 1 1 0 0 1 0 1 1 0 0 0 0 0 1 0 0 0 0 1 0 0
0 0   1 0 0 1 1 0 0 1 1 0 0 1 0 0 0 0
1 0   0 0 1 1 0 0 0 0 1 0 1 1 1 1 0 0
0 0   0 0 0 0 0 0 1 0 0 0 1 1 1 1 0 0
1 1 0 1 1 0 0 0 1 1 0 0 1 1 0 0 0 1 1 0 0 0 1 1 0 0 1 0 0 1 0 1 0 1 1
1 0 1 0 0 0 1 1 1 1 0 0 1 0 1 1 1 0 0 1 0 1 1 0 1 0 1 1 1 1 1 1 0 0
0 1 0 0 1 0 1 0 1 1 1 0 0 0 1 0 1 0 1 0 0 1 0 0 0 0 1 1 1 0 1 0 1

CHAPTER NINETEEN

A T 0532 THE next morning, Tom was warming up for his morning workout when Yuri tapped on the door.

Tom stepped out, careful not to wake Vik, mostly because the very sight of the Vik filled him with a strange loathing right now. He didn't like Yuri any better.

He eyed the larger boy warily. Between the incident last night and his newest download, he was having trouble this morning remembering why he'd ever been able to stand any of these people.

"Ah, excellent, you are awake, Tim," Yuri said genially, as though he didn't even notice the loathing on Tom's face. "I've noticed you are now very concerned with physical fitness."

"Responsible people take care of their bodies," Tom informed him.

"Exactly. Just as I have always believed. So I am here to suggest we go running together."

Tom felt a sudden burst of suspicion. He didn't trust Yuri at all. "I prefer to run on my own, thanks."

Yuri nodded. "Ah, I understand. You worry you will not be able to keep up with me." He turned and started jogging.

Indignation exploded through Tom. Not keep up? He hurled himself forward after Yuri, matching him pace for pace.

Yuri was in better shape. He'd been running every morning for years, and Tom had only gotten into this in the last few weeks. But he gritted his teeth every time he began to lag behind, and charged after Yuri through the corridors and staircases of the Spire. Yuri dashed through the Calisthenics arena and then slid open the door to the weight room beyond. He headed straight for the weight bench. Tom vowed to match him pound for pound.

"I'll spot you first," Yuri said.

"No, I'll spot you," Tom growled.

"Fine. If you are too tired to go first, I'll be glad to."

"I am not too tired." Tom flopped down onto the bench.

Yuri slid weights onto the bar. Tom watched him add more and more.

"Er . . ."

"What, Tim? I was setting it at my usual, but perhaps this is too heavy for you?"

Tom gritted his teeth. "No. Maybe put on more." He regretted it when Yuri nodded.

"I'll do that." And he slid on more weights.

Tom bit the inside of his cheek, nervous. But he'd lift it. If he had to bust a few joints, he'd lift that bar.

But after Yuri helped him lift the bar from the bench, then released it to Tom's grasp, Tom's arms buckled and it took all his strength to stop the weight from crushing his chest. His arms shook as the bar sank down, then settled against his ribs.

"Okay, maybe not." Tom could barely talk, straining against

the bar, fighting for breath. "Yuri, a little help?"

"You will have to wait for that, Tom."

Yuri ducked out of his sight, and that's when Tom realized he'd been tricked. "Yuri . . . Yuri!" He began struggling to dislodge the bar, to get out from under it, but he was stuck there, trapped in place on the bench.

A new set of footsteps marched in. "Is he stuck?"

Wyatt.

"What—what—" Tom sputtered.

"He is stuck." Yuri's face appeared above his, scheming.

"See, I told you he'd be dumb enough to try to lift it," Wyatt said.

"What are you guys doing?" Tom snarled at them. "I told you—"

"Not to mess with you, right?" Wyatt bent down toward him. "You didn't really think I'd leave it alone after what you pulled last night, did you?"

"Let me go!"

"No. See, we're dealing with New Tom," she said. "We hate him."

He tried to thrash his head away from her, but Yuri clamped his hands on his cheeks to hold him still.

Tom spotted a neural wire in her hands. "What is that for?"

"I hoped Lieutenant Blackburn would debug you himself, but you stopped that, so I had to finish my program early. It's a firewall of sorts."

"The mother of all firewalls," Yuri said, admiration in his voice. "She programmed it."

"It's all coded in Klondike," Wyatt said. "It has some antivirus functions. It searches out rootkits, removes malware. Mostly my coding. It might have some problems I haven't found yet. If so, sorry, Tom, but you're still getting this."

287

"No!" Tom wasn't allowed unauthorized software. A warning beacon flashed in his head over and over again, electric jolts telling him not to allow this. "Stop!"

"Quickly, Wyatt," Yuri urged.

"You'll thank us for this," she promised, and clicked the wire into his brain stem.

Tom was half aware of Yuri lifting the bar back off his chest. His brain buzzed with the stream of codes searching for every last trace of Dominion Agra's software and behavioral modification. All the data implanted over the course of thirty-one days was neutralized, removed, and replaced with security subroutines. The procedure lasted forty-seven minutes. It took that much time for Tom to wrap his head around what was happening, what had happened.

Debug complete, flashed in his visual cortex and Tom opened his eyes. Yuri and Wyatt both straightened, their murmured conversation fading. They were both frozen stock-still, waiting for his reaction.

"Tom?" Wyatt ventured meekly.

"It's me." He sat up. "Actually me."

"I knew there was some software problem in your head," Wyatt cried. "What happened?"

"Dominion." His voice shook with fury. "I am going to murder Dalton Prestwick."

Comprehension flooded Wyatt's face. "That's the guy you saw parents' weekend, right? Your stepfather?"

"He's not married to my mom." Tom rubbed at the bruised skin over his chest. "He works for Dominion Agra. They did something to me." He felt like there was a furnace igniting inside him, his anger burning hotter and hotter. The nightmare of the past month flashed in front of his eyes.

Barking for Karl . . . trying on suits for Dalton . . . smiling and being polite to those Dominion Agra execs . . . agreeing that his dad was asleep in his own vomit somewhere . . .

Tom ripped to his feet and hurled a dumbbell, sending it crashing into an equipment rack. Yuri jumped to his feet, startled, when it all came crashing down in an earsplitting jumble. Wyatt just sat frozen on the weight bench.

Yuri's mouth hung open. "Do you feel better now, Tom?"

"No!" Nothing was going to be better. Not until he tore them all apart. Until he ripped Dalton's face off and clawed out Karl's guts.

Tom clamped his fists over the steel bar of the bench, feeling like he could break it apart with his hands. Fury pulsed through him, and his fingers tightened on it until they hurt. He was so angry he felt sick. So angry he—he didn't remember something. But then he did. He remembered it.

He released his grip on the bar, the shock of it clearing his head. He looked at Yuri.

"You called me Tom. You said it. Just now. You used my name." The implication raced through his brain.

The mother of all firewalls.

"Wyatt," Tom breathed.

Yuri sighed, and looked at Wyatt. She nodded stiffly.

"I have this firewall, too, Tom," Yuri said.

"I tested it on him last night." She folded her arms. "I had to see if it would neutralize sophisticated malware like Yuri's, so I'd know if it would work on yours. And afterward, well, I couldn't just take it away from him again."

"You unscrambled him," Tom said, shocked.

"He's not a spy," Wyatt said heatedly.

"I am not, Tom," Yuri pledged.

He must've seen the apprehension on Tom's face, because

his big, broad-shouldered body stirred uneasily on the weight bench.

"I was born in Russia, yes, but I have lived here many years now. I always wanted to be a cosmonaut, but no people go into space now. So when my father moved us here, I tried to join the US Intrasolar Forces in case that changed one day. My father's friend, he heard about this ambition and helped me come here . . ."

"Vengerov." Tom spat the name, remembering the man from the Beringer Club.

Yuri dipped his head, conceding it. "He has influence, because when my country began experimenting with neural processors, Vengerov defected with this technology to America. He helped develop the program, so out of friendship to my father, he was able to get me in here. I have always tried to be a good trainee. Even when I did not get promoted after two years, I stayed, and I tried harder. Why would I spy? It is one thing if I believed I was fighting for Russia, and you for America, but my parents, they are always saying this is not the case with this war. War is not about countries now."

Tom thought suddenly of what his dad always said. "It's about companies."

"Exactly," Yuri agreed. "So what is it to me who wins? It has never mattered."

Tom rubbed at his pulsing forehead. He wasn't sure what to think of this. He couldn't really think right now.

Yuri grabbed hold of Wyatt's hand, and she jumped, startled, like she'd forgotten for a moment that he was there.

"At least I know your name now," Yuri told her.

There was a wistful note in his voice that made Tom feel like a terrible person. Yuri saw everything now for the first time, and he knew his friends had gone along with it, too.

"Look, I'm sorry, man."

"To be very honest"—Yuri's gaze dropped to his fingers, linked with Wyatt's—"I almost wish I'd stayed that way. It was very strange to realize I did not know the names of any of my friends."

Wyatt stood there, rigid, for a few moments, then reached out and gave Yuri a few rough taps on his shoulder. Tom realized after a moment that she wasn't halfheartedly punching him, she was trying to comfort him.

"You can't tell anyone, Tom," Wyatt said severely. "Yuri and I would both get charged with treason."

"I won't. I owe you both."

"Thomas will not tell." Yuri leaned forward, his eyes gripping Tom's. "I know he will keep our secret."

"I would die before I'd tell anyone." And he meant it with every fiber of his being.

CHAPTER TWENTY

W HEN TOM STEPPED into his bunk, he had twenty minutes left until morning meal formation, and his brain was still a mess. He couldn't stop thinking of the video Karl had sent him, the video of him crouched on the floor, barking like a dog.

Tom settled onto his bed, the images of Karl laughing at him over the video camera and Dalton wreathed in cigar smoke burning his brain.

Vik stood by his bed, getting dressed. He threw Tom a sullen look, then turned away from him. "What, not gonna gel up your hair and make yourself pretty today?"

"Nope." Tom's chest felt like it was going to explode. He scrunched the bedsheets with his clenched fists, trying to think through the blinding rage that kept morphing and twisting into confusion and this bone-deep misery.

"See you later then, Spineless Disgrace to Mankind."

Tom saw Vik head toward the door, about to disappear back into the hallway. Despair crashed over him like a living force of its own. Out it came, one word: *"Doctor!"*

Vik halted, his shoulders drawing up like some alert predator. He turned, a strange gleam in his black eyes. "Doctor?"

"Doctor," Tom confirmed.

Hope leaped into Vik's face. "Seriously? Seriously, Tom?"

Tom nodded, and swallowed hard. "So as it turns out, some Dominion Agra people have been planting stuff in my head to make me a good little boy. I need vengeance. I need blood-vendetta, massacre-style vengeance."

Vik bellowed a sudden laugh. To Tom's shock, his roommate leaped forward and crushed him in a fierce bear hug before hurling him back down onto the bed. "Good to have you back!" Vik dropped down next to him. "So, vengeance, huh?"

Tom gazed bleakly at the wall across from him. "Vik, I'm supposed to see the Dominion Agra people on Saturday. I have until Saturday to figure it out. Vik, right now I can't even think of a revenge scheme that won't get me sent to prison for the next forty years."

"That's why there are two Doctors of Doom, buddy. Can't think? I'll think for you."

"Right. Right." Tom scraped his hands through his hair over and over again. He rose, fumbling in his drawer for his uniform.

"Forget that." Vik knocked Tom's drawer closed with his heel. "We'll skip morning meal formation. Tell me what happened. And then we'll plot some glorious revenge."

TOM AND VIK had the time of their lives in the days leading up to the Dominion Agra soiree. The first thing they did was check the limit of the credit card Dalton had given him. It was fifty thousand dollars.

Good little Zombie Tom was trustworthy enough not to abuse it.

Regular Tom was delighted to.

He convinced Wyatt to hack the credit card company's database and change Dalton's contact information so he wouldn't find out what Tom was doing in time to stop it. She didn't want to be party to credit card fraud beyond that, so Tom had to spend fifty thousand dollars without her help.

Vik nobly offered to help.

Tom put down ten thousand dollars for his father the next time he stayed at the Dusty Squanto Casino. Then he and Vik decided to have some fun of their own.

They spent an evening in the Pentagon City Mall, and made the acquaintance of a group of girls who were unimpressed with them until Tom paid for every purchase they made at the most expensive stores. The girls liked them after that. Then they took the girls out to dinner at Chris Majal's Indian Hall, and Tom left their waiter his first-ever thousand-dollar tip. He also treated everyone in the place to their dinners, too.

Then the girls found out they were fourteen and fifteen, and all the money in the world couldn't get them a second night out after that. Tom and Vik didn't care, though. There were other great things they could do with a ridiculous amount of money and very little time to spend it. They bought suits for some homeless people hanging around Dupont Circle. They played the most expensive VR sims that cost a few hundred bucks a pop. Friday night, they rented out a fusion club and arcade to put on the first ever Spire party, due to end thirty minutes before the 2300 weekend curfew.

Tom showed the bouncers a digital image of Karl. "If you see this guy, I have special instructions. First of all, bring him to the coat room."

"And after that?"

"Don't be gentle," Tom said, drawing out the words in vicious delight. "Then come get me."

The bouncer wasn't gentle. He called Tom over and pointed out Karl's unconscious body, sprawled on the floor. Tom swiped him a thousand-dollar tip just for that. Then he whipped out his portable data chip and neural wire, and set to work on Karl.

No one knew who was behind the last-minute party. Tom, Vik, Yuri, and Wyatt sat together on a table overlooking the rest of the club.

"What is the total now?" Yuri asked him, surveying their opulent surroundings.

"We've spent $47,912," Tom said. "If you think of something I can drop another two grand on tonight, let me know."

"Don't they suspect fraud yet?" Wyatt asked.

Vik laughed. "Yeah. The company's called three times now, but his retina scan and voice imprint checks out, and his name's on the card. Nothing Dalton Prestwick can do but . . ."

"Pay," Tom finished, relishing it.

It was Dalton's misfortune that he had no idea what was happening with his credit card, and he wasn't even due to get a statement for several weeks.

It was Karl's misfortune that he didn't hear who was behind the Spire party before getting in a limo with Tom the next evening at 1800 for their ride to the Beringer Club.

Tom grinned at the large boy as he piled into the other seat. He couldn't help it. He could see streaks of orange on Karl's rough skin where he'd tried to cover up the bruised face.

"Hiya, Karl!" Tom said, delighted. "Wow, are you wearing makeup? It looks real pretty on you."

"Shut up, Fido," Karl muttered.

Tom had gelled up his hair before flushing the rest of the stuff down the toilet. He'd donned the suit Dalton bought him, worn the tie, and as far as Karl was concerned, he was a nice little zombie. Tom had believed it would be hard, being civil, playing Karl's respectful, mindless underling, but it wasn't. His whole body thrummed in malevolent anticipation. He knew what was coming.

When they walked into the Beringer Club together, Dalton clapped eyes on them and demanded, "Karl, are you wearing makeup?"

It was all Tom could do not to crack up.

"Go wash your face," Dalton said.

Karl's cheeks flushed purple. "But—"

"Go! Before anyone sees you!"

Karl scrambled away.

Dalton's gaze moved to Tom. His eyes swept him up and down, like he was regarding a piece of property.

Tom went along with it, his blood boiling with malice, his face as calm as he could keep it.

"Tom, you know anything you do here reflects on me," Dalton said.

"Of course I know that, Mr. Prestwick." He was counting on it.

"So does anything Karl does, unfortunately, though I'd never have chosen him as one of our CamCo Members." His hand began to rub Tom's shoulder. "Try to keep him in line, will you?"

It was hard not to bust out laughing, just thinking of how Karl would react if he ever heard that. Tom suppressed it by biting the inside of his cheek. "Of course I'll definitely keep Karl from embarrassing you, Mr. Prestwick."

Dalton nodded appreciatively, his hazel eyes searching

Tom's. "Good. You're a good boy, Tom. You've made me proud. You've become a very respectful, polite young man."

Tom felt his nails digging into his palms. It was all he could do not to puke all over him.

"Karl, on the other hand . . ." Dalton gave a sigh. "His father was an exec here. We had to take him as one of ours. He was friends with Elliot, so we were hoping he might connect us with him. No help with that. Nobridis, Inc., snapped Ramirez up like hot cakes. So we were stuck with Karl. That is, until I acquired you. You've shaped up well, haven't you? I think I'll have a golden opportunity for you not so far in the future."

He patted Tom's cheek. Tom wanted to clamp his teeth down and rip some fingers off.

"Too bad Mr. Vengerov couldn't be here," Dalton lamented. "He'd be impressed to see the end result of his software. I think once the lot of you are public, I may have to slip some behavior modification into Karl's datastream, too. Just"—he winked—"some secrecy between us, eh, sport?"

Tom winked back. "Totally between us, Mr. Prestwick. Too bad about Mr. Vengerov."

Too, *too* bad. He would've loved to get that guy, too.

"Now, I've got some last-minute etiquette instructions, and a who's who guide waiting in the neural access booth. Go download that." Dalton paused, looking him over again, congratulating himself for destroying the old Tom and replacing him with this one.

Tom fought to keep the placid look on his face as he headed off. If he gave into his feelings, he'd end up leaping forward and ripping Dalton's face off, gorilla-style.

He shut himself in the private neural access room. He felt sweat break out on his forehead at the sight of the neural access port, but he knew this would be okay. It would be.

Wyatt had tweaked his firewall to higher levels to ensure he resisted anything he was exposed to tonight. He still felt a sick wave of apprehension when he contemplated the open port. It was hard to lift his legs, to force himself to stretch out on the lounger. His hand shook so much when he tried hooking himself up that he kept missing the brain stem access port.

Tom closed his eyes, took a deep breath, and tried to force his hands to stop trembling. God. He was *acting* like a pansy. At this rate, he'd need another one of Vik's interventions.

"Do it already. Plug it in, you coward," Tom growled.

He jammed the wire into the port.

The connection swept over him, his body going numb and senses dimming, lines of code rushing toward him, which almost sent him over the edge into terror until he felt them resound against Wyatt's firewall. He tuned into the process, because watching it made him feel better, seeing every line deleted as it was added, neutralized when it could not be by a few extra 0s and 1s. Tom relaxed. His expensive suit was plastered to his body with sweat.

Time ticked itself down as Tom watched, waiting for the moment he could yank out the wire.

And then it happened.

Text planted itself in his vision center:

You've stopped dueling me, Mordred. Have you finally realized you can never defeat me?

Tom stared at the text, shocked. Medusa. She'd used net-send. She'd figured out somehow how to hack in and drop something in his neural processor, the way he'd done to her.

In the last couple weeks, he'd completely stopped checking the gaming message board he used to arrange meetings with Medusa. It hadn't seemed like something worth doing, not while the Dominion Agra programs were jammed in his head.

He'd thought of it as a pointless, needless risk.

Now he felt a sick, swooping sensation, realizing how close he'd come to severing their connection.

Tom rolled up his sleeve, glad he'd brought his keyboard, and messaged back quickly, *Is that wishful thinking I see? I'll never surrender. How'd you hack my firewall, anyway?*

I'd kill you before telling you, she retorted.

That made Tom chuckle. *I will live to duel you another day, but I don't have time now. I am about to carry out an elaborate vengeance scheme. Everyone with Dominion Agra is going to have a really, really bad night.*

She didn't reply for a long instant. He wondered again how she'd hacked him.

What are your GPS coordinates? she asked finally.

Why?

Because I like revenge. I can help.

Tom began laughing suddenly. He couldn't help it. It was brilliant. *Yes, Medusa, I think you can help.*

CHAPTER TWENTY-ONE

A s the etiquette installation ceased, neutralized entirely by Wyatt's firewall, Tom knew it was time. He set about the elaborate scheme that he'd planned thanks to an idea of Vik's. Following the directions Vik had given him, he hacked straight into the city's central septic system.

"So at my primary school in Delhi, we played a prank, once," Vik had told him, and Tom thought the idea was sheer genius.

Now he isolated the system for the Beringer Club. There he stopped. Vik had given him a complicated sequence of coding, but Tom didn't even recognize this system. It wasn't like the schematic Vik showed him of the other septic tank.

He faltered, dismayed. And then he decided to try that thing *he* could do. The same way he'd linked to the Spire, to the satellites, to the security cameras. . . .

Tom gritted his teeth. Concentrated. Sensed the connection, sensed the elaborate system of codes and commands and algorithms controlling that machine. The electrical impulses in his brain sparked . . .

And he wasn't all in his brain anymore. His organic body grew distant. It was a cold, numb thing unlike the cortex controlling the wastewater for the Beringer Club.

Panic spiked through him in this disengaged state, because there was so much data, streams of code pulling him in every direction and he wasn't sure what he was—

Tom Raines. I'm Tom Raines.

And the thought saved him. Saved him enough to begin using that thing he had that no machine did. A will. He had a will and the machine only had a single, fixed program dictating its functions, and he seeded Vik's codes to alter its function. It all fell into place.

TOM ENTERED THE club for the first part of the show. He walked through the well-dressed executives, their pet US congressmen, their trophy spouses. He saw Dalton and Karl in conversation with Mr. Carolac, Dominion Agra's CEO, and headed over to them.

Dalton swept Tom into the conversation. "Mr. Carolac, this is him. Our newest acquisition. Thomas Raines."

Mr. Carolac was a sickly-looking man with bags under his eyes, and a grayish tint to his skin. He shook Tom's hand, looking him over. "I've heard a lot about you, Tom."

"I've heard a lot about you, too, Mr. Carolac." Tom smiled, aware that the Trojan he'd planted in Karl while he was unconscious last night was about to activate right . . . *now.*

"You and Karl are both making us very—"

Karl farted.

Mr. Carolac swung his watery gaze to Karl's, shocked.

Karl flushed bright red.

He farted again, a loud one that rumbled all the way across the room.

Karl's eyes widened and swung toward Tom, because Frequent Noisome Farts had to be flashing across his vision center, and only now did he understand what was going on.

"You!" Karl jabbed an accusing finger at Tom. "His programming's not working!"

Tom made a show of furrowing his brow, all cavemanlike, as Karl farted again. "I don't know what you're talking about, Karl. Don't blame me if you need a change of diet."

Karl took a menacing step toward him, farting with each movement. The stench mounted in the air.

Dalton seized him. "Karl, for God's sake, go to the restroom."

"It's not my fault. It's Raines! I'm telling you, he—"

"GO!"

Karl dashed through the crowd of silent partygoers. Everyone in sight had hands clamped over their noses at the ghastly smell pervading the air.

They didn't realize it wasn't Karl they were smelling.

It was the septic tank Tom had reprogrammed. Gallons and gallons of sewer water were pumping in reverse, filling the sinks, the toilets, soon to be overflowing on the floor.

Tom cleared his throat. "Well, that was just awkward." He gave a canned laugh, and looked at all the adults around him. "I'm going to fetch you ladies and gentlemen some drinks so we can pretend it didn't happen."

Mr. Carolac seemed mollified. "At least you got it right with one of them, Dalton."

"I have to apologize for Karl, sir," Dalton was saying as Tom headed off.

But Tom didn't go to the bar. He strolled out the door and

was beyond the portcullis when Karl began screaming from the bathroom about the sewage. Tom reached out and swiped the portcullis closed, and then modified its default password to a thirty-number password of his own.

Karl's shouts were followed by Dalton's, then by shouts from the other partygoers. The smell grew so nasty Tom fought back the urge to gag. He settled on the steps and watched the Dominion Agra execs through the bars. He listened to the cries of disgust as the sewage backing up in the toilets burst out of the bathrooms and seeped through the door into the club.

Mr. Carolac yelled at everyone to evacuate, and then when no one could get the mechanized portcullis open, yelled for someone to call technical support. Tom began to laugh. He laughed harder when he heard people shouting that their cell phones weren't working. That must be Medusa's touch. For a moment, Tom's mind was blown. She'd hacked in and disabled satellites. Satellites! He wasn't sure even Wyatt could do that.

Thanks, Medusa, Tom thought with a grin.

But apparently, she wasn't finished. Loud music began blaring. It wasn't music so much as a shrieking of metal scraping along metal from the speakers, ear-piercing and painful. Fists began pounding on the exits, hands yanking on the portcullis.

Dalton appeared between the steel bars, his turn at trying to yank it up. Tom swaggered into his view. Dalton spotted him, and seemed relieved. "Tom. Tom! Thank God, it's you. You're not trapped in here. Go outside and get us some help."

Tom dug his fists in his pockets and looked over Dalton's predicament with a long, lazy sweep of his eyes. "Hmm. I don't think I will."

Sewage seeped up around Dalton's leather shoes. Tom reveled in the shock on his face.

"Tom!" He hammered on the portcullis. *"Get us help right now!"*

Tom shook his head, eyes on Dalton's. He leaped down to the bottom of the stairs, his shoes squishing through the sewage bubbling across the floor.

"I might open it, Dalton." Tom leaned in close to the portcullis, staying carefully out of arm's reach. "You know, if you get on your knees and beg me."

"OPEN IT NOW, TOM!"

Tom shook his head, knowing he was grinning like a madman. Dalton's helpless outrage was so wonderful he couldn't stop himself. "No, Dalton. Get on your knees and beg me. Beg me to let you go. Otherwise you can stay there in the sewage all night. And your boss along with you." He made a show of scratching his head. "Gosh, what's he going to think of tonight? First Karl's digestive problems, and now this . . . Everything we do reflects on you, right?"

Dalton gaped at him, like he couldn't get his head around to his obedient little Tom turning on him.

"Your choice, Dalton. Now, even if you don't beg me, the sewage will stop backing up in about half an hour, so you won't drown. You'll have to endure the stench until someone out there realizes you guys need rescuing. And hey"—Tom winked at Dalton the way Dalton had earlier, like they shared an inside joke—"at least you've got an open bar."

"Don't you dare leave us!"

"Wrong thing to say." Tom swiveled around and sauntered toward the stairs.

"Wait, wait! Tom, please." A note of hysteria climbed into Dalton's voice.

Tom swung a careless glance over his shoulder but

didn't come back. "You're not on your knees, Dalton. I'm not negotiating that condition. I figure after a month of groveling to you, the least you can do is get on your knees for me."

"This is a twenty-thousand-dollar suit."

"That's not my problem."

Dalton stared at him, the music blaring from behind him, the stench of sewage thick on the air. Then he lowered himself to his knees in the muck. "Please open it." His face was set with hard, furious lines, his voice a whip of anger and hurt pride. "Please let us out, Tom."

Tom gazed at Dalton and thought of the smoke and the camera and how very close he'd come to being destroyed. "No." He headed up the stairs.

The screams followed him: "I'LL KILL YOU FOR THIS, RAINES! YOU'RE DEAD, KID, DO YOU HEAR ME? I'LL KILL YOU! YOU'RE DEAD! I'LL MAKE YOU SORRY YOU WERE BORN, I'LL—"

But Tom just headed up the stairs as Dalton's voice grew distant. When he hit the street, he made sure to lock the door behind him, and twisted the sign around to show BEWARE OF DOG so no one else would walk into the club and find the trapped Dominion execs.

Tom drove his hands into his pockets, kicked off the soiled leather shoes, and strolled down the Washington, DC street toward the distant dome of the Capitol. It was the time of year when the cherry blossom trees lining the concrete were blazing in full bloom. When Tom came across a fountain and dipped his head in, pink petals swirled into the gurgling water washing away his hair gel. He saw a vendor at a stand selling Washington, DC memorabilia to tourists. He traded the guy his eleven-thousand-dollar suit for a large "Made in the USA" shirt, American flag jogging pants, and the vendor's own pair of sneakers.

And then Tom hit the subway, leaving Dominion Agra and the Beringer Club far behind him.

DESPITE TOM'S ACCOUNT of what happened, and Karl's supermurderous glare when he returned to the Spire the next morning, his friends were on alert for any reemergence of Zombie Tom. But Zombie Tom wasn't the problem. Each day, old Tom grew more and more miserable like there was some storm cloud he couldn't escape. He tried acting normal by laughing and joking around and throwing himself into sims. But it didn't change the way he felt.

In Applied Simulations one day, he didn't charge across the fields with the rest of the Roman legion to battle Queen Boudicca. Wyatt searched him out and found him slumped against a tree, sandals buried in the mud. "You're not New Tom again, are you?"

"No."

Wyatt shifted back and forth. "But people are fighting, and you're here. You love fighting."

"I'm thinking, okay? Am I not allowed to think?"

"You don't generally do that." She settled next to him, taking care to avoid the mud.

Tom watched her dully. She hadn't been herself lately, either, and he was pretty sure it was because of what had gone down with Blackburn. He'd heard enough of their conversation in that office to get it: they'd had some sort of rapport. And then he'd gone and demolished it.

He rubbed at his forehead. "Did I ever say sorry? About making Blackburn think that—"

"I told you, that wasn't you." She wrapped her arms around

her knees. "I still don't even know what Roanoke means. You know, other than the obvious thing: that colony in early America."

"Vengerov knew," Tom muttered. "I heard him. He knew just what buttons to push. He put it there." He shook off the thought. "Look, Wyatt, I'm going to tell him what really happened—"

"No! Don't mention that again, okay? I'm sure Lieutenant Blackburn will start talking to me again one day, if you just let it drop. He has to, doesn't he?"

Tom couldn't answer that for her. So he raised his hands. "Fine. It's all you."

"Is that what's been bothering you, then?"

"Nothing's bothering me."

"Something is. That's why I'm here. It's so we can talk about your feelings."

Tom gave an incredulous laugh. "Talk about my feelings?"

She shifted her weight, practically squirming with how uncomfortable she was. "Elliot told me about using more emotional sensitivity. It sounds pretty straightforward. If you want to try it, you can use 'I feel' statements and I'll listen in a calm and nonjudgmental manner."

Tom snorted.

"He also said I could lead this discussion by saying empathetic things such as: 'I feel like you are sad, Tom.'" She nodded. "Are you sad, Tom?"

"No," Tom snarled, suddenly furious. "I'm not *sad*. I'm angry, okay? You want an 'I feel' statement? I feel like killing someone. I keep thinking of how completely snowballed I was by that whole thing, and I feel like I should have burned that club down with Dalton Prestwick inside it, okay? I didn't even get that anything was wrong! I went for weeks on end gelling my hair and sucking up to Karl and I didn't even know that anything was different!"

"The program had a rootkit. It was designed to hide itself from you."

"That's not the point, okay? I should've realized something was up because I just started trusting Dalton. *Dalton Prestwick* of all people! I hate this guy, okay? He treats my mom like garbage. He's the reason I don't have a family! And suddenly, what, I get one program in my brain and I think he's the greatest guy in the world? I mean, I seriously thought he was doing everything for my own good! I thought that, and I didn't even wonder about it!"

"Again, program. Designed that way."

"I don't do that, okay? I always know when people are scamming me. I just don't do the blind devotion thing. I've never even trusted my dad like that!"

Wyatt looked at him sharply, then bit her lip, because this was something even she knew better than to ask about.

Tom glared across the field, feeling sick over it all. He kept thinking of Dalton showing him how to put on a tie—and he just wished he could go back in time somehow and strangle him with it. He felt like he'd done something awful, like he'd committed some terrible treason against his dad, because even now he could remember how it felt for that fleeting instant to trust someone so absolutely, to believe so unquestioningly everything Dalton did was for his own good. . . .

And most shameful of all, he missed that feeling so much he felt hollow inside.

Tom thrust himself to his feet and drew his sword. "This is stupid." He needed to fight. Some fake violence against fake people would cure everything. "Just forget it all."

"So you don't have any more 'I feel' statements?"

Tom laughed harshly and headed toward the battle. "Wyatt, no offense, but you suck at playing therapist. How about you go back to being you, I go back to being me, and we forget this ever happened, okay? But thanks anyway."

CHAPTER TWENTY-TWO

A WEEK LATER, WYATT still received no sign of forgiveness from Blackburn. He deposited a curt message in her vision center, assigning her a room to work alone in the basement, and so much tedious reformatting that she had to start leaving dinner early every night to make headway on it.

Tom knew his payback was next.

The first few days back in Programming were agonizing, knowing something bad had to be coming. Blackburn confirmed it for him by veering off his planned discussion of compilers and introducing a repertoire of new weaponized viruses, which Tom studied with a mounting sense of unease.

And then the day came.

"Today in class, we're going to apply the knowledge of the last week." His eyes found Tom, promising death. "Consider this exercise like a fox hunt, though if you want a formal name for it, I'll call it Crossing the Wrong Person Is Bad for Your Health."

Confused mumbling filled the room, as people looked at one another, trying to figure out who this was aimed at. Tom slouched down in his seat. Well, they'd know soon enough.

"All of you are hunting down one target," Blackburn went on, "one fox. Use whatever programs you'd like to take that fox down. Hopefully, this will teach that fox a valuable lesson."

In other words, Blackburn was declaring it open season on him.

"Tom Raines," he announced, "you have a very exciting job today. You get to be the fox."

"I'm so shocked," Tom said sarcastically.

"If you manage to evade your fellow trainees until the end of this class, you win," Blackburn said. "Use whatever means of escape you want. The rest of you will be competing against one another to see who gets the fox first. The winner can skip a day of class."

Everyone sat up straighter. Even Vik, next to Tom.

"Traitor!" Tom said.

"Call me Doctor Benedict Arnold," Vik answered.

Tom waited for his neural processor to call up the reference.

"*You're* the American here. What's the matter with you?" Vik said.

"Look, Vik, you're my buddy. You can destroy me before anyone else does."

"That's what friends are for," Vik agreed.

"So, Mr. Raines?" Blackburn said, elbows on the podium. "Are you going to run for it? It's really no fun for anyone if you make this too easy."

Tom shrugged and stayed right by Vik, content to let his friend hit him with a virus first. "No point, sir. I can't win. Almost every trainee in the Spire is here. I might as well not bother."

Blackburn considered it a moment, and then nodded. "Fair enough. Let's give you more of a chance. A good programmer on your side. Mr. Harrison? You're fox number two."

Nigel Harrison, closer to the front, sat up in his seat, horrified. "This is completely unfair!"

"Really?" Blackburn said drily. "I didn't hear you screaming injustice to the skies just a few moments ago when it was just Raines. *Now* it's unfair?"

The black-haired boy gazed up at him with open loathing.

"Go, you two," Blackburn said. "You get a five-minute head start."

Tom didn't move. Neither did Nigel. Five minutes was nothing. Nothing.

Blackburn looked directly at Tom again. "Or is the challenge too much for you?"

Blood roared up into Tom's head. Oh, that was *it*.

"Don't fall for it," Vik warned in an undertone.

Yeah, he knew Blackburn was just goading him. But the accusation that Tom wasn't getting up to fight because he was afraid just wasn't something he'd let stand. He was going to prove Blackburn wrong. Prove them all wrong.

Tom leaped to his feet, ignoring Blackburn's ferocious smile, and headed toward the front. "Come on, Nigel. Let's get out of here."

Nigel Harrison's face twitched. "Ten minutes or it's no deal. Sir."

Blackburn waved his hand. "You can take fifteen, even." His tone said, *It will make no difference.*

Tom knew it wouldn't, but he bolted for the doors. This time Nigel followed.

TOM RACED DOWN the corridor to the elevator. "This is what I figure, Nigel . . . Nigel!"

He realized suddenly he was alone. The slim, black-haired boy was following him at a maddeningly slow pace, his pale face blank. Tom rushed back to his side, and matched his steps.

"This is what I think." Tom practically hopped in place, fighting the urge to sprint, knowing he needed the other kid cooperating if they were going to win this sucker. "We should pick somewhere secure where we can control who gets in, like the Census Chamber, and then we make a stand. We can do it. We can stomp them all."

"No, we can't," Nigel said.

"You and me, we're going to be like those three hundred Spartans, okay? This is our glorious moment where we take on a vastly superior enemy force and win. Ever played that game, Sparta 300?" He fought the urge to grab Nigel's arm and hoist him over his shoulder to move him faster.

"You're such a child," Nigel muttered. "You and your dumb friend, Vik. Life isn't a stupid video game. Do you realize that? And seriously, who calls themselves the Doctor Dooms? You stole that from *The Fantastic Four.*"

Tom pounded on the button for the elevator. "First of all, we're Doctors *of* Doom—there's an 'of' and it's *plural.* Second of all, that doesn't have anything to do with the here and now."

The elevator doors slid open. Nigel slumped back against the wall, wasting precious time that Tom knew they couldn't afford to lose if they were going to have a chance of surviving the class period.

"Come on. Come on, Nigel! We've gotta go somewhere we can defend ourselves."

Nigel fixed him with cold, blue eyes. "Is it true you blew up the Beringer Club?"

"You know about that?" Tom said, startled.

"Dominion Agra did the whole song and dance with me, too," Nigel said. "They acted like they were going to sponsor me, let me come to the club when I wanted to, then nixed my nomination to Camelot Company and banned me from the premises. So did you do it?"

"I didn't blow up the Beringer Club. I just flooded it with sewage. With the Dominion execs in there."

Nigel studied him, then his mouth quirked. He slid past Tom into the elevator, hit B for basement. "I'll work with you. And I know how we can win this."

"Let's do it, man." Tom offered him a high five, but Nigel just shot his raised hand a slicing look, and Tom dropped it to his side.

They emerged from the elevator. Tom started for the Census Chamber, but Nigel didn't follow. Tom found the small boy standing instead before the Spire's primary processor: a refrigerator-sized computer chip swamped by wires, blasted on both sides by cooling hoses. "First, let's disable the tracking system so they can't find our GPS signals, and—"

An idea crept into Tom's brain. "Wait. No, keep it on. The internal GPS system is the first thing they'll access once they start hunting us, don't you see?"

Nigel looked at him, catching onto the idea. "So we plant a Trojan there."

"Exactly."

Nigel darted over to a computer fixed to the wall, began typing away at the keyboard. "I've got the perfect one." A strange gleam appeared in his eyes. "It's my own creation. Grand Mal Seizure."

"You're joking, right?" Tom said. But Nigel was still typing. Tom grabbed Nigel's skinny arm before he could execute the command. "You can't plant that virus. That's a serious medical problem."

"So?"

"People die of seizures. You could kill someone."

Nigel's smirk was nasty. "I know." He reached for the keyboard again.

This time, Tom shoved him away from it. Nigel crashed against the wall. He righted himself, staring at Tom like he had just betrayed him somehow.

"What's the matter with you?" Tom bellowed. "Do you think Marsh will let us get away with doing something like that?"

"I wouldn't use it on CamCo. That's all Marsh cares about." Nigel's blue eyes glowed fanatically. "I'll just use it on the others, the dead weight, and let Blackburn fix it later. He'll know better than to mess with us again after that, and so will the rest of them." His voice shook with hatred. "Don't you get it? Neither of us have a chance to be Camelot Company now. Dominion Agra is going to blackball you for what you did, and I got nixed because of this defective neural processor."

"Defective?"

"I didn't have this twitch before," Nigel railed. "It's a hardware problem with my neural processor. They'd have to cut open my head again to fix it, so General Marsh has just decided for me that it's too much of a risk even if *I'm* willing to do it. It ruins everything! I can't get to CamCo because companies think I'd look bad on camera. And Marsh just thinks it's fine and great. He even told me, 'Son, you can just do something else for the military. Not everyone's Combatant material.' But I don't want to do something else. I want *this*. And now you're in the same situation. You can't be CamCo, either. So let's go for it another way."

"What, by wiping out the competition?"

"No, we show Marsh we're ruthless." Nigel's fist clenched in the air, gripping something only he saw. "Don't you see? Look at the Russo-Chinese Combatants. Medusa doesn't have a corporate sponsor, but Medusa is a Combatant anyway because he's just that good. We can be like that. They're looking for people who are different, who aren't mediocre like the rest. We'll show them we're so deadly, the military *has* to make us CamCo even without sponsors!"

"Not this way." Tom planted himself between Nigel and the keyboard. "I have friends here."

Nigel's face twitched, his expression like a storm cloud. "Good for you."

"I wasn't saying you don't—"

"I don't," Nigel hissed. "I don't have friends here."

Gee, I wonder why, Tom thought, but he just said, "Okay, so maybe you don't, but that doesn't mean I'll let you hurt mine."

"What reality do you live in?" Spit flew from Nigel's mouth. "In a few minutes, your so-called friends are going to be hunting you down. Your friends helped you mess with the entire board of Dominion Agra. That's one of the chief companies in the Coalition of Multinationals, do you get that? Those are some of the most powerful people in the world, and you swamped them in sewage! If you had *real* friends, they'd have told you that you're an idiot for even thinking about doing that!"

Tom bristled, indignant. "My friends do tell me I'm an idiot. All the time!"

"Fine, Raines. Play it your way."

Tom didn't trust him. He turned to the keyboard himself, careful to block Nigel's path to it, trying to call up from his memory Frequent Noisome Farts. He'd stick that in the tracking system, and maybe the others in the Spire wouldn't be so quick to search for them if a few of them came down with some major flatulence.

"That's really an impressive firewall you've got," Nigel remarked from behind him. "Enslow make that for you?"

Tom ignored him. He was laboring to type in the correct source code.

"Impressive," Nigel went on, "but flawed. You should've sided with me. You might've stood a chance."

Tom whirled around, saw him raising his forearm keyboard. He leaped forward, but not in time. The virus initiated and his head thrashed back and slammed into something hard. His vision blurred into darkness.

TOM AWOKE LYING on the stage of the Lafayette Room, pain drilling behind his eyes. He gazed at the empty rows of benches, blurring in and out of his vision.

He tried to push himself up, but found his wrists pinned against his chest. "Hey!" he yelled out, fighting to free himself. He could feel something bunched up against the back of his head, too, and the front of it slipped down over his face, and blinded him.

Blackburn yanked the uniform tunic off his head. "Calm down," he ordered.

"Let me go!" Tom cried.

"I'm freeing you right now. Stay calm."

He reached behind Tom and tugged at something—and the constriction loosened around him. He saw then that his bonds were all made of uniform tunics.

"You were thrashing," Blackburn explained.

Tom jolted to his feet. The movement made his stomach turn. "What happened?" He swallowed against the dry ache in his throat. "Who won?"

"I've been dismantling Mr. Harrison's program. It seems he took you out before anyone else could get to you. You were one of the two foxes, so he won the competition."

Tom hadn't even thought of attacking Nigel and winning that way.

"What did he get me with?" Tom rubbed at his head. "Grand Mal Seizure?"

"No. Who would program something like that? He hit you with a nasty variation of Nigel Harrison. Your twitching manifested itself as a sustained thrashing, and you knocked yourself unconscious."

Tom laughed, his head whirling. His legs felt a bit funny beneath him. "You're kidding. Nigel Harrison Nigel Harrisoned me?"

"That's right." Blackburn sounded annoyed. "And if he'd written a self-termination sequence, I would've given him a day off. Since I was stuck dismantling it, I revoked his victory."

Tom's eyes riveted on a smear of blood on the stage below him. He raised a shaky hand to the side of his head and pressed the stinging bump gingerly.

"Don't poke at it," Blackburn warned, plucking Tom's hand away.

Yeah, like he cared. Tom ripped out of his grip and jumped down from the stage. The floor gave way beneath him, and he tumbled to the ground.

"Graceful." A thump of boots behind him, and then a large

hand seized the back of his tunic and hauled him to his feet.

"Let me go. Stay away from me!"

Blackburn steered him jerkily down the aisle. "You have a head injury, Raines. You're going to the infirmary."

"I'm great. I'm perfect. Let go!"

He turned Tom around and clasped his shoulders. "You were unconscious for fifteen minutes, Raines. Your pupils are uneven. You need to see a doctor."

Tom felt awkward, seeing him this close, hearing him actually speak softly. He turned his head away. "So you got what you wanted, huh? This was bad for my health."

Blackburn considered him. "No. This went too far. Come on."

Tom stopped trying to break away from him. Blackburn remained silent the rest of the trip to the infirmary.

Tom swayed dizzily when Blackburn delivered him to Nurse Chang, who urged him into one of the beds and flashed a penlight in his eyes. Then Tom pressed his cheek against the mattress, and it felt solid and calm when his head was so jumbled. He was suddenly glad to be here. He didn't feel like delighting Karl by puking all over himself in the middle of the mess hall.

"Stay awake, Mr. Raines," Nurse Chang ordered.

Tom forced his eyes back open, watching the bedside table blur in and out. He felt so sick. The lights were too bright. He didn't like that Blackburn was still there, standing over him. He tried to shut out the sound of his voice as he asked, "How long do you expect he'll be here? I should inform General Marsh."

"I'll let you know after his CT, but he's young. Something that would floor you or me for a few weeks, they can shake off in days."

"You don't need to tell me. Two boys, one year apart. There

were more than enough trips to the ER." He was silent a long moment. "Just keep me informed."

Heavy footsteps, and then the hiss of a door sliding open and closed again. Like some dark cloud had dissolved, Tom was finally able to relax, certain Blackburn was finally gone.

CHAPTER TWENTY-THREE

AFTER A COUPLE days, Tom was allowed to leave the infirmary, but he was ordered to remain on bed rest. That's why his GPS signal was situated in his bunk, while he hung out in the VR parlor of the Pentagon City Mall.

He'd spent all Saturday morning fighting Medusa in Pirate Wars. He was the leader of the Black Flag pirate fleet, and she was Ching Shih, the Chinese pirate queen leading the Red Flag Fleet. Despite the low, persistent headache left over from his concussion, Tom fought valiantly and managed to board her ship. Just as he set about massacring her crew, he noticed Medusa's dark head bobbing in the water beyond the ship, her huge grin filled with expectation.

She waved happily. It was his only warning.

Her ship exploded, taking out Tom, the ship, and the bulk of his Black Flag Fleet.

They met back in the RPG, and Tom slipped into his ogre avatar. Medusa's Egyptian queen was turning a series of backflips on the couch, celebrating her victory.

"You're still celebrating?" he asked.

Medusa laughed and spun toward him. "You'd be gloating much more if you ever won."

Tom laughed. "A hundred times more, at least." His ogre tromped forward, and they started circling around each other, another duel in the making. "Tell me something." He fixed his gaze on her avatar, as though a few megapixels could give him a clue to the real person behind it. "Did you grow up speaking Mandarin?"

"Cantonese."

Tom congratulated himself for weaseling her nationality out of her. She'd conceded the girl issue, since her voice was a girl's, and he'd figured she was Chinese, but he wanted to be sure. Now he was getting a mental picture of her—shiny black hair, lively black eyes. Short, he thought.

"I figured you weren't Russian."

"Russians only train in the Forbidden City two weeks a year, or we go to their underground facility beneath the Kremlin."

"Only two weeks a year, huh? Some of the Indians train here with us all the time. So do the—" Tom stopped before he could tell her about the handful of trainees at the Spire from the Euro-Australian block.

Medusa was quiet a minute. They always had to walk a careful line between their strange friendship and the treason charges they'd face, giving away military secrets.

"That's probably not so classified," Tom said, reconsidering it.

"Everyone knows about the underground Russian facility," Medusa said, sounding a bit uneasy. "Just like the Bombay facility for the Indians."

"What about the other countries you're allied with?"

"They tend to want to live in Moscow, not with us. You have to join our military to be in our program."

"Really? We're not military here. Not till we're eighteen." Tom's ogre leaped up onto the couch. His massive weight tilted it, and with a gale of laughter, Medusa's avatar fluttered off, letting it unbalance and flip on top of Tom's avatar. "Are the Russians military?" he asked.

"Yes, but they don't take it seriously. They can quit anytime they want. They have a real problem there, because so many rich Russians buy their kids a place in the program just to get a neural processor in their brains, and then pull them out." She began taking advantage of the way Tom's ogre was pinned down to stomp on his head. "Most of the time, they don't even get the neural processors taken back out of them, even if it's early enough."

"Clever. So parents send them there to get turned into instant geniuses, huh?"

"Well, you'd think that's why they do it. But one time a family got investigated for it, and it turned out the girl who got the neural processor wasn't even their kid, just some girl they paid to impersonate her. And by the time the military realized this, they'd already had the girl's head cut open, and sold the processor on the black market."

"Wow."

"We just don't approach things the same way they do. That's why the Russians hate it when they visit us. This year they kept complaining because they wanted to sleep every single night."

Tom paused in his struggle to throw off the couch as her boot descended into his face over and over. "Wait, you guys don't sleep every single night?"

"You do?"

"Sleep is good, Medusa. Sleep is great."

"We have scheduled slow-wave sleep periods. But daily sleep isn't necessary with the neural processor."

Tom waved his gloves and resumed trying to move the couch. "But it's sleep."

"We put the time to better use." She bent down to smile tauntingly in his face, her dark hair wreathing her head. "Maybe that's why we're winning."

Tom laughed. "Maybe that's why the foreign Combatants would rather live in Russia!" He hurled the couch to the side, and then leaped to his feet and punched her.

"Are you from Texas?" Medusa asked him out of the blue, punching him back.

"Why Texas? Do I seem like a Texan?"

"Texas and New York are the only places I've heard about in America. Oh, and California."

"Not from Texas, but I know a guy from Texas. He's named Eddie."

"Did he live on a ranch?"

"Nah. He's not a cowboy, either. I think he's a doctor. He and my dad got in a fistfight once, and then they got beer afterward. They're still buddies. I guess it's how they make friends down there or something."

"Isn't that how we made friends, too? Fighting?" She knocked him through the wall.

Tom found his feet, charged back into the room, and tackled her. "Yeah, but we didn't just fight. We wrecked the Beringer Club together. Oh, and I died horribly at your hands. Gruesome murder always builds the foundation for a beautiful friendship."

She laughed, and her Egyptian queen roundhouse kicked his ogre across the room, slamming him into the stone wall and collapsing it. Tom's ogre got buried, and he couldn't help the mental picture his brain was forming: a pretty Chinese girl who loved video games, shooting fire from her eyes, and fighting him. Oh, and who also happened to be the greatest warrior in the world.

He was glad Medusa couldn't see him right now, just his ax-wielding ogre avatar, buried in stones, because he'd feel embarrassed if she saw his huge grin.

THAT TUESDAY, TOM received a ping as soon as Tactics ended: *Report to Elliot Ramirez for semester evaluation.*

"Oh. Oh, great." Tom knew how this was going to go.

The plebes were all being evaluated for the promotions to Middle Company, a small but important step up the ladder. The decision was in the hands of Marsh, but their Applied Simulations instructors had a say, too. Tom had been avoiding Elliot, hoping to put off the inevitable lecture about his lack of teamwork, his inability to play nicely with others, and something else like his lack of self-actualization or something. But Elliot was obviously sick of waiting for Tom to come to him on his own time.

He'd never been to the fourteenth floor where the Combatants in Camelot Company lived. He heard rumors the way everyone else did: that the CamCos didn't have their own rooms, they all slept in one massive barracks-type place. They also had a swimming pool, feather beds, a hot tub where all the CamCo girls romped about wearing nothing, a private bar, and a masseuse. When the doors parted to reveal a common room like on every floor, and private rooms like on every other floor, Tom felt a twinge of disappointment. He stepped out onto the soft carpet, his eyes trained on the massive window overlooking the green expanse of Arlington fourteen stories below them. He turned in a slow circle, looking at the doors.

"Tom."

Elliot's voice made him jump. The dark-haired boy stood in the doorway to his bunk, and he gestured Tom inside.

Tom followed him into the private bunk. Single occupant. Nice.

Elliot must've been lounging on his bed, because he flopped back down and slung his legs across the sheets, a silent screen running on the ceiling over his head—the battle at Mercury from a few months earlier.

"So, your first evaluation," Elliot said, eyes trained on the ceiling.

Tom shifted his weight. "Yeah."

"Sit."

Tom lowered himself into Elliot's plush leather chair.

"Sorry to rush this, Tom, but we've been busy trying to prep for Capitol Summit. General Marsh keeps sending me messages from India, telling me to urge CamCo along in nominating my proxy. And here I was, hoping maybe I could play as myself this year."

Tom looked up at the screen, because he wasn't sure what to say to that. Of the members of CamCo, Elliot's fighting was the most rote and predictable. There was a good reason Marsh never let him serve as his own proxy.

Elliot was gazing at the image again.

"Tell me something, Tom, what do you think I did wrong here?" Elliot waved his finger and rewound a segment where his ship grazed Medusa's, swerved at the last minute, then caught a missile she blasted back at him. His ship exploded, a fiery mass of flames streaking toward the surface of Mercury.

"Uh, you got blown up."

"Obviously. But why did it happen? How did I mess up?"

"You're asking me to play armchair quarterback?"

"Exactly. Armchair quarterback me."

Tom shifted in the chair. He'd be glad to tell Elliot why he'd messed up, but it didn't seem like the right time to rub in his failings. Besides, ever since Elliot let him fight Medusa in Troy, he didn't feel the need to do it.

"Um, you would've gotten blown up anyway. Even if you'd done everything right there."

"But I might've taken Medusa with me if I'd played my cards right. What should I have done?"

"You did everything by the book. You'd know better than me. You're much farther along in tactics than I am."

"But . . . ?"

"You should've kamikaze'd her," Tom blurted. "You had the chance. Knock out Medusa and the rest would've been in shock. You could've just picked them off."

"*Her*?"

Tom winced at the slip. "I think of Medusa as a girl for some reason."

"Me, too. Kind of funny. To be honest, ramming her didn't even occur to me at the time. But it would've occurred to you, wouldn't it have?" Elliot pondered him, rubbing his thumb across his chin. "That's something about you, Tom. I've seen it time and again, the way you aim straight for the throat. You have the killer instinct. At the end of the day, I don't. I don't have teeth and claws and the hunger for it, I suppose."

"You're not vicious like me, you mean."

"I suppose that's one way to put it. Do you know why I wanted you to pay fealty?"

Tom had theories at the time. Some need for power, some deep-seated egotism. It didn't feel fair saying anything about that now.

Elliot answered his own question. "Because that's as much

a part of advancing here as your battle performance. All the killer instinct in the world won't get you anywhere if you're not willing to play the social game. There's not a person in history who achieved greatness without choking back some pride, without ever smiling at someone they despised, without playing along even if they hated the very idea of it."

"I get it. I'm not a team player."

"You could be." Elliot leaned toward him. "You can be. A very valuable, effective team player. Exactly the kind of player who leads teams to victory. But you need to play that other game, too. You need to learn to—"

"Suck up?" Tom said before he could stop himself.

"That's right. Suck up."

Tom stared at him, caught off the guard, the ships still dancing on the screen overhead.

"You can think anything you want, Tom, but you won't get anywhere unless you learn on occasion to act like a pathetic little suck-up. The way I do."

Tom wasn't even sure what to say to this. It had never occurred to him that Elliot was completely aware of the way he came across.

Elliot went on. "I admire your integrity. I admire how you hold your ground. But I'd also like to see you win some ground, not just hold it. I'd like to see someone with your creativity, your drive, really get somewhere. You're not going to do that unless you learn to bend."

For a moment, Tom was too caught off guard to reply. And then he remembered that this didn't matter. Not really. "I'm not going to get anywhere, anyway."

"You're referring to the Dominion Agra execs and the Beringer Club?"

Tom started.

Elliot smiled. "I've heard a few whispers. Your new infamy's an obstacle to getting a sponsor. I'll admit it." He rose to his feet. "But there are four other companies on the Coalition that invest in Indo-American Combatants. Dominion Agra is not the only act in town. Don't give up hope this soon."

Tom rose to his feet, confused. This hadn't gone as he'd expected. "Thanks for the advice."

"Don't mention it." Elliot paused by the door. "Tom, I'm going to recommend you for Middle. I want you to think about what I said, though." He winked. "And good luck."

Stunned, wondering if he'd never understood this guy, Tom shook the hand Elliot offered. He was reeling when he left Elliot's bunk and headed back toward the elevator—and that was how he missed Karl where he was sitting on a couch, downloading his homework.

Karl stopped the download and bounded to his feet. "Lassie."

Tom wasn't in the mood for this. He hit the button for the elevator, hoping it would get there soon.

"What, trying to ignore me? Taking the higher ground's so unlike you." He heard Karl's slow, steady footsteps drawing up behind him and turned his back to the elevator.

But Karl didn't attack him. He hung back in an unsettling manner, lips fixed in a strange, lopsided grin.

"What?" Tom blurted.

"Getting my last look at you."

"You going somewhere? Remind me to throw a party."

"No, no. You see, a few days ago, Dalton got the credit card bill for your last party."

Tom gave an inflammatory laugh. He couldn't help it.

"I'd thank you for the black eye," Karl said, "but I guess I don't need to. Let's just say, Fido, you're already dead."

"Yeah, yeah. You say that a lot, but I'm still here."

"Not for long. You're going to be gone very, very soon. So I wanted to enjoy this. It's like watching a guy you hate about to drop off the edge of a cliff."

Tom felt a wave of foreboding at the veiled warning but forced a smile to his lips. "Yeah, the anticipation's mutual. I keep looking at you, Karl, and thinking of how very excited I am about what Dalton's going to do to you."

"You don't scare me."

"I don't care. It's fantastic enough knowing what's coming to you. And knowing you don't know it."

The first uncertainty flickered over Karl's face. "What, Benji?"

"Dalton told me about the behavioral subroutines you've got coming your way. I wonder if he'll have you gel your hair?" Tom considered him, then shook his head. "Nah. Let's face it, he can't play that same angle. I'm prettier than you."

Karl's face twisted like he tried for a sneer and couldn't manage it. "He wouldn't do that to me."

"You have no idea, do you?" Tom said. "Dalton said the only reason they took you on was to get to Elliot, but that didn't happen. So they're going to—what was that word you used? Oh, yeah. 'Neuter' you. Don't believe me? I could head right down to the census device. Send you a memory of it."

Karl didn't speak.

The elevator door slid open. "Rather live in the dark? Too bad." Tom turned for it, pulsing with triumph, but Karl seized his collar and yanked him back.

"You're lying!" Karl aimed a fist at him. Tom ducked his head, and laughed at Karl's cry when his knuckles slammed the wall.

"Can't believe you fell for that aga—"

The second fist caught him mid-gloat, drove the breath right from his stomach. Tom doubled over, black spots in front of his vision, his legs sinking beneath him.

"Admit that you're lying," Karl snarled down at him.

"What—you want—me to lie—about lying?" Tom choked out.

"Karl? What are you doing?"

Tom had never been so happy to hear Elliot's voice. Karl flung him to the carpet fast enough to make Tom's head spin. He clambered to his feet, hearing Karl argue, "This isn't your business, Elliot. He's provoking me. He keeps saying—"

Tom staggered upright, fighting for breath. Elliot stood in the middle of the hallway, his steady, dark gaze fixed on Karl's. "What could possibly justify beating up a fourteen-year-old kid?"

"But, Elliot—"

"Tom's one of my plebes. I'd like you to leave him alone from now on."

Karl's cheeks grew crimson. "You don't get to tell me what to do."

"Actually, I do, Karl," Elliot said, his voice soft. "If you want to retain any influence in Camelot Company, you'll listen to me when I tell you to leave Tom alone. Understand?"

Karl made a face like an angry pit bull. For all his talk to Tom about being the big man in charge, he suddenly looked like an angry little kid.

"Understand?" There was steel in Elliot's velvety voice.

Tom watched, fascinated, the way Karl's cheeks turned a dark shade of scarlet. Then Karl jerked a nod.

"That's a yes?" Elliot said.

"Yes." Karl's teeth were gritted.

"Thank you, Karl. Now leave."

Tom watched, awestruck, as Karl slinked away. He was like some vicious Doberman that had been admonished by his master. It had never occurred to Tom that Karl might listen to anyone. That Karl respected anyone enough to do what they said.

Tom looked at Elliot, understanding for the first time what the other guy had been trying to tell him. Some people didn't have to fight to hold their ground, to get their way. There were other games to play, other competitions to win.

"You okay there, Tom?" Elliot said.

"Uh, yeah. Thanks."

He heard the elevator slide open behind him. Before Elliot could disappear back into his bunk, Tom called, "Wait."

Elliot glanced back at him.

Feeling foolish, Tom looked at the windowed wall. "Elliot, maybe you're not vicious because you're not messed up enough." He darted Elliot a quick glance, saw the calm, thoughtful face. "Maybe you're too"—he tried to think of an Elliot Ramirez–appropriate word—"too *self-actualized* to act all savage."

Elliot smiled. "You think so?"

"Yeah. Anyway, that's all." Tom waved and bumbled into the elevator, hoping Elliot had figured out that this moment was as close as Tom would ever get to apologizing for never having given him a chance.

0 0 0 1 0 1 0 1 1 0 1 1 0 0 0 0 0 0 1 0 0 1 1 1 0 0 0 0 0 1 0 1 1 1 0 1 0 0
1 0 0 0 0 0 1 1 1 1 1 0 1 0 0 1 1 1 1 0 1 1 0 0 1 1 0 1 0 0 0 1 0 1 0 0
0 1 0 1 1 0 0 1 1 1 1 1 1 1 0 0 1 1 0 1 0 1 1 0 0 0 0 0 0 1 0 0 1 1 1
0 1 0 0 0 1 1 0 1 1 0 1 1 1 0 0 1 1 1 0 0 0 0 0 0 1 0 1 1 0 1 0 0 1
1 1 1 0 1 0 0 0 0 1 1 1 1 0 0 1 0 0 1 0 1 1 1 0 0 1 1 1 0 1 1 0 1 0 0 1
0 1 0 1 0 1 0 0 0 1 1 0 1 1 0 0 0 0 1 1 0 1 0 0 1 1 0 0 0 1 0 1 1 1 0 0
0 1 0 1 1 0 0 1 1 0 1 0 0 0 0 0 1 1 1 0 1 1 0 0 0 0 0 0 0 1 0 1 1 0 0
1 1 1 0 0 0 1 1 0 0 0 0 0 1 1 1 1 0 1 1 0 1 1 0 1 0 0 0 0 0 1 0 0 1 1 1 0
1 1 1 1 1 1 0 0 1 0 1 0 1 1 1 0 1 1 1 0 1 0 1 0 1 1 1 1 0 1 0 1 1 0 1 1 0
1 0 1 0 0 1 1 1 1 1 1 1 0 1 1 0 0 0 0 1 1 1 0 1 1 0 1 1 0 1 1 1 1 0 0 0
0 0 0 1 1 0 1 1 0 0 1 1 0 1 0 0 1 0 1 0 1 0 1 0 0 1 0 0 0 0 1 0 0 1 0
1 1 1 0 0 0 1 0 0 1 0 1 1 0 0 1 0 0 1 1 0 1 0 1 0 1 1 1 0 0 0 0 1 0 1 1 0
0 1 0 0 0 0 0 0 1 1 1 1 1 0 1 1 0 0 1 1 0 1 1 0 0 0 0 0 0 1 0 0 0 0 1 0 0
0 0 0
0 1 0
1 0 0

CHAPTER TWENTY-FOUR

THERE WAS NO policy against fraternization. They weren't military regulars, after all, and Marsh was realistic enough to understand what happened when a large group of teenagers lived in one place. There was nothing to encourage it, though. No dances like in an actual high school. If people wanted to go on a date, they had to wait until the weekend and hit Washington, DC, or settle for the romantic glow of the Pentagon City Mall's food court.

Every so often in the summer, though, the Spire held Open Evenings when the roof of the planetarium parted to reveal the night sky overhead. Officially, the Open Evenings were meant to help the older trainees who were studying astrophysics, but mostly they provided a nice view and the couples or potential couples migrated there whenever possible. Tonight, Yuri and Wyatt were going, and Vik was planning to go there to try to snag a seat next to a Machiavelli named Jenny Nguyen. She'd been "making eyes at him" in Applied Sims, he claimed, and he was going for it. He even had the perfect line ready.

"What line?" Tom asked.

"Not telling. It'll jinx it."

"It's that bad, huh?"

"It's all in the delivery, Tom!"

His roommate spent half an hour brushing lint off his pants and changing shirts while Tom made fun of him.

"Displace your Y chromosome?"

"Shut up. This is different."

"Sure it is, buddy. Don't let Jenny get past first base today. She won't respect you in the morning."

Vik swiped out a fist and socked his arm, but he was grinning, his crazy-eyed look back. "I look good."

Tom pressed his hand over his heart, testifying to his honesty. "You look insane."

"Insanely good," Vik said. "She is going to be all over me."

"Tell yourself that, Vik."

"Die slowly, Tom."

Tom waited until Vik left to wring out maximum embarrassment, then he started playing video games. Something kept bothering him, though—and when he started up a game that offered a two-player option, he realized what it was: he liked it better when he was playing games against Medusa.

The nagging emptiness of the bunk and the silence of Alexander Division pressed in around Tom. He couldn't help imagining Medusa as some girl who lived just down the hall. She'd be someone he could play games with anytime. Maybe she'd even be someone he could ask up to the Planetarium some night . . . if he dared.

VIK RETURNED TO his bunk with a black eye and refused to tell Tom what had happened with Jenny. So Tom made up wild, and increasingly absurd, ways he could've gotten it, until Vik plugged in his neural wire to escape the conversation. Grinning, Tom hooked in for the night, too, and dropped off to sleep.

Early the next morning, he ventured through the crisp, morning darkness to the Metro. Pentagon City wasn't open yet, so he hit another Arlington VR parlor. He had an hour to meet with Medusa before she needed to log off.

"So you want to know something stupid?" he said to her.

They were fighting as Siegfried and Brunhilde again today, because Tom had explored the sim enough on his own to figure out a new strategy for killing her. Unfortunately, Medusa had snuck in another add-on she used to full tactical advantage: whenever they stepped on certain bricks, fire spouted up around them.

She circled around him, sword gleaming in the burning chamber. "What?"

Tom concentrated on her sword rather than her avatar's face. "We have this thing sometimes where people in the Spire look at the stars. It's a thing where boyfriends and girlfriends go together. I had this weird thought. I wished you lived in the Spire so I could've asked you."

He darted Medusa a quick look. Her smile had dropped off her face.

"Stupid, right?" Tom said with a forced laugh.

She didn't say anything. Tom hacked at her with his ax, hoping to make her forget all about it. Medusa parried his blows, then with a violent slash, gutted him. She kicked his body onto one of the booby-trapped bricks and set him on fire.

Medusa didn't speak again until she returned with a basin and dumped water on his burning body. "You wouldn't like me in real life. I bet you like pretty girls."

"Girls always say they're not pretty when they actually are. I bet you are, too." Tom just knew it.

Medusa considered him for a long moment. And then she did something unexpected: she leaned toward him and pressed a rough kiss onto his lips.

Tom wasn't hooked in with his neural processor. He didn't feel the sensation. It was VR, an illusion supplied by his visor of Brunhilde's beautiful face inches from his, her eyes closed, her lips pressed where his would have been. His wired gloves vibrated with contact when he pressed his palms to where her virtual arms were. But when Medusa started to pull back, he clutched at her avatar, feeling chills all over like he'd actually kissed a girl for the first time.

"Not so fast." He pulled her back to him, pressed his virtual lips to hers to return the kiss.

Medusa laughed and squirmed out of his grip. "Hey, I'm hooked in here. Your teeth just hit mine."

"Sorry." Tom didn't even care that this was a public VR parlor, and people could probably see he was kissing someone through the gauzy curtain hiding him. Lightning bolts struck all through him. "Does this mean we're boyfriend and girlfriend?"

"We don't even know each other's names."

"Yeah, but we've killed each other so many times, I figure that counts for something." Tom took a breath, then a daring chance. "Do you want to know what I look like?"

Medusa stared at him through Brunhilde's brilliant blue eyes.

"We can both do it. Just drop the avatars." The words strangled him, because he never did this if he could help it. He never went in his real skin into VR. But he wanted to see her, even if it meant she'd have to see him, and he knew, just knew, that Medusa wouldn't pass his image on to anyone else. "It won't give away our identities. I won't show anyone if you won't."

Medusa retreated, her avatar slinking back farther in the sim.

"I'm not gonna show anyone what you look like if you're worried about your identity," Tom pledged, sensing her retreat. "I wouldn't."

Medusa gazed at him in the flickering torchlight. "You have to know something. Capitol Summit's coming soon."

"Um, yeah, I kinda know that," Tom said. It was all over the news, after all.

"Elliot Ramirez will be fighting there, but everyone here knows he'll have a proxy."

"Yeah, the way Svetlana always does."

"A proxy like Alec Tarsus."

Tom's heart stopped. How did she know that name?

Her next words made the blood drain from his cheeks. "Or Heather Akron. Or Cadence Grey. Or Karl Marsters."

Those were Camelot Company people.

Their identities were classified. Medusa couldn't know them. She wasn't supposed to.

Unless there'd been some breach.

Some serious, serious breach.

"I've heard all of the Camelot Company names now. Their IPs, too. It's going to be on the news today. Maybe you should go." She gazed intently at him. "It might be safer for you."

Tom understood her. He swallowed hard. "Yeah, I should probably go."

He pulled off his VR visor. The humming voices around him weren't soothing, reassuring. Tom saw the blank screen on the wall, his mouth dry, knowing there was no real privacy on the internet, even with all his planning, all his care to meet her only out of the Spire.

CamCo's identities had been leaked. Something like this was going to be big.

He knew, just knew, that something bad was going to come of it.

CHAPTER TWENTY-FIVE

THE NEWS BROKE on his way back to the Spire. He heard snatches of those names on people's lips in the Metro. The names the general population shouldn't know. Heather . . . Alec . . . Ralph . . . Emefa . . . He'd heard all of them by the time he reached the Pentagon. Every Combatant in CamCo had been leaked.

And once he was in the Spire, it was as cataclysmic as he feared. The place was in chaos with the breaking news, trainees swarming around tables in the mess hall, the room buzzing with frantic voices. The screens built into the walls had all been turned on, the news playing.

Tom passed a few CamCos. Snowden Gainey of Napoleon Division was practically bouncing in place, and he was talking excitedly to Mason Meekins of Hannibal, who was scowling at the nearest screen. When Tom stepped into the elevator, he saw the news playing on its normally inactive, emergency-only screen. The reporter spoke as the image panned over photographs of various newly revealed CamCos taken from yearbooks, the internet, and other places. One yearbook photo of a bucktoothed girl with glasses and heavy bangs caught him up short. The caption said she was Heather Akron.

When Tom reached his bunk, Vik filled him in on everything people had been talking about for the last hour: the Chinese state news had aired all the identities of the members of CamCo, and even purported to have matched them to the "IPs of their personal computers." Those in the military who knew about neural processors realized the true meaning of that statement: they could glean the real names of the Camelot Company Combatants just using their IP addresses now.

"Elliot Ramirez has to be dying inside," Vik said. "He's not going to be the only famous face here anymore."

Tom's head pulsed. "This is bad."

Vik dropped onto his own bed, slinging his boots over his mattress. "Yeah, especially for Blackburn. Someone must've hacked into the Spire and gotten the identities."

"You think so?" Tom knew he shouldn't sound hopeful. If it was all Blackburn's fault, maybe there wouldn't be an investigation.

"That, or we've got a leak."

A leak. Tom felt cold. If Blackburn wasn't responsible, he'd be fanatical in investigating who that leak could be. This would be a thousand times worse than when he hunted down the person who hacked the personnel database. This was *treason*. Tom headed to the window and stared out bleakly onto the roof of the Old Pentagon. He was in trouble. His meetings with Medusa were like a gigantic red flag.

Vik's hand clapped on his shoulder, making him jump. "Cheer up. Think about the Summit."

"What about it?"

Vik sounded gleeful. "Russo-Chinese intelligence has got CamCo's IPs and names. Don't you see? There's no deniability once they have the names. If Elliot gets proxied at the Capitol Summit, they can plaster the face of Elliot's real proxy on the news. Either we're going to get embarrassed at Capitol Summit, or Elliot's got to have someone who's still got a secret identity come and fight for him. One of us non-CamCos. There's gonna be some movement up the ranks."

"It's not going to be us, Vik. We're plebes. Nigel Harrison will probably get to do it because he's next in line for CamCo."

"Still, it'll be someone. They haven't promoted any new CamCo members in ages." Vik flopped back onto his bed, his face dazzled. "Imagine that. Your first fight in space—against Medusa. Imagine fighting Medusa."

It took all Tom's self-control not to blurt out everything.

PEOPLE WITH NEURAL processors did not dream. They opened their eyes at a time preprogrammed, wide-awake. But when Tom opened his eyes at 0513 hours, he knew it was too early, and something was wrong.

He bolted upright in bed and realized what the problem was: Lieutenant Blackburn towered above him in full uniform, gripping the wire he'd pulled out of Tom's brain stem. A pair of armed soldiers waited behind him in the open doorway.

Tom's mouth grew dry. He'd thought about maybe confessing his meetings with Medusa before anyone found out about them, but he wasn't going to have the chance.

"Mr. Raines, do you know why I had to drag myself up here at this ungodly early hour?" Blackburn demanded. "It's because some establishment called the Beringer Club heard about yesterday's leak, and they felt it was their patriotic duty to wake me up and inform me that you were on their property recently. They claim you were communicating with an online acquaintance while there. Someone in China."

And then it all made terrible sense.

Dalton. Of course, it was Dalton. This was all Dalton.

Tom should've said something in his own defense. He probably should've done most anything other than start laughing, but that's what came out of his mouth.

"Something funny about this?" Blackburn said.

He clamped his hand over his mouth, aghast at himself. "No, sir." His voice came out muffled. But his brain kept connecting the dots, and that hideous impulse to laugh wouldn't go away.

Dalton, who'd as good as told him a few months ago that CamCo would be going public soon.

Dalton, who'd warned him through Karl that revenge was on its way.

Now Dalton was doing his "patriotic duty" and setting Tom up. The Beringer Club must've had some way to detect Medusa net-sending him. The leak was out, and so was some incriminating information about Tom. It was *all* so very *Dalton*.

"Do you even have the slightest understanding of how serious this situation is, Mr. Raines? Whoever leaked those names committed treason. There's a mandatory ten-year prison sentence for treason."

The word "prison" did it. The horrendous urge to laugh dissolved. Tom dragged his gaze up to Blackburn's. "Look, I *do* have an online friend in China, but it's . . ." He hesitated, knowing this was just going to make his case look worse, but honesty was the only thing he could offer. "Sir, I was meeting Medusa, okay? But I can explain. I didn't leak anything, I swear."

"Medusa." Blackburn scrubbed a big palm over his mouth. "The Russo-Chinese Combatant, Medusa. Even you can't be this stupid, Raines."

"We just hung around and talked and played games." The words spilled out of him. "I was just curious about her, okay? But I never said anything classified. It wasn't me."

Blackburn knelt down so they were at eye level. His voice was softer. "And she never sent you a link to a third-party website? Never directed you somewhere online that required you to run a script? Raines, are you very sure she couldn't have snuck a Trojan into your processor that opened a back door into our system?"

"She wouldn't do that." It couldn't be her. It had to be Dalton.

But . . .

Involuntarily, his brain turned back to Medusa net-sending him a message in the Beringer Club. She'd managed to penetrate his firewall and leave a message in his vision center, the way he'd done to her.

He knew how he'd done it. He'd done that thing where he hooked into the satellites, where he floated right through the firewall of the Sun Tzu Citadel. That was the thing he could do. But come to think of it, he still didn't know how she'd managed it. How she'd penetrated the firewall and gotten to him.

No. He shook his head. No, Medusa wouldn't do that. She'd kissed him. It couldn't be her.

"But she likes me. We're not . . . We're . . ." He stopped, his cheeks burning.

He'd said enough. Blackburn reared back to his feet with a great sigh. "The honeypot is the oldest trick in the espionage book, Mr. Raines. Pretty faces have taken in presidents and generals, and it's not outside the realm of possibility that one could take in a teenage boy. You need to get dressed and come with me."

Tom rose from his bed and numbly pulled on his uniform,

his mind racing over every encounter he'd had with Medusa, trying to pick out some hint she'd been manipulating him. He couldn't see it. The leak couldn't have been his fault, could it have?

Vik was still snoring softly in the other bed when Tom followed Blackburn from the room. In that moment, he would've given anything to be sleeping again, too.

When he stepped out of Alexander Division into the plebe common room, he found armed soldiers waiting. Their guns reared to attention at the sight of him, and Tom's blood froze in his veins. The utter seriousness of the situation sank in. His heart began pounding wildly. He couldn't seem to take another step. He couldn't move.

Ten years in prison.

"Put those down. All of you," Blackburn ordered sharply. "Raines, pay them no mind. We're going downstairs to talk."

Tom's throat was bone-dry. He felt rooted in place.

"I'm not a spy."

"I believe you," Blackburn said. "I'm fully convinced that if the Russians or Chinese wanted to sneak a double agent into the Spire, it would not be you. So ignore the guns and focus on me." He pointed two fingers at his eyes, and Tom focused on them. "I'm sure this wasn't intentional on your part. You won't go to prison for being a dupe. But we have to go downstairs, and I need to see your processor so I can check for malware. They could be accessing the Spire right now."

"Right now?"

"Yes, Raines. So we'll do a system scan and see. And then we'll use the census device to check your meetings so I can get proof you did nothing intentional here. Understand?"

Tom swallowed, and swallowed again. He felt like there was a mass jammed in his throat.

"Y-yes, sir." He moved his legs that suddenly seemed to weigh a ton, and followed Blackburn into the elevator.

IN THE INFIRMARY, a tired-eyed Dr. Gonzales strapped a blood-pressure cuff to his arm and began giving him a physical for what Blackburn told him would be a neural culling with the census device.

"A neural culling is much like a regular memory viewing," Blackburn explained. He was hovering over a nearby computer that was connected to Tom's brain stem port by a neural wire. The screen flickered with data, Tom's scan in progress.

Tom just watched that screen from afar, his skin prickling all over with anxiety as he waited for Blackburn to find something.

"The census device will sort through your processor's indexed memories using an alternative search algorithm," Blackburn went on, eyes on his screen. "You don't steer the device this time. It steers itself and looks for memories and mental images you try to hide. *There!*"

His exclamation made Tom jump. He watched the lieutenant type rapidly at the keyboard. "And there it is." His voice was triumphant. "This must be the malware. It's certainly not mine."

Tom's heart lurched. He leaped to his feet and rushed over to see it, because he had to witness Medusa's treachery for himself. Dr. Gonzales cursed, and Tom realized he still had the blood pressure cuff on, and the equipment trailing behind him had upended a box of supplies.

But he couldn't focus on that right now. He grabbed the back of Blackburn's chair and looked over his shoulder, his eyes picking frantically over the data on the screen. Relief surged through him when he glimpsed the suspicious file name. He shook his head. "That's not malware, sir."

"Raines, this is a sophisticated piece of software. I don't expect you to understand—"

"I'm telling you, it's not malware. It's Wyatt's." He thought quickly of a reason for it to be there. "I asked Wyatt to write it for me after the war games. You know, because my programs suck."

"They do," Blackburn agreed absently, studying the program.

"Is that all you've found?" Tom asked hopefully. "There's nothing else?"

He flipped off the screen. "Yes, that's it."

Tom could've whooped in triumph. No honeypot. No treachery. Medusa hadn't been using him to spy on the Spire. It wasn't his fault. He hopped back up on the examination table, feeling like he could soar up into the stratosphere, he was so relieved. Dr. Gonzales resumed his physical exam.

"So we've just gotta do this neural-culling thing, then I can go?" he asked Blackburn as Dr. Gonzales listened to his back with a stethoscope.

"We'll stick you in the census device, and then you're off on your merry way."

Tom found himself grinning. He couldn't help it. It was the best news he'd ever heard. He was sure of it.

Blackburn's eyes narrowed. "But if you think I'm not at least putting you on restricted libs for being a colossal idiot, you're sadly mistaken."

Tom shrugged it off. Restricted libs was nothing compared to ten years in prison.

Dr. Gonzales stood up straight and ripped off the blood pressure cuff. "He's healthy, Lieutenant. I'll sign the authorization forms now."

"Authorization forms?" Tom echoed.

Blackburn reached back, and retrieved a pile of papers. "A neural culling requires physician consent."

"Will you need anything else?" Dr. Gonzales asked, flipping through one paper, signing it, and then the next. Then the next. On and on the stack went, and Tom wondered why there were so many papers for this. "Should I send someone down with incontinence supplies?"

Tom looked at Blackburn sharply. "Incontinence supplies?"

Blackburn shook his head. "It shouldn't be necessary."

"*Incontinence supplies?* I thought you said this is just like a standard viewing!"

Blackburn considered him. "It is, Raines. As long as there's no resistance on your part, it *is* just like a standard viewing. But sometimes, especially in the beginning of the culling, people tend to fight the census device. A neural culling is intrusive. It brings up things you may not want to share, memories you may only half recall. It also brings up private mental images."

"Private mental images," Tom repeated, understanding it. "Like, uh, daydreams."

"Yes."

"And other things like that."

"Yes," Blackburn said impatiently.

"You're going to see them," Tom repeated.

"Yes, Raines, and if you can't get over that, I'll end up seeing a lot of them. For both our sakes, embrace immodesty."

Tom's head throbbed. "So why incontinence supplies?"

"Prolonged resistance leads to a prolonged culling," Blackburn explained. "The device is designed to search for memories you actively conceal. If you resist, it begins digging out other, unrelated memories in an attempt to neutralize your ability to resist. It strips away your psychological defense mechanisms in a systematic fashion. Theoretically, it could break your mind. But that won't be an issue. If you didn't commit treason, you have nothing worth hiding from me, and this will be over very quickly."

Something nagged at Tom's brain, though. And he didn't figure out what it was until they were out of the infirmary, heading down the hallway toward the elevator. Blackburn waved away the armed soldiers again, grumbling something about overkill, so the soldiers lowered their guns again and fell behind them at a distance.

Halfway to the elevator, Tom stopped dead in his tracks.

He was remembering something: jogging through these hallways with Yuri.

With *Yuri*.

Yuri, who had a new firewall.

Tom's vague worry morphed into real horror. He knew Yuri's secret, Wyatt's secret. He hadn't committed treason, but *they* had. If he knew it, Blackburn would soon know it. The neural culling would find that in his brain.

"Wait. I don't want to do this."

Blackburn turned. "Refusal's not an option here, Raines." He studied him a moment. "I realize you're afraid—"

"I'm not scared," Tom protested.

"Good. You shouldn't be. Let's go and get this over with."

"I don't want to get a neural culling, sir!"

"This is not a choice." Blackburn spoke slowly, like he was explaining something to a young child. "You don't have right of refusal when national security is concerned."

Tom could hear his heart pounding, it was beating so hard. He hadn't worn his forearm keyboard, so he scanned the nearest wall for a computer. Maybe he could net-send Wyatt a warning. Then she could rescramble Yuri and cover up evidence or whatever.

"Can I contact someone first?"

Blackburn's eyes narrowed. "Who?"

Tom couldn't answer that.

"You're beginning to seem very suspicious right now, Mr. Raines, do you realize that?"

Tom was breathing hard. He looked at the soldiers, then at Blackburn, a sense of doom crashing over him.

"Okay, I'll go," Tom said. He started to follow, waiting until Blackburn bought it and turned away from him. Then Tom whipped around and sprinted off down the hallway.

Cries rang out behind him, *"After him!"*

TOM WASN'T STUPID enough to think he'd be able to escape the Pentagon all on his own. There was one person who could step in right now and avert disaster, a person even General Marsh couldn't touch. He just hoped she was there. He threw himself against Olivia Ossare's glass door, and pounded his hand against it. He heard boots thumping toward him.

Moron, moron, moron, Tom's thoughts beat. *It's not even 0700, of course she's not here yet. . . .*

And then she rose up from the other side of the desk, where she'd been leaning down, going through her drawers. Relief gushed through him. As soon as she slid aside the glass door, he bolted inside, fighting the wild urge to grab her and whirl her in a circle or something.

"You're here in case we have a problem with our military custodians, right?" Tom said, all in a rush. "Well, I've got a *huge* problem with my military custodians."

Her brow furrowed. "What's going on?"

"You have to help me. You *have* to." Tom heard pounding on the door, and jumped a foot in the air, stumbling into her desk away from the sound.

Outside the door, Blackburn's soldiers were staring in at them. Tom felt sickened by the enormity of what was happening here.

"What is it?" Olivia stepped toward the door.

"Don't!" Tom grabbed her arm. "Don't open it."

But she took his wrist and gently eased his grip from her. "Tom, sit down. I am going to tell them to wait."

"What if they won't listen to you?"

She squeezed his hand, then released it. "They'll listen." There was steel in her voice. "Now sit down."

Tom couldn't seem to catch his breath. But there was a calmness, a self-assurance in her voice, that made him somehow believe her.

When she turned toward the soldiers, he grabbed her computer, called up net-send, and started to type in a message to Wyatt, then he realized it. No, he couldn't do this, either. Blackburn could track it. He deleted it quickly. His brain went blank. He couldn't think of anything to do. He didn't have any way to save himself.

His eyes riveted to the soldiers beyond the glass, arguing with Olivia. Her soft voice persisted, and then amazingly, miraculously, they backed off. Tom never would've thought some guys with guns would listen to her. She closed the door and settled behind her desk.

"Want to fill me in, Tom?" she asked him.

Tom closed his eyes, trying to sort it all out. He knew he'd made a mistake, running from Blackburn. He didn't know what else he could've done.

"Blackburn thinks I'm the leak and he's going to use the census device on me." His words began spilling out faster and faster. "I'm not the leak. I swear it, I'm not. And it's not like a regular memory viewing. They're going to rip memories out of my head. Blackburn said it could break your brain if you use it long enough. Dr. Gonzales said it could make you incontinent. I don't want to be incontinent, okay? I don't!"

Olivia's brow knit like she was pondering it. "They have no right to force this on you, Tom. I'll speak to Lieutenant Blackburn."

"He won't listen to you. Look, do you have any civilian resources that can help? Any at all? Because I don't know what to do."

"I'll talk to General Marsh."

"He's in India right now meeting with some military guys about the Capitol Summit."

And then Blackburn himself was at the door, speaking to the soldiers. Tom clenched his fists on the desk in front of him, watching with a knot of dread in his throat the way Blackburn lifted his forearm keyboard, and typed something.

Click. The lock snapped open.

Blackburn strode through the door.

Olivia leaped to her feet. "What do you think you're doing?" she shouted at him, rushing around her desk and planting herself between Blackburn and Tom. "This is my office. You don't have the right to break in here!"

"And that's one of our plebes."

"You can't do this." When Blackburn moved toward Tom, Olivia stepped in his way. "I'm this boy's advocate, and I am not letting you seize him and subject him to that device. He's a civilian, and you don't have this authority. You are breaking the law, Lieutenant!"

He was unimpressed. "A law's a piece of paper unless someone's willing and able to enforce it. Let's ask the folks with the guns, shall we? I'm breaking the law here. Anyone care to arrest me?" He threw up his hands in mock surrender and glanced back at his troops, who just stood there in silence. "No? Well, that answers that. Move aside, Ms. Ossare."

He started forward again, but she stopped him by planting her hands on his chest. "How dare you." Rage made her voice shake. "You are overstepping your jurisdiction. These are his legal rights—"

"Before you lecture me about rights, tell me, really, how have you been here for three long years without figuring out the way things work? He's not at a summer camp. He's a military asset. His rights begin and end with that neural processor in his brain, and that's still more than most of the rabble can claim. As for my jurisdiction? I have brute force. You have words. One trumps the other. I'll show you which." He plucked her hands from his chest, then whirled her around, and shoved her out of his way.

She started for him again, but one of Blackburn's men caught her around the waist. Tom jumped to his feet, because Olivia looked ready to fight them all, and he wasn't going to let her get hurt. He'd done everything he could, coming here, seeing if there were civilian resources. There weren't. It was done, and it would only get worse if he didn't stop this now.

"Ms. Ossare, don't! It's okay. I'll go with them."

"Thatta boy, Raines," Blackburn said, closing the distance and seizing him. This time, he didn't tell the soldiers to lower the guns they'd raised. He dragged Tom from the room with a firm grip on his arm.

Olivia rushed after them as soon as she was free. She reached out, and her dark hand enveloped his, just briefly. "Tom, I will get you out of this," she pledged. "I swear it."

"Thanks," Tom said, before Blackburn jerked him forward and out of her reach. He didn't think she could, though. He knew nothing could save him from the census device now.

CHAPTER TWENTY-SIX

Today, the Calisthenics Arena resembled a tropical island. Tom charged forward, faster and stronger than anyone else in the simulation. At a quiet, sunlit cove, he waited to help Heather over a fallen palm tree. She leaped over the log, then stumbled, and gave a squeal of surprise. Her uniform had fallen off!

Her beautiful eyes rose to his. "Oh no, what do I do, Tom? It's so cold without my clothes. And zombies are attacking me!"

A bunch of zombies began attacking her. Tom felled them all with blows of his mighty fists. Heather gasped in fear of the zombies, then in admiration at Tom's prowess.

Tom turned around and strode forward, towering over her by a foot, his shoulders as broad as Siegfried's. Heather's beautiful eyes feasted upon the sight of his perfect six-pack, bared where his tunic had been torn open by the zombies. "Oh, Tom, you're so buff and brave. You're ten *times the man Elliot Ramirez is."*

Wyatt walked by and said, "It's true! He is!" Then she walked away.

Tom gathered Heather in his muscular arms. "Don't worry. You don't need clothes. Not when Tom Raines is around."

Another girlish shriek.

It was Ching Shih, the Chinese pirate woman Medusa played in Pirate Wars. She'd tripped over the same palm tree and lost her uniform, too. But she wasn't actually Ching Shih. It was a younger, much more beautiful version of her. It was Medusa the way Tom imagined her.

"Oh no, Tom," Medusa said. "I'm cold now, too!"

"Well, well." Tom chuckled. "It's lucky for you that I've got two arms." He reached out for her, and Medusa pranced over and happily joined them.

Heather pouted. "Tom, I don't want to share you."

"Maybe I don't want to share Tom with you, Heather." Medusa pressed up against Tom's powerful chest.

Tom smiled at the two girls in his arms. "Don't fight over me, ladies. Big Tom's got enough loving for both of you."

They blushed, murmuring about how good-looking and charming he was, and then they looked each other up and down.

"ALL YOUR FANTASIES go the same way," Blackburn complained. He was seated next to the census device, coffee in hand, Tom's mental images on the screen overhead. "Don't you ever get bored?"

"Feel free to stop watching!" Tom screamed at him.

"Calm down. You're getting hysterical . . . Big Tom."

Tom closed his eyes. He wanted to be shot right now. But first, he wanted to see Blackburn shot. No, eviscerated.

He sat beneath the census device, arms strapped down to keep him from fleeing again, the points of light blaring into his temples from the suspended, upside-down claw. He hoped a meteor would hit the Spire and obliterate it around them. Anything, anything to stop this.

As the fantasy took its natural course, Blackburn let out an exasperated breath and said, "Enough already." He launched himself to his feet, reached overhead, and turned off the census device.

"Are we done?" Tom asked hopefully.

"We haven't started, Raines. You and I have wasted three hours on these inane fantasies of yours. When will you get it through your head that you can't hide anything from me while you're in that chair? If you're already fighting me on something so mildly embarrassing as these—" He seemed to fumble for the right phrase. "—these implausible encounters you've imagined with various female trainees, then this is going to be a long ordeal for both of us."

Tom glared at the screen, his fists balled up against the armrests.

Blackburn snapped his fingers to draw Tom's attention back to him. "Try this, Raines. Don't think of an elephant."

"What?"

"Don't think of an elephant. I repeat, do not think of an elephant." He let those words hang in the air a moment. Then, "You're thinking of an elephant, aren't you?"

"Yes, I'm thinking of a stupid elephant now! Why?"

"That's how this works," Blackburn told him, pointing at the screen. "You're trying not to think of that elephant, which gives you a keen awareness of that elephant. The census device can sense that awareness. It knows you're hiding something. It won't stop digging through the rest of your memories until it senses that you've stopped hiding that elephant from it."

"So you're saying if I don't stop caring that you're going to see everything in my brain, you're going to end up seeing everything in my brain, is that it?"

"Yes, that's it, so you'd better desensitize quickly. If you hold out too long, I guarantee you, you won't have much of a mind left after this is over. You can't fight a census device."

Tom's chest ached as Blackburn flipped the census device back on. He tried to duck his head, but he knew it was useless. The beams followed him and found his temples again. A sense of futility seeped through him. He was already so sick of this. He just wanted to go back to his bunk.

"Progress," Blackburn noted. "Very good."

Tom lifted his head and saw that the fantasies were finally gone. He'd desensitized to the idea of Blackburn seeing them, he supposed. But the next image the census device called up wasn't any better.

It was Tom's first day of school ever. He was eleven years old and staring down at the claws of his Lord Krull avatar as Ms. Falmouth yelled at him for being insolent. Then she asked him to read something off the board. Tom hedged and made excuses, but she pressed him relentlessly, cornered him. Tom knew the letters a bit, so he tried, "Li-in-co-le-in . . ." staring at the text of "Lincoln." The classroom filled with laughter when his classmates realized he couldn't read.

Heat blasted his face. "That didn't happen." He couldn't stop his lips from moving, forming the urgent lie, because he would've torn out his stomach before showing this to Blackburn. "That wasn't any more real than the fantasies."

"Truly, Raines, I don't care." Blackburn sipped at his coffee, looking bored.

Tom relaxed just a bit, realizing he meant it, and the

Rosewood memories slipped away. The scene transformed again.

Neil.

No, not his father. Not in front of Blackburn. *Please* not his father.

And Tom tried to fight it so the census device stuck on that theme. *It was that night when Tom was little and the two guys busted into their room. They shouted at Neil about money, they clobbered him. They took Neil's watch since it was all he had left. Tom got so scared, huddled under the bed, that he peed on himself. Neil kept trying to coax him out afterward, telling him it was okay, they were gone now, but Tom wanted his mom and he put his hands over his ears when Neil explained again that she wasn't coming, she wasn't going to be here ever again. . . .*

Tom's every muscle was clenched, and his teeth were grinding together. He hadn't thought of that night in so long, in so many years. He must've forgotten it, really, and now it was there in his brain like it had just happened moments ago.

Blackburn swung his chair around and studied him over his coffee cup. "I warned you that the census device pulls up buried memories and dismantles your psychological defenses. This is going to get worse and worse if you don't give up whatever you're hiding."

Tom's thoughts flashed to Yuri and Wyatt, and he forced them away just as quickly. "I'm not hiding anything."

"If you weren't, this would be over by now, and we'd both be at breakfast."

The census device kept digging, bringing up more and more memories, an endless catalog of them. Tom decided he hated the census device, hated it so much, he felt like he was choking. He wished he could fry the thing. Go into it just like the septic tank in the Beringer Club and make it blow

357

up from the inside . . .

And then the neural culling began digging into that memory. It plastered itself across the screen: *The mesh of wires, the electricity, Tom's consciousness diving into the septic system at the Beringer Club and interfacing with it. The sewage bubbling up as the gauges pumped in reverse* . . .

At first, Blackburn just cast an idle glance at the image. Then he sat up ramrod straight, and by the time the screen showed the sewage seeping over the floor of the Beringer Club, he was on his feet with his mouth hanging open.

"What is this, Raines?" He turned, his eyes blazing in the shadowed, projected light of the screen. "What did I just see?"

Tom's head pulsed. Great. Now Blackburn knew what he'd done to the Dominion Agra execs, and then he'd tell Marsh. "Look, I know they put a ton of money into the war effort, but those Dominion guys had it coming!"

"Not that. The machine. What was that?"

Tom blinked, realizing that he wasn't even asking about the place he'd flooded. "I was reprogramming a septic tank."

"That wasn't programming. You were *interfacing* with it!"

"Oh. Sort of."

Blackburn reached overhead and manipulated a few controls on the census device. The bands of light bearing into Tom's temples vanished, and Tom felt like some rubber band, pulled taut, and been snapped. An overwhelming sense of relief surged through him.

Blackburn replayed the memory of the septic tank again and again. "How is it possible? That tank couldn't have been designed for a neural interface. Was it some freak hardware error?"

Tom realized it: he was far more interested in this than in whether or not Tom was a traitor.

Hope reared up inside him. He could use it. He was sure of it. If he just got Blackburn caught up in this, Yuri and Wyatt would never even become an issue.

"This has to be doctored somehow," Blackburn was muttering to himself. "It can't be the true recollection."

"Actually, it can," Tom spoke up. "It is. I used my processor to control the septic tank."

Blackburn turned back to him, shock written on his face. "You've done this more than once."

"A couple other times, yeah."

He drew a sharp breath. "At will?"

"More or less."

Blackburn just gaped at him for a long time. Then he seemed to recover his ability to speak. "Show me the others."

"Stop the culling."

"Raines—"

"I am not the traitor, sir. You know it. Swear you'll stop the culling, and I'll show you everything you want."

Blackburn's smile was ironic. "You realize you're threatening to keep a secret from me while strapped down under a census device."

"Why take all that time to dig it out of my brain if I'm willing to just give it to you, huh?"

Blackburn considered that. "Fine, Raines. You show me the memories, and I'll break procedure and stop the culling. We have a deal."

"I need a guarantee."

"There are no guarantees. I can only give you my word."

"At least take off these straps!"

Blackburn stepped over and undid the straps. "Don't run."

Tom's stomach was twisting in knots. He didn't have any way to force him to abide by their agreement, but if he didn't give the memories willingly, Blackburn still won. He'd just resume the culling and force them out. All Tom could do was give in and hope Blackburn meant his promise.

Blackburn tapped a button on the claw and reactivated the census device, but now it wasn't forcing memories out of Tom's head. He steered it to that time he sought out the satellites during the war games, and that time he sought Medusa, and even that first connection to the internet he made, back while he was unconscious after surgery. *The views of Rio, the Grand Canyon, the reservoir, the Bombay highway . . .*

"Look at that," Blackburn murmured, replaying the satellite one again. "Right through the Citadel's firewall as though it doesn't even exist. There isn't a technology in the world that can do that."

"I don't really know how that happens," Tom admitted. "It's the way I messaged Medusa the first time. I sort of went through the firewall and net-sent a hello to her neural processor."

Blackburn insisted on seeing that one more in detail, so Tom went back to it. Then Blackburn replayed them all, again and again. The coffee sat stagnant in his cup. Hours dragged by as he flipped between the memories. Tom started to wonder if he'd been completely forgotten. His throat grew parched. His stomach growled like it was ready to start digesting itself.

After another cycle of replaying the memories, the screen went dark.

Blackburn sat there in the dimness, staring where the images had just been. He spoke for the first time in hours. "Who else knows about this?"

"Vik, kind of. I told him about it, but he didn't believe me."

Blackburn regarded him searchingly. "This really means nothing to you, does it? You don't have the slightest understanding of the magnitude of this. You did something that shouldn't be possible."

"Sure, I know being able to interface with other tech is . . . it's something. I just haven't really thought about it much, uh, or really sat down and figured out what that something could be."

Blackburn's gray-eyed gaze slid back and forth between Tom and the census device. "So you're ready to talk about this. You weren't hiding these memories. What exactly were you concealing during the culling, then?"

"Just private stuff, okay?"

But Blackburn was stroking his chin, eyes on him, speculative. "I looked into your records, Raines. You never had a psych screening before coming here. That's standard procedure, did you know that?"

"Uh, I hadn't heard, no."

"A trainee who was recruited even though he has no relevant background," Blackburn murmured to himself, turning back to face the screen. "A trainee with no education, no screening tests, no medical records . . ."

"My dad always moved us around, and I've never even been that sick, that's why! I haven't needed a hospital since I was born."

"And now this. How does it connect?"

"Freak coincidence, sir. Are we done here?"

Blackburn turned on him suddenly. "Have you ever had dealings with Obsidian Corp? Or a man named Joseph Vengerov?"

Tom's brain flickered back to the Beringer Club.

"You have," Blackburn breathed, seeing his face. A light stole into his eyes. "*When?*"

"It didn't have to do with this."

"Show me," Blackburn demanded, turning the census device back on.

Tom started to give the memory. Vengerov and Dalton appeared on the screen, and Vengerov was looking at Tom and speaking those words, *"And how is this project coming?"*

And then he realized it: they'd been talking about his reprogramming. Blackburn would never let that rest either. He'd want to know the whole story of a Coalition company messing with a trainee's neural processor.

And it would lead to Wyatt giving him the firewall.

And that would lead to Yuri's firewall, and their treason.

It could lead to Wyatt down here, strapped in for a culling. Then Yuri, getting his mind torn apart. It could lead to prison for both of them, and probably for Tom, too, because he was covering for them.

He couldn't let it happen. He forced his mind away from the memory.

"What are you doing?" Blackburn demanded when the image froze.

Tom was sitting in the chair, his eyes screwed shut, realizing there was no way he could do this. He thought of Wyatt again, and wondered how much worse it would be for her—after she'd trusted Blackburn, after Blackburn had turned on her . . . "No, I'm not showing that one."

"Excuse me?"

"I said no." Tom opened his eyes, determined. "We had a deal: once I showed you the other memories, we'd be done. Well, I showed you all of them. We're done here."

"First, Vengerov."

"No."

"I want the rest, Raines."

"No!"

Blackburn closed the distance between them, looking like some psycho from a horror movie in the projected light of the census device. "You will show me that memory, Raines!"

"*I WON'T!* It has nothing to do with this!"

When Blackburn moved in to tie him down again, Tom's self-control vanished. He kicked wildly out at him. Blackburn's fist flew toward his face, a ringing blow connected with Tom's jaw, sending him reeling back into the chair. He recovered his bearings as the straps were already tightening on his wrists again, and he desperately tried to escape, but they trapped him in the chair.

Blackburn backed away from him. "So here it is. You have a choice, Raines." The projected image of Vengerov rippled over his face like he was some distorted mirror. "Either you show me the rest of that memory willingly, or I cull it out of you. So help me, I'm going to see it if I have to rip apart your mind to get it."

Tom gritted his teeth, his face feeling numb from the blow. "Come on, why aren't you listening to me? It has nothing to do with any of this!"

"Have it your way."

His tone sounded like a death sentence. He activated the culling and set it to full power. The lights blared into Tom's temples and eradicated the world around him.

Tom slammed his head back into the headrest so hard prongs of pain jolted up his neck, and the restraints on his wrists scoured his skin. Memory after memory passed by, terrible things that felt like organs ripped from his body.

Hours of it dragged by, as the memories flittered from one subject to another. Sometimes, a particularly nasty one hit him like he'd just broken some bone he hadn't been aware of before. He swam back to awareness when Blackburn began pressing a cup to his lips around 2000. "You must be thirsty."

On the screen: *Tom was nine and trying to sleep on a bench at a bus station, but Neil stood in the middle of the morning crowd, still drunk from the night before, railing stupidly at people walking past him, "Going off to vote Milgram today? He's Obsidian's man. Or Wantube? He's owned by Dominion!"*

He didn't want anything from Blackburn. He tried twisting his head away, but Blackburn caught his jaw firmly and poured—and as soon as the water touched his tongue, Tom realized he was dying of thirst. He swallowed huge mouthfuls as . . . *His father kept ranting at people hurrying by him. "Ha! Either way you vote Coalition! Don't you get it? You aren't making a choice! Doesn't anyone else see that?"*

Blackburn set the glass back down as *the policeman came over. Neil ranted, "What do you mean, public disturbance? Is freedom of speech a public disturbance now?" Tom sat up from his bench, realizing where this was going. . . .*

"This is needless, Raines. Why are you fighting me?"

Tom stared at Blackburn's fatigues, where the projected light was now playing the image of Neil brawling with three policemen. He closed his eyes, not wanting to see his dad get tasered like the last time.

"What hold does Vengerov have over you?" Blackburn said, lowering himself down before Tom's chair, far too close. "Money? Threats? Blackmail? You can tell me. There has to be something."

Tom could hear his father roaring in anger. He heaved in great breaths, suddenly feeling like he was drowning, his dad yelling on-screen and Blackburn pressing in before him.

"This ability you have . . . Is that the project he mentioned? Vengerov is obviously involved somehow. Is this Obsidian Corp's next great experiment? Is that why he got your screenings waived?" Anger lined his voice. "Just tell me, Raines. A trillionaire doesn't need the protection of a fourteen-year-old boy!"

"I've told you," Tom croaked.

"No, you haven't! You've lied!"

I am not protecting him! Tom wanted to scream at him. *I DON'T CARE about Vengerov!* But it would be like screaming into a strong wind. Useless. So useless.

"Vengerov isn't worth this." Blackburn leaned closer, his voice right in Tom's ear. "You can't trust him. He's the one responsible for all those deaths. Not just the soldiers in my testing group. Others."

Tom's dad's shouts and the policemen's shouts were dying down, and he knew on the screen, he'd see himself *standing in the middle of the train station watching his father get carried away in handcuffs. He started to follow, and then he stopped, realizing where he'd end up if he did. He'd find himself in some foster home somewhere. His dad wouldn't want him to follow.* And Tom still remembered that feeling of being hopelessly lost in the middle of a busy crowd, wondering what he was supposed to do now, where he was supposed to go, feeling like he was slipping down some drain. It took him a moment to realize he wasn't remembering the feeling. It was there right now inside him.

"We weren't the first whose minds he butchered," Blackburn went on. "One thousand Russians were, back when Vengerov was in charge of LM Lymer Fleet. He'd just inherited his old man's company, and he figured he'd make a name for himself by taking a bold step with other people's lives at stake. Most died, just like with us. The difference was, the Russians killed the broken survivors to bury the whole project. That's why Vengerov had to come here. They would never have let him do it again, and he needed living subjects, living adults. He told our military that all he needed was a few hundred. Surely at least a handful would survive the neural processors, and that was all he needed. So they assigned a few hundred of us to the great experiment."

Tom found himself staring at the new image on the screen, a smiling blond woman. . . . *His mother, looking so young, back when he was so little he'd forgotten this. She was looking at him and smiling, her hair spilling over her shoulders. Tom clung to her, getting a piggyback ride down the dark street. . . .*

Blackburn must've seen something on his face. He stopped talking and his eyes followed Tom's, to the screen.

She spun him around in a circle, streetlights whirling before his eyes. "So what are we gonna get for dinner?"

"Ice cream, Momma!"

His mother whirled to a stop, laughing, and staggered a bit. "We'll get a tub of ice cream bigger than your head, Tommy. And hot fudge, too." *Her hair was all scrunched up against his face, and . . .*

The memory scorched its way through his head. Tom was aware of the beams digging into his brain, but he couldn't stop looking because he didn't remember even living with his mother. He didn't have any memory of his mother, well, loving him. He didn't remember her like this. He couldn't bear to see this.

"It's that painful seeing her, is it?" Blackburn remarked, looking at him again. "Then I can guarantee you, you'll see more of *her* in the hours ahead if you don't give me—"

And then something happened.

Tom was looking through his own eyes and he was not, he

was seeing fire, and then the census device was fused to his brain and sparks fountained from the controls. With a spike of rage, Tom sent an electrical current whipping from the metallic claw.

Blackburn yelled out and crashed to the floor.

Tom snapped back into himself, the stench of smoke in his nostrils, his heart jerking against his rib cage. Blackburn lay, heaving ragged breaths for several stunned moments. Then he struggled back to his feet, one arm clutched uselessly to his side.

He surveyed the census device, his eyes wild. Dark smoke curled up in a twisting line. Comprehension flooded his face. "That was you, wasn't it?" His gaze dropped to Tom's. "You interfaced with it."

Tom didn't know. He didn't know anything right now, except he was tired and sick and he wished he'd killed him. "I'll fry you again if you turn it back on!"

Blackburn circled the census device, singed arm clutched to his torso. "You burned out one of the legs to stop me." He paused a moment, a strange smile on his lips as he took a moment to absorb the idea. "Who knew you could do that? Thatta boy, Raines."

"I'll do it again, I swear!" Tom screamed at him.

Blackburn just seemed intrigued. He raised his good arm and grabbed one of the still-functional legs. "Go ahead. I'm touching it. There's no way you can miss. Do it again."

"I'm not bluffing! I'll electrocute you!"

"And I'm waiting with bated breath." Blackburn didn't even sound sarcastic. "Do it, Raines."

But Tom couldn't. His chest felt tight. He couldn't seem to get enough air in his lungs. He felt like he was going to break down, and he'd rather be flayed alive than let Blackburn see that. "You're insane."

"Yes, I've heard that tune." Blackburn released the leg and lowered his arm back to his side. "And I see you can't do that on command. That's useful to know for tomorrow morning."

CHAPTER TWENTY-SEVEN

TOM WOKE UP still strapped in the chair, his brain aching in his skull, his head stuffy like it might burst. His thoughts were scattered, strange things to him after hours of culling. He stared dully at Olivia Ossare, who stood in front of him, jerking the straps off his wrists, muttering to herself. "This is savage . . . just a child."

His voice came out scratchy. "You came."

"Tom!" Her warm palm cupped his chin. "Are you all right?"

His head pounded. He closed his eyes because it was easier than answering that. She helped him stand and then wobble down from the chair on rubbery legs.

"Is this over?" he asked.

Her grip tightened on him. "I'm working on it, Tom. Right now, Lieutenant Blackburn can't be reasoned with. It took me this long just to get in to see you."

Tom's vision blackened and he swayed. She eased him down

to the floor. He sagged to the ground, his head flopping against her arm, the ceiling spinning overhead in frantic circles.

He felt her fingers threading through his hair. The memory of his mother, so close to the surface, flickered up as she stroked his hair. He kept his eyes closed, a knot rising in his throat.

"Please let this be over soon."

He didn't realize he'd spoken aloud until she told him, "I'm doing my best. I've been trying to get in touch with your father."

"My dad can't help me."

"He can, Tom. He can sue for custody of you."

Tom's eyes snapped open. He sat up quickly enough to make his vision blacken. "Custody?"

"The military can't retain custody of you if your father withdraws consent."

Tom's head ached. He felt like he might vomit. "I'd have to quit to get out of this?" Blood buzzed up in his ears. "But the neural processor can't come out. Not ever."

"Your brain becomes dependent eventually, but you only had it installed five months ago. I spoke to Dr. Gonzales, and he said it's early enough to allow for a phased removal. They're doing something similar with your friend Stephen."

No. *No.* He couldn't go back to that. Loser Tom moving casino to casino with nothing ahead of him, nothing behind him, nothing, nothing . . .

But if he stayed, and Blackburn kept culling his brain . . .

He'd go insane. He couldn't take more of this. He'd go insane and he'd give away Yuri and Wyatt.

Hot frustration roared up inside him. Tom curled a hand into a fist and slammed it into the floor. The world sharpened into focus around him. He slammed it again and again. Then Olivia caught his wrist.

"Tom, stop that. You'll hurt yourself."

He didn't care. The pain was distant in his awareness, fury swamping everything. Short of punching Blackburn's face over and over, it was the only thing that made him feel better. He tried twisting out of her grip, but he was too worn out to keep it up for long.

"I am not contacting my father," Tom said. "I need an option C."

"There is no option C, Tom. I need your father on our side if I'm going to get you out of this."

Tom's gaze drifted up to the census device, burned out, looming in calm menace over the chair and arm straps. "It's option C or nothing."

THE NEXT MORNING, Blackburn sent soldiers in to strap Tom into the chair, a fully repaired census device looming overhead. Tom tugged at the arm straps, surveying the metal claw morosely. His head remained foggy from his fitful sleep. He watched Blackburn glide into the room, a bandaged arm clutched to his side. The sight flooded him with venomous glee.

"Does your arm hurt?" he asked Blackburn as he prepared the device.

"Not a bit," Blackburn answered.

As Blackburn shifted, Tom swung his boot toward the bandaged arm. Blackburn hissed and flinched back just in time.

Tom smiled at him maliciously, taking a horrible, dark pleasure from it. "It hurts."

"Not like this will." Blackburn flipped on the census device, the most stinging retort of all. The bright beams of light bore into Tom's temples, digging, digging into his brain, his memories, flipping open one, discarding, flipping open another, discarding all like pieces of trash, searching for Vengerov.

Neil . . . his mother . . . Karl . . . his mother . . . Dalton . . . his mother . . . He was a few minutes into it this time before a loud clang shut the machine off.

It took Tom's fuzzy brain a moment to focus on General Marsh's voice.

"What exactly do you think you're doing, Lieutenant?"

Tom jerked in his seat, elation sending his brain soaring. He saw Marsh and Blackburn facing off, the screen between them. "I'm investigating the leak, General. As you ordered."

"I didn't say you could strap Raines into the census device. Get him out of that chair. Now!"

Blackburn didn't move. "No, sir."

"Excuse me?"

"He stays."

"This is an order!"

"And I'm disregarding it, sir."

Marsh swore, and charged over toward Tom. His leathery face was twisted in fury, and Tom sagged back, so relieved he felt like he could hug the old general.

Blackburn trailed behind him with a slow, deliberate stride. "Before you release him, there's one thing I'd like to make clear, sir."

"What?" Marsh whirled on him, his knobby fists clenched at his sides.

"If you take him out of that chair," Blackburn said, "I leave. I walk away."

Marsh was silent a long moment. "Are you threatening me?"

"Yes, that's exactly what I'm doing, sir. I won't just walk out, though. I will rig up this entire place with a good-bye present that all of Obsidian Corp. won't be able to fix."

Tom couldn't believe Blackburn, a lieutenant, was just standing there threatening a *general*. That wasn't how it worked. Hatred and anticipation surged through him. Marsh was going to make him so sorry for it!

"James, you wouldn't do that," Marsh said, a note of pleading in his voice. "I know this leak has to hurt your pride, but this is taking it too far."

"Try me," Blackburn replied simply.

Tom stared disbelievingly at Marsh's back. Why wasn't he ordering some soldiers in to arrest Blackburn? Or doing something even remotely general-like to a lieutenant who dared to talk to him like that?

And then Blackburn actually stepped out of the room and left them alone, like he was so confident in his threat he didn't have to bother staying to enforce it.

"General!" Tom said, desperate. "Please, General, come on . . ."

Marsh heaved a great sigh and turned around. "I'm afraid what you just saw, Tom, was my hands being tied."

Tom stared at him in naked disbelief. Marsh walked out of the room, leaving Tom there, strapped to the chair. Minutes dragged by as Tom stared into the emptiness of the room, feeling numb and alone.

He heard Blackburn's slow, deliberate footsteps and closed his eyes, because he couldn't stand to see him. Blackburn didn't flip the census device back on right away. First he unstrapped one of Tom's arms and gave him water, but Tom's arm shook too hard to hold it. So Blackburn strapped it down and held the glass for him.

A wild thought occurred to Tom. The longer he was drinking water, the longer he'd have before the culling started again. So he asked for more, and then more. Even when his stomach felt like it was going to burst, he pleaded for more.

"Enough. You'll make yourself sick," Blackburn said finally, refusing to give him another glass.

That did it. *Make yourself sick* . . . It was suddenly the most hilarious thing he'd ever heard. Tom started laughing. The wild, hysterical laughter rocked his whole body. He laughed until his stomach hurt, until tears streamed from his eyes, until he actually was sick, and even after that he couldn't stop laughing until the beams were back on and boring into his head.

Blackburn stood there watching him, rubbing his palm over his mouth over and over, and ripping Tom's mind apart.

TOM FOUND HIMSELF locked in a small cell that looked onto the census device. He stood in the middle of the room, over-stimulated by the humming electric light overhead, by the bright bite of its rays, by the pounding in his head, images swimming like ghosts in his vision. He resorted to the only thing that seemed to unify his brain again—his fist crashing against the wall over and over again, until the pain exploding in his knuckles mounted in his awareness and the blood smeared on the walls connected him with his vision center again.

Then someone slipped through the door, and a gentle but firm hand clasped his wrist. Olivia Ossare gripped his arm and urged him to sit down on the bed, offering him a glass of water. Tom gulped it greedily, only half aware of Olivia inspecting the damage to his bloody knuckles. He felt so strange, so strange, like he was about to explode out of his skin.

He wasn't aware of slumping back against the granite wall, but he drifted to himself when he felt her fingers threading in his hair again. Tom pressed his eyes closed even tighter, because even if he didn't quite understand why her touch was so soothing, he had this strong suspicion opening his eyes would make it stop.

"I think," Tom confessed when he could finally speak, feeling flat and empty, "I'm up for option B." He couldn't take much more of this. "Please find my father. Please get me out of here."

"Tom," she whispered, "I already have."

BLACKBURN COULDN'T LAY a finger or a use single device on him now that Tom's father was suing to remove him from the Spire. When Olivia arrived with the military police, Blackburn stood there in the middle of the dark Census Chamber, following Tom with his eyes as he was led from the room. Now Tom slouched in Olivia's office, listening to her argue over legal issues with General Marsh and a military lawyer. The words were over his head. He didn't want to hear them.

He knew what this meant. A gradual phaseout of the neural processor. Removal from the Spire. Going back to living with Neil.

He'd never betray Yuri or Wyatt then. Blackburn could never again pillage his mind with the census device. He'd hold on to his sanity.

Maybe.

Maybe.

There was a part of Tom that wanted to pound his head against the desk in front of him. He couldn't bear the thought of going back to his old life. Not after all this. Not after what he had here. And it killed him to think of how Dalton had won. Dalton had maneuvered him right out of the Spire. It was so much worse, getting the world and then having it taken away. It would've been better if he'd never come here.

"May I speak to him alone?" Marsh asked Olivia.

Olivia looked at Tom. "It's up to you."

Tom shrugged a shoulder. It wasn't until the lawyer and Ms. Ossare were both out of the room that he raised his eyes to General Marsh and gazed upon him with open loathing. The guy with his hands tied.

"Why didn't you give me the screening tests or the psych tests like everyone else?" Tom's voice shook with fury. "Blackburn thinks I'm part of some conspiracy because I didn't have the tests everyone else did! Why didn't you just give them to me and stop this from happening?"

"To be honest, son, I didn't get you psych tested because I didn't think you'd pass."

"*I'M NOT DERANGED!*" Tom screamed, knowing how deranged he sounded.

"Easy, Tom." Marsh rose and circled around Olivia's desk, examining an ink blot framed on her wall. "The truth is, I didn't search you out through official channels. You were a side project of mine. After all, I don't go personally to retrieve most recruits."

Tom stared hard at Marsh's tired reflection in the glass pane over the ink blot.

"I was looking for something very different. You've seen Camelot Company in action. Those kids are the best this country has to offer. Well-rounded, bright, personable."

"Like *Karl Marsters*?"

"Well, most of them." Marsh dipped his head, conceding that. "They're America's straight shooters who will get somewhere in life. That's who we recruit. That's the type of kid we usually attract."

"Unlike me."

Here it was again, that issue Tom had wondered about from the very start. He knew how strange it was that Marsh would recruit him, of all people in the country. He'd ignored the wrongness of it. And only now, now that it was about to implode, was Marsh answering him. Tom wanted to tear him apart for it.

"Unlike you," Marsh agreed. "Do you remember the scenario with the tank, Tom? The one I ran you through at the Dusty Squanto? There are several steps involved there. The testee first has to decide to go for the tank directly, rather than the antitank guns. And then comes the critical next step, the one most of our trainees in the Spire fail."

"What?" Tom asked miserably.

"They get the hatch open and drop inside. That's when they screw up. They drop into the tank and find the operator in the process of dying from exposure to the Martian atmosphere."

"And then they kill the guy."

Marsh shook his head. "That's not what most trainees do. It would be easy if they could simply shoot the man, but it's not possible with an iono-sulfuric rifle in a closed space. So they count on the man dying on his own. They don't take into account the backup systems in the tank: the autosealing hatch, the pressurizers, and the operator's hidden weapon. The operator recovers, and he kills the test taker. The only one here in the Spire who passed that phase was you."

"I didn't even know about those backup systems."

"You bludgeoned the man before it even became an issue. You won the scenario. You beat a dying man to death. You did something the others flinched from."

"It was just a video game, though."

"It's the instinct it reveals. That's what I was looking for."

"You can't tell me Karl Marsters would flinch from bludgeoning a dying guy."

"Karl Marsters didn't go for the tank. That was the

problem. I ran thousands of teenagers through that scenario. I found plenty who would bludgeon that operator—plenty with that killer instinct—but invariably, they failed to go directly for the tank because they failed to anticipate the best move for their opponent. Those cruel enough to bludgeon a dying man never had the same capacity to foresee the moves the operator was going to make. You not only passed, you nailed it on the first try. I thought you would. That's why I honed in on you."

So that's why Marsh hadn't helped him. The thought stung him. He'd had these high expectations, and Tom hadn't lived up to them. "I must've been a huge disappointment to you."

"Not at all. You have poor impulse control, and you're too arrogant for your own good. You're also shaping up into exactly what I wanted to find. Exactly the type of Combatant we've been lacking."

Tom remembered something Elliot had said, something Nigel had said. About how they were looking for someone different. "You want vicious."

"Yes, Tom." Marsh leaned toward him, eyes intent. "Vicious. Ruthless, but only when you need to be. Someone who strikes when they know it will hurt. Someone who lands the lethal blow. Those are the people who win wars. Those are the people who take down the Medusas of this world. Look at Achilles—he wasn't toppled by a warrior who was stronger than him, faster, better. He was felled by an arrow to the weak spot in his armor. You have an eye for those weak spots. You could be something. You could take down the other side's best. I was willing to risk recruiting you through unofficial channels. And if you were as good as I hoped . . ."

"It would be your icing on the cake?" Tom mocked.

"Don't mouth off. I'm your senior officer until the day you walk out of the Spire, Plebe."

"So seniority matters now?" Rage ignited in his chest. "It didn't in the Census Chamber! Lieutenant Blackburn got away with threatening you!"

"That's a very different matter."

"*How?*"

"Because he knows I can't afford to lose him. He does something invaluable around here, and he does it for very cheap."

Tom blinked. "The programming?"

"Obsidian Corp. built your processors. They used to handle all your software, too. Because they were the only ones who wrote Zorten II, they charged us through the roof for it. We tried cutting costs by training our own people, but Obsidian Corp. always hired them away. We tried to force our officers to finish their terms of service, but soon we'd get the angry calls from senators on behalf of Obsidian ordering us to let the programmers resign. To add insult to injury, Joseph Vengerov always turned around and tried to lease our own programmers back to us as consultants. It wasn't financially sustainable. Lieutenant Blackburn *is*."

"This is all about money, then."

"It's always about money, son. War is expensive. We cut costs wherever we can. That's why all our shipyards are in space. That's why Combatants need sponsors. The fact is, the only people in this country who can afford to pay taxes to support the military are the very people powerful enough to avoid paying them. As for the resources we win in space? We're lucky to see a dime. We haven't even seized Mercury yet, and Senator Bixby's promised first drilling rights to Nobridis. That's why I need Lieutenant Blackburn. He does everything Obsidian did, and he does it for an officer's salary. Not only that, but he does it better. And the best part is, Joseph Vengerov could throw his entire fortune at him, and Blackburn would still turn down a job with Obsidian Corp., because *they* were the ones behind the neural processors. In fact, Lieutenant Blackburn had only one condition when he came to the Spire: he wanted to teach the trainees how to program with Zorten II."

"He came here just for that?"

"That's all he wants. That's why I stuck my neck out to get him on my staff. If he quits on me, or worse, follows through on his threat, every assurance I gave the Defense Committee gets discredited and so do I."

"I don't believe it." Tom's voice shook. Blackburn had to have some other reason. He was twisted and evil and . . .

"It's true, Tom." Marsh raised an open palm in the air. "He wants you to learn. Look what happened to him with his own processor."

"Yeah, I know it drove him crazy."

"More than that. All three adults who survived the neural processors reacted in different ways. The other two had serious problems, but they were either lucid or lucid most of the time. Major Blackburn was never lucid."

"Major," Tom repeated.

"He was a major in the US Army. First in his class at West Point, in fact. Once he got the processor, he had that psychotic break, but he refused to believe he was sick, and he wasn't responding to medication. Obsidian Corp. stepped forward and offered to take custody of the survivors. It was their project, so they were willing to foot the expense of treating them with their own therapies. The other two survivors went willingly. Major Blackburn did not. He escaped their custody and disappeared right off the grid, and I'll tell you, Tom, that's not an easy feat in an age of universal surveillance. He even retrieved his family."

Tom opened and closed his mouth. "Lieutenant Blackburn has a family."

"*Major* Blackburn did," Marsh corrected. "A wife, two kids, a house in Wyoming. We stationed soldiers at their home, waiting for him to show, and he still got them right out from under our noses. We heard nothing for years, and then one day out of the blue, his wife tipped us off. She'd realized by then that he'd lost his mind. He was paranoid, erratic, and she was afraid of him. She let us know that he'd taken the family and holed up in a compound outside Roanoke, Texas."

Roanoke. The word sent a chill through Tom. "So what happened?"

Marsh tapped his fingers on his desk. "He was armed to the teeth. His wife knew when we came to retrieve the processor, Major Blackburn might turn it into a bloodbath. She was willing to stay near him during the siege to keep us informed of his movements, if we were willing to smuggle out the children before the shooting began. On the day of the operation, she was able to slip the children out back where we had a team waiting to transport them out of harm's way. And when that team drove from the house, they found out the hard way that Major Blackburn had rigged the surrounding area with land mines."

Tom was stunned into silence, realizing it. It took him several seconds to speak. "His kids were in the car?"

"Yes."

"He blew up his own kids."

"Yes, Tom."

Tom couldn't get his head around to that.

"When we did finally move in, Major Blackburn didn't put up a fight," Marsh said. "As far gone as he was, even *he* understood what had happened. And even after he'd fixed his own neural processor, it was years before he was able to gain the slightest freedom of movement—he'd proven that dangerous. So you appreciate now, I hope, just how far out I had to stick my neck to get him in here. The army would never have had him back. Their boys drove that car onto that land mine. So James Blackburn's now with my branch, and he's my responsibility. He goes down, I go down, and he knows it."

Tom's head throbbed. "So I'm done." The implications of all this sank like a lead weight in his gut. "He has one over you, so if I stay, Blackburn's going to drive me out of my mind with the census device and you can't stop him. I have to quit."

"There's one other way. It can't come through me, but if he received an order directly from the senators on the Defense Committee to back down, he would have to leave you be. If you want them to step in for you, Tom, you have to become too valuable to let go. And you have to do it somewhere public enough to make an impression on them."

Tom sat up, his insides twisted into knots of anxiety, apprehension. Hope clawed its frantic way up from the murky depths where he'd banished it. His palms and forehead pricked with sweat.

"How? General, I'll do anything."

"You're coming with me to the Capitol Summit. You'll be the one to proxy for Elliot. You'll be the one to beat Medusa."

0 1 1 1 1 1 0 0 0 1 0 0 0 0 1 1 1 0 1 0 1 0 1 0 1 0 0 1 0 0 1 1 0 1 1 0 0 1 0 0
0 0 0 1 0 1 0 1 1 0 1 1 0 0 0 0 0 0 1 0 0 1 1 1 0 0 0 0 0 1 0 1 1 0 1 0 1 0 0
1 0 0 0 0 1 1 1 1 1 0 1 0 0 1 1 1 1 1 0 1 1 0 0 1 1 0 1 0 1 0 0 0 1 0 1 0 0
0 1 0 1 0 0 1 1 1 1 1 1 1 0 0 1 1 1 0 1 0 1 1 0 0 0 0 0 0 0 1 0 0 1 1 1
0 1 0 0 0 1 1 0 1 1 0 1 1 1 1 0 0 0 0 0 0 0 1 0 1 1 0 1 0 0 1
1 1 1 0 1 0 0 0 0 0 1 1 1 1 0 0 1 0 0 1 0 1 1 1 0 0 1 1 1 0 1 1 0 1 0 0 1
0 1 0 1 0 1 0 0 0 1 1 0 1 1 0 0 0 0 1 1 0 1 0 0 1 1 0 0 0 1 0 1 1 1 1 0 0
0 1 0 1 1 0 0 1 1 0 1 0 0 0 0 0 1 0 1 1 0 1 1 0 0 0 0 0 0 0 1 0 1 1 0 0
1 1 1 0 0 0 1 1 0 0 0 0 0 1 1 1 1 0 1 1 0 1 1 0 1 0 0 0 0 0 1 0 0 1 1 1 0
1 1 1 1 1 1 0 0 1 0 1 0 1 1 1 0 1 1 0 1 0 1 0 1 1 1 1 0 1 0 1 1 0 1 1 0
1 0 1 0 0 1 1 1 1 1 1 0 1 1 0 0 0 0 1 1 1 0 1 1 0 1 1 1 0 1 1 1 0 0 0
0 0 0 1 1 0 1 1 0 0 1 1 0 1 0 0 1 0 0 0 0 1 0 1 0 1 0 0 1 0 0 0 0 1 0 0 1 0
1 1 1 0 0 0 1 0 0 1 0 1 1 0 0 1 0 0 1 0 1 0 1 0 1 1 0 0 0 1 0 1 1 0
0 1 0 0 0 0 0 0 0 1 1 1 1 0 1 1 0 0 1 1 0 1 1 0 1 0 0 0 0 1 0 0 0 0 1 0 0
0 0 0 1 1 1 1 0 0 1 0 0 1 1 0 0 1 0 0 0 0 1 1 0 0 1 0 0 0 0
0 1 0 1 1 0 0 0 1 1 0 0 1 1 0 0 1 1 0 0 0 0 0 1 0 1 1 1 0 0
1 0 0 1 0 1 1 1 0 0 1 0 1 1 0 0 0 0 0 0 0 1 0 0 0 1 1 1 1 0 0
0 1 1 0 1 1 0 0 0 1 1 0 0 1 1 0 0 1 1 0 0 0 0 1 0 1 0 0 1 0 0 1 0 1 0 1 1 1 1
1 1 0 1 0 0 0 1 1 1 0 0 1 0 1 1 1 1 0 0 1 0 1 0 1 0 1 1 1 1 1 1 0 0
0 0 1 0 1 0 0 1 0 1 1 1 0 0 1 0 1 0 0 0 1 0 1 0 0 1 0 0 0 0 1 0 0 1 1 0 1
1 1 0 1 0 0 1 0 0 0 0 1 0 0 0 0 0 0 0 1 0 0 0 1 0 0 1 0 1

CHAPTER TWENTY-EIGHT

Tom sprinted across the Calisthenics Arena and caught up to Vik midway through the Battle of Gettysburg. His roommate lifted his bayonet to impale him, then realized who it was and lowered it again.

"Tom! Hey, man. You done being disappeared now?"

"Not yet. Run faster."

"Aah," Vik agreed. The Confederates in Pickett's Charge were nearly upon them.

They picked up the pace, sprinting through the grass. In front of them, the Union soldiers fired at their position. The two armies pressed in on them like a steel trap springing shut.

"So where have you been?" Vik screamed the words to be heard over the booming canons. "You should hear the rumors about you, man. I'm talking alien abductions and secret CIA mind-control experiments here."

"Basement." Tom couldn't say much more than that. Not because it was classified, but more because he was out of breath. Two days, no sleep, little food or water, and constant neural culling had left him a wreck.

Olivia had offered to write him an excuse for Calisthenics, but Tom didn't know how much time he had left at the Spire. He wanted to spend as much of it with his friends as he could.

Now the sky turned black above them, and the dead Confederate and Union soldiers rose and revealed themselves to be zombies, descending upon the trainees for a bloodbath. Tom used his bayonet to behead one, but a pair of Union zombies seized him and tore his throat out.

Session expired. Immobility sequence initiated. Tom's body went numb below the chest. He dropped to the grass.

Vik dropped dead on the grass next to him. "So tell me everything," he shouted over the roar of gunfire.

"You never die in Calisthenics."

"I pulled a Beamer and suicided."

Pulled a Beamer. Tom sighed, a bleak mood sinking over him as the zombies trampled his body to get at the rest of the trainees. He had to beat Medusa or *he'd* be the one pulling a Beamer—booted out of the program, getting the neural processor phased out of his brain.

"Well, Tom?"

"It's a long story." And he didn't want to talk about it. He really didn't.

But Vik insisted. "This is a long battle. Come on. Talk."

Worn boots scrunched the grass next to Tom's head, and a familiar voice rang out: "Timothy."

Tom opened his mouth to ask why he was going back to the wrong name, then remembered that Vik didn't know Yuri was unscrambled. So he settled with, "Hey, man."

"Tom was going to explain who disappeared him," Vik said. "Drop dead with us."

"Very well." Yuri tossed aside his musket so the nearest zombie could come kill him.

But he miscalculated his death. The zombie pounced on his large back, tore out his throat, and his immobility sequence engaged. Yuri dropped like a falling tree, and landed sidelong across Tom and Vik's stomachs, knocking the breath out of them.

"Oof!" Tom struggled against the weight. "Yuri, did you have to land right on top of us?"

"I am sorry, Tim. I'll try to drag myself over." Yuri clawed at the grass, hauling his immobile body inch by painstaking inch, but his progress was sluggish.

"Wyatt, help us!" Vik shouted.

Nearby, Wyatt dodged a zombie—which went on to kill a plebe behind her. She staggered over to them. "Tom, you're back!" A big grin broke over her face. "We thought you fell down a hole and died somewhere."

"Close. I was with Blackburn. Hey, can you drag your boyfriend's body off us before we suffocate?"

Yuri said apologetically, "My very great muscle mass makes me heavy."

She tugged at Yuri's arm, dragged him to the side—far enough to relieve them of the worst of the weight. Then a zombie got her from behind, and Wyatt dropped across Yuri, her weight making up for the few inches she'd dragged him. Tom and Vik both groaned.

"Sorry," Wyatt said. "At least we can hear each other. Where have you been?"

"Census device." Tom shoved at Yuri's immobile mass, but it wasn't going to budge again now that Wyatt was on top of him. "Blackburn thought I was the leak. I have this internet friend in China. It looked bad. Actually, the friend's Medusa."

Stunned silence. Tom turned back to see the other three dead trainees gaping at him. That, more than anything, reminded Tom how stupid he'd been to befriend Medusa in the first place.

"Look," he said, "I was curious about seeing Medusa again after the incursion. We played games and she killed me a lot and stuff. Oh, and Medusa *is* a girl. Yeah, I found that out, too."

"A girl?" Wyatt said, frowning. "Like a girlfriend girl?"

Tom's cheeks flushed. "No. I mean . . ." He still wasn't sure what to say to that. "No!" He considered that kiss. "Well, maybe. I'm not sure."

"How long has this been going on?" she mumbled.

"Not so long."

"You never told us."

"So? Why's it such a big deal?"

"It's not," Wyatt said. "I don't care."

"Good." Tom was distracted then. A new Machiavelli plebe with stubbled hair ran past with Jenny Nguyen. The new girl, whom his processor identified as Iman Attar, pointed at them. "Why are they all lying on top of each other?"

Jenny glanced their way, then urged her onward. Her voice drifted their way, "Alexander boys are weird. That kid Vikram sat next to me the other day in the planetarium . . ."

Vik groaned and clamped his hands over his face. Intrigued, Tom raised his head up to see. Wyatt and Yuri did so as well.

". . . and Vikram said, 'Uh-oh, looks like you have spicy Indian on your lips.'"

"That's your great line?" Tom burst into his first laughter in days.

"Shut up," Vik muttered.

Jenny's voice reached them over the screams and the

gunfire. "I was like, 'You're creepy,' and got up to leave, and then he head-butted me."

The girls moved off. Utter silence hung in the air for a taut moment. Tom gaped at Vik. Wyatt's lips were tightly pressed together like she was straining not to react.

"Well?" Vik said. "Just get it out of the way."

"We're not going to laugh at you, Vik," Tom assured him. "I have bigger things to worry about right now"—his voice started shaking with suppressed laughter—"so it doesn't matter if you're a SPICY INDIAN."

Yuri and Wyatt broke into laughter, and Tom threw his head back, cackling helplessly. And for a few wonderful moments, it felt like the census device never happened and he had no cares in the world.

"Thanks, everyone. You're good friends," Vik grumbled.

"And I can't believe you head-butted her after we saw that happen with Wyatt!"

"It's surprisingly easy to do, Tom!"

"Yeah, maybe when a girl's desperate to run away from you."

"Do not take her rejection personally, Viktor," Yuri said gently. "Maybe she has a phobia of spicy Indians."

Vik raised up his arm and thwapped Yuri, then Tom. Tom kept laughing.

"Vik," Wyatt objected. "Stop thrashing. You're getting spicy Indian on us."

Vik made a frustrated noise and waved his hand impatiently in the air, gesturing for them to get all the laughter out and over with. Then, when it died a bit, he finally said, "We done?"

"Spicy Indian will never be done," Tom vowed.

"Yeah, well, right now, you *do* have bigger things going on."

Any desire to laugh drained away. Tom's thoughts spiraled

back to the last two days, a dark pit in his stomach.

"Here's what I want to know," Vik went on. "Medusa. Tell us. She's a girl. So, is she hot?"

Tom was relieved, because talking about Medusa wasn't nearly as awful as discussing Blackburn or his treason charges. "She wouldn't let me see her," he admitted.

"Oh no, young Skywalker. The ugly is strong in that one."

Wyatt glared at him. "Or perhaps she has a classified identity? You know, the same way we do?"

"Nah. Ugly. Face it, Tom," Vik said, "no girl who fights like that can be hot, too. It would cause a huge imbalance in the cosmos that would unravel the space-time continuum and make the universe implode. And she won't show you. That's a red flag. Big, bright, waving red flag."

Tom shook off the thoughts of Medusa's hypothetical ugliness, because really, he was an idiot even wondering about this right now when he had much more significant, life-changing issues plaguing him.

"It doesn't matter, anyway, Vik. I can't see Medusa again. I got caught, and now Blackburn's out to fry my brain in the census device."

Wyatt gasped. "He's seen your memories?"

Yuri looked over at him, openmouthed.

Tom knew what they were worried about. "He hasn't seen everything," he said meaningfully, watching them. "But he knows I'm hiding something from him, and he won't stop until he gets it."

"So just show him," Vik said. "Whatever it is, buddy, it can't be that bad."

Wyatt and Yuri were looking at each other, though, realization on their faces.

"You don't get it, Vik," Tom said. Vik wasn't clued in. He

didn't realize two of his friends were facing ten years in prison if Blackburn got that memory. "I have this under control. There's a way I can get out of this: Marsh is having me face Medusa at the Capitol Summit. He wants me to proxy for Elliot. I beat her, he defends me to the Defense Committee. I lose, and I'm stuck either getting my brain fried or getting my neural processor removed."

Stunned silence followed this.

"That's a great deal," Vik said.

"That's an awful deal," Wyatt said, at the same time.

"It's great. He gets to fly at Capitol Summit! I can't believe you're a plebe and Marsh is letting you do that," Vik said, sounding envious. And out of breath, too, due to the being-crushed-by-a-pile-of-bodies thing.

"It's not great at all, Vik," Wyatt said. "Tom can't possibly beat Medusa. He doesn't have enough training, and even if he did, no one with enough training has managed to beat her."

She sounded so dubious about it that Tom's pride prickled. "Hey, I pick up sims quickly. Everyone says so. And I've faced Medusa in other battle sims. I swear, I always come close."

"Do it, then," Vik said. "Stomp your online girlfriend. Stomp her good, Tom."

Tom's head slumped back. "I'll need to be lucky. She's better than me. She's faster, smarter, all-around deadlier."

"So cheat," Vik said.

"Cheat?" Yuri cried. "He does not need to cheat! He can triumph over Medusa as an honorable warrior."

Vik groaned and turned back to Tom, as though he'd decided Yuri was now an utterly hopeless case. "Doctor, you must cheat until you win. Winning is the noble thing to do."

"Vik, if I knew how to cheat, I'd be on it in a second. I don't even know what military scenario we're going to be fighting."

"I can program a virus for you," Wyatt spoke up, sounding quite eager for the chance. "You can scramble her CPU midfight."

"The summit's in two days."

Wyatt scoffed. "Have you ever met me? That's more than enough time."

"To-Timothy, you are ignoring the obvious solution," Yuri said, his massive weight shifting, crushing Tom farther into the grass. "Why not ask Medusa to lose on purpose?"

Tom stared at him. "What?"

"Ask Medusa to lose on purpose," Yuri repeated.

Tom stared at him. The concept seemed perfectly rational and yet, it simply made no sense to him. "Why would she ever agree to that?"

"Isn't this obvious? She cares for you. If she knows you are to face a treason charge, she may consider losing. This is not a real battle. This is a show battle. No countries will be harmed by losing."

"But I can't do that," Tom said, aghast.

"You'd rather scramble her CPU?" Vik pointed out. "Tom, I hate to say it, but you should probably listen to the Android here. Go for emotional blackmail."

"But my virus!" Wyatt said.

"He can use a virus if it fails, okay?" Vik said. "You're bloodthirsty with those things, aren't you, Evil Wench?"

"At least I don't have tiny, delicate hands."

"What? What about my hands? Where is this coming from?"

Tom tuned out their argument. Emotional blackmail. On Medusa. He frowned up into the stormy black night.

It wouldn't work. Medusa was a competitor. It didn't matter if they'd become friends, or even kissed once. Even the thought of asking her to do it made him feel like a chump. She'd never go for it.

After all, he wouldn't.

THAT NIGHT, TOM, Vik, and Yuri woke at 0200. They met Wyatt in the shadowed common room. She'd already disabled the Spire's transmission tracking and surveillance program.

She waved for Tom to hook into one of the neural access ports in the wall. "You have ten minutes, Tom. I don't think we should risk disabling the Spire's firewall any longer than that."

"It'll be quick," Tom assured her.

"Good luck, Doctor." Vik handed Tom a neural wire.

"Thanks, Doctor. See you guys in a few minutes." Tom hooked himself in.

Numbness and darkness enveloped him as he transitioned from real Tom to an internet avatar. He dropped a message onto the community message board, and the timing was perfect—mere minutes later, he received a private message confirmation from Medusa with a new URL.

Tom resolved into their private, password-protected program. He glanced around the ornate chamber she'd chosen for the simulation. The program informed him this was Hatfield Palace in Renaissance England. Medusa flared to life across from him as a slim redhead with dark eyes and a cool, superior smile, her floor-length dress twirling when she spun in a circle.

"Nice," Tom said, looking her up and down. "Who are you supposed to be?"

"Princess Elizabeth Tudor." She moved toward him. "We can joust or plot to overthrow Queen Mary. Or we could switch characters and fight the Irish, Scottish, and French . . . or fight as the Irish, Scottish, or French against the English. There's even a battle with the Spanish Armada later. It's a flexible program. With lots of beheadings."

"Who am I?" He glanced down at his body. He had tight stockings on. He frowned and stretched his virtual legs experimentally. Stockings didn't seem manly to him.

The information algorithm from the program informed him he was *playing Robert Dudley, the man Queen Elizabeth I of England loved the entirety of her life*. It was a good sign, he supposed. He'd noticed Medusa sometimes picked programs and scenarios pointedly.

Still, he felt twitchy and uneasy when Medusa sauntered up to him, dark eyes twinkling into his beneath her lion's mane of red hair. "I thought the worst when you stopped showing up."

Tom's stomach churned. "The worst happened," he admitted. "One of the officers at the Spire found out about me meeting with you."

Her face froze. "Oh."

"They think I'm the leak now."

She turned away from him. "What's going to happen to you?"

"Well, I'm either going to end up, um"—he fumbled for a way to explain the census device without revealing the truth, and settled for—"'questioned' about you until I lose my mind, or I'm going to be out of the Spire. Forever."

"Maybe this was a bad idea."

"Hey, it was my bad idea, okay?" And this was his moment. His moment to reveal that he'd be the one facing her in the Capitol, his moment to tell her she was the one who could save him by taking a fall for him.

So why couldn't he talk?

All Tom could think about was how humiliating it would

be when he begged her to lose for him. And how pathetic it would be when she laughed in his face, because who did that? People didn't do stuff like that. Not in real life. He didn't know what world Yuri lived in, but Tom's insides clenched up at the very idea of begging Medusa to please help him when he knew she'd just think less of him. She'd think he was pathetic for needing help like this. Ask her to lose for him? He might as well ask her to donate some vital organs, too. She wouldn't do it.

"We can still meet online, can't we?" Medusa said, peering at him. "Once you're out of the Spire, it's not treason anymore if we meet."

Tom stepped back from her, feeling cold, thinking of how he'd end up if he lost the neural processor, lost the better Tom who'd been born in the Spire. What kind of person he'd be if he was that kid following Neil around again. That ugly, stupid kid who was worthless.

He'd rather tear off his arms than show her that guy.

"It wouldn't be a good idea," Tom said.

"I see." There was something flat in her voice. "So once you're gone from the military, you can't be bothered. I get it."

Tom's head wasn't in the right place for this stuff. "What? Where did you even get that?"

"Maybe this was a bad idea all around." And then she fizzled out of the program, leaving Tom alone in his stupid stockings in Renaissance England.

Tom yanked out his neural wire and sat up. His friends were all settled on nearby chairs in the dark common room, watching for his reaction.

Vik spoke first. "No go?"

"No go," Tom confirmed.

Wyatt was sitting with her knees drawn up to her chest, and she seemed to be bouncing in her seat a bit. "Virus, then?"

Tom nodded resignedly. "Virus."

"I've already got most of it ready for you." She sounded oddly cheerful about that as she set about hacking into the Spire's defenses, erecting them again.

"Great," Tom said faintly.

Sure, he hadn't actually had a chance to ask Medusa about taking a fall for him, but he felt like a weight had been lifted off his chest, knowing she was angry at him now, knowing it couldn't happen. If he'd groveled like some pathetic wimp and then been laughed at, it would've killed him. She never would've respected him after he asked her for something like that.

"The Android was wrong, then," Vik murmured. "Sorry, buddy. Guess Medusa isn't that into you. Hey"—his hand thumped Tom's shoulder—"all the more reason to stomp her."

"Sure. Stomp her." Except for the part where she always beat him.

Wyatt nodded in the darkness, typing in the finishing touches before the Spire's defenses snapped back on to full. "The one I've started programming is called an adware virus."

"Adware virus?" Tom echoed.

"It works by basically taking up more and more CPU until it's too slow to really do much of anything. It'll trigger the moment you send it to Medusa, so I'll set it to delete itself from your CPU at the same time so it doesn't slow you down, too. You unload it once, early in the fight, and then beat her before she can recover from it. You probably won't have access to a keyboard, so I'm going to try a trick Blackburn showed me and set it up to respond to a thought interface."

"Is that the only way?" Tom asked her. "Vik and I tried

net-sending with a thought interface during Programming once, but I couldn't concentrate on just one thing at a time."

Vik nodded. "His programming questions were always like, 'Vik, how do steak boobs function?'"

Tom elbowed him. Hard. Vik sniggered.

Yuri had been very quiet this whole time. Now he raised his head. "Steak boobs?"

"No, Yuri," Wyatt cried. "No steak boobs. And, Tom, I'm giving you one phrase for this. You can focus your brain for the time it takes to think out one phrase, can't you?"

Tom shrugged. "All right, hit me."

"When the time comes to send out the virus, I want you to think this: 'tiny spicy Vikram.'"

Vik's smile dropped away. Despite the seriousness of his situation, Tom started laughing.

"Wait, no," Vik said. "I don't like this phrase."

"Don't think it too early," she warned Tom. "You have to have Medusa's ship in your sights. Focus on her, and think 'tiny spicy Vikram' over and over until the virus deploys."

"That's it?" Tom said. "What about firewalls?"

"You're both going to be on the same server for the summit, so that shouldn't be an issue. And once the virus deploys, trust me, she's not going to be flying anywhere for a while."

"Vikram is not tiny," Vik declared belatedly. "I'm taller than both of you."

Wyatt ignored him. "I think plan B is going to work."

Then Yuri spoke up. "Or perhaps we should try plan C." He was sitting farthest from Tom, leaning his chin in a hand, large shoulders slouched.

Tom wasn't sure what Yuri had in mind, but Wyatt guessed. She sprang to her feet. "No, Yuri! Your plan sucks."

"I have not said my plan."

"I've guessed it, and I know it sucks."

"I will not let Thomas take the fall for me," Yuri told her.

Vik gave a sudden start. He stared at Yuri for a long moment, then pointed at him, looking wildly between Wyatt and Tom. "Did you guys hear that? He said 'Thomas.'"

Wyatt bit her lip and looked at Tom.

Vik noticed. "All right." He dropped his voice. "Why aren't you two gasping in shock? What am I missing?"

Tom turned on Yuri instead. "I owe you. I am not going to give you away."

"You don't have to, Tom. I will reveal myself. I'll confess."

"He said 'Tom' now! I know you guys heard that," Vik insisted.

"If Blackburn finds out you're unscrambled, he'll think you're the leak, Yuri," Wyatt pointed out.

"Unscrambled?" Vik echoed.

"But you will be safe," Yuri replied.

"You won't just be compromising yourself," Tom pointed out, ignoring Vik, who looked ready to tear his hair out. "Wyatt made your firewall. She'll get thrown in prison for ten years, too, for committing treason. I'll go to prison for aiding and abetting her. We'll *all* lose our neural processors."

"Yuri, you've had your processor too long," Wyatt said, horrified. "You'll never survive it if they take it out."

"So let's not risk it," Tom said, looking between them. "You're keeping quiet, Yuri."

Vik was rubbing his head. "Wait . . . wait . . . Let me get this straight. Yuri's not scrambled anymore? And you guys both knew?"

"He's not," Wyatt said, drawing to her full height. "So what? How is this a problem?"

"How is this a problem?" Vik echoed. "Do you live in the

real world with the rest of us? This is a huge problem, Wyatt!"

Yuri found his feet. "I am not a spy, Vikram."

"It doesn't matter, Yuri!" Vik said. "Don't you people get that? How is this going to look? The military is a hierarchy. You can't dismantle their security because *you* think your boyfriend's trustworthy. It's not your call."

"But you're okay with dropping the Spire's defenses because you think your friend is trustworthy?" Wyatt pointed out.

"That's different. We did it for ten minutes, and no one is going to find out about it. This? Is permanent. Do you seriously think Blackburn's going to miss Yuri's new software forever?" He turned to Yuri. "I know you're not a spy. I know you, man, but you're delusional if you think Blackburn won't figure it out!"

Wyatt raised her forearm keyboard. "At least you won't remember."

Vik's eyes shot wide open. Tom leaped forward and batted her arm down. "Don't." And as soon as he reached her, Yuri seized him in a headlock and clasped him against his broad chest.

"Thomas, do not," he warned him.

Tom yanked at the massive arm. "I'm not gonna touch her, Yuri! But she can't use a virus on Vik. No one's brain is getting fried today, okay?" Yuri's grip eased up, and Tom jerked out of his arms. He looked around at all them, heaving for breath. "Okay?"

Wyatt stared down Vik, and Yuri loomed over Tom, ready to leap in if anything escalated.

"Vik, if Yuri goes down, Wyatt and I go down, too," Tom said. "I get that you're committed to this military stuff, but this has to be our secret. Do you want to send all three of us to prison? You want to risk Yuri's life?"

Vik groaned. "Tom, I don't even want to be in this position!"

"I know. I know. None of us do. But life's about ugly choices, right? You either stay quiet and be complicit with us, or you take us all down and live with it. Which one will it be?"

Vik spun away from them, gripping his hair.

"Well, Vik?" Tom pressed, watching his back anxiously.

"Fine, but on one condition," Vik said, whirling back around, "I'm going to think of a manly version of 'evil wench' and you have to answer to it."

"Deal," Tom agreed, secretly relieved. He knew this was Vik's way of saying he wouldn't turn on them. He addressed Yuri next. "And you get how important it is to keep your mouth shut now? For me, for Wyatt? You understand?"

"Yes," Yuri said, a troubled line between his eyebrows. "I'll stay quiet."

"Good. So this is what happens from here: Wyatt, you program a virus. Yuri, you try not to do anything stupid like tell the truth. Vik, you keep thinking about a manly equivalent of 'evil wench.'"

"I've got ideas," Vik grumbled.

"And I just have to answer to it. Oh, and show Marsh and the Defense Committee that I'm the guy who can take down the greatest warrior in the world."

Put that way, it almost sounded easy.

0 1 1 1 1 1 0 0 0 1 0 0 0 0 1 1 0 1 0 1 0 1 0 1 0 0 1 0 0 1 1 0 1 1 0 0 1 0 0
0 0 0 1 0 1 0 1 1 0 1 1 0 0 0 0 0 0 1 0 0 1 1 1 0 0 0 0 0 1 0 1 1 0 1 0 0
1 0 0 0 0 0 1 1 1 1 1 0 1 0 0 1 1 1 1 1 0 1 1 0 0 1 1 0 1 0 0 0 1 0 1 0 0
0 1 0 1 1 0 0 1 1 1 1 1 1 1 1 0 0 1 1 1 0 1 0 1 1 0 0 0 0 0 0 1 0 0 1 1 1
0 1 0 0 0 1 1 0 1 1 0 1 1 0 1 1 1 0 0 0 0 0 0 0 1 0 1 1 0 1 0 0 1
1 1 1 0 1 0 0 0 0 0 1 1 1 1 0 0 1 0 0 1 0 1 1 1 0 0 1 1 1 0 1 1 0 0 1 0 1
0 1 0 1 0 1 0 0 0 1 1 0 1 1 0 0 0 0 1 1 0 1 0 0 1 1 0 0 0 1 0 1 1 1 1 0 0
0 1 0 1 1 0 0 1 1 0 1 0 0 0 0 0 1 0 1 1 1 0 1 1 0 0 0 0 0 0 1 0 1 1 0 0
1 1 1 0 0 0 1 1 0 0 0 0 0 1 1 1 1 0 1 1 0 1 1 0 1 0 0 0 0 0 1 0 0 1 1 0
1 1 1 1 1 0 0 1 0 1 0 1 1 1 0 1 1 1 0 1 0 1 0 1 1 1 1 0 1 0 1 1 0 1 1 0
1 0 1 0 0 1 1 1 1 1 1 0 1 1 0 0 0 0 1 1 1 0 1 1 0 1 1 1 0 1 1 1 1 0 0 0
0 0 0 1 1 0 1 1 0 0 1 1 0 1 0 1 0 0 0 1 0 0 0 1 0 1 0 1 0 0 1 0 0 0 0 1 0 0 1 0
1 1 1 0 0 0 1 0 0 1 0 1 1 0 0 1 0 0 1 1 0 1 0 1 0 1 1 1 0 0 0 1 0 0 1 1 0
0 1 0 0 0 0 0 0 0 1 1 1 1 1 0 0 1 1 0 1 1 0 0 0 0 0 0 1 0 0 0 0 1 0 0
0 0 0 1 0 0 1 1 1 0 0 1 1 1 0 0 1 0 0 0 0
0 1 0 1 0 0 0 1 0 1 1 1 1 0 0
1 0 0 1 0 0 0 0 1 0 0 0 1 1 1 0 0
0 1 1 0 1 1 1 0 0 0 1 1 1 0 0 1 1 1 0 0 0 0 1 1 0 0 1 0 0 1 0 1 0 1 1 1 1
1 0 1 0 0 0 1 1 1 1 0 0 1 0 1 0 1 1 1 0 0 1 0 1 0 1 0 1 0 0 1 0 1 1 0 1 1 1 0 0
0 0 1 0 0 1 0 1 0 1 1 0 0 1 0 0 1 0 1 0 1 0 0 0 1 0 0 0 1 1 0 1

CHAPTER TWENTY-NINE

N IGEL HARRISON WASN'T stupid. On the day of the Capitol Summit, he figured out the moment Tom and Elliot joined him in the private car that he wasn't the one who'd be fighting Medusa.

"Oh. Great." His delicate face twisted with disgust. "I guess this means I'm the token proxy here."

"Tom is here if you can't take Medusa, Nigel," Elliot said. "He's very good for a plebe."

"He's still a *plebe*," Nigel railed. "He's in first-year tactics. He is going to hook into an actual ship in space and face off against another actual ship in space—and he's going to do it for the first time at Capitol Summit? How does this make sense to you, Elliot?"

When Nigel put it that way, it suddenly didn't make much sense to Tom, either. He felt a strange, dropping sensation. Marsh and Elliot had told him that, yes, he'd be flying actual ships in space. But they'd said it wasn't a real battle, it was more like a game. Tom had been sure he could win a game.

It only hit him now that this game was real. A real ship. A real game.

"Tom's downloaded everything he needs to know about navigation," Elliot told Nigel, "and General Marsh let him hook into one of the ships in orbit to practice. He picked it up right away. Tom's a natural."

"Is Marsh going senile, Raines? How'd you talk him into it?" Nigel shouted.

"I didn't," Tom snapped. "This was his idea, not mine."

"We're supposed to support each other, Nigel," Elliot reminded him.

"I'm supposed to be okay with getting thrown out for a plebe?" Nigel cried. "I'd understand an upper since we've got some training with the ships. I'd get it if Marsh picked a middle even—since they've done ride alongs with CamCo and have seen battles up close. But he's a plebe. A plebe! It boggles my mind!"

"I don't like that attitude, Nigel."

"And I don't like people who talk like they're day camp counselors," Nigel sneered.

"Now you're just being petty . . ."

Tom let the two argue it out, his nerves sparking like live wires. Although Elliot was disappointed he had to have a proxy, he seemed pleased to hear it was one of his own plebes who'd be doing the bulk of the fighting. He'd even watched Tom try out navigating one of the ships, and it really was a lot like Applied Sims. He told him he'd done a great job afterward. But Elliot was like that. He probably would've encouraged him even if he'd accidentally crashed the ship into the moon. But now Tom was thinking about Nigel's words. He'd been so eager for this chance to vindicate himself, he hadn't really considered whether he was ready. He'd flown that test ship around the moon for maybe twenty minutes with Elliot and General Marsh watching. Not in a battle. Not in any sort of high-stress situation. His stomach began to ache.

"What kind of game will this be?" Tom asked, trying to calm his nerves.

"A pathetic farce," Nigel answered bitterly.

Elliot ignored him. "It changes year to year, Tom. The Capitol Summit exhibition isn't a real battle. It's more of an excuse to entertain the members of the Coalition and give the public a show. Odds are, you and Medusa will be competing with one small goal in mind. Winner is the one who completes it first, and the winning country gets the prestige."

Tom stared at him. "So if I lose, I damage our country's world prestige."

"Right," Nigel said nastily. "No pressure, though."

"No." Elliot leaned toward him, clasped his shoulder with an encouraging hand. "Don't think of it that way, Tom. No one expects our side to win this year."

"Oh. That's real reassuring," Tom said.

"Well, I meant it to be. If you, or if you"—Elliot nodded to Nigel, too, remembering to include him; Nigel rolled his eyes, seeing it for the perfunctory gesture it was—"end up taking down Medusa, it'll be a great surprise for everyone. We all know Medusa's something better than the rest of us. The Coalition knows it, too. So don't let the pressure get to you. It's not the end of the world if you lose."

Elliot didn't know the details, then. For Tom, it was the end of the world.

If he lost this, he lost everything. His place at the Spire, his neural processor, his friends, his future. Everything.

Near the Capitol Building, Elliot slid out of their private

car and switched to a limousine, prepared for his public entrance and his photo op with politicians, Nobridis execs, and the fawning media.

Tom and Nigel sat in silence as their car rolled toward their destination. Tom was too consumed by a mounting anxiety to really care that Nigel was glaring at him. They were heading to the same place as Elliot—the Capitol Building—just in a more secretive manner. Their identities and IPs hadn't been leaked. Since their names were both state secrets, either of them could proxy Elliot. There was no risk of the Russo-Chinese embarrassing America by telling the whole world who the real pilot of Elliot's ship was.

Their private car stopped by the Hart Senate Office Building. Tom sat frozen in his seat. The ride had gone by too quickly.

"You're sweating, aren't you?" Nigel said, relishing it.

"Shut up." Tom shoved his way out of the car.

General Marsh waited inside the lobby for their arrival. "Good. Good. Come on, you two." He hastened them through the metal detectors, which buzzed as they passed through, then across the marble hall to the elevators.

They piled into the members only elevator normally reserved for US senators and descended into the basement. Then they shuffled into a small, underground subway car. It charged down the tracks, whisking them toward the discreet, interior entrance into the Capitol Building.

The general surveyed Tom as the tracks thundered beneath them. "You two feeling ready?"

Nigel's face twitched. It was his only answer, because he knew he wasn't the one being asked.

"Yes, sir. I'm ready." Tom was glad his voice didn't shake.

Marsh led them through private passages in the lower

floors of the Capitol to a hidden room beneath the Rotunda. It was long, narrow, and soundproof, with two chairs and a wall that doubled as a viewing screen of the massive dome in the middle of the Capitol Building.

Tom stared at the screen's image of the place. The Rotunda was a cavernous room with an intricate painting ringing the top; statues, and oil paintings depicted scenes from eighteenth century American history. A crowd of onlookers milled throughout the room, their seats positioned around the central ring where Svetlana and Elliot would face off, a circular screen overhead ready to display the space battle.

"This is a private room where the two of you will stay. Here is the neural access port." Marsh tapped briskly on a discreet nook in the wall. "I'm giving you the schematics for a satellite. It's an antique. It's been in orbit since the early days of the space program, and now we want it in a museum. This year, you're competing with the Russo-Chinese Combatant to retrieve that satellite first. No missiles, no weapons. You have to be tricky to win this. The victor will be the one to grab it and deposit it on the lawn of the Smithsonian. Once the action begins, Ramirez will hook himself in. He hits the upper atmosphere, and then Mr. Harrison hooks in. You have two minutes to impress me, Harrison. Then Raines takes over."

Nigel's lips twisted. "Great. Two minutes to beat someone who has never been beaten before. What a fantastic opportunity that's not rigged against me at all."

Marsh looked at him. "Excuse me, young man?"

"Nothing, sir."

Marsh turned around to face the screen and listed the identities of the Summit's attendees as they strode in, men and women in suits worth more money than what most people made in a year or two.

"Take a look. These are the world's power players." He gestured at them with his thick forefinger. "You know President Milgram, Vice President Richter, and the Secretary of Defense, Jim Sienker. And talking to them, that's—"

"Joseph Vengerov," Tom said sourly.

"That's right. Founder and CEO of Obsidian Corp. You two actually have Vengerov to thank for the neural processor technology."

Tom had Vengerov to thank for his time as Dalton's stooge. Not to mention Blackburn's decision to fry his brain in the census device. His eyes scanned the crowd, and then he saw him—Lieutenant Blackburn in full dress uniform, at the very edge of the gathering. Watching Vengerov.

Tom shuddered. He had to win this.

"On Svetlana Moriakova's side," Marsh was saying, "you can see the South American, African, Chinese, Nordic, and Russian contingents. On Mr. Ramirez's side, you'll see some of our allies—the Indians, Europeans, Australians, Canadians. Ah, and those are representatives of the Coalition: the Russo-Chinese contingent: Lexicon Mobile, Harbinger, LM Lymer Fleet, Kronus Portable, Stronghold Energy, and Preeminent Communications. Over there, those are Indo-American allies on the Coalition, our power players: Obsidian, Nobridis, Wyndham Harks, Matchett-Reddy, Epicenter Manufacturing, and—"

"Dominion Agra," Tom finished for him, bursting with hatred at the very sight of the tall, disdainful man striding into the crowd.

Amazing how the most powerful people in the world were gathered in the Rotunda, yet Dalton still looked at those around him like he owned them all.

"Good, son," Marsh said. "You know your friends on the Coalition."

No, he knew his enemies. And Tom knew Dalton was more his enemy than anyone from Russia or China. Determination filled him to the brim. He was going to win today. He had to. Just so he could stay in the Spire and rub it in Dalton's face.

"I trust you two are old enough to handle yourselves in here," Marsh told them. "If there's a problem, send a message to Lieutenant Blackburn. He's on standby in the crowd."

"I didn't bring a keyboard," Tom said, wondering how Marsh could expect him to message *Blackburn* for help, of all people. If he broke all his bones and then caught on fire, he still wouldn't ask for Blackburn to come and help him.

"Good thing I did," Nigel replied, tugging back his sleeve to show Marsh.

Marsh nodded. "I'll see you two after it's over."

After General Marsh left to join the summit, ordering them to pay attention and hook in as soon as the challenge began, Tom stood there in the isolated, hidden room with Nigel, watching the guests. Nigel didn't bother. He just clicked and unclicked the neural wire into the access port in the wall, his slim legs jouncing restlessly.

Tom regarded his resentful face, his hooded expression. "You know, you may not believe it, but I need this a lot more than you do right now."

"Really?" Nigel's pale eyes flipped up to Tom's. "So you had your last chance at Camelot Company taken away *for the second time*?"

Tom wasn't sure what to say. He hoped Nigel wasn't going to resist when he took control of the ship in space. Nigel was a small guy, and Tom didn't feel right about the idea of punching him just to get the wire from him.

He'd do it, he just didn't want to.

Activity in the Rotunda stirred on the screen. Nigel straightened. Tom turned to look. On the screen, the attendees of Capitol Summit fell silent. The only sound in the chamber with Nigel and Tom was the buzzing of the speakers, filtering voices in from the Rotunda. Elliot and the tall, blond Russian girl, Svetlana Moriakova, stepped toward each other and shook hands. Then they strode to stations outfitted with controllers, even steering wheels, to allow them to launch the ships themselves and complete the show that they were the ones piloting the ships in space. The public didn't know about neural processors. They probably wouldn't find the comalike stillness of a real Combatant all that exciting, after all.

Tom's heartbeat picked up. *Just a few minutes from now.*

He turned to Nigel, and saw that the other boy hadn't hooked in. Instead, he held a slim wire in his hand, his eyes on Tom's face.

"I don't want to bother if I'm going to get kicked off in two minutes. Take it from the start."

Tom blinked, feeling dull and rather stupid. It was only two minutes, but it felt like being catapulted right into the action before he was ready. "Seriously?"

"Seriously." Nigel's voice sounded hollow. "You know why Marsh wants me out there first? It's so if you lose, it'll still make him look good, like he took it by the book and gave me a chance, and I couldn't cut it." His lips twisted. "He's a coward. He should just have you do it if that's what he wants."

And Tom could agree with that suddenly: Marsh was a coward. He'd gone out of his way to get Tom into the program, but now he didn't have his back, not really. Tom's only chance lay in pulling off a miracle and beating Medusa.

He remembered his father's words, suddenly, from the day they parted: *Tom, whatever happens, you take care of yourself.*

So he'd do it. He'd beat Medusa, and if he didn't, well, then Marsh wasn't going to wash his hands clean like he'd played no role in getting Tom in the Spire, in getting Tom to fly at Capitol Summit. He took the wire from Nigel, and reached up to plug it in. Out of the corner of his eye he noticed Nigel's toxic smile, and the keyboard he unveiled from beneath his sleeve.

"What are you—" Tom began.

It was his only warning Tom had before the text flashed over his vision center: *Session expired. Immobility sequence initiated.* Feeling seeped away from Tom's chest on down. He crashed to the ground, just like in Calisthenics.

Nigel stepped calmly over him and retrieved the wire. "Really, Raines, did you think I was going to sit back and let you be the big hero today? Did you really?"

Tom looked up at him, shocked. "Well, yeah." He clawed uselessly at the carpet below him. As always, the Calisthenics immobility program allowed use of his arms, but no weight-bearing. He couldn't even drag himself up.

"It's not going to happen!" Nigel whirled back toward the Rotunda. "I thought when I leaked the CamCo names, that would be enough. Marsh would have to use me. He'd have no choice once the IPs were public!"

The gears of Tom's brain ground to a halt. "That was you."

Nigel grinned sickeningly. "Back when Dominion Agra was working with you, Dalton Prestwick offered to sponsor me, too, if I just helped him make CamCo public. They probably figured the same thing I did: that as soon as everyone knew the current Combatants, the military would need more who were still anonymous. And wouldn't it be so easy for Dominion to move you up the ranks if that happened? They had names they could leak, but they didn't know what IPs went with them. They asked me to do the rest. But once you destroyed the club, Dalton told me the deal was off. It didn't make a difference, though. I'd already decided to leak the information myself. I sent one untraceable email with just enough neural processor-specific lingo to convince the Chinese ambassador I was legit, then a second with the list. It was that easy. I told you, I'm going to be CamCo whether I get a sponsor or not."

Tom threw a desperate glance toward the image of the Rotunda, where Svetlana looked in control as she pretended to steer a ship, and Elliot was coated with sweat, fighting for real for the first time ever at the Summit. He was jerking violently at the controls, his vessel in the upper atmosphere barreling toward the satellite in a direct course, all determination and no imagination.

Medusa was too clever for that. She used her engine exhaust to propel debris his way, knocking him off course. Sometimes she simply toyed with Elliot, ignoring the satellite altogether. She'd veer in, about to ram him, then sweep to the side after he panicked and jerked his ship wildly off course. Then, with a taunting wiggle of her vessel, she'd hang back to wait for his next attempt as though the whole process amused her. She was psyching him out. It was like a cat dangling a mouse from its claw. It was obvious that both Combatants knew who was going to triumph.

"Nigel, you can't trust Dalton. Dominion Agra won't sponsor you. They'll just make you a fall guy! That's probably what they had planned all along!"

Nigel whirled on him ferociously. "You don't get it, Raines! I *don't* trust Dominion Agra. Of course I don't. I'm not stupid. *I* was supposed to be CamCo. Sure, Dominion Agra gave me the idea, but I knew it benefited me, too. I knew leaking the names and making CamCo public would move me up. Even when they revoked their offer, I knew I was going to do it anyway. But even that blew up in my face, thanks to Marsh's apparent need to advance you, so *this* is my chance. Right now. After today, the military will have no choice but to let me fight."

"What are you planning?" Tom asked him warily, gazing at the wire in Nigel's hand.

Nigel turned toward the screen, regarding the crowd with an exultant glow in his eyes. "I've got a starship at my control, Raines. And you have to say one thing about the Spire: it's a pretty easy target."

Tom stared at his back. He couldn't be serious. He wasn't seriously going to use Elliot's ship to attack the Pentagonal Spire.

"The Pentagon won't even see the attack coming. They'll think I'm"—Nigel leered back at Tom—"well, they'll think you are doing some bizarre maneuver. I guess that's what happens when you put a plebe in charge. And a plebe deranged enough to bite the head off a scorpion, too." He shook his head. "I can hear it now. 'What was that Marsh thinking?' He'll get a court martial for this. For sure."

"There aren't any missiles on that ship. Remember?"

"I'm not using missiles. I'm ramming it. Pow. Big explosion, right at the base. If it doesn't wipe out everyone in the building, it'll at least take out a good chunk of them."

Tom grew cold. That plan could work. "You won't get away with this."

"Actually, Tom, I will." Nigel knelt down carefully out of arm's reach, smiling tauntingly into his face. "Remember how Blackburn planted that memory of the scorpion in your head? I thought it might be useful, so I figured out how to implant memories, too. As soon as the Spire's in flames, I'm planting a new memory in both our heads. You'll get my memory of destroying the Spire for the census device, and I'll get your memory of being unable to stop it, however hard I tried. The public will blame Elliot, the military will blame you, and I'll be the only hero here. As one of the only surviving Combatants, I'll have to be CamCo. I'll even have a clean conscience about it. Isn't that the greatest?"

Tom's mind was blown. Nigel was some kind of diabolical mastermind, and he'd been turned down for CamCo?

"Yeah, that's right, Raines," he sneered. "I am much, much smarter than you."

"Nigel, come on, wait!"

With a last, taunting smirk, Nigel hooked himself in.

Tom watched him fade into the program, raging at his useless legs, the arms that refused to let him heave himself up. He pounded his fist on the floor, frustrated. He craned his head up as far as he could to see Nigel's slack face, and the screen looming over the Combatants. Then his gaze riveted to Elliot. Tom saw the moment Elliot lost control of the fighting, because he gave what looked to be a relieved laugh, and a certain happiness washed over his features. He had no idea that this wasn't his proxy come to his rescue but rather the doom of them all.

Tom saw Nigel's ship spinning around in the upper atmosphere, whirling away from Medusa altogether. An ignorant observer might've thought it was some clever tactical ploy or even showmanship, the way he aimed it right into the Earth's atmosphere, the fire blaring around the heat shields. Tom heard a few appreciative murmurs from the spectators as Nigel streaked down toward the land mass below.

Then Tom realized with sudden, dizzying shock that Nigel was through the upper atmosphere, that his ship was hurtling toward the ground at breakneck speed, setting coordinates for Virginia. The lights of Washington, DC, veered into sight as he dipped lower, and then beyond that to Arlington. The Spire rose over the land.

Nigel was really going to do it. No one knew that ship was an enemy. No one knew they had to stop it. Nigel was going to take out the Spire and destroy everything Tom had.

Tom did the only thing he could, unleashed the single weapon he had.

He gazed straight at Nigel, gritted his teeth, and thought out the phrase *Tiny spicy Vikram . . . TINY SPICY VIKRAM!*

And then it happened. The adware virus file unloaded from his processor like a hydrogen bomb rolling its way out of a bomb bay. A sense of lightness snapped through Tom's brain, the virus deleting itself from his processor as the stream of code danced across his vision, deserting him, slamming Nigel, triggering.

He sprang out of his seat like he'd been slapped by some giant, invisible hand.

"'Your computer is infected,'" Nigel read, seeing something in his vision center. "'Click here to download protection for your PC.' . . . I'm not a PC! I don't need a . . ." His voice changed again, something else scrolling before his wide blue eyes. "'Free money. Click here for details.'" He fumblingly tore out his neural wire, but it didn't stop the barrage of ads. "'Learn the ultimate belly fat-busting secret.' . . . What is this, Raines?"

"Sounds like it's the ultimate belly fat-busting secret."

"That's not what I meant!" Nigel's face grew cloudy again as he seemed to see something else, his voice growing deeper and thicker. "'Become a mystery shopper.' . . . 'Get paid for your opinions.' . . . 'Find out who's searching for you.' . . . 'Congratulations, you've won a free' . . . 'Swat the fly and win a hundred' . . . 'Make money from home.' . . ."

His voice grew slower and slower, like the wheels of a train chugging to a stop, and his slim fingers threaded through his black hair and tugged on it, as though he hoped gripping his head would stop the ads Wyatt's virus was unpacking in his brain. The screen overhead showed Nigel's ship whirling out of control, hurtling toward the Spire.

"Whaaat isss thiiiiis . . ." Nigel stepped toward Tom as if wading through some thick swamp. Slowly, sluggishly, he keeled toward him, reached out to grab him. "Raaaines . . ."

He staggered right into arm's reach. Tom punched him.

Nigel reeled back, his head crashing against the corner of his chair. He crumpled to the ground and stayed there.

Tom couldn't drag himself over to Nigel with the immobility program stopping his arms from bearing his own weight. So he grabbed Nigel's skinny leg, dragged him over, tore the neural wire out of his slack grip, and then shoved it into his own brain stem.

The program enveloped him. Tom's brain was sucked straight into the navigation system of Nigel's ship, a jarring shift of consciousness. His senses zinged with the machine's sensors, the logical parameters of the vessel's computer warring with Tom's human brain. He forced himself farther, the machine humming around him, plunging deeper into the command system. He became enveloped by every connection, every stream of code, even as the view on the Rotunda's screen jolted toward the target. He flashed between the ship and his organic body, where his heart was pounding with terror. For the briefest instant through his eyes, he saw the screen, with the uneasy stirring in the Rotunda and Elliot's shocked expression as everyone gazed at the screen where Tom's ship was on a collision course with the Pentagonal Spire.

And then Tom veered, pulling out of the death plunge, soaring back up through the silken clouds into the upper atmosphere again. The blue sky drained into stark darkness around him. Tingles of excitement climbed up his spine as the Earth curved beneath him and the stars resolved in vibrant life about his vessel.

Medusa's ship had clamped upon the satellite they were competing to seize. Tom gazed at her vessel—a sharp, scythelike thing—through the thermal sensors of his own, and he was glad the virus, the easy cheat, was gone. This was how he wanted to face her. His kind-of girlfriend, his idol, his archenemy. Warrior to warrior.

This was going to be their first real battle.

CHAPTER THIRTY

T OM FOUND INTERFACING with a machine in space strangely similar to interfacing with the body of an animal in Applied Sims. The commands and controls registered themselves in his thoughts as soon as he hooked in. He knew how to crank his engine to full the same way he knew how to lift his leg and step forward. It came so readily. Another flexure of his thoughts, and he sent his vessel charging straight at the satellite, determined to deploy his own clamps and grab it. He'd either tear it from Medusa's grip—unlikely—or destroy it. If she took off with the prize, it was over. If he destroyed it, at least they *both* lost.

She veered aside just in time to avoid a collision. When she made for Earth, though, he veered in to block her way and made another grab at the satellite.

She used net-send, targeting his ship with her message, since she couldn't know what IP address she was dealing with. *Are you turning this into a zero-sum game now?*

Tom messaged back, *What's a zero-sum game?*

Are you an idiot?

Sure I am. Deranged, too.

A pause. Then, *You. I should've known.*

Should you have?

No one else would've risked destroying that satellite.
Medusa dipped a wing at him. Tom felt sure she was amused,
even as she dodged his next attempt to barrel in and destroy
the satellite. *No one but you. Oh, and me.*

And then with one sharp twist of her ship, she flung the
satellite at him. He dodged just in time to avoid the sure
defeat of losing both his ship and the prize. But Medusa was
heading toward him, obviously having decided upon a new
strategy: destroy his ship and *then* take off with the satellite.
Tom frantically reoriented himself as Medusa's vessel veered in
behind him and then hung back against the black tapestry of
stars like a calculating predator.

So who were the idiots flying before you? she messaged.

Tom changed his strategy, too. If she'd let go of it, maybe
he could try just bolting in quickly, grabbing it, and hoping to
beat her down to Earth. He used the American satellite grid,
trying to find the target satellite's new position. *It's a long story.*

Brace yourself for a tragic ending.

Just as Tom found his position, space junk appeared on
his thermal sensors. Medusa had twisted around and used the
wake of her engine to hurl a mass of steel toward him. Tom's
heart jerked, but he didn't dodge in time. The steel rocked the
vessel he was steering, knocking him off course, then forcing
Tom to bank downward to avoid her next improvised weapon of
space debris. Medusa passed Tom's ship, then slowed abruptly,
trying to catch him in the fiery plume of her engine. Tom
banked downward, letting her shoot far past him.

He tried to twist and evade her sensors, but she whipped

around and cut back into his path. He looked at the data coming from the Indo-American satellite grid again, searching for space junk he could use as a weapon. He located the remains of an orbiting space telescope he could use to damage her. But when he tried to force her toward it using the wake of his own engine, she neatly evaded the trap by dropping toward the upper atmosphere, using gravity to propel her out of harm's way, and Tom almost careened into it himself.

He was aware of his heart slamming in his body, shocked by the near miss. The Russo-Chinese satellite grid must've been more comprehensive than the Indo-American grid. Medusa seemed to know every floating piece of debris in the area, where to find it, where to steer him, where not to get maneuvered herself.

He felt his distant body, his teeth grinding in frustration, because he would kill right now for access to the Russo-Chinese satellites so he could see what she was seeing.

And it occurred to him that he could have it.

Maybe one cheat wasn't so bad.

Tom headed farther from the old satellite they were chasing, then he took a chance. Wyatt's virus was gone, but he concentrated on his neural processor, buzzing in his head, only half aware of how to do this. He sensed his processor's connection to the internet, and then let his brain do the work for him. Those bolts of electricity joined with the signals of his brain, the signals of his neural processor. He snapped from his own flesh. Both the vessel he controlled and the body he owned grew distant and cold as he groped frantically through the internet toward that Russo-Chinese satellite subsystem he knew had to exist.

His consciousness jolted into an old, clunky satellite with primitive thermal sensors. He couldn't see Medusa, couldn't orient himself, so he jumped to the next one.

Then it happened.

His brain melded to the satellite, or tried to, and encountered another mind reaching for the same one. Another consciousness, another set of neural impulses free-floating in space, maneuvering outside the scope of a physical body.

Tom snapped back with shock into his vessel, and he stared with his vessel's sensors toward Medusa's vessel in space, shaken to the core of his being. He had a sense, an unsettling sense, that she was doing the exact same thing.

Medusa messaged him. *You're like me.*

Tom couldn't think for a full second, so stunned it was like his brain and his neural processor had gone totally silent. Then, *We're the same,* he messaged her.

And it all made sense.

Medusa was extraordinary, because she *was* extraordinary. She accessed satellites. She could delve into the Indo-American systems just like the Russo-Chinese systems. She could enter machines the way he could. She could see ahead because she *could* see ahead where other Combatants could not. She could even interface with the ships around hers, the ones connected to the internet but not connected to her brain, because she was just like Tom. She had the same ability he did.

As though the realization galvanized her, Medusa bombarded him with an artillery of space debris, ignoring the satellite altogether—as though she'd realized Tom was more of a threat than she'd ever supposed. Tom evaded the trash—old satellites, chunks of rock—much more easily now, attuned to the same satellite system she was, using the same advantage she was using, the Russo-Chinese and Indo-American satellites relaying information straight into his neural processor.

Medusa suddenly decelerated, forcing him downward

toward a hunk of granite orbiting the Earth. Tom steered so quickly to evade it, he sent his vessel hurtling in an uncontrollable circle. But his sensors picked up something else, then—the satellite. The very one they were out to collect, jolting straight into his electromagnetic sensor sight. He deployed his clamps and seized it as he rocketed past, dragging it down with him toward the vast blue sphere of the Earth.

Medusa charged after him as he descended into the atmosphere of the planet, heat shields lighting up on all sides of his vessel, around the satellite. Tom sped up his descent as much as he dared, knowing that if he went too fast, he'd burn up the satellite and his ship with it.

Medusa grew dangerous now, truly dangerous. Out for blood the same way Tom had been when she held the satellite. She hurtled toward him, and he knew now this would be a fight to avoid mutual destruction. She shot straight toward him, threatening him with a collision. Tom swung downward to avoid it, found himself accelerating too quickly, the heat sensors lighting up madly in his vessel. He decelerated but still plunged off course, trapped by gravity, well away from Washington, DC, and was torn down toward a chaotic mass of storm clouds.

Medusa retreated just as Tom's vessel plunged into the eye of the storm. Black clouds enveloped him, lightning crashing around him. Turbulence pounded his vessel on all sides. He adjusted course, dodging the thunderheads, the flashing of lightning that would end this in an instant, and then tried to tap back into the Russo-Chinese satellite system to orient himself—

And found Medusa's consciousness waiting there for his, inhabiting the satellites. She struck at him like lightning, ripping him out of the satellite systems and into the vast miasma of the internet. Chaos rocketed Tom as his brain zinged through the tangle of connections among billions of machines, Medusa dragging him down some unknown pathway.

New connections flashed through him. Tom jerked suddenly into the neural processor of Elliot Ramirez.

Tom could see the Rotunda through Elliot's eyes, too, and feel his shock when Medusa planted a command into his brain from the inside. Elliot stopped pretending to control the ships and his body began twirling and dipping like he was ice-skating in the middle of the Rotunda. Across from him, Svetlana Moriakova gaped at his pirouettes, his leaps, then dissolved into laughter.

So Tom focused on Svetlana with Elliot's eyes, her IP address scrolling across Elliot's vision center. That sent him lurching into her processor, and he ordered her to open her lips to scream, "I'll eat your souls! And bathe in your blood!" He felt her cheeks heating up and saw through her eyes the spectators glancing at one another, puzzled by the strange behavior of the two young people.

And then with a thought of his vessel, Tom snapped back into it. One last violent jolt, and his ship freed itself from the grip of the storm. He felt Medusa's consciousness following him, grappling for control of his ship. He felt her mind trying to access the clamps, trying to get him to release the satellite—to drop it into the ocean, destroy it, before he could win.

A thought crawled into Tom's brain. If Medusa could access Elliot's neural processor, and he could access Svetlana's, why couldn't he access hers? He abandoned the fight for the clamps and made for her ship. Just as he interfaced with it, Medusa moved her consciousness to defend it.

But Tom didn't access her ship. It was a feint.

He delved instead into the connection between her ship

and some neural processor somewhere, Medusa's processor transmitting from somewhere on Earth. He pursued it and found himself interfacing with a network based in Washington, DC, even. His consciousness interfaced with the network, brushing past the security measures of the Chinese embassy, and there he found himself in the surveillance subsystem, dancing between various rooms inside the embassy. Then he found a private one, with a girl hooked in with a neural wire into an interface port. He gazed through the security cameras, his human brain making sense of what the cameras were seeing.

At first glance, the girl in military fatigues was almost what he imagined—thick black hair in a braid, full lips, a small, delicate face. And then the camera shifted to take in the rest of her face and he finally knew why her call sign was Medusa.

A mythical female monster so hideous to behold men died if they looked on her face . . .

The rest of her face was mottled like the cratered surface of the moon, bulging up around one of the dark eyes. Fleshy patches covered one side of her skull where the black hair had been seared off, the scalp scarred over. She must've been in some terrible accident. Her lips and nose twisted down as though they'd melted into the rest of her face. Tom forgot all about the fight in one mind-numbing instant as he gazed upon the disfigured girl he'd grown so obsessed with.

Then it came to him.

He knew how to win.

Tom almost couldn't do it. Almost. Because he was vicious, yes. But this was only a weapon because she liked him, and because she knew he liked her. He knew this was crossing some line he could never step back from again.

Another part of Tom's brain, connected to his ship, knew

it was hurtling toward DC. He knew even now he was losing control of it as Medusa fought to wrest it from him. He knew they were plummeting toward the ground, and either he would win this or she would, and he couldn't lose. He'd be done for. Blackburn would destroy him.

He aimed straight for her heart.

I see why you're called Medusa.

He maneuvered the cameras toward her and let her feel him maneuvering the cameras, and in the Chinese Embassy the disfigured girl returned to her human body just long enough to snap open her eyes and look up toward the cameras. Naked horror blazed over her face.

And Tom knew he was the bad guy Marsh wanted him to be.

He could almost feel her scream through that other consciousness touching his, a blinding jolt of pure rage and humiliation tearing at his core. He swore her thoughts were screaming in his head.

You've ruined it! YOU'VE RUINED EVERYTHING!

Tom knew what she was going to do before her consciousness deserted his. There was no dodging it as she hurtled toward him in her suicidal, kamikaze attack—so he threw it all into fate's hands and released his docking clamps, the momentum of his flight propelling the satellite forward toward the Smithsonian's lawn just as Medusa's vessel crashed into his.

The sensors fizzled into darkness.

Tom's eyes snapped open and he yanked the wire out of his brain stem.

He was in the hidden room with Nigel's unconscious body in front of the vast screen overlooking the Rotunda. The crowd was frozen, Elliot no longer fake ice-skating and Svetlana no longer screaming, everyone gaping at the rounded screen overhead, wondering if Tom had destroyed the satellite.

And then the screen flashed to the lawn of the Smithsonian, where the satellite lay smoking—but intact—near the smoldering remains of the two vessels. An American flag crossed with an Indian flag like two swords flashed across the screen, noting the winner.

Tom had done it. He'd won.

The Indo-American contingent roared to its feet, and Elliot gave a theatrical wave and a bow, basking in applause.

Tom's head slumped back against the carpet. He lay there alone, thinking of the girl he'd humiliated. The girl whose secret he'd viewed against her will. She'd been the greatest warrior in the world, Achilles, and he'd driven his sword into her heel.

He couldn't get Medusa's dark, horrified eyes out of his mind.

CHAPTER THIRTY-ONE

W ITHIN MINUTES GENERAL Marsh and Lieutenant Blackburn snapped the door open.

"Excellent job, Mr. Raines—" Marsh stopped, shock on his face as his watery eyes took in the scene: Tom lying on the floor near an overturned chair, Nigel crumpled against the wall, a neural wire strewn on the carpet. "What happened in here?"

"That guy's your leak, General." Tom nodded toward Nigel. He looked at the other surprised face, and his gut contracted with sheer hatred for Blackburn. "Maybe you should stick *him* in your census device and see for yourself! Oh, and he tried to destroy the Spire, too. Just FYI."

Blackburn and Marsh exchanged a look.

"I didn't get a message," Blackburn noted, his eyes sliding down to Tom's. "You were supposed to net-send me if there was trouble, Raines."

"I didn't have a chance," Tom said defensively.

Blackburn locked the door, then he and Marsh began

working in tandem. Marsh lifted the overturned chair and hoisted Tom up into it, then he pressed a finger to his earpiece and spoke quietly to a team, ordering them to clear the corridor. Blackburn knelt down to check Nigel's pulse and then turned to Tom. Tom forced himself to hold still as Blackburn deactivated his immobility sequence. He couldn't bring himself to thank him.

"The exit route's clear," Marsh told Blackburn. "Take Harrison to the holding area, then get back before anyone misses you."

"Yes, sir." Blackburn hoisted Nigel up over his shoulder, and disappeared into the hallway with him.

Tom watched the door shut, relieved it was Nigel getting hoisted away to the census device rather than him.

After Tom's quick explanation, Marsh congratulated him, clapped his shoulder, and instructed him to wait here until the Rotunda cleared out. Marsh dipped back out of the room, and Tom saw him reappear in the Rotunda, embarking on a hearty round of handshakes with various Coalition executives. Tom looked at the floor, not in the mood to watch the schmoozing.

An insane relief warred with a sinking realization of what he'd done to win. He didn't even think of celebrating his first victory ever over Medusa. The thought of it made him feel almost sick.

Maybe that was why it was hard to muster a triumphant smile when the door opened again, and this time Dalton strode inside.

"Who invited you?" Tom said.

"General Marsh knows I'm a friend of your family." Dalton kicked the door closed, hard.

Rather than challenge that, Tom remarked, "Guess you've heard about Nigel."

"You surprise me, Tom." Dalton whirled around and leaned back against the door, arms folded. "You live at the Pentagon, and yet no one's told you about a doctrine called mutual assured destruction."

"Major Cromwell's talked all about it, actually, but our destruction's not mutually assured, Dalton. My buddy Nigel"—Tom jabbed his thumb back at the empty chair behind his—"really had some interesting stuff to say before I clocked him."

Dalton drew an audible breath.

Tom smiled at him with bald-faced insolence. "Yeah, he talked all about *you* getting him to leak CamCo names and IPs. I think there's a word for that. What is it? Oh. Of course. Treason."

"You can't prove anything."

"I disagree. You have one, maybe two hours tops before Lieutenant Blackburn sticks him in the census device and finds out all about you."

"Yes, and he'll pass his findings on to his superiors, who will speak to my superiors. A campaign donation or two later, and we'll have an order from President Milgram himself sweeping this all under the rug." Dalton gave a snakelike smile. "That's the way the world works."

"Fine. Then I'll use the census device, retrieve my own memory of Nigel telling me Dominion's plan to leak Combatant names—your plan, Dalton—and stick it on the internet." He saw Dalton flinch like he'd just been slapped. Tom smiled. "That's also the way the world works."

This threat did it. Tom watched Dalton sweat and fumble for a retort. He knew that the internet killed any hopes of burying a secret. As much as the internet had been regulated, as much as it had been censored and filtered over the years, there were too many programmers and too many mobile hubs for the Coalition to subdue it.

Dalton finally managed, "You're remarkably ungrateful. I offered you the chance of a lifetime."

"Offered? I've got a problem with that word, Dalton. It implies you gave me a choice."

"I had to force you. You were too stupid to cooperate! You could have been the next Elliot Ramirez if you'd simply worked with me."

Tom slid his eyes toward the screen, the view of the Rotunda where Elliot was busy pumping hands, exchanging pleasantries. Showing the same face to everyone, no hint of his real feelings, playing the game. Elliot could do it somehow, could manage to keep that smile on his face without losing his soul.

But Tom couldn't.

He knew what it meant now, throwing away something of himself to win. He saw how meaningless it was. Maybe he'd saved himself, saved Yuri and Wyatt, by tearing out Medusa's throat, but the taste of victory was bitter on his lips, and the thought of going out into the world now and smiling at people he loathed just made him feel ill. He couldn't do it. He'd choke on it. It wasn't worth being somebody if it meant hollowing himself out to win a place with people like Dalton.

"Elliot's an okay guy." That admission still surprised Tom. "But I would never want to be him."

"If you really think that, you're as much of a fool as your father is."

"My dad is not a fool."

"I know all about him, Tom. He can't hold a job, so he deludes himself into thinking it's rebellion against society. He can't make it so, he pretends he doesn't want to. But I know better. This is cold, hard reality: everyone wants to be an Elliot Ramirez."

Tom just stared at him, amazed that Dalton couldn't even imagine someone not caring about the same things he did. But why was it a surprise? A guy like Dalton could never understand a guy like his dad. Neil had faults. Many, many faults. But he saw some things perfectly. He never bought into the image stuff, the power stuff. He never accepted he was prisoner to a society stronger than he was. Even when he was kicked down time and again, he never "stuck his neck in the corporate yoke." His dad was way too stubborn, too proud.

And for the first time, Tom realized there was something to admire about that. It took guts to be his dad; it took courage to charge down a path the rest of society dared not follow. Dalton Prestwick played the game exactly the way he was supposed to play it, and he didn't even see that he was trapped by it. He had to live out the entirety of his life as Dalton Prestwick. It was really a worse fate than anything Tom could inflict on him.

Tom rose to his feet. He just wanted this man out of his life. Forever.

"Here's the deal, Dalton. You stay away from me, got it? You and I never speak to each other again. Don't mess with any more of our brains. Not even Karl's, as much as he deserves it. He starts gelling his hair and wearing cologne, and I'll tell the Pentagon to look for some Dominion Agra software in his processor. And as for my father, he doesn't exist to you anymore. Never even say his name again."

Dalton's expression grew narrow and calculating. "Is that all?"

"You do all that, and I won't send a copy of my memory to anyone. You don't do it, and I'll post it on the internet. I swear I will."

"Fine. We have a deal." He offered his hand. "Shake?"

Tom turned his back to him. "I'm not shaking your hand, Dalton. Just go away."

Tom, like all the other non-CamCos in the Spire, was a state secret. So he waited in the private room until the non–Indo-American affiliated crowds departed. Once the only people left in the Capitol were military and the representatives of Indo-American companies, he emerged.

Tom ventured out into the Rotunda and headed over to Elliot. "How's it going?"

Elliot's collar was stained with sweat. He yanked it open, like it was suffocating him. "Remember what I said about wanting to fight my own battles? Yeah, forget it. I am happy—no, *overjoyed*—to have a proxy." He reached up and gripped Tom's shoulder. "Good job, Tom."

"Hey," Tom said, "I couldn't have won if you'd been destroyed earlier. You held out against Medusa, man. That's something."

Elliot beamed at him. "Thanks. And, hey, Marsh filled me in about Nigel. You saved the day, didn't you?" He chuckled. "One of my plebes, saving us all."

"I had some help. Wyatt's virus took Nigel down. I was going to cheat. I didn't get the chance."

Elliot glanced around, then leaned closer to him, his dark eyes probing his. "Something odd happened. I can't explain it. I swear, I lost control of my neural processor for a while there. I think Svetlana did, too."

Tom tried to think quickly of an excuse so Elliot would forget all about that. "Maybe you just—"

"Raines."

The voice from behind him made his heart jump into his throat. Tom's every muscle tensed. He turned slowly, seething with hatred, to see Lieutenant Blackburn, just feet away.

I just won Capitol Summit, Tom reminded himself. *He can't do anything to me.*

And then it hit him: Blackburn really *couldn't* do anything to him. And Tom found himself grinning, a sense of power washing through him.

"Great to see you," Tom said. "I was hoping for a chance to talk to you, sir."

Blackburn blinked, disconcerted, like he didn't know how to react to this. It gave Tom fierce pleasure.

"Is there a problem?" Elliot spoke up, looking between them, his brow furrowed.

"None at all. See you later, Elliot." Tom drove his hands into his pockets and walked from the Rotunda into the dim, statue-strewn corridor beyond, knowing by instinct that Blackburn was right behind him.

As soon as they were out of earshot of anyone else, Blackburn demanded, "Did I just interrupt you in the process of telling Elliot Ramirez about your ability?"

Tom turned around, anger frothing in his veins. He'd never hated someone so much.

"No, sir. That didn't work out so well for me the last time, did it?"

Blackburn's eyes narrowed. "You don't even realize how lucky you are that I'm the one who found that first."

"Yeah," Tom agreed sarcastically. "I'm so lucky you tried to rip my brain apart. I can't imagine what a company like, say, Obsidian would do instead. Gosh, they might actually do something *evil*."

"If you'd just given up that memory—"

"We're not having this discussion anymore!" Tom roared at him. "I am not tied down under the census device!" He dropped his voice to a poisonous whisper. "Besides, I know what you want."

"Do you?"

"This is all about Obsidian and Vengerov. He messed up one group of adults in Russia, and then he came over here and messed up you guys, too. That must burn you that he got away scot-free with what he did to you, and all you got was Roanoke."

Blackburn's body tensed.

"I know all about Roanoke." Tom leaned against the wall behind him. He watched Blackburn's face, cold calculation like ice in his veins. "And don't get me wrong, it's not because Wyatt told me. She *never* looked at your personnel file. Actually, the only mistake she ever made, sir, was having some sort of trust in you. Good thing you took care of that quickly enough." He let that sink in, eyes on Blackburn's inscrutable face, then added, "No, I heard about it because of *Joseph Vengerov.*"

Blackburn glanced sharply behind him, back toward the rotunda where Vengerov had just been, almost as though he expected him to be sneaking up behind him.

Tom smiled. "Yeah, my old pal Joe. I hung out with him once in the Beringer Club. And you know what? That's it. See, there's no human experiment going on here, no conspiracy. I was never hiding anything about that from you. I only met Vengerov that once. But you know what? I think I could start a conspiracy with Joe now that you've got the idea in my head. Maybe Joe and I would have a lot to say to each other. After all, I figure what you'd hate, more than anything else in the world, would be if Joe got richer and more powerful—and he'd definitely do that if he got his hands on an 'ability' like mine. You've gotta admit, it would be so easy for me to just walk back into the Rotunda and tell him all about it."

Blackburn took a menacing step toward him, and Tom just kept leaning on the wall, refusing to be intimidated. "That would be the most profoundly stupid thing you could ever do, Raines. You'd live to regret it."

"That's funny," Tom said in a hard voice, "because I think I'd take my chances with Joe before I'd get my brain ripped apart by you. And knowing just how much you'd hate it? That just makes it all the better."

"You little fool," Blackburn hissed. "You think I couldn't just hack into your brain and stop you?"

Tom shrugged. "But then you'd miss the other secret. The one I was keeping from you. Here it is: I'm not the only one who can do this."

Blackburn reared back a step like he'd just stumbled upon some venomous snake. "There are others," he breathed.

"That's right. The trigger's there, and I don't have to be the one to pull it. Any one of us could go to Joe and hand over what we can do to Obsidian and make him CEO of the year. You can stop me, sure, but you can't stop all of us. You know what I think this means, sir? I think it means you never, ever mess with me again."

Blackburn considered him for a long, tense moment, obviously trying to gauge whether Tom'd go through with it. He must've seen something he didn't like on Tom's face, because he lifted his hands and took a step back. "Fine. We're done. I'll leave you be."

Tom felt like he was on fire. That was all he wanted. That, and to rip Blackburn's head off—but he didn't think he was going to get that.

"What are you waiting for?" Blackburn snapped. "Shoo, Raines. Get of my sight."

Tom shook his head. "No, see, that's not how it works. I won this one. We both know it. That means *you* get out of *my* sight. *Sir.*"

Blackburn raised his eyebrows at that. And then his expression shifted, the faint twist of his lips seeming to say touché. Without another word, he turned and disappeared down the corridor—and the surrender in the sound of his retreating footsteps made dark triumph flood Tom's chest.

Sometimes things just worked out.

TOM SPOKE WITH Olivia Ossare as soon as he returned to the Spire. She advised him to wait until the next meeting of the Defense Committee to back down on the lawsuit. Finally, the word came: the Defense Committee had seen the evidence from Nigel's memories, and they officially assigned the blame for the leak to him. Any further investigation of Tom was prohibited.

Olivia squeezed Tom's hand when she heard. "We won."

"You saved my life here," Tom told her.

"Protecting you kids is my job. I'm glad I finally had a chance to do it."

Clearing his name proved the easy part. Getting his dad to back down was another matter.

Neil didn't know the specifics, just that Tom faced some threat at the Pentagonal Spire, and that was enough to enrage him. Weeks passed and he wouldn't abandon the custody suit. Tom had to meet with him in VR just to talk him down, and Neil insisted on seeing "my boy the way he looks," and not "some fancy avatar."

Tom had expected his father to choose a casino or maybe the Las Vegas strip as the setting for their conversation, but when he hooked into VR, he found Neil on top of Mount Everest, gazing down at the vast snowy mountaintops around him.

His dad looked older than he remembered, smaller somehow, in the whitewash of the scenery. He turned around when he heard Tom's footsteps crunch their way over. He gazed at him. "My God, is that what you look like now?"

"Scanned myself in today." Tom glanced down at himself, self-conscious. "Just a growth spurt."

"Your face. Look at that." Neil closed the distance. "Your skin . . ."

The knots in Tom's chest loosened, because this was his father. He didn't need to worry about this. He could reason with him. "Regular showers, Dad. They help. You get the money I put down for you at the Dusty Squanto?"

"Just tell me the person you ripped off deserved it," Neil said wryly.

"Trust me, he did."

The eyes of Neil's avatar narrowed. He studied Tom very closely. "Smile, Tom."

"Smile?" Tom echoed.

"Yes. Smile."

Confused, Tom smiled.

"Raise your eyebrows," Neil said, eyes still narrowed.

And Tom knew exactly why Neil was asking him to do this: just like when he'd seen that interview with Elliot on the TV, he must've noticed something *wrong* about Tom's face, about the way he was moving, the neural processor regulating his expressions. The last thing his dad needed to know about was the computer in Tom's brain.

"Dad," Tom lied, "this is an avatar. If I look different, it's because this is a projected image. This isn't what my face actually looks like."

"You sure?"

"I'm sure. Megapixels distort things. The science is really technical and I doubt you want me to go into it." Tom didn't know the science, but he nodded like he did.

Neil rubbed at his chin.

"You've always hated VR stuff, anyway," Tom said.

"The real world's an ugly place, Tom. But I'm not gonna hide from it. Your grandfather was that way—paid more attention to some World of Warcraft than he did to us. Now, are you sure, are you absolutely sure . . ." He made a vague gesture, but Tom knew what he was asking. It was about the lawsuit.

"Yeah, I'm sure you should drop the lawsuit. I had this situation, but it cleared up. I'm staying at the Spire, after all."

Neil dropped his voice and inched closer, as though that made any difference in VR if someone was eavesdropping on them. "Tom, you're sure? If the military's giving you a problem, I'll figure something out."

"Dad, it's really okay now. I only needed you to give me a trump card in this one situation. I was . . ." He fumbled for a way to say it that Neil might appreciate, a way that wouldn't reveal anything classified. He came up with it. "I was bluffing."

"Bluffing, eh?"

"Yeah. Gambling for something. And I won."

His father studied him for a long moment. Then his lips cracked in a knowing smile. "I bet I know what you were gambling for."

Tom wondered what his theory could be. "Do you?"

Neil leaned toward him. "You were aiming to fly in that Capitol Summit thing, weren't you?"

Tom jerked. "What?"

"It was everywhere, clips of the way we won this year. I knew with one look it wasn't that Ramirez kid. Flying right at that satellite? I saw that, and I knew it was my boy."

"How did—" Tom stopped, realizing he'd given away too much.

"I've seen you play thousands of those games. Think I don't know how your brain works, Tommy?"

Tom stared at his dad's collar. Neil *had* seen him play games over the years. He'd noticed him.

"Uh, I found out something yesterday," Tom said. "We have promotions twice a year, right? And I heard I'm getting promoted." He wasn't sure why he suddenly wanted Neil to know. "It's to Middle Company. It's not Camelot Company yet, but it might be soon. I might be one of the call signs on the news one day."

Neil turned away from him and squinted into the sunlight. "Rising up the ranks, huh?"

Tom watched Neil's back, waiting for some jab about serving the "corporate war machine."

But Neil surprised him with, "Sorry I can't be there to see that."

Tom couldn't speak. He could not say a word.

He turned to stare into the distance, just like his dad was, aware of his chest aching as he stood next to him on top of Mount Everest. For the first time, he knew that even if his father hated what he was doing, he was still proud of him.

CHAPTER THIRTY-TWO

"**G**ORMLESS CRETIN."

Vik's words, spoken a few weeks later as they stood in formation outside the doorway to the Lafayette Room, made Tom jump. "What now?"

"It's your new nickname," Vik said.

The long-awaited manly equivalent of Evil Wench didn't make much sense to Tom. The formation of a dozen plebes began marching forward into the room. His brain was not sorting out the reference. What did "gormless" mean?

"Not stored in your neural processor, right?" Vik raised his eyebrows as the doors parted around them. "I picked it on purpose just for that. We have a deal—you have to answer to it."

Tom laughted. "Fine, but, Vik, nothing in the world can top Spicy Indian."

"Die slowly, Tom."

Tom laughed as they marched into the Lafayette Room

and began heading down the aisle in single file At the front of the room, Marsh, Cromwell, and Blackburn waited on the stage. The rest of the trainees stood at attention in front of their benches for the ceremony.

Tom caught eyes with Yuri in the plebe section—and received a faint smile. As much as Yuri had tried to put on a cheerful show when he heard all his friends were getting promoted, it obviously bothered him. First he'd been scrambled, and now this: more confirmation he didn't have a chance of moving up in the ranks. Tom turned back to the stage and arranged his face into a stiff, formal, getting-promoted-type expression. A quick glance at Vik told him he was doing the same. He was straining so hard for a serious expression that he just looked constipated.

They stood in a line in front of the stage while Marsh launched into a speech about patriotism. Major Cromwell's lids drooped, like she was about to fall asleep. And Blackburn was standing rigidly in place, like he'd braced himself for an impending root canal.

The best musicians among the trainees played a march when the speech ended, and the plebes scheduled for promotion filed up to the stage. Vik was the first to received his promotion—a neural chip with upgrades from Blackburn, a new rank badge from Cromwell, and then a handshake from General Marsh. Tom searched Vik's face as he left the stage for any sign of pride, but something was off there. He looked a bit pale. It wasn't until Vik's eyes darted to Yuri in the plebe section, that Tom realized why: Vik was worrying about the treason they'd committed together. Wyatt was the next to stand before a granite-faced Blackburn. She stared below him and he looked above her as he thrust a neural chip with a new set of software updates into her hand. She almost stumbled in her eagerness to move on to face Cromwell.

Tom's name was called last. Blackburn's jaw clenched. He stared at him with an intent, unblinking gaze as he handed him the neural chip. Tom took it, and decided he was going to get Wyatt to scan this whole thing, directory by directory, before hooking it into his brain. He saw a flash of satisfaction on Cromwell's face as she switched the old rank badge on the collar of his tunic with a new one: same eagle, only with two arrow-type lines beneath it instead of one. Marsh shook his hand, pride in his face.

As the ceremony concluded, and the trainees applauded the newly promoted, Tom scanned the reactions in the Combatants assembled in the front row. Karl was sulking. Then Elliot nudged him, and he began the world's most halfhearted clapping.

As Heather clapped, her gaze moved to Tom's and locked on, and he found suddenly that he couldn't tear his eyes from hers. There was still something mesmerizing about the intensity of her stare. He broke away then, his ears growing hot, feeling foolish. The band played them from the room as the assembled trainees stood at attention.

Tom felt like he could breathe again once in the main lobby beneath the enormous, outstretched wings of the golden eagle. Vik plodded up behind him, so Tom turned and elbowed him, hoping to knock some life back into his face and get him over whatever it was troubling him. "Come on, man. Cheer up. Doctors of Doom aren't supposed to worry about stuff."

Vik turned to him, his voice dropping to the faintest of whispers. "Tom, what if we regret this?"

"What, you think Yuri is actually an evil spy?" Tom said just as softly.

"No, I just—" Vik looked around quickly, checking again to

make sure no one was close to them. "Come on, Tom! We did something we don't have a right to do. It's treason."

Surviving the census device and winning Capitol Summit had left Tom feeling near invincible. He'd been there, done that. "Look, if we're just careful, no one will know. If they start to suspect? Then we get Wyatt to change him back. And if that doesn't work, then I'll take the blame, okay? You're safe. I'll be the idiot here."

That seemed to mollify Vik. His voice rose to a normal volume. "Well, of course you're the idiot here, Gormless Cretin."

"What *is* a gormless cretin?" Tom burst out.

"A redundancy." Wyatt's voice rang out from behind them. She emerged from the crowd filling the lobby, Yuri behind her. "A 'dim-witted dumb person.'"

Tom groaned. "Really, Vik?"

"The fact that you needed Wyatt to explain it for you supports my 'gormless' theory," Vik argued.

Wyatt spoke up. "We've got break coming up. Can we do something our last night other than stand around here?"

Yuri smiled, all earnest, goofy adoration of her. "We should all go out. I have found an appropriate promotion ritual. It's called wetting down."

"Wetting down?" Wyatt said. "Where you buy us drinks and throw us into a body of water?"

Yuri's smile dropped off his lips. "I was going to buy dinner instead."

"Dinner's fine, but forget throwing us in the water."

"Yeah," Vik spoke up, completely in agreement with Wyatt for once. "Every company in the world dumps stuff in the Atlantic. We'd have kids with five arms."

"They could form one-person bands," Tom told Vik.

He saw Vik's eyes light up with the possibilities.

Wyatt cried, "No. No throwing us in the water! You're still buying us dinner, though, Yuri." There was no question in her tone.

The others headed upstairs to change clothes. Tom lingered, staring at the golden eagle, amazed that he'd thought it was glaring at him his first day in the Spire. It had been so intimidating. But it looked smaller now, somehow. Or maybe he'd just grown.

A shadow slid over the marble floor behind him. He turned and met yellow-brown eyes and a starship-wrecking smile.

"Heather."

"Congratulations, Tom. I knew you'd go places here."

"Oh, you mean Middle?" Tom fingered his new insignia self-consciously. "Yeah, thanks."

"No, I'm talking about that other thing." Her eyes twinkled, and he knew she was congratulating him for winning the Capitol Summit. "Looks like you're going to be with us in CamCo someday."

Tom straightened and held her eyes, awed by the thought. It really looked to be a sure thing now, didn't it? Marsh's look on the stage, his reaction, Elliot's support, now this. . . . He'd make his way here. It was only a matter of time.

"Are you heading out with your friends?" Heather stepped closer. "I thought I'd take you somewhere to congratulate you." She let out a breath that fluttered her dark hair. "Of course, I've also been asked to talk to you about opportunities down the road with my sponsor, Wyndham Harks, but really . . ." Her eyes flickered downward and then traveled back up to his in a way that made him aware of how hard his heart was beating. Her voice sounded a bit breathy as she said, "I'm just so excited for an excuse to hang out with you."

The glitter in her amber eyes dared him to do something reckless. Tom found it a bit hard to catch his breath suddenly, keenly aware of how close she was, close enough for him to smell her shampoo. Coconut. He realized suddenly that she could still do this to him. She could still make him feel like that shrimpy kid his first day at the Spire, so thrilled a girl was talking to him. Maybe she'd always be able to do it.

But his thoughts kept wandering away from her toward something else, something much more compelling. *Someone* else.

And suddenly, Tom's brain was working again, and he found himself answering Heather with a shake of his head. "Sorry, I've got something I have to do."

Tom DIDN'T KNOW why tonight would be any different. He'd hooked into VR every day since the Capitol Summit. He wasn't sure why it mattered so much, this hope of finding her. He knew he'd destroyed whatever he had had with Medusa, and even if he hadn't . . . if he hadn't . . . that pretty Chinese girl he'd built up in his imagination didn't exist. And she knew the guy she'd met over the internet didn't really exist, either. What could have prepared her for the person he turned out to be? Nothing in their conversations, in their battles, in those moments when they smiled at each other over their bared swords, could've readied her for the truth about him: that he was someone who could do something so vicious, so personal, so cruel, just to win against her.

It bothered Tom to think about it, so he tried not to. And maybe he would've been a better person if he'd just left her alone after what happened. But whenever he closed his eyes, he still saw her flying, fighting with ferocious genius. He still remembered that kiss.

So he still returned to the internet. He hooked in straight from his bunk. Maybe it was reckless overconfidence, but he couldn't bring himself to fear much of anything after the events of Capitol Summit. General Marsh had called him up to his office to congratulate him again. Members of CamCo suddenly waved to him in the corridors, and upper-level Alexanders had all started talking to him like he'd been inducted into some club he didn't even know about. Lieutenant Blackburn was careful never to bother him in class, not even for demonstrations. He'd taken instead to watching Tom from across the mess hall, across the lobby, but still never breathing a word to his face.

So Tom lay on his bed and checked their message board, then he visited their simulations. Siegfried and Brunhilde's stone castle stood empty, no queen of Iceland waiting, sword in hand. No luck in the old RPG of the Egyptian queen and the ogre, either. Prepared for disappointment, he hooked into the Renaissance England simulation, and found himself snapping into character.

He was facing her again.

She stood by a throne at the head of the English royal court, her back to him, simulated courtiers milling about on all sides. Tom stood before her, tension making his every muscle clench. He glanced down at his character, and the simulation informed him he was *Robert Devereux, the Earl of Essex*. When Medusa turned toward him, he was greeted not by the pretty redheaded princess, but the aged face of what the program informed him was *The sixty-seven-year-old Queen Elizabeth I*. Her lips curled into a thin, downward twist and her cold eyes glittered like polished onyx, black and hard.

Tom closed his own eyes, the information spinning in his head.

The young Earl of Essex flattered and flirted with the much older Queen Elizabeth. He took advantage of her affection and betrayed her. As he began to fall from favor, he fought her guards and charged desperately into her chamber. He burst inside before she'd been made up for the day, and beheld her aged face, her white hair without a wig. All pretense of flirtation between them shattered in one instant. Shortly after, she ordered him beheaded.

She must've edited it. It was too pointed. Tom opened his eyes again and faced her unflinchingly. "I need to talk to you."

"What could you possibly have to say to me?" Her voice was cold.

He'd prepared for this. He waggled his fingers, accessed an image file from the Spire's database. His guise as the Earl of Essex vanished, replaced instantly by another: the Tom Raines who had walked into the Spire. The short, skinny kid with terrible acne, flat blond hair, a slouched posture. Tom stood there as that guy, the guy he'd sworn not to show her, and then opened his arms wide to let her see him in all his complete lack of magnificence.

"This is me. Okay?"

"That's not you." Medusa waved Elizabeth's wrinkled hand, and her own appearance morphed. A boy Tom almost didn't recognize stood in her place.

The boy was him. Tom as he was now. A taller, clear-skinned guy with cold blue eyes, who stood there with a confident posture controlled by a neural processor, whose muscles had been honed during Calisthenics, whose self-assurance radiated from every plane of his face.

Tom stared at his other self, feeling like he was regarding a stranger. "When did you see me?"

"I peeked at the security cameras in the Beringer Club."

Tom raised his eyebrows at her: she *had* to see the irony.

"Yes, I'm a hypocrite. It doesn't change anything." Medusa sagged back into the throne. "You can't do this. You can't pull a move like that, be cutthroat like that, and then come here and be nice."

"I just want to make it right."

"Then let me hate you."

He felt like he'd been punched. "You hate me now?"

Medusa raised a finger, and Tom found himself standing there as his newer self. She morphed back into the girl he'd seen briefly, and he fought the urge to look away. He fought the urge to stare, too. He felt trapped by those eyes that gazed out from her ruined face. He couldn't imagine moving through the world like that. Like a monster.

"Haven't you ever, you know"—he blurted the rest—"tried to get it fixed?"

For a moment of silence, she just watched him squirm. "Eight surgeries. Five skin grafts, two face transplants. After the neural graft, I was done. I'd had enough. It was fine until you came. Until you let me pretend I could be normal."

"I'm sorry." It was all he could think to say.

Medusa shrugged. "I can't blame you."

She was walking away now, toward a door hidden in the far wall. Once she stepped through it, he'd never see her again: he knew it in his gut.

He took a sharp step toward her. "I had to win. I *had* to. They thought I was a traitor, so it was win or I was losing my neural processor and going to prison, okay? Come on! It's not like I could've asked you to lose for me!"

She looked back at him, her eyes gleaming. "Maybe I would have."

His throat closed. "You wouldn't have." People didn't do that. They didn't.

"I guess you'll never know now. Just a word of warning, Mordred: next battle, I'm going to stomp you so hard that afterward, you'll make *me* look pretty."

Tom's uneasiness melted away. Implicit in that remark was a promise, though maybe she'd meant it as a threat: they'd meet again.

He felt his lips pulling into a grin. He'd take it. Take it and run. "You'll try."

Medusa's lips split with that challenging smile, and for a second he recognized her somehow, he knew her on some primal level, the same way he'd recognized her behind the face of Brunhilde, the helmet of Achilles, or in that ship maneuvering in space, and then she flickered away. The simulation darkened around him. Tom pulled out his neural wire, Medusa's dangerous smile lingering in his brain.

A fist hammered on the door, and then Vik, Yuri, and Wyatt came piling in.

"Come on, man, we're starving," Vik said. "I'd estimate we're ten minutes away from cannibalizing someone here."

"This is true." Yuri thumped Tom's bed. "And it will not be me. I am paying for dinner."

Vik nodded. "And it can't be Wyatt, since we'd look like real jerks if we killed and ate a girl. It's also not going to be me since this whole thing's my idea. That leaves you, Tom. Death by Indo-Russian cannibals. Beamer would love it."

"Indo-Russian?" Wyatt said. "Oh. So *I* don't get to eat now, is that it?"

Vik threw up his hands, exasperated. "Come on, Enslow. What do you think? Of course you get to eat Tom with us. Death by *Americo*-Indo-Russian cannibals just sounded too wordy."

Tom met their expectant grins with one of his own. He'd

never expected to have a future a year ago. He'd never expected to have friends.

And he'd definitely never expected to ever have to tell someone, "All right, no killing and eating me, okay? I'm ready to go."

ACKNOWLEDGMENTS

Figuring out the dedication was the hardest part of this, because there are so many amazing people involved in this process. Specifically, I have to hone in on Mer and Rob, since you guys have been incredible to me both during this process and in life in general, and I really don't have words to thank you enough. You both should be up front, too.

Meredith, you were the first person apart from my agent to give the book a read, and you've given me amazing advice and insight throughout this process. Thank you!

Rob, thank you, thank you for reading over so many things that were entirely over my head, and always providing another perspective when I was trying to understand things.

Thanks also to:

Jamie, for cowriting that first mauscript with me many moons ago that got me started, and for all the silly stories over the years. Oh, and for being around all this last year during various, unnecessarily angsty moments, and being a voice of reason.

Jessica, because you've been there since we were little and you put up with that whole year of me trying to convince you I was a Martian. It's rare, I think, to find all of one's childhood memories tied to another person, and I look forward to many adulthood memories, too. You are awesome, Jessie!

Betsey—I'm so lucky to have you as a sister-in-law, and I can't wait to see the girls grow up!

Judy and the Persoffs (you're a bit like having a second family), Toddaroo (for having firm opinions at exactly the right time), and the Hattens.

David Dunton, who pulled me out of his slush pile and stuck with me until we had a winner. You've always been such an amazing advocate for my novels and I am incredibly lucky to have you as an agent. Also, Nikki, for "lighting a fire" under him to read over that first manuscript, even in the middle of a very major event for you all. Thank you both.

Molly O'Neill, the only person who's read the book over as many times as me, and honestly, you've been a dream editor. Your instincts are dead on, you've believed in the book wholeheartedly, advocated for it, and you always believed in my ability to shore up the weaknesses.

Katherine Tegen and the KT Books/HarperCollins team: Anne Hoppe, Sarah Shumway, Claudia Gabel, Melissa Miller, Katie Bignell, Laurel Symonds, Jean McGinley, Barb Fitzsimmons, Amy Ryan, Joel Tippie, Sammy Yuen (thank you for the cover!), Lisa Wong, Esilda Kerr, Kathryn Silsand, Lauren Flower, Megan Sugrue, Stephanie Stein, Alison Lisnow, and Casey McIntyre.

Thanks also to Sara Crowe and all the foreign publishers who have purchased rights to the story, especially Sarah Odedina and Hot Key Books, who put *Insignia* on their launch list. Thanks to Kassie Evashevski, Johnny Pariseau, Drew Reed, and Zander Bauman, and those at Fox who optioned the manuscript.

Thanks to Suzanna Hermans, Cathy Berner, and Jill Hendrix for being the first booksellers to read and support!

Also, there are lots of people who make this world more awesome: Alice & Tim, Christiane, Duncan, Maxine, Jan, Jackie, Shelley, Cristina, Allison, Amy, Stina, and Forever Tie-Dyed Blue Girls, Rachel, Ashley, Jennylle, & SDAP folks.

All the extraordinary teachers I've been lucky enough to learn from, and there are just a few here: Mr. Terry, Mr. Ott, Inna V., Mr. Shapiro, Ms. Stinner (who rendered the human body a perfectly logical thing), Mr. Sevilla.

Professor Muir: thank you for those study projects and discussions. Years later, and I can fully appreciate how amazing it is when a professor with your level of expertise takes the time for an undergrad. I was privileged to have a chance to study with you.

Ms. Pettigrew, because you encouraged a tenth grader to seriously pursue writing.

If I've left anyone out . . . Come on. Seriously? Look at the daunting list above. I really tried.